By Path of Night

By Stan Simmons

PublishAmerica
Baltimore

First printing

At the specific preference of the author, PublishAmerica allowed this work to remain exactly as the author intended, verbatim, without editorial input.

ISBN: 1-4241-2164-7
PUBLISHED BY PUBLISHAMERICA, LLLP
www.publishamerica.com
Baltimore

Printed in the United States of America

Chapter 1

Dark clouds grew threateningly in the west, ominous, oppressive. Evil, rust-colored monsters, they rolled along the ground gathering sand and debris. They smothered the horizon, swelling tall and furious above Cash, Texas, three miles away.

Faye Cowen stared at the storm clouds through single-pane glass. They would be fierce, full of darkness and stifling, choking, grabbing...she clamped her teeth together so hard her jaws ached. It would require a concentrated effort not to panic. She would fight for each breath, a never-ending battle within, trying to not lose her mind, fighting the feeling of being buried alive.

And so it was, for hours, alone in the dust-choked house. By ten o'clock, she had turned on every light. By noon dampened sheets sagged against the walls, brown and crusty, weighted at the bottom by invading sand and dust. Outside where a green field of cotton had flourished, only leafless stems remained, bent in the wind. Ruined.

Oma had not died on a windy day. It had been quite beautiful, actually. So pretty, in fact, Faye tarried a few moments after hanging out the clothes...paused to pet the dog, and to pick at a young dandelion. It was long enough for Oma to engross himself in the new *Venetian* blinds Allen bought her. Long enough for Oma to...he had always been so inquisitive.

Staring out the back door, she no longer saw the storm. Faye Cowen's storm lay malevolent, deep inside, malignant. A tear escaped from beneath her plastic-framed glasses, leaving a tiny, muddy rivulet down a white cheek with no makeup.

Faye sat, beaten down by the roaring noise outside, the eternal gusts of wind threatening to blow the house from its foundation; by the constant, never-ending flow of dust as it filtered through the walls, around doors, through vents, under the floor…relentless. Dust floated everywhere, spiraling down over everything…over the hand-washed bedding, over the hand-waxed hardwood floors, over the kitchen table, over Faye Cowen.

Two miles away her son Jeff Cowen gazed out the window of school bus number 6, watching dark, thick lumps of something rolling across the ground. The lumps became tumbleweeds, scurrying frantically across the road from right to left. Some passed in front of the bus, while others slammed into the side with a crunching, scratchy "thump."

The windows on the right side of the bus wheezed with each gust. Wind fought for a way in, winning, groaning against every tiny crevasse, crease, and seam.

Although Jeff's and Randy's house was only thirty yards east of the two-lane highway, neither could see it as the bus clattered to the right shoulder of the road.

Mr. Hughes slipped a gloved hand over the door release knob before braking to a complete stop. It was a motion as involuntary as taking one breath after another. He had driven the same route for seventeen years, and had worn lots of door openers slick.

Both boys in the front seat braced themselves for the blast, as Jeff grabbed several books from his younger brother's lap. The fierce wind momentarily drove them against the straight-backed seats, but they shuffled back and forth and struggled upright, leaning into the blast of sand and debris. Jeff couldn't even hear the colored kids lining up behind him.

Holding tightly to Randy's books, he slid against the right front fender of the bus, then around the tall black front bumper. He could feel his younger brother nudge up closely behind.

They were half-way across the highway when Jeff heard the bus begin to pull away. In that same instant, he heard a voice over the wind. He was not certain he had heard anything at all until later that night when he closed his eyes to sleep...to try to sleep.

The bus stopped suddenly, he saw faintly through squinted eyes. Mr. Hughes, slightly visible through the large bus window, appeared to have frozen in place. His face was a picture of confusion. He looked forward, then at his mirror, then forward again, then into the blankness of nowhere.

"Mone!" yelled Randy. Come on.

Jeff couldn't move. Beneath the bus, toward the rear, he saw feet. The Negro kids, instead of rushing for the two houses on their side of the road, were clustered around one of the rear wheels. Jeff knelt down, peering through the haze, directly into the wind.

Gall erupted in his mouth...an acrid sickening emotion of taste. She was a bundle of rags blowing in the wind, a sight that froze itself to his consciousness, an ugly portrait stained into his brain.

It was obvious, fighting the wind, she had lost—had been thrown beneath the bus an instant before the big yellow thing roared away...crushing her like a pile of twigs.

Jeff didn't want to go to her. Every emotion told him not to. Why go? To see her, brains spilled out onto the gravely sand, eyes staring up at him? See what?

His feet became the sand, pouring themselves slowly across the highway, back to where her body lay motionless. Each step had to wait for the next to pour itself along the pavement. The bus driver should be there, he thought, stepping in front of them, blocking out the view, yelling for the kids to get back. But Mr. Hughes still sat in the dusty green driver's seat picking at something on the back of his left hand, his mind trying to escape from the day.

Jeff stopped at the little girl's feet. There was a space between the colored kids who stood around, some bent over her, others looking around nervously. Her body lay behind the right rear tire, a six-year old with stupid looking paper things curled up in her black hair. Little pink stupid looking things, sand-covered, blowing against her little blank-staring, lips slightly parted, no soul in there, too little face.

Her book, pages flying in the wind, stopped for an instant. Jeff glanced down at "See Dick run." And immediately Dick was gone as the pages twisted and turned to other stories of other kids running and playing with Spot.

There was not the blood and guts he feared. Her torso was twisted, but mostly she just looked asleep; until he got close enough to actually see her eyes. They were slightly opened, sand already sticking to her eyeballs, building up in her ears.

His mind failed to register at first, then a scream overwhelmed his consciousness. It was loud, even over the roaring of the sandstorm; and not so much a scream as a wail. A tormented explosion of emotion, it evoked from one of the girls standing nearby.

Jeff Cowen feared he might vomit.

Faye bolted upright when the door slammed open.

"Mama!" yelled Randy, "Mama! Somphun's wrong!" His dark, expressive eyes spoke even more than his words. Faye's knees buckled slightly, her earlier silent thoughts lost for the moment.

"Where's Jeff?" she asked, sharply. "Where is your brother?"

"The bus," he pointed in the direction of the still open door. Sand and dust poured in, blowing a table lamp over. Before it stopped rocking on the hardwood floor, Faye Cowen was half way to the road.

Jeff fought back the desire to scream out. He found himself oddly angry—angry with Mr. Hughes…angry with him for running over the little girl…angry with him for making Jeff ride in the front seat every day…angry with him for not making this go away…for not being here telling them to get back.

Then one of the older colored boys was there, kneeling over the still figure. He lay down beside the broken child, absorbing the blasts of cutting wind. Tears flowed down both his cheeks, covering them with muddy rivulets of sorrow and sand. Wind whipped his yellow nylon shirt up over his head, exposing a smooth, muscular back.

The boy stroked his little sister, petting her head, brushing his hand over tight curls that sprang back lively even in death. Jeff saw the boy's lips moving—talking to the face of the body that used to be a person... soothing her...patting her like a puppy.

Jeff mechanically pulled the boy's shirt tail down. The unreal feelings of being whipped back and forth by wind, swirling crazily around the bus; the boy lying on the ground by the little dark-skinned girl...the silence brought about by the enormous noise of the wind... the dream-like feeling of watching—of seeing a dead person...it was too much.

Then Faye was there, down on both knees touching the shoulder of the boy on the ground. Jeff couldn't hear her words, but it appeared she called the Negro boy by name. Whatever she said, the boy moved back and made room for her. Faye swiftly had the girl in her arms and hurried away.

The girl's cheek pressed against her shoulder as long, thin legs draped loosely over one arm like pendulums while Faye strode toward the farm workers' house. She did not glance in the direction of Mr. Hughes.

Jeff was surprised his mother had lifted the little girl so easily. She gave no indication of being aware of the wind, although it tore at her, whipping brown hair in every direction, sticking the cotton dress to her body as if she had been doused with water.

He walked five feet behind her and the colored boy followed him, he knew, although he didn't look back and really couldn't hear him. The bus was quickly lost in the sandstorm, as were all the other kids. They were alone now, the three of them...the **four** of them, he corrected, remembering his mother's load.

Darkness in the old house was pervasive. A sixty-watt light bulb hung from a wire in the living room ceiling. Its meager beams fought but failed to bring light to its four corners.

Faye placed the little girl on the dusty old sofa, resting her small head on a wadded up shirt from the floor nearby. Mr. Wilson's shirt, she assumed...the dead girl's father.

Mr. Wilson liked the old house. Ever since his Leta died...since the first minute he heard of his wife's death...he promised himself, and the kids, they would stay here. He thought of that even at this moment as he drove the John Deere over acre after acre of Mr. Bradley's ruining cotton stalks, the rotary hoes throwing up dark soil to mix with that being blown away. He thought of that just as Faye Cowen laid his dead daughter on to the sofa he had found in the ditch near Crowell last year.

"Get a wet rag," Faye managed through a straining throat. She was speaking to the colored boy, a little harshly, Jeff thought. "I need to clean her up before your daddy gets home."

"Yessum," the boy answered, hurrying into the kitchen. Jeff saw him swipe at the muddy streams on his cheek.

Faye's hands were busy, shuffling over the girl's clothing, brushing away particles real and imaginary.

"Jeff, go tell your daddy. Tell him to call the Sheriff," she added, not looking up. Her hands had not stopped moving. "Then check on Randy. I think he was pretty upset when he went back to the house."

Jeff was glad to leave, happy to be free of the little body on the sofa. Happy to be out of the dreadful, bleak house. It smelled of old dirt, and—in his mind—of death. The wind slammed into him like a rampaging bull. But it was better than being in that house.

Chapter 2

Allen Cowen watched his oldest son from the window of the back door. He was proud of Jeff, of the way he had taken so much responsibility now that Allen's time was so limited. He was proud, but he hadn't told Jeff, of course. He did not know how to tell people his feelings, even if he had been predisposed to do so, which he wasn't.

From a distant room he heard a muffled sound. It was Randy falling into a heap in the living room floor, still trying to get dressed through a fog of sleep-filled eyes. Randy. His baby. His loving, kissing, hugging, frustrated, little boy. Allen caught a swell of salt rising from his chest into his throat. His baby **again.** He choked it back, eyes moistening for an instant.

He turned slowly from the back door, Jeff forgotten for the moment, Randy pushed back as well. Oma, also. There was work to do. Breakfast, then work. It would be a slow day at work, the harvest not yet in swing. Nevertheless, there were things to do. And, what about the colored boy…what was his name? He would have to do some more thinking on that today. Johnny? He thought that was it.

There was no way he could do what the sheriff asked of him. It wouldn't be fair to the family. It wouldn't be right. Why can't things just stay normal? Allen hoped Faye wouldn't bring it up again at breakfast.

The return spring on the screen door squealed a complaint as Jeff jerked it open. Pushing the door open, the smells of the fresh outdoors, the milk in the bucket he carried…all disappeared. Fried bacon, huge eggs bubbling in bacon grease, toast, jelly; those things captured him now.

"Wash your hands," said Faye. She placed a square of home-churned butter on the table and gave Jeff a glance he didn't understand. She turned immediately and went into the small living room, knelt down and untied a knot on Randy's shoe.

Allen was sitting at the head of the table when she and Randy came in. The table was, in fact, oval, but it was referred to as the "head" because it was where he sat. The butter was next to his plate. All sat for an instant of silence, looking at Allen. "Randy," he spoke, and four heads bowed.

Randy wanted someone else to say grace. He didn't really feel too thankful in the mornings anyway. "Favher," he began, "phank you for vis food…and…uh…ever fang. Jesus name, amen."

Jeff had just filled his plate when Faye spoke. "Allen, I really think we should talk about it with the boys."

Allen's first bite hesitated an instant, the white of an egg hanging from the fork tines, then continued into his mouth, giving him a moment of rumination. He didn't look up. Not at first. Jeff wondered a little frantically what he had done wrong. Randy ate.

"I don't think it's the right time, mama. This thing may work itself out without us anyway."

Faye sat quietly, not eating, trying to think of the right thing to do…to say. "I don't think so." She put a pat of butter on tan toast and spread it meticulously.

"It just don't feel right about getting the boys tied up in this. Not to mention you. He's almost a man. You know how people talk." Allen was not even pretending to eat now. His full attention was riveted upon his wife. So was that of both boys. It wasn't like mama to question dad's decisions.

What?" demanded Randy. Faye looked at him but did not answer.

"Eat your food. You're gonna be late for school." It was Allen's dismissal voice, but Randy did not dismiss easily.

"What? Talk 'bout what? Whadayamean?"

Allen groaned. He wished Faye had not brought it up today. He wasn't through thinking about it. The matter would probably take care of itself anyway without them doing anything. He would help in whatever way he could…any **other** way, but not this. It was too much to ask.

"It's nothing really," he began. "Colored man across the highway got himself into trouble. Nothing to concern us." Allen tried to get back to his breakfast. It didn't look so good any more. He put the fork down.

No one moved. Both boys still looked at their dad, as Faye studied something in her plate. When Allen looked up, Jeff looked away. Randy would not be put off. He looked right into the eyes of Allen Cowen, ready for a real answer.

"Listen," and the man cleared his throat. "'Scuse me. Now listen. It's just that Mr. Bradley's colored man got into some trouble. He, uh…well, after his little girl…after she passed away…remember how he was when he found out what happened?"

Jeff didn't want to hear more. The breakfast was already beginning to spoil in his stomach. He didn't want to talk about this. Didn't want to hear it.

"The other night," Allen continued, "Saturday, I guess he got to drinking a little…anyway they arrested him for…he broke into a place and was trying to steal some stuff."

"Wow!" Randy exclaimed, impressed they lived so close to a criminal.

"What'd he get in to?" asked Jeff..

"They caught him coming out of Blackmons," Faye said quietly.

A puzzled look from both boys caused her to elaborate. "You know, Blackmons'…over at Hoover." They still gave no indication of understanding. "Blackmons' Monuments…you know, sort of behind the Dairy Queen in Hoover."

"Monamints?" Randy said.

Jeff did not know why, but an uncomfortable feeling struck him again. Like his dad, he did not want this conversation to happen.

"Wayne...Deputy Tinsley, was going to take him home, I think," Faye added. "But Sheriff Hand insisted they put him in jail."

Allen glared at Faye, but continued as though she had not spoken. "He was carrying on about, I guess, his little girl...he kept trying to say her name, they thought, but the Sheriff couldn't understand him too well...he was crying and drunk, and they couldn't tell for sure."

"Then why did they think it had anything to do with...you know, the girl?" Jeff asked, a little angry with himself for some reason.

"Well," Allen cleared his throat again. "They think he was jabbering something about her not having a headstone. They caught him coming out of there with one under his arm...a stone, I mean. I don't know. I don't know what he was thinking. It wasn't even wrote on."

"Just like them, I guess," began Jeff, "Instead of staying home he goes and gets drunk."

"Jeff!" his mother spewed out his name. "You don't know what that man..." but her words failed. There was a slight quivering of her lower lip, and her eyes reddened.

"I didn't mean anything mama. I just don't think he shoulda' got drunk." His explanation fell on deaf ears. Faye was far away in another place. It would be several minutes before anyone spoke again.

Jeff could feel the deep burning of his skin as he flushed. He knew he had hurt his mother. He was considered by others in school to be too tough to mess with, but he didn't feel too tough this morning. He wished Randy would say something to her. He could always make her laugh.

And, just on cue, "Mama, what's a monamint?" Randy asked as though nothing else had been said.

Jeff lowered his head so no one could see him roll his eyes. Maybe that wasn't the right question. But it was the right question.

"A mon-u-ment," she began in her best teaching voice, "is a headstone that is placed over a grave."

"You know, like the one on Oma's grave," put in Allen quickly, wanting to move on to other things.

"Yes, like that one," Faye completed.

Then Jeff remembered the beginning of the conversation. "What's all that got to do with us? We don't even hardly know Mr. Bradley's hired help."

"Mr. Wilson…" began Allen…

"Who?" Randy demanded.

"Shut up. Quit buttin' in," barked Jeff.

"Listen, both of you," said Faye, "Mr. Wilson is still in jail. He may be going to prison."

Then to Randy, "Mr. Wilson is Isaac Wilson, Mr. Bradley's hired man."

"The one 'at got drunk?" he wanted to know.

"Yes. The one who tried to steal a gravestone for his daughter…for his daughter's grave," she answered.

"And," Allen was having difficulty choosing his words, "he…uh…he doesn't have a place for his boy, you know, if he does go to prison."

Both Allen and Faye caught themselves staring at the boys, waiting for a reaction. There was none.

"And Mr. Wilson asked us if we would take care of Johnny for him if that does happen…prison, I mean." Faye said.

"You mean like check on him if he's got food and stuff?" asked Jeff, sitting taller in his chair now.

"No," sighed his mother. "I mean like live here with us…probably just for a while."

"No!" blurted Jeff. "I mean…what could we…where could we put him?" His stomach was churning. What would his friends say? What would the people in town…

"You and Randy sleep in the same room. Oma's room is empty and we could…" began Faye.

"Oma's! You said **I** could have that room. I've been thinking about moving in there!"

"Jeff, it's been years. You could have moved in any time," Faye responded.

"I just couldn't yet. But I'm ready now. Really," he answered weakly. There was an unfamiliar expression on his face. "I don't want some stranger in our house...in his room. And sure not some ni...a Negro we don't even know."

"I agree with him, mama." Allen spoke softly, "Jeff should get the spare room. Besides, I never even considered putting the boy in the house. At best, maybe put him in the barn for a few days till they locate family or something."

"Why not me?" piped in Randy. "Why can't I have Oma's room?"

Ignoring the question, Allen continued to look at his wife. "Honey...we could put Jeff's twin bed in there...maybe get some new curtains..."

"Yeah, mama. I could make a chest in Ag class...it'd be nice. I could fix up Oma's room really, you know, nice," Jeff offered, feigning excitement.

"Let's do it then!" Allen spoke, dismissing the conversation as though they had just closed a business deal.

Faye arose from her chair, plate in hand, and carried it to the sink. She began tracing and retracing her steps, gathering up salt and pepper, butter, utensils—Randy gulped his milk, afraid he would lose it to his mother's sudden clean-up binge.

Breakfast had not gone the way Allen wanted, but maybe this thing with Faye was finally over. He hoped so. He knew he was not a prejudiced man. He bore no hatred for the boy...didn't even really know him. And he had nothing at all against colored people, as long as they knew their place. Allen didn't like turmoil. And this boy didn't belong here. That was obvious from Jeff's reaction, wasn't it? Besides, the people in town...

Chapter 3

Faye Cowen stood silently at the kitchen window, watching the school bus ramble out of sight. Her jaws, clamped tightly, shoulders rigid, were the only visible indications of her inner turmoil. A fire blazed in her eyes: a resolute stare into the future. She would not fight against Allen. She **could** not. She had never taken a stand in opposition to him in her life. Never. Just as her mother had remained subservient to **her** husband, Faye had learned her role.

No, she would not oppose Allen, but she would not be pushed aside about this. Not this time. She would convince Allen, somehow. She would win this battle, not to prove a point, but because she was right. She would go back to the Wilson's house…when Allen went to work…today.

She never considered the front door might be locked. It wasn't. Faye glanced quickly, involuntarily, at the sofa, then away. A fly landed on her forehead and was swept quickly away with an absent flip of her hand. The smell in the old house was dank, old, moist. A dirty pair of denim overalls, faded to pale, dusty gray, lay abandoned on the arm of a ragged, green arm chair. One circular spring exposed itself through the worn fabric of the seat. A work boot, tilted over on its side, displayed a leather sole no longer intact. Without realizing it, Faye searched the living room with her eyes, the dying room, her mind whispered.

The walls still bore the cinder, darkened stain of many years of coal-oil lanterns. Electricity had been added six years before, emphasizing the blackened spots on the ceiling from the lamps, making starker the appearance of the cluttered rooms.

She felt a sudden surge of guilt, of intrusion upon those who had lived here. Who still lived here. She waved it off. She could feel guilty later.

Suddenly, a sound! A rattle. Someone in the kitchen. Frozen, her breath stopped, half-drawn, lungs hungry for air. Her first act was of retreat…one step backward. But the calf of her leg touched against some object, and her knee jerked quickly away in reflex.

She stood silently, erect. Caught in the trap she had made for herself, she wanted to think, "What am I doing here? How stupid! Mind your own…" but her brain could not process feeling into thoughts.

What her brain did do was rationalize. Maybe just imagining things. No one there, really. Then the sound came again, rattling, more distinct, followed by a loud "thump!" on the floor. Her mind raced, heart exploding with each beat. Not one fiber of her body moved.

Then he was there. Large, black, and fat, his feet padded silently against the old kitchen linoleum. Green eyes looked directly at Faye Cowen, unconcerned…bored. His long tail whipped twice, some kind of feline indication of irritation. And then he was gone, slinking into a back bedroom.

Faye slumped onto the broken arm chair, the one she had bumped against, not remembering the fright its touch gave her earlier. The exposed spring went unnoticed as it pushed against her. She pressed a quivering hand against her heaving chest. The other arm lay lifeless, her hand mere inches from the floor.

When she could finally speak, the words were strained through breathless lungs, "hate…cats…I…hate…"

She saw the book. Only the spine was visible beneath the center sofa pad, obviously hidden there. Still weak from fright, she shuffled over to the book, pulled it tentatively from its hideout, turning it over and over in small hands. There was no writing on the cover. An old gray ledger, it was frayed at the edges, and rough in her hands. Many of the pages were rumpled and stained.

She lifted the front of the soiled sofa pad to return it, then stopped. She lowered the pad and sat slowly back onto the chair. The ledger was private, she knew. Private and none of her business. She opened it.

May 14th

*It been most two year now. Isaac has been good to me just like he promised. Two year. I ain't wrote in so long...can't even find my old writing book. It seems so long, so far away from Virginia. Mama hasn't written since before Christmas. I don't know how anyone is doing back home. My only salvation is Jesus and my wonderful, precious children. (Isaac Wilson, just in case you snoop into my writing, that don't mean nothing against you). I see changes in Johnny boy. I guess I should call him a man now. He hates me to call him Johnny boy. Habits is hard to undo. His voice changed a couple year ago, and he done lost most of that smooth Virginia sound I like. I know he's lonesome. The kids here, the other Negro kids, still make fun of him. Say he's putting on "airs." But he got most of that lazy Texas talk down now, trying to be like them. He still has troubles with that tempter he got from his daddy, though. I'm so proud of him anyways. He treats Isaac like he was his own daddy. I've heard him, late at night, snubbing in his room. That was several years ago, of course. I guess he just about ran out of little boy tears over his real daddy, if he's alive or dead, back in prison, or just shacked up somewhere not caring about nothing or nobody. I hope he **is** dead. And if he is, I know where he is, and it sure ain't heaven. I know God don't won't no low-down shiftless womanizing drunk up there with the angels.*

July 19th

Isaac been working non-stop these days, mostly trying to keep Mr. Bradley's wells running and the irrigation tubes pouring water full-time. Gets up once in the middle of the night to change tubes. You'd think a half mile of cotton could soak up enough water to keep for the night, at least. But Isaac is excited about this job, and about this house, too, and I know he will kill himself working if he has to.

I hate the way he acts around Mr. Bradley. Most like bowing and scraping and saying yowsa boss, and nawsuh Mr. Bradley, like some low crawling slave. But he says he'll do what he have to do to keep this here job. Season jobs is just too hard on a family, running here and there. And it's true, we been here over a whole year now. With me and the kids helping with the hoeing and picking it makes up for two outsiders Mr. Bradley don't have to hire to help. (Dear Lord that man gives me the willies.) Course, little Mattie Mae, she don't cause no trouble at all. She helps right along side us, but she's young and all and don't make up for much. But she tries.

I know it made Isaac upset with me, but I told him these children are going to school. They can help after. A lot of the Negro hands don't have their kids in school now, but I just know this is best. I can do enough extra during the day to make up for them being gone. My kids is going to get a education.

November 1957

The darkness of depressing thoughts has almost overcome me. My folks back home used to tell me it was just a case of nerves when I felt like this. So hard to get out of bed, much less go outside. I will put on, like I always do, for Isaac and the kids. They don't understand. Nobody does. There's nobody around here for me to talk to anyways, so I guess it don't matter if nobody understands or not.

Isaac is good to me. He does the best he can to take care of me. And Johnny and Little Matt's are good kids. It's just me, I know. There must be something awful wrong with me. Maybe just weak, but it seems worse than that. There are big old holes inside me. Black holes in my sprit. Places in my heart where it seems like the devil hisself has hold.

I guess he does at that, thinking about it. I hate that white man more than anything in the world... way he looks at me. What he does... how he is. He sure is the devil.

On these days it seems like nothing goes right. Every little thing in my mind seems big and terrible. I just can't help it. Dear God, I know it's probably wrong for me to think this, but I wish so much I could just go to sleep and not wake up ever. Peace of death seems so good to me now...so much better than this living. I'm sure the kids and Isaac would all be better off if I was gone. Oh, they would be sad for a while. But before long, Isaac would meet someone else...somebody lots better for him and the kids. They would forget about me soon. Everybody would be better off. Except for working in the house and helping in the fields, I ain't no real use.

What's the matter with me? Jesus help me. My soul is rotting. My spirit is dead. I ain't been happy since...? I don't even remember. This is just awful. Here I sit feeling sorry, but the real reason I opened up this writing book today is because I'm just busting. It's the first real newsy thing I done knowed about in years.

*Of all the places in the world we could have landed, God brought us right here. And guess who lives across the highway? It's a family last name of Cowen. Could it be? Could they be **the** Cowen we know about from back in Virginia? It don't seem possible, I know, but I seen Mr. Cowen in town today, and dear sweet Jesus, he does look like I thought he would. Exactly like his daddy's pictures. If I could just know for sure, it would almost make it worth being here in this flat, dirty, ugly place.*

Faye Cowen read, and re-read the script without looking up, the cat forgotten. Her trespass forgotten. She slammed the book closed then, lost for a moment as she sat in silence, eyes looking beyond the walls of the house.

"Dear God," she whispered. She jumped up and ran back across the road, the ledger gripped firmly in tan hands with white knuckles.

What **about** Allen? What could this woman know of him? It had to be a mistake. After all, the woman wasn't sure. Faye wondered absently about the way Mrs. Wilson described her feelings...feelings Faye recognized in herself since Oma's death..."the death I caused" slipped into her mind as she pushed away the thought. Tears welled in her eyes. She dabbed at them with the corner of her pillow-tick apron.

Faye held tightly to the ledger. The colored woman who wrote the pages seemed so terribly sad. Her sadness seemed almost a sickness, something for which she should be able to take a pill. Nevertheless, she could not shake the feelings of uneasiness over the mention of Allen. She must know more. Knowing she would continue digging, something deep inside told her to stop.

Throw the book away!

Against her will, she kept the ledger closed. She did not want to know more now. She had to think. She also knew there was no power on earth that would keep her from eventually re-opening it.

A knock at the front door startled her. Guilt had her on edge, and she quickly slipped the ledger in a bureau drawer under a small stack of papers. She realized she had been holding her breath.

"Just a moment!" She took two gulps of air into her lungs, trying to relax. From the kitchen window she saw a sheriff's car in the driveway near the corner of the house, the driver's door still ajar. She rushed to respond to the knock and was relieved to see Deputy Wayne Tinsley standing on the porch.

"Is something wrong, Wayne?" Her dark eyes searched his for an indication of why he was there. "Are the boys okay?"

"Relax, Faye. I didn't mean to startle you," he began. "It's nothing really." Deputy Tinsley was a year older than Faye and had known her since her first year at Cash Elementary.

At thirty-five, his Indian-black hair was already sprinkled by a large dose of silver. A western *Resistol* hat in his hand explained the disheveled dents in his hair. He had, of course, removed the headgear before knocking on Faye's door.

"It doesn't have anything to do with y'all at all. I was just wondering if Jeff said anything to you about an incident that happened Friday night in town." Wayne shifted slightly, uncomfortable around Faye, as always. His trim body was hard as old brick, and although very slender, he had never really looked skinny, not even as a kid in school. He reminded Faye of a new, stiff lariat.

"No. I don't recall him mentioning anything at all about Friday night," she answered.

"What kind of incident?"

"Little girl was almost hit by a car on the highway last night…just outside of town." "Really? Is she all right?" she asked.

"Yeah, she will be," he answered. "As well as possible, considering."

"You said she was almost hit. Did something else happen?"

Wayne hesitated a moment, shifting weight from one Acme boot to the other. "There's a lot of stuff we don't know yet…uh, Faye…could I maybe get a glass of water?"

"Oh, I'm sorry Wayne. Where's my manners? Come on in. I'll get you some…would you prefer tea?" she called back over her shoulder.

"Tea would be great. Thank you."

"Sweet?"

"Sweet would be fine, yes." He followed her into the kitchen and sat at the table, hat in his lap. He moved it then, carefully placing it, upside-down, on the chair next to his. Not satisfied with that, he removed it from the chair and put it on the table. Perhaps he should leave that chair empty, he thought.

Faye, however, sat in the chair across the table from him after setting iced-tea glasses down in front of each of them.

"I just thought maybe Jeff had heard something at school about what happened. You know how the kids talk." He continued as if there had been no break in the conversation. "We took her to the hospital. Somebody molested her. She hasn't spoken a word since they found her. Whoever it was, scared that poor little girl to death."

"Dear Lord. That poor little thing. How old…?"

"Six. Six, maybe seven. First year of school. Her folks are hired people on the McMasters farm."

"I know the farm. I don't guess I know the hired hands." Faye shook her head wearily.

"How did this happen? Who could have…?"

"Don't know, Faye. We're just searching for needles in the proverbial haystack. That's why I'm here."

"Did you get a description? Anything?"

"No. Like I said, she can't talk. That monster scared her plumb to death."

"You'll find him," Faye said.

Wayne shook his head, staring into the weak iced tea. "We have to, Faye. This was bad. Really bad. And..." he paused.

"What? What is it?"

"This is going to sound awful, I'm afraid." He breathed in deeply. "Sheriff Hand says we'll work this thing to the...well, till the guy is caught and in jail."

"Of course."

"Things aren't looking too good for the sheriff's election. If we don't have this animal in jail in three weeks..."

"The new sheriff...if there is one...he'll keep looking also, won't he?"

"Jack Edson is the most prejudice man I've ever met, Faye. And the little girl is Negro. He won't turn a tap to find out who did this. And he probably will win the election."

"So, you've got a child molester on the loose, a little girl too afraid to speak, an idiot running for sheriff...and three weeks to save the day...sounds like your average, run of the mill small town business."

"At least we haven't had a murder."

"Careful of what you're thankful for," she smiled over her glass.

He paused and took a long pull on the cold drink. He glanced over the rim at Faye who was looking at him. He quickly looked away. "Anyway, I thought I'd just...you know...check with you. About Jeff, I mean."

Faye suddenly felt uneasy. It was no secret Wayne had a crush on her in school. Of course that had been years ago. He married a girl from Hoover when he returned from the Army. Faye was already married to Allen by then. She smiled again, a tiny smile, amused with herself for even imagining such a thing. Wayne Tinsley was there on business.

She glanced down at her folded hands. They were small, but strong and rough from physical work. She looked back up at the deputy.

"What are they going to do about Mr. Hughes?" she asked without preamble.

"Mr...who? Hughes?"

"You know, the bus driver...the little girl..."

"Oh, yeah. Well, nothing I guess. It **was** an accident." He looked into the glass for a moment. "I'm sure he feels bad about it."

"I'm sure," she agreed. " I was just wondering, you know, if he was responsible for making sure she was safe…something like that?"

"Why, sure. He's suppose to be careful. Sure. But the wind was terrible. It was just an accident."

"Okay," she responded, not looking at him.

"Is something wrong?" he asked carefully.

She shook her head. "I suppose not. I just didn't know how that sort of thing works. You're the first person I've had to ask, that would know, I mean."

He watched her for a moment; her face, her breathing. She was upset, he could tell. Should he ask why? "Thanks for the tea," he said, rising from the table. He lifted the hat gently from the table. It embarrassed him that she thought he knew things about law. He was a sheriff's deputy…had been for five years—ever since his farm failed. But he had no training. He had broken up family fights and served papers. Occasionally he would stop a traffic violator or check on underage kids drinking beer…that was about it.

He liked her thinking he was more important than he really was. He knew how immature those feelings were, but they were there just the same.

He opened the screen door, wishing he could say more, and wishing he had said less. "Thanks again for the tea," he called back over his right shoulder.

"Any time," she answered. She watched him walk back to the sheriff's car and slide all his six feet two inches behind the wheel. He moved like a cat…lithe, strong, and unpretentious. The car backed slowly from the drive and onto the highway. She saw Wayne look back at the house, then quickly away, as he sped off toward Cash.

Faye watched him out of sight, then slid her eyes toward the clock on the living room wall over the sofa. Allen would be home soon. Allen, whose name was hidden in the tattered pages of a ledger written by a young Negro woman. A **dead** woman.

Chapter 4

William Bradley brushed the toe of his right boot against the back of his left trouser leg. The sixty-five dollar western-cut slacks reflected the sun with whispers of a sheen blended into the dark luxurious material. He cuffed his hand over his mouth and blew into it, sniffing immediately. He could smell none of the lingering perfume which had been so noticeable earlier.

He **had** washed his hands twice since leaving Mary Sager's house. He wished she wouldn't wear that cheap stuff. He told her so, and she promised to leave it off next time. Shouldn't complain, he thought. She wasn't exactly his first choice, anyway. One of his hired hands had a fifteen year old girl who had blossomed unbelievably. He had wanted to see her, but her sick kid brother had ruined that plan.

She excited him more than he liked to admit. She **was** colored, of course, but that didn't really bother him. He repeated what he heard as a young man. "You're not a true Texan until you've had sex with a nigger woman."

He walked carefully across the weed-laden front yard of his house where the Wilson family lived. He paid the man a hundred dollars per month, and there was only a slight chance there might be something left behind. The idea of going into their house appealed to him anyway.

There might be some pictures behind…maybe even some naked women magazines. He knew how those men liked to look at nude white women.

The door wasn't locked, nor was it shut. The screen door was held closed with a spring, but it was impossible to see inside because of the bright sunlight. He strode inside without hesitating, the same as he would have done if the Wilsons were still there.

Johnny jerked his head up as the screen door slammed open. He was sprawled across the sofa, one leg dangling over the cushioned armrest. A text book lay nearby, unopened.

"What the…!" Bradley erupted.

They stared at each other for an instant. Johnny bolted to a sitting position, leaning forward slightly. The whites of his eyes were bright in the dimly lit room. Bradley's breathing was loud, and his eyes, too, could be seen from afar, ablaze with rage.

When he found his tongue, Bradley cursed again. Then, "What are you still doing here? You don't understand English or something?"

"Yowsa' Mr. Bradley, sir. I does," Johnny replied, trying to sound as subservient as his step-dad.

"I'm calling the sheriff! You can just go along to prison with that old thief."

"Mr. Wilson ain't no thief!" Johnny snapped.

"He got caught stealing. He's a thief." Bradley never considered that Johnny Wilson was three inches taller than he, and outweighed him by twenty pounds. None of his workers had ever back-talked him in his life, nor to his dad before that.

"No, sir. He is **not** a thief!" Johnny had now dropped the affectations of illiteracy. Something inside him seemed to be rushing for an exit, with nowhere to go. He glared back at Mr. Bradley, who didn't notice.

"Don't argue with me, boy! You're on dangerous ground here… trespassing, and I can shoot you and nobody would think a thing about it."

Johnny Wilson drew silent for a moment, knowing Bradley was right. He tried to regain composure before speaking again. White people were all like this. He had been a fool to cross the man. It truly was up to his step-dad's former boss whether he would be sent to jail or just killed outright.

"I'm sorry, sir. Didn't mean no disrespect." Johnny hated himself for his weakness, but continued. "Ya' see, sir. I just ain't got no place to go. Not jest yet. I was hoping maybe I could do some work for you around here…least wise till you get another family in to farm the place." His voice was soft, and had lowered in volume as he spoke, the last few words almost inaudible.

"No can do, boy." Bradley stroked his chin, more comfortable than a moment before. "Your dad's a drunk and a thief—probably worse if I just knew. It's in your blood. I got nothing against you, personally. You just can't help it. If I let you stay here, you'd have half the place sold off before I knew it."

"But, sir…"

"No buts! You got thirty seconds to get out of here. After that I call the sheriff."

"Ain't no call for that, Mr. Bradley, sir. Jest let me get my stuff."

"You got no stuff. You're trespassing, and this is my property. You're lucky to get outta here with your skin. So, git!"

"I'm gittin', sir. I was just wondering if you would let me just take a minute or two…you know…to see to my mama's stuff." His head was bowed, eyes riveted on the floor.

"Your mommy's **stuff**? Boy you got some nerve. You can't be that ignorant. I said get out, and I meant it. You're doing nothing but wasting my time. I've got important things I need to be doing." Then, he lowered his voice to an almost whisper, and hissed, "Besides, if you want to know about your mommy's stuff, I can tell you about it. I know more about her **stuff** than you do."

Johnny's head shot up.

Then Bradley added, "Or, maybe I don't."

"What're you saying?" demanded the younger man.

"I'm not saying nothing. Just that I knew your mama **very** well. I knew her stuff…intimately, I guess you might say."

In the darkness of the smoky old house, Bill Bradley could not see

28

the rage in Johnny's face, the twitching of jaw muscles, or the deadly look in his eyes. A look of murder. Both fists were clinched at his side. Was Mr. Bradley saying what Johnny **thought** he was saying?

Stupidly, Bradley answered the unasked question. "Right in there," he pointed to the nearest bedroom. "Right there on your parents' bed. And she liked it. They usually do. I've had lots better, though. Most nigger women are pretty good, but she mostly just laid there, enjoying it."

Before Bradley finished the sentence, Johnny crossed the room, slamming the older man backwards with a vicious blow to the chest with his fist. He fell backward, tripping over a small footstool, landing hard on his back in the floor. His head snapped back and bounced off the hardwood with a resounding crack.

Johnny jumped astraddle the man before he could lift himself from the floor. Shock was replaced by terror in the eyes of Bradley. >From the light of the open front door, he could see the face of the enraged Johnny Wilson above him. He didn't see it for long. Johnny slammed a large fist into his face, then another. Then again. The first blow hurt Bradley, as did the second. But soon, he could only feel the pressure of the blows striking his face. They didn't hurt anymore, and he wasn't sure what was happening.

Bradley could no longer see the man on his chest. He couldn't see anything. He felt his head rocking from side to side, knowing he was still being beaten. Then he knew nothing at all.

Johnny stopped beating the man beneath him when he could no longer swing his arms. The rush of adrenaline, and the activity of the brief encounter, left him gasping for air. He closed his eyes tightly, trying to catch a breath of air, trying to erase what he had just done.

But when he opened them, the body still lay beneath him on the floor, not moving. Where Bradley's face had been was a mass of blood and destroyed meat. The dark red flow still streamed from his broken nose. Johnny Wilson looked at his hands, turned them over and inspected the palms. They were covered in blood. Mr. Bradley's blood. A **white man's** blood.

Chapter 5

May 22

Desperation presses hard against the inside of my skin. How much more can a person endure? Big baby, that's me. Others, they get by. Parents losing children...how terrible for those who don't know about a better life later. How do they do it? Why even ask why? I already know. Because there ain't no choice. No way out. No breath of air. Daily turn myself over to God...His will be done. Is it His will, all these things?

Is it okay for me to even question? Do I ask the awful question? Would that make me even more evil, or just less faithful...or are they the same things?

*Depression eating at my flesh, rotting my soul. Killing the joy I long for so much...so awful much. The joy I believe I'm **supposed** to feel. And if I don't, does that mean something? What about Mr. Cowen? Why was we put here so close? And why Mr. Bradley? What would Isaac say if he knew about Mr. Bradley. Would he kill that horrible man for me?*

Why this total loss inside me? Why try to find blame, anyway? It just steals away in dark corners. It doesn't even really exist. If only there was something to attack. Not fair...Like trying to get a loan. Who can

*get them? Those white people that don't even need one. Beat the poor.
Kill the poor. Rape the poor women who can't say to her husband what
happened 'cause he might lose a sorry job.*

*I know now I'll never talk to Mr. Cowen about his past. His wife she
seems real nice, always waving at me from across the road. Caint see
no good in causing her trouble...or him either for that matter. Some
things should just be left alone.*

*I did write home though. I told Evelyn I done found our half brother,
right here in Texas. And just like mama told us, you can't hardly even
see he's got any colored in him at all. His hair is real wiry, and he keeps
it cut close. His lips are a little full. That's about all, though. Skin white
as snow.*

*I remember that first day I saw him in town. We was just meeting on
the sidewalk. His build, the way he walked and moved...I guess my
mouth just dropped open. He even nodded to me, but I couldn't say
anything or even act like I saw him. I thought, if that ain't **him**, then Mr.
Hall done dropped another sprout somewhere, cause he was a spitting
image of him.*

*Then, when I found out his name is Cowen, I just about dropped
dead in my tracks. The same last name as those folks that mama said
came and took him away that night. She said they seemed real nervous,
being in colored town and all...like we was going to rub off on them or
something. But she said they was also nice. And they would take my
older brother as their own baby...keep it a secret like he was adopted
out of a orphanage.*

*Course, I wasn't born yet, but I used to see Mr. Hall from time to
time in town back in Virginia, and I always wondered if his little boy
looked like him or like mama. She couldn't keep him, that was sure, him
being white and all, and Mr. Hall said he couldn't have a new baby all
of a sudden, just like that. He wasn't even married.*

*He didn't come around after that, mama said. And when she talked
about him sometimes her eyes would get all teary. I think they were
really in love, though I don't really know how that was possible. Mama
was never really happy after that, I don't think. She tried to put on, and
she was always good to daddy. But all my life seemed there was an*

empty place inside her. I guess she could feel I was—you know, kinda knowing something was wrong. Maybe that's why she told me the story. She cried and cried. She cried about Mr. Hall, but mostly she cried about little Jefferson. Colored people didn't want him cause he was white and white folk didn't want him cause he was colored. Only people seemed to want him was the Cowens. Mama said they wanted a baby so bad they would have taken a goat in diapers.

I promised her I would never tell, but I couldn't help it. I told Evelyn when she was eleven or twelve, right after daddy died. Mama never did cry over my daddy like she did Mr. Hall.

So, that's out of the way. I won't tell Mr. Cowen. People around here don't seem to notice anything different about him. I do, but maybe that's cause I'm looking for something. With that done, there is only two things left to do. Two real important things.

I don't know if God can forgive me for either one of them.

Faye Cowen closed the ledger gently, quietly. The remaining pages were blank. Her head was fuzzy inside, thoughts would not clarify.

"My dear God," she whispered. She leaned back in the kitchen chair. The ledger was heavier than she had ever noticed before, and she put it on the table before her. And again, "Dear God." She thought she would faint as the room seemed to darken, and her thoughts became even more disoriented.

"My husband is colored," she whispered to herself, hearing the sound of her own voice mutter the unimaginable. "Allen is half Negro…a, what do they call them? Mulatto?" Then another thought drove itself into her consciousness. Her boys! Her boys were part Negro!

Immediately her mind raced, picturing her sons in her mind, watchful for any tale-tale signs of their…what?…their heritage? Bloodline? Their coloredness? Jeff was blond. His eyes blue. No, there was nothing there to give it away. Randy? Oh, my…Randy! Randy's beautiful, curly black hair…and his nose! It was broader than most…they had always joked with him about acquiring the old Cowen light-bulb nose.

Things that seemed cute yesterday were suddenly threatening, shameful. The last date in the entry ledger was the day Johnny Wilson found his mother hanging from the tree in their back yard.

Chapter 6

Jeff enjoyed Saturdays more than ever since Mr. Bradley hired him and two of his friends to break his horses. He loved the Bradley place, its corrals and huge barns looking more like a ranch than a farm. Farm implements lined up outside the barn spoiled the effect somewhat, but still it impressed him. The smell of horse manure and fresh hay struck him as he neared the sprawling red barn. It was still cool at 6:30 a.m., and quiet.

It would be hot later, however, and he already had the order of horses he would ride scheduled in his mind. More difficult animals would be first, and the easier ones later in the day.

Around ten o'clock, Mrs. Bradley would bring them some iced tea to drink. She always did. Jeff did not know her before he began working on their place part-time. No one knew anything about her. No one ever saw her.

She still seemed a little uncomfortable around Jeff and his friends, but recently had engaged them upon occasion with light conversation. To all their surprise, she was very pretty.

At least she was pretty to be that old—probably in her thirties—and the three young men had found themselves drawn to her. Jeff recalled the Saturday one week earlier when she brought them lemonade instead of tea. They talked for a few moments, and Ray made a funny remark. All four were laughing aloud when she seemed to catch herself. Lowering her head, the ever-present straw hat covering her eyes, she turned and hurried back to the safety of her house.

Jeff pushed open the pedestrian door of the barn, hesitating a moment for his eyes to adjust to the darkness. Mr. Bradley had installed the light switch fifteen feet inside the barn instead of next to the door.

He stepped inside and immediately heard a noise. It wasn't the typical sound of a rat scurrying through feed sacks, but something large, the unmistakable clop-clopping of horse hooves on the concrete floor of the barn. One of the thoroughbreds was out of his stall.

"Somebody's gonna' be in trouble," Jeff whispered. Bradley **never** allowed horses to run loose in the barn. They were either in the pasture, or—if being worked—in one of the eight stalls inside the barn.

He eased across the room, taking in more of his surroundings. He could tell the horse had been on the far side of the barn, but the sound of hooves on the floor seemed to draw nearer, the animal perhaps drawn by the opening of the door Jeff had opened.

He flipped the switch. A dark chestnut horse stood trembling two feet from Jeff. The animal lurched, bowling him over. Like a freight-train, the tall animal covered the short distance and rushed out the door, slamming his left side against the door jamb, hooves skidding on concrete. Then he was gone.

Jeff realized he was holding his breath, and let out a sigh of relief. It would take a while gathering up the animal. One of the more sedate horses on the place normally, it was strange for him to act so wild. He shook his head, thinking again how much trouble Mr. Bradley's hired man would be in. Probably lose his job, he thought.

Then he saw him. Jeff gasped, his heart pounding immediately in his ears. He could not breathe. He could not think. He could only stare. A pool of dark red blood spread across the concrete around Mr. Bradley's head. The thick liquid had congealed into masses of *Jello*-like curds, dull and lifeless, darkening…sticky.

But the blood was not what held Jeff's attention. In the center of the pool was Bill

Bradley's head, a wooden-handled ice pick stuck to the hilt in his left eye. The right eye was half open, cloudy and puffed out. His face was a pulp of smashed and bruised flesh. Both ears were torn and battered. Blood had trickled out of his right ear, leaving a dried scab-like line from the ear opening parallel to the floor toward his jaw. Bradley...he was sure it was Bradley because of the clothes and familiar expensive boots...lay on his back, the front of his white western-cut shirt covered in blood.

His hands were covered in blood also. His right hand clung to his shirt front, the material wadded in his death grasp. The other hand gripped loosely at the ice pick.

Jeff's mind said run for help, but his eyes could not remove themselves from the scene before him. The ice pick was only partially visible behind Bradley's bloody fingers, and he couldn't see any of the metal spike. But the shape of the wooden handle was common...and the thing was stuck in Bradley's **eye**!

Finally he turned away, then realized...what if someone's still in the barn? The killer! . He ran. He sprinted, banging against the side of the door just as the horse Oklahoma had done earlier.

The brightness of the early morning was surreal after the artificial light of the barn. The nearest house, of course, was Bradley's. It was a hundred yards to the house, and Jeff was gasping for air as he ran up to the back door.

"Oh, no! Oh, man. Ohhh..." A thought came to Jeff as he raised his fist to pound on the door of the farm house. **Mrs.** Bradley. What if somebody had...had done something to her, too? And if not, what would he tell her? He couldn't tell her what he found in the barn. He held the screen door open in one hand, his other cocked. His mind raced. What to do?

"Jeff?"

He jumped. She had pulled the door open and was standing right in front of him.

"Jeff, what's wrong? You look white as a sheet."

"I, uh..." he gasped. He needed a minute...gather his thoughts.

She wore a modest terry-cloth robe, her feet were bare. Black hair was combed straight back and wet. A tiny trickle of water inched its way from behind her ear and down a long, slender neck. Jeff stared at her, puffing. He never realized…her hair was long. What was he thinking? Her husband lay murdered a hundred yards away, and he couldn't take his eyes off her.

"Need to call…uh…I need to call…dang…call, the uh…the sheriff."

"The sheriff? Jeff, calm down. Come in and just calm down. Tell me now," she reached for his hand, remembered a hot cup of coffee which she placed on the cabinet, then reached for him again. "Jeff, are one of the other boys hurt?"

He accepted her hand, and stepped inside the back door. "No, they're okay. Not here yet." Her hand was so gentle, fragile. "Mr. Bradley…" he began.

"No, I'm sorry Jeff. He's not here."

"Not here?"

"No. He left last night for Ruidoso. Can I help?"

"Mrs. Bradley…uh, please just sit down for a minute. Let me call the Sheriff. I'll tell you about it…you know…in a minute. Okay?"

She seemed perplexed, but sat as Jeff had requested.

"The phone is in there," she said, pointing toward a room down a small hallway. "The bedroom."

"Thanks. Be right back." He hurried into the room, glad to be momentarily out of Mrs. Bradley's presence. He would still have to tell her, he knew, or put her off till the Sheriff arrived. He found the phone and dialed "O." The operator had him connected to the Sheriff's Department in Hoover in less than a minute.

"You've got to get somebody out to the Bradley place," he whispered hurriedly. "There's been a murder!" He hesitated, then answered, "It's on the same road as the Cash cemetery…two miles past. Just ask your deputy over here. He knows…just tell him to go to Bill Bradley's place…go to the barn."

He listened intently to the black phone, bent over because of the short cord. His eyes wandered over the bed, still unmade. It smelled good, clean.

"No," he said suddenly into the phone, "We don't need an

ambulance…seventeen…I'm seventeen…what difference…?" He stopped for a moment. "Of course I'm sure. Yes, **dead**! I'm positive. Who? Mr. Bradley! Mr. Bradley has been murdered. I found him in his barn…"

The quick intake of breath from across the room spun Jeff around in his tracks. The telephone, jerked from the table, landed loudly on the hardwood floor. He saw her in the doorway, staring at him. Her large eyes looked at him, but didn't seem to see. Her face paled. She had heard him. She heard it all!

"Mrs. Bradley…" he began.

Beneath the thick robe, Jeff saw a quivering of her legs. He started to speak again, but stopped. She leaned against the side of the doorway, then slowly, quietly, slumped to the floor, unconscious.

Chapter 7

Hensley County Deputy Sheriff Wayne Tinsley had never worked a homicide. He had helped his fellow deputies in Hoover with a couple of murders in the past, but both of those had been "smoking gun" cases. The dead guys and their killers were still at the scene, and there wasn't much investigation to it.

Other deputies were on their way from Hoover to assist, but he would be responsible. The Sheriff was out of town on vacation, and it was his policy that "Whoever catches the crime carries the baby." Tinsley wasn't sure what that was supposed to mean exactly, but he understood the gist of it. If you got the call, it was your case till it was over.

He consciously calmed himself as he pulled into the driveway at Bill Bradley's farm. Driving past the house, he sped directly to the barn as instructed by his dispatcher. He had driven past the Bradley place a hundred times, but had never been on the property before.

The pedestrian door to the barn still stood wide open, and he stepped gingerly through it. He moved cautiously, not knowing what to expect. The light was on, and it took only seconds for his eyes to adjust. As an afterthought, he removed the revolver from its holster and held it loosely at his side, not really expecting a murderer to jump out from behind a stack of hay; however, just in case.

Although emotionally prepared to see a dead body, Wayne jerked to a halt when he saw Bradley in the floor of the barn. He was aware of his own heart as it pounded harder against his chest. He felt his breath increase, and tried to slow it. "Calm. Be calm. Just do your job."

He walked slowly around the body, trying to concentrate on any evidence that might be present; but the battered face, and the ice pick in the man's eye, kept Tinsley's attention as over and over again he found himself staring at the heart of the violence. Wayne replaced the revolver and removed a small notebook from his left shirt pocket. He needed to make notes…focus.

The barn was quiet except for an occasional stirring of horses behind stable doors. At least he hoped it was horses. Why weren't the other deputies here yet? It was only nine miles to Cash from Hoover, and another three or four miles to the Bradley place.

He went back to the entrance. Beginning there, he back-tracked slowly toward the body, bowing low toward the floor, searching…trying to see, trying to understand. He didn't know exactly what he was looking for, but he knew to look. Just inside the door was a dark skid mark, as though someone had hurried out the door and slid their shoe heel in their hurried escape. He tore a blank piece of paper from the notebook and placed it beside the skid mark.

He felt a little better, having now found what he thought might be evidence. Easing toward the body, Wayne Tinsley looked even closer at the floor, hoping to have some other evidence before his back-ups arrived. He noted that the barn floor was of finished, smooth concrete, except for where the horses walked from stables to the big sliding doors. That floor was roughly textured to give the horses better traction.

Tinsley knew that fact had nothing to do with this murder. He just liked barns, and this one had been built right. He acknowledged that fact in spite of how he personally felt about Mr. Bradley. Bill. Everyone within fifty miles knew what a womanizer he was. Ran around on his wife all the time. Messed around with his own hired help…their women, and even young daughters. That was what Wayne had heard anyway.

He didn't doubt the stories. In his patrol duties, Deputy Tinsley had seen Bradley's pick-up parked in alleys, or behind houses where he had no business being, and—frequently—parked right in front of a house where a husband was known to be absent. Most of his indiscretions seemed to occur in the town of Hoover—not out of any sense of propriety, Tinsley knew—but because there weren't but about three hundred and fifty homes in the entire town of Cash. Not a great selection.

Bradley's wife, on the other hand, was almost never seen in town; didn't go to any church he was aware of. Bill even bought the groceries. It was as though he kept her prisoner. Tinsley knew that was not the case, of course, since he had seen her outside her home many times when he was on patrol, working in the yard, or just sitting in the large rocker on the front porch.

He often waved to her from the road…everyone in the county waved to everyone else. Most of the time she did not appear to see him, but occasionally she would wave back, although timidly.

He closed his mind and his eyes for an instant. Concentrate, he thought. A man has been murdered here. Returning to the body, Tinsley began taking notes:

1. Left eye. Ice pick to the hilt. Wooden handle, so no fingerprints
2. Right ear, blood…dried blood. Trickled down…sideways (what's that about?) The blood is parallel to the floor. Why? Because he was standing or sitting upright while it bled. It dried before this happened?
3. Blood coagulated. Smells. (They told me blood doesn't have an odor.) Lots of it
4. Face. Hammered. Battered. Left ear almost torn off. Nose obviously broken. Lips swollen. Right eye blackened and puffed out.
5. Right hand holding shirt…death drip. Left hand on murder weapon
6. Both boots on. Belt still fastened. Shirt fastened, except top two buttons. Hat not present (Haven't checked his pickup yet).

7. No blunt instrument found yet—haven't completed search of area. Too much blood for one puncture wound?

8. Be sure to take plenty pictures

9. ?

Wayne Tinsley kept the small notebook open where he had written, but replaced it in his pocket. He should search the barn further. Perhaps there was a bloody club...something. He looked once more at the dark pool surrounding Bradley's head. At one edge of the blood was a pattern of some kind. He knelt beside it and recognized immediately the unmistakable print of a horse shoe. It was curious, since no horse was evident, but no more than that. Horses seldom used ice picks to murder their owners.

He heard the distant sounds of a siren. They would be here soon. He wished the sheriff was available. Sheriff Hand had worked in a large metropolitan police department years before, and probably had experience with this sort of thing. None of the deputies were really qualified for this, he knew, including himself.

A thorough search of the barn interior turned up nothing suspicious. Two deputies showed up together, their wailing sirens taking forever to finally wind down to silence. It irritated Tinsley, but he wasn't sure why.

"What 'ya want us to do, Wayne?" asked Bill Lightsey, the older, and much paunchier of the two new arrivals. Then he saw Bradley. "Holy Je...what the...oh, my good Lord!" He stared at the body, mouth agape.

"Hi, Bill. Reckon y'all could maybe check around outside? See if you can find any tracks, blood...anything like that?"

Bill nodded without speaking. His partner, Ralph Palmer, was twenty-one and had been on the job three months. He had never seen a fresh body before. He stared, not speaking. His chin quivered, and a small tic at his left eye indicated he might still be alive.

"We probably should do that pretty soon," Tinsley reminded them. "People will be curious about the sirens, and we'll have a mob on our hands in less than an hour."

Bill nodded again, and began to turn his body toward the door. However his head would not follow. His eyes transfixed on the scene before him. "Wayne, you know this guy?"

"Yeah, a little. Know more **about** him than anything else. Haven't spoken to him very often. Didn't particularly like him."

"Okay. Well, guess we'll get busy outside." He shook his head slightly. "Glad you didn't like him. Makes it a little easier, I guess. You gonna' be okay in here?"

"Sure. I'm almost done, actually. Just need a bunch of pictures."

"Oh, man," Lightsey groaned.

"You do have the camera with you, don't you? I specifically told the dispatcher…"

Lightsey held up a beefy right hand, palm outward toward Deputy Tinsley. "She told me, Wayne. Dang it! She told me. I just got in a hurry, had to pick up the rookie…my fault."

Tinsley let out a long sigh. He lowered his head in thought for a moment. "Here's what we'll do. Bill, you go ahead and check the area outside. Palmer…" Ralph Palmer still stared at the body on the floor. "Palmer!" Tinsley snapped.

Deputy Palmer jerked his head up and looked at the angry Tinsley.

"Pay attention, Ralph," he began, calming his voice. "This is very important. I'm going down to the Bradley house. I may be there a while 'cause I know I'm going to have to talk to Bradley's wife."

Palmer acknowledged with a slight head movement, not removing his eyes from the body.

Tinsley continued, "I don't know how long I'll be. I'm going to see if I can borrow a camera from Mrs. Bradley."

Bill Lightsey was almost to the door, when he spun around on cowboy boots. "You're gonna' borrow a camera from the widow to take pictures of her dead husband?"

"If she's got one, I am. You got a better idea?"

Lightsey thought a moment. "Nope."

Tinsley returned his attention to Palmer. "So, here's what you do. When we leave this barn, you are going to stand in front of that door. No one is to get by you. Nobody!"

"Okay," Ralph acknowledged. "How about Bill, though?"

"Did you hear what I said…I mean the part about **nobody**?"

"Yes, sir."

"That means nobody. Not Bill. Not a newspaper reporter. Not the justice of the peace. Not the President of the United States. Not so much as a tumble-bug. Do you understand?"

"Yes, sir. I understand now. I won't let you down."

"I'm sure you won't, Ralph. Besides, you've probably already heard what I do to rookies who disappoint me." Tinsley was walking toward the farm house.

"Uh, no deputy. I don't guess I heard," called Ralph.

"Believe me, you don't want to find out," he said without turning.

Bill Lightsey had started his search of the area outside the barn. Ralph looked at him for support, caught the older deputy's eyes, and found nothing there but a shrug of his thick shoulders. Ralph closed the door and leaned against it, touching the hardware at his side to assure himself the thirty-eight was still there.

Chapter 8

Tinsley tapped quietly on the back storm door. Hearing nothing, he knocked louder, calling out.

"Come in! We're back here! Help," came a male voice from the back of the house. The storm door was unlocked, and the kitchen door stood ajar.

Wayne Tinsley hurried through the kitchen, past the living room, and down the hall. In the last doorway at the end of the dimly lit hallway sat a man holding the lifeless body of a woman.

"Jeff! Jeff, is that you?"

"Yeah," the young man responded, breathless. "Look. She's been like this ever since I called." He nodded down at the woman. She lay still, breathing slowly, eyes closed. There was a strain in Jeff's voice which was similarly obvious in his face. He cradled her head in his arms, her back and shoulders resting against his thighs. His legs had lost feeling, but he wouldn't move.

"There's an ambulance coming," Wayne said. "They should be here any time."

Jeff nodded. The deputy inched closer to her.

"What happened to her?" he asked, finally. "Is she hurt?"

"No, I don't think so. She heard me tell the sheriff's department about Mr. Bradley. When I turned around she just went white and fell down. I thought she was dead." As he spoke, Jeff absently brushed the woman's hair away from her face. "I didn't know what to do."

"Well, I guess you did just fine," said Tinsley, looking around the room. "Jeff, have you ever been in the house here before?"

"No. This is the first time."

Wayne continued looking. "I was just wondering if they have a camera. Think I'll take a look around for a second. Do you think they'd mind?"

Jeff shrugged. How would he know? He was just their…a revulsion poisoned his stomach…there wasn't a **them** anymore. He could see Mr. Bradley in his mind…vividly…the body…the ice pick. There was no them. Only her.

Wayne knelt down beside them again, reaching out a dark brown hand to her pale white throat. He felt gently for a pulse at her carotid artery. He found the pulse slow and strong. He already knew she was alive, from the rhythmic rise and fall of her chest beneath the bath robe, but it seemed the thing to do.

"She'll be fine, Jeff," he said, answering the unasked question. He rose again and continued his search for a camera…hopefully one with film. "You can lay her down, if you like. I'll get a pillow for her head," he added.

"No, I'm okay. I'll wait for the ambulance."

"Whatever you want to do."

"Deputy Tinsley, have you been out to the barn yet? I heard some sirens a while ago."

"Yeah, I was out there."

"Do you know who…?"

"No idea yet, boy. We're just sorta' getting our investigation started. How about you? You got any ideas?"

Jeff shook his head. "No. I ain't never seen anybody beat like that before." He looked back down at Mrs. Bradley. She hadn't heard. He lowered his voice. "I found him. I'm the one that called."

"I know. What're you doing out here this early anyway?" Tinsley didn't look at Jeff as he talked. His search had taken him to the master bedroom closet.

"Breaking horses for Mr. Bradley. A couple of my friends were supposed to be here too. Sometimes they sleep late though."

"Ever see a dead body before, Jeff? A fresh one, I mean."

"Yeah, once before. That bus accident."

"I remember. That was a bad business, too." Tinsley shook his head as he reached over a *Parcheesi* game in the top of the closet. "That's about two more than most boys your age. Sorry it had to be you that...here it is!" He pulled out a black box camera, rolling it over in his hands, inspecting the mechanisms.

The camera was similar to one Wayne had used before. He flipped out the small crank and wound it clock-wise till it stopped, advancing the film to the next frame. He wasn't sure if it would even take pictures indoors, but he had already considered how to increase light in the barn.

They would open the big doors, then bring a squad car up close and shine a spot light on whatever needed photographed. It was the best he could do. He needed to talk to Jeff more, but that would have to wait. He had to get back to the barn before Ralph accidentally shot somebody.

Chapter 9

Deputy Tinsley stayed in Mrs. Bradley's hospital room much of Saturday night. She rested quietly, with occasional bouts of stirring and mumbling. She had not regained consciousness but, according to Dr. Mack, they had sedated her anyway "to calm her emotions."

"Excuse me, Wayne," said the nurse in a whispered voice. The heavy wooden door slid quietly open into the room. She was robustly built, her slightly graying hair and spectacles finishing out the appearance package. The white nurse's uniform was heavily starched, her hose also white, but transparent. He heard an unfamiliar sound as she walked across the room...a swishing that occurred in rhythm with her legs as she walked.

"Sure," he responded. He slid his chair away from the bedside and stood beside it. "Do I need to leave the room?"

"No. I'm just going to check her vitals." She began her task with quiet efficiency. Occasionally she spoke to Mrs. Bradley as though she were awake. "Let me see your arm here, Sweetie...just a minute... okay, there we go."

"Do you think she can hear you, Mrs. Richards?" Tinsley asked.

"Don't really know. Most people don't seem to think so."

"Why do you talk to her, then?"

"Just in case. I sort of have this theory that somewhere in there someone is listening. She may not **know** what's being said, or understand the meaning, but I think deep inside I may be offering some comfort. Silly, I know." She finished charting her numbers and replaced the clipboard at the foot of the bed.

"Mrs. Richards…what exactly is wrong with her? I keep hearing all this mumbo-jumbo, but I don't get it. A person can't just faint and stay…well, fainted. Can they?"

She stifled a laugh, and quickly removed the smile from her face when she realized he was serious. "It's not like that. It's not so much that she fainted, but more the **reason** she fainted."

Tinsley nodded. "Okay…and?"

"The brain is a very fragile organ. I'm not talking about the physiological brain, either. I mean the part of our mind where emotions are. Sometimes things happen that our brains are just not ready to accept. They just sort of shut down. Like overloading an electric plug. Bang! It blows a fuse."

Wayne Tinsley scratched his head, thoughtfully. "So, hearing about Bill's death just put her into overload, so to speak?"

"Something like that."

"How long will she be out?"

"No way to tell. Probably not long. Maybe an hour, maybe a couple of days. You really should get a little rest. We can call you when she comes to."

"Yeah, I guess that would be the best thing. I've written my report, but I haven't given it to the Sheriff yet. He'll be wanting something for the newspaper Monday."

"Well, my heart goes out to this little lady," said Nurse Richards. "But to tell you the truth her misery is sure misplaced. Bill Bradley was the sorriest excuse for a man I ever knew."

"Did you know him well?"

Lord, forgive me. I shouldn't speak this way of the dead," she twirled on stubby-heeled white shoes toward the door, "but I think she's better off. Anyway, ain't none of my…" her voice trailed off as the door closed behind her.

Wayne agreed with Mrs. Richards. Most of the people in Cash

probably did, he thought. But in his position as a deputy he couldn't be too outspoken about his opinions. One of the first things he learned about law enforcement when Sheriff Hand hired him was deputies don't embarrass sheriffs...not if they want to stay deputies.

And the second thing he learned was...well, thought Tinsley, I'm still waiting on that second thing. He looked long into the ivory-colored face of Mrs. Bradley. Mrs. Ivy Jean Bradley.

He had found a driver's license in her purse at the house after the ambulance took her away. Oddly, it was a recent issue. Why would she even **need** a driver's license, he wondered. Then he remembered someone saying she went to the city on rare occasions.

What had she seen? Probably nothing. The murder took place in the barn, after all. But he did know enough about investigating to know he needed to talk to her as soon as possible. He put his hand on hers, "I'll be back. It'll be okay." He pulled his hand back, suddenly aware of the intimacy of being alone in the room with her.

Wayne spoke to a few people in the hospital lobby on his way out. He knew most of the residents of Cash and the surrounding farms, the main reason he had been hired as a deputy. With Hoover—the county seat—being several miles away, it was easier having a local man handling calls in the area than sending deputies all that distance for every little thing.

Besides, Cash contained some of the wealthiest constituents in the county and a significant number of voters. They liked having one of "their own" handling local problems. With Wayne being a military veteran, that made him even more appropriate for the job.

He took the murder report to the sheriff's office. The long drive and the cool night air bore down on his weary body like a huge weight. By the time he arrived home two hours later, he could have slept on nails. He put on the emergency brake, turned off the key, and leaned his head against the window for a moment.

Through a deep fog in his mind, Tinsley considered the new murder case...and he had done nothing on the child's sexual assault case... time was running out.

He awoke in the exact same position hours later.

Chapter 10

Jeff was in a foul mood. In fact, everyone in the family had been a little testy that morning; on edge. Allen had seemed in a particularly bad mood. That was most unusual of all, thought Jeff. His dad usually didn't seem to feel too much one way or another. At least, not so it showed.

Dixie trotted alongside, looking up at Jeff as they walked the 50 yards to the barn. Her bobbed tail wiggled furiously.

"What're you looking at?" snapped Jeff, but she continued watching him anyway. She was a good mouser, but she was too little, and she was Randy's. Jeff had wanted a big dog, but Allen had found Dixie somewhere and gave her to Randy.

The rusty chain held the snap swivel which kept the door hasp closed on the barn door. Only today it held nothing. It hung loosely, not attached to the hasp. The door was closed, but not secure. Jeff's face heated as blood rushed to it. Frantically, he tried to remember exactly what he had done the previous night after milking.

He tried to go over what had happened, why he might have left the door unlocked. If the cow had gotten into the barn, she would have foundered for sure on the molasses-sweetened feed inside. She would probably have died, and it would have been his fault.

He couldn't think of anything that had diverted his attention the evening before. He had been doing chores for so long, he did them mostly without thinking. The steps he took each day at the barn were always the same. Perhaps it was just that he had had the murder on his mind a lot since finding Mr. Bradley.

More than that, he had **Mrs.** Bradley on his mind.

Dixie scratched at the tin-covered door, returning Jeff's attention to his task. He had held the chain in his hand as he day-dreamed. Jerking the door open, he watched Dixie bolt through the narrow opening. Jeff heard the usual scurrying of many tiny mice feet as the rodents ran for cover from the quick predator.

Jeff pulled the door only partly closed behind him, needing some light from outside to get the feed for the cow. Mildred was tame as any house pet, and she would follow him right into the barn if he gave her a chance. Pushing her back out was like moving a nine hundred pound brick.

He lifted the stained galvanized bucket from a nail in the rafter and dipped it into the sweet feed for Mildred to eat while he milked. He stopped, the bucket only partially full. Something was out of place...not right. The square bales of alfalfa hay were out of order. He peered at them a moment, frozen in his task.

Then he realized they were not so much out of order as they were **different.** Moved.

Askew from their usual exactly squared piles. Then he saw the foot! Dixie's sniffing at the object drew his attention. The shoe was barely visible from behind the stack of alfalfa, against the far wall. Jeff let go of the bucket and straightened. Maybe it's just a shoe, he thought. But as soon as he thought it, he saw a small part of a foot in the worn down brogans.

Jeff walked slowly toward the still limb. His first thought was that he had found another body. A chill went through him when he remembered Mr. Bradley with the ice pick stuck in his eye. Then the foot moved!

It was a slight movement only. A twitch. It was the foot of someone not dead. Jeff was immediately relieved, then frightened. Why would someone be hiding in the barn?

"Hey, you!" he barked in the deepest voice he could find. "You, there in the hay…I see you! Might as well come on out." The foot remained still.

"If you don't get out of there right now, I'll call the Sheriff."

The muffled sound of a voice buried deep in the hay was unintelligible. The foot began slowly backing out of the cover as a leg emerged, then another. Jostling the hay out of the way, Johnny Wilson crawled to his knees and knelt there in front of Jeff.

"Please, don't call the Sheriff."

"What are you doing here?" Jeff asked, ignoring the other young man's plea. Then he saw the blood…a lot of blood. Without taking his eyes from the intruder, Jeff reached back and pushed the barn door open wider. Light rushed in.

"Holy…! What happened to you?"

Johnny looked toward the floor, still kneeling. His blood-covered hand scraped absently at a dark red crust on his cheek. "It's not my blood," he said quietly.

Jeff froze. His eyes widened, the whites showing in the shadows of the barn. "You! It was you! You did that to Mr. Bradley!"

Johnny didn't speak. He waved his head from side to side slightly. Otherwise he made no movement. Finally, he spoke. "I'm real hungry."

Their eyes held for a moment. Jeff could not believe it. He was facing a murderer, covered in blood. And all the man had to say was he was hungry. "What?" he said weakly. He realized he should be running away…getting Allen…doing something. But he just stood there. Jeff had had an image of the murderer in his mind, and this didn't fit. But the blood…so much blood.

"I got to get the Sheriff, uh…Johnny. We have to get him here. He can get you something to eat."

"I cain't, Mr. Jeff, sir."

"But you have to. They're looking for you."

"I didn't mean to hurt Mr. Bradley. We was fighting, and I got real mad."

"Just tell the Sheriff that," said Jeff.

"Do you think Mr. Bradley might not file charges, if I work for him for free or something?"

"Mr. Bradley?" Jeff stared at the man knelt before him. He couldn't see Johnny's eyes very well, but something in his voice…"You don't know? Bill Bradley's dead. How could you not know?"

Johnny's head jerked up, his eyes now widened. "Dead? He cain't be dead. I hit him. I hit him a lot. I think I knocked him out. He didn't move, but…"

"You really don't know?" Jeff's head spun. "Wait a minute! What about the ice pick?"

"Ice pick?"

"Yeah. The ice pick. What about that?"

Johnny stared blankly at Jeff. "I didn't take no ice pick…not anything else, either. I didn't even take what was mine. I just ran away."

Jeff hesitated, then, "I got to get the sheriff."

"They'll kill me!" the bloody man barked, harsher than he intended, and he reached for Jeff's arm. His grip was stronger than Jeff expected, but he still managed to jerk away.

"Don't!"

Johnny's eyes were wide, darting from Jeff to the partially opened door. "Sorry, Mr. Jeff, sir. Didn't mean to be putting hands on you. I'se just scared…real scared."

"Stop that," snapped Jeff, "That thing you do with the 'Mr. Jeff, sir.' I don't like it."

"Yes, sir. What you gonna do, though? They'll kill me sure."

"Well, maybe they **should** kill you. You can't just go around killing white ranchers and expect to walk away scott-free. You can't stab a man in the eye with an ice pick and leave him dead. He has…had a wife and everything."

"I didn't stick nobody in no eye! We just had a fight. That's all. He was still in the house when I left…he was in bad shape, but not stuck in no eye."

"The house? Then who…?" Jeff felt himself waiver. He was in over his head with this whole thing. He just wanted the sheriff to come take care of this business. But he also knew the colored boy was right. They would probably give him a trial, then electrocute him. Why did he have to come to this barn?

"What are you doing here? Here in our barn, I mean."

"Didn't know where else to go. Cain't go home. Don't know no other place...least not around here. I thought I might find some food. I'm real hungry."

"Steal some food, you mean."

"Yes, sir."

Jeff felt himself soften and was angered at his weakness. The boy looked awful, covered in blood, filthy. Maybe he was telling the truth. But the **blood**! He had said there was a fight.

"I have to think," he said finally. "In the meantime, I'll get you something to eat. I really think I need to call the sheriff, though." He held his hand up, palm outward, when the bloody man started to protest. "I won't call the law just yet."

The other only nodded.

"Now clean yourself up. Use the faucet at the stock tank." Jeff spoke gruffly as he walked away.

"Yes, sir."

Chapter 11

Tinsley pulled briskly into the small hospital parking lot. Although the town of Cash wasn't large, it bragged of two excellent doctors, and patients came from as far as 60 miles away to be treated there.

The ride to the hospital was quick, as was the donning of his uniform. But Wayne sat in the county car several moments gathering his thoughts before entering the hospital. Mrs. Bradley was awake. As promised, a hospital nurse called him as soon as the patient regained consciousness.

He was in over his head. He had no training or experience for this kind of thing. And, worse, the sheriff had called Hoover the afternoon before to tell his secretary he was extending his time out of town for a "few more days." Right in the middle of a tough election, too. Had she even told the sheriff there had been a murder?

He eased out of the patrol car and stretched to his full height. He groaned slightly as he stretched still higher, lifting himself up on tip toes. He let out a sigh as he settled back down to earth. Grabbing his hat from the dash, he placed it absently over the salt and pepper thatch which thickly covered his head. Finally, he patted his left shirt pocket and slammed the car door. Yes, the note pad was in his pocket.

Wayne was surprised at the visceral affects Bradley's murder had on him. He saw a lot of dead people during the war—some of them his friends. But this was very different. Perhaps because violent death was a part of war. That kind of thing just wasn't supposed to happen here, though. There had never been a murder in the Cash, Texas, area. Never.

There was something else, too. People were afraid. A woman had been widowed. A man was murdered. And the killer was still out there. People were—for the first time—locking their doors at night. And Deputy Tinsley knew it was up to him to make things right again.

Wayne could feel the eyes of the town's people watching when he drove past them. What were they thinking, he wondered. They still waved at him when their eyes met, but it seemed to Deputy Tinsley there were fewer eyes meeting his than before the murder two days ago. Perhaps Mrs. Bradley could finally shed some light on the case.

Then she was there, still lying in the same bed where he had knelt over her, patting her hand before. She looked so different now. Nurse Richards was brushing out her patient's long black hair. They were talking quietly as he stood halfway in the door opening.

The morning of the murder, and later at the hospital, Wayne remembered her hair looking like it had been wet, then dried without care into little ringlets. It was now full, hanging in swells over slender shoulders.

"Hello, Wayne!" called out Nurse Beatrice Richards. "Good thing we weren't talking about you." She laughed a small laugh, glancing down at her patient who managed a strained smile.

Deputy Tinsley realized then that the amazing difference in the appearance of Mrs. Bradley was not only her hair. She had been unconscious before. He had never seen her eyes! And as she looked up at him, a sudden, totally ridiculous image struck him. Bambi!

"Deputy Tinsley?" she asked.

"Yes, ma'am." He quickly removed his hat.

"They tell me how kind you've been, sitting up with me here." She ended the statement out of breath. Lying back against the double pillows Mrs. Richards had fluffed for her, she placed the palm of her left hand high on her chest. She took in two deep breaths.

"I'm sorry," she said. "I'm afraid I'm a little weak."

"Oh, no. I probably shouldn't have come so soon." He glanced at Mrs. Richards who only shrugged.

"It's okay," Mrs. Bradley responded. "I wanted to talk to you, too. I have so many questions." She brushed the wrinkles from the hospital blanket and tugged it higher under her chin. When she lifted her eyes again, Tinsley saw the unmistakable welling of tears as they glistened, on the verge of spilling over.

"Are you sure you're up to talking just yet?"

She dabbed at the corner of each eye with the sheet edge and took another deep breath.

"I need to know things, Sheriff. People are not talking to me." She glanced at the nurse who was emptying a trash can. "Can you excuse us, please?"

Nurse Richards looked at her, then at Tinsley. "I'll just be down at the nurses' station."

"Okay, Beatrice, thanks." He turned back to Mrs. Bradley. "I'm just a deputy," he said. "Not the sheriff."

"But you are in charge of this...this case?"

"Yes, ma'am. But I can get more help. All I need. Don't worry about that."

"I wasn't. How do we do this?"

"Maybe, if you don't mind, ma'am, I'll ask you a few questions." He removed the note pad from the shirt pocket, along with a pencil. "Then I'll answer whatever questions you have—at least whatever ones I **can** answer."

"Okay," she said quietly. "I'll do my best."

"Mrs. Bradley, uh, I guess the most obvious question is, do you know who killed your husband?"

"Of course not."

"I'm sorry. I have to ask."

"I didn't mean to be short with you, Sheriff—uh, deputy. I'm on medication, but I'm still a little edgy."

"Of course, ma'am." He stepped closer to the bed so he might better hear her. "Do you know anyone who would want to harm your husband?"

She hesitated several moments, then sighed deeply.

"I'm afraid you'll need another note book." She looked toward the curtained window. "Please understand, this is very difficult for me. I've been married to Bill since I was fifteen—seventeen years. Wayne did the quick math and jotted down "32 YOA." She continued.

"Bill made a lot of enemies. He was not what people would consider a good man...Mr. Tinsley, this **is** private, isn't it? I mean, this won't be in the newspaper or anything?"

"'Course it's private ma'am. You can trust me."

She looked at him for a long moment. He became uncomfortable, cleared his throat, and glanced down at the pencil in his right hand.

"Yes. Yes, Mr., uh...deputy Tinsley. I believe I can."

"So, you were saying a lot of people didn't like your husband? Why is that?"

"If you don't already know the answer to that question, I fear this investigation may be in a lot of trouble."

"I just need to know what you know. Sure, I've heard some things...seen some things. I just need to know what else you can tell me. The smallest thing could make the difference...to get justice for Mr. Bradley."

"Justice! You want justice for Bill? Deputy..." she fought mightily to control her emotions. "Deputy, what would you think of me if I told you he probably received just that recently? Justice, I mean."

"It's not mine to judge, ma'am."

"I know. It's just that...how does one begin? How do I open up emotions that have been sealed for seventeen years?"

He didn't answer. Her eyes were locked on his when she continued. Was she measuring him as he was her, he wondered.

"I want the killer found. Regardless of my feelings for Bill, I want the killer found. In spite of everything, he **was** my husband."

"Yes, ma'am."

"Bill wasn't faithful to me, deputy. I guess you know that?"

He nodded but didn't comment.

"I don't know how many there were. Lots. Sometimes when he was angry—which was often—he'd tell me of some woman—some girl he'd been with."

Tinsley could see the muscles in her jaw snap as her teeth clinched between breaths.

"Did he mention names, ma'am?" he asked, feeling like a voyeur.

"Names? Oh, yes. Names, addresses, car descriptions, who their husbands—or fathers—were. Everything. As much as possible. That way, when I saw them, I would know...I would know he had been with this girl, or with that man's wife."

Tinsley stared, not realizing it. How could a man...her eyes...her, what?...her small...meek...a victim of that...that...

"Deputy?"

"Yes, ma'am?" His eyes quickly returned to the pad as he scribbled something unreadable.

"I need to continue. I need to do this while I can," she added, almost frantically.

"Go ahead, Mrs. Bradley."

"This next part is even more embarrassing, I'm afraid," she began.

He flushed. "I apologize, ma'am. Would you feel more comfortable if I bring in Mrs. Richards—a lady to be with you during this?"

"No, it's okay," she answered. "The fewer people the better. I just wanted to warn you, and—more likely—give myself another moment to build up courage."

"Go ahead when you're ready," he said quietly.

"Mr. Bradley...Bill...didn't just have these, uh, encounters. He brought them back to me. Over and over. I honestly don't believe he ever received the real satisfaction he wanted until he came home."

Wayne made a few notes, then looked back at the woman in front of him. A question formed across his face, and she answered before he could ask aloud.

"When he came home—often drunk—after one of his...well, you know." She sighed, picking out a spot on the curtains again upon which to focus. "He would...he...this is even harder than I expected. I'm sorry."

"It's okay, Mrs. Bradley. Maybe it's not that important to the investigation anyway."

"But it is," she sighed, not looking at him. "What I'm about to tell you will give you your best suspect."

"Okay."

"Bill told me everything. Literally everything that happened with his…lovers." Her eyes teared again but she plodded forward. "He reveled in telling me every sordid, disgusting thing he did with them." She seemed almost in a trance, thought Wayne.

"Every smell. Every touch. Every vile, evil thing they did. How much he paid, or how he used leverage on some of those poor… sometimes he would threaten them with losing their own homes…those he owned, at least…things like that.

"He would stand over me, slumped, swaying…his foul-smelling breath often overpowering even the stench of his body…the odor of his sins. He would look at me…he stared at me…never into my eyes… lower…rip the covers back…stare and tell me…he got so excited…no, wrong word. Not excited. What's an evil word for aroused? If I screamed—years ago—if I screamed, he choked me. If I moved away, he choked me. I was positive he would murder me, eventually.

"So, I stopped screaming. And I stopped trying to move away. My eyes looked his way, but I didn't see. I didn't hear. I went…some place. I don't know. After that I didn't have so many bruises on my neck. He still slapped me often…when he didn't think I was revolted enough by his actions, I guess. I didn't care. It was being choked that I…"

Then she was back. She looked quickly at Wayne and her face, which had been ashen, immediately flushed rose. "Uh…" she managed, looking at him like a cornered rabbit.

"It's okay, Mrs. Bradley," he whispered. He suddenly realized he had her small hand in his own. He squeezed it gently and placed it back on the blanket, patting it as one would an infant. "It's okay. All over now." He thought of Mr. Bradley and was glad someone stuck an ice pick in his eye.

"Yes. Yes it is over. You want to know when it began, Deputy Tinsley?"

He nodded.

"Seventeen years ago last February 19th. On our wedding night."

Wayne looked into, through the timid creature beneath him on the hospital bed. He wanted more than anything to hold her against him…to take away her pain…her history. His desire was not physical, not a feeling of lust. It was the most basic emotion among creatures of higher order…to protect the innocent. He wanted to help. He had never seen a human being so much like a tiny, injured animal. He did not want to question her further.

"Mrs. Bradley, one more thing. You said I would get my best suspect from what you just told me. Do you believe one of the husbands of a lady friend…someone he was seeing…I mean a specific man…?"

"No. No, Mr. Tinsley. Not a husband. I've given you the best suspect by what I just told you. The person who hated Bill Bradley more than anyone in the world…who wanted him dead."

He hesitated, looking down at her without understanding.

"Me," she said. "I am your best suspect."

Chapter 12

Johnny snatched the biscuits from Jeff's hands without speaking. One went into his mouth whole as the other lingered close behind.

"Umm…" he mumbled, nodding his head slightly. "Good." He held up one hand, observing it curiously. "Sticky."

"I poked a hole in the edge and poured syrup in. That's how I like 'em." Jeff watched the other boy stuff the second biscuit into his mouth, savoring it longer, chewing slower.

Johnny stepped past Jeff and strode to the stock tank. He washed the syrup off, then scooped up a drink from the tank with cupped hands.

"You look better, at least, with all that blood washed off, but you still smell awful." "Ain't had no bath since I don't know when," answered Johnny defensively.

"We got some lye soap chunks at the house," Jeff said. "I'll get one of them out here later." He glanced at the stock tank. Nodding at it, he added, "You can bathe in there—wash your clothes, too."

"Okay."

"Be sure when you're through, though, you run the water over the side for awhile…get all that junk out of the water. Stuff might kill the cow."

"What stuff? I ain't got no stuff that would kill a cow."

"I was talking about the lye soap. Why are you so touchy? I'm trying to help here."

"Yes, sir. I know. I'm sorry, too. I been on a real edge, thinking about all this killing talk."

Jeff looked back toward the house. "We'd better go back in the barn."

They sat on alfalfa hay bales, several feet apart, not looking at each other. Finally, Jeff cleared his throat.

"About that killing. I shoulda' already turned you over to Sheriff Hand. The way I figure it is I might already be in trouble just helping you."

Johnny remained silent, his slow, rhythmic breathing the only indication of his presence in the darkness of the windowless barn.

"You need to tell me some reason not to turn you in. I need to know what happened."

Again there was a long silence. Johnny started to speak when Jeff interrupted. "I'll know if you're lying!"

"Ain't gonna' lie, Mr. Jeff." He sniffed. "I was in our house 'cross the road—sleeping—when Mr. Bradley came in. If I was awake, I'd a just run out the back when he drove up."

"Okay, and…"

"The door slammed, and I sat up scared like. I don't remember exactly what he was saying, but it was mean stuff. He said I had to leave right then…wouldn't let me get none of my mama's stuff."

"So you jumped him?"

"No, not yet." His voice had lowered to a husky whisper. "He said some stuff about my dead mama. Real nasty stuff."

"What kind of stuff?"

"Can't say. I remember, but I can't say it."

"But bad, huh?"

"Awful. That's when I jumped on him. He tried to fight back, but he was weak. I never been like that before. I been mad plenty. But not like that. I just beat him and beat him and beat him. Next thing I know I'm just beating a bloody face…can't even see him no more." They sat quietly a moment, each processing his own thoughts.

"So, how'd he get killed?" questioned Jeff. "How did he get an ice pick in his eye?"

"Don't know. I thought maybe he was dead when I ran away. But I didn't stick him."

"So, you're saying you left him at **your** house? You didn't go to his place?"

"No, sir. I never did."

A deep sigh escaped from Jeff's chest. "I don't know what to do. Mama would want me to help you, I think. Dad would skin both of us if he found out."

"I could just maybe go someplace," offered Johnny.

"Like where?"

"Don't know. Long way off, maybe."

"Oh, sure. Colored boy traveling alone on the South Texas Plains. They'd have you strung up before breakfast."

"So you **do** believe me? You said, Mr. Jeff, you could tell if I lied. You can tell I ain't lying, can't you?"

"That's what I said, but I don't know whether to believe you or not. I know you been through a lot lately…first your mama, then little sister…now your dad going to prison, more than likely." He frowned in the darkness. "I'm afraid maybe I just feel sorry for you—like I want to believe you. I'm not sure."

"Yes, sir."

"Then I think of Mr. Bradley—I found him dead, you know—and you with blood all over you. Mostly, though, I think of his wife. I never saw a prettier lady…and she was, I don't know, just in awful shape."

"Are you afraid of me, Mr. Jeff?"

"No, why?"

"If your insides thought I was a killer, wouldn't you be afraid…here in the dark, alone with me?"

"I don't know. Maybe. I'm probably just too dumb to be scared."

"What should I do, Mr. Jeff?"

"First off, stop calling me **Mr.** Jeff. Sounds retarded."

"Okay. Just meant it as respect."

"I know. Second…well, second, I don't know what you should do.

Except I know you need a bath. Better do it tonight after dark…less chance of being seen."

"Okay, Mr…okay."

Jeff could not believe he was allowing Johnny to stay in their barn. Other than Allen, Jeff had opposed helping him more than anyone else. And there was more reason than ever now not to have him here. Jeff had to talk to somebody. Maybe his mother could advise him who to talk with. Deputy Tinsley, perhaps.

Chapter 13

Faye sat at the kitchen table staring vacantly across the room at a floral patterned wallpaper without really seeing it. What she saw was an old ledger, and a baby born shamefully out of wedlock. And, not only that, a mixed child…a Negro-and-white infant taken away by her husband's parents—her in-laws—many years ago.

Allen's birth certificate had been destroyed in a house fire, they had said. He was born in their house before the doctor arrived. It had been a stormy night. Oh, a little town you've never heard of…in Virginia.

Faye was ashamed of her own thoughts, of her feelings. What would her family say if they knew? What would people in town think? How would they treat her family then? If they knew.

She had been so pompous…so self-righteous, about the colored boy across the street. Why did she even think of him as the **colored** boy…why not Johnny? Or, that nice young man. She was so tired. Her mind was so tired. Faye wanted to lean her head on the table, nestled in folded arms,. but what if she couldn't raise it again?

She heard the back screen door squeak, then the door open. Jeff had been doing chores, and she knew it was him at the door without looking. Faye felt the strain in the relationship she and Jeff shared. He was so much like his dad. His Negro dad! She tried to focus. Jeff had been their only child for several years. Then Randy, their baby. Then a new baby came and went. Oma. And Randy was the baby again.

Jeff had always been so independent…not so much in need of a mother. He always seemed to be on the outside of the family looking in. His words surprised her when he spoke.

"Mama, can we talk about something? Something important?"

She was already standing, pushing her chair away. "What's wrong? Is something wrong?"

"No. Can we just sit here a minute and talk. I need some advice."

Oh, Good Lord, he knows. Somehow he knows, she thought.

"Advice. You want advice from **me**?" She slumped slowly back into her chair.

He sat down across the table from her, and took a deep breath. "When you hear what it's about, you'll know why I didn't go to dad."

She remained speechless. He **does** know!

"It's about that boy from across the street…Johnny."

She nodded, relieved. "Okay."

"Mama, he's out in the barn right now."

She stared, unknowingly, briefly. "Well, I **was** preparing a little space in there for him to sleep. But Allen hasn't approved yet."

"You don't understand," he snapped. "He may have been involved in what happened to Mr. Bradley. His murder."

"What? Why? Why would you say that?" The steel in her shoulders would not relax. Her neck ached.

"I found him out there—Johnny, I mean—yesterday morning. He was covered in blood…had it all over him."

"He's been in there since **yesterday**! Jeff, you could have been killed…we all could have been murdered in our sleep!"

"Mama, I said he **may** be a suspect. I don't know that he killed Mr. Bradley. I sorta' think he didn't."

"Why? What did he say?" she leaned forward, straining on his every word.

"Well, he didn't say much. Told me what happened…his version, anyway."

"Jeff, you'll have to turn him in. If he didn't do anything, they'll turn him loose."

"But he did do **something**," he answered. "And I'm not sure it'll matter whether he actually killed him or not. He beat Mr. Bradley…beat him pretty bad, apparently."

Faye appreciated her son's concern, and experienced a strange pride that he had come to her.

"Jeff, what do **you** think would be the right thing?"

"I don't know. I don't want to be in the middle of this. I don't want him—Johnny—to be in our barn. I don't want him depending on me."

"But…?"

"I don't know, mama. I was kneeling right beside him that day his sister got run over. I saw the look on his face. I thought about Oma and how that made me feel."

"I see."

"I don't. Not really. I don't know why that one thing should make a difference. It's not like we're friends."

"No. But maybe…maybe on that day when the little girl got killed, something happened to make Johnny a **person** in your mind. He was no longer just a Negro hired hand with no name or face. He was Johnny, and you shared a terrible moment. Maybe it is nothing unusual at all. Maybe it's common when people are thrown into a terrible situation together, they just naturally grow…I don't know, closer maybe."

He considered her thoughts. "I don't think so. I think maybe I just feel sorry for him. I don't think it's anything more than that."

"Okay. So you're going to turn him in, then?"

"I think so. I think maybe I should talk to a cop or somebody."

"Wayne would be a good one to talk to. I think he's fair…strict, but I believe he also has a good heart."

"That was my thinking, too. I'll call him tomorrow. Should I tell dad?"

"I don't like going behind your dad's back, son. I never have. But I do think this one time…in this instance, it might be better to just not mention it."

Chapter 14

Wayne began putting his notes away when Mrs. Bradley stopped him. "Deputy, you said you would answer some questions for me."

Yes, ma'am, if I can. What would you like to know?"

"I want to know about my husband's murder. What happened? What do you know? What do you think?"

"I'm afraid we don't have much." He cleared his throat. "We can't get fingerprints off concrete, where he was found. We also can't get prints off the wooden ice pick handle…"

"What ice pick handle?"

"The one in his…the one he was killed with."

"An ice pick?" She sighed heavily, then continued. "I knew he was murdered. I guess I assumed he had been shot."

"I'm sorry, Mrs. Bradley," Tinsley said quietly. "I'm afraid I'm not very good at this."

"Not your fault, deputy. What else? Please." Around her lightly tinted lips was the tale-tale whitening of her skin. Otherwise the tension in her face was well hidden.

"I think he was killed in your barn." Her brow furrowed, and he continued. "You see, there was a lot of blood around his bod…around Mr. Bradley. But it was mostly a single puddle. Almost no other blood spots around anywhere."

She seemed to be laboring at controlling her breathing, breaking words into small segmented parts of a sentence. "I...don't...know...what that, uh-what-that tells you."

"I'm not an expert, ma'am, but he...somebody beat Mr. Bradley severely, but not in the barn. And, though I have to wait on the autopsy report to make it official, I'm pretty sure he died from the ice pick wound." He looked at the young widow. "Is this more than you want to know?"

"I have to know sometime."

"Yes, ma'am. I'm pretty sure he came into the barn on his own two feet...either that, or was carried in. There were no marks on his boots like there would be if he was dragged.

"Also, his pickup was just outside the barn, and there is blood on the steering wheel and all around the driver's side of the cab. He drove himself to the barn. Whether he was alone or not, we don't know. We **did** pick up a few fingerprints on the other side of the cab, but they may be yours." He looked at her questioningly.

"No, they're not mine," she said. "I've never been in his pickup." Her face flushed again. "One of the few women in Cash who hasn't been, I suspect."

"We'll need to fingerprint you later, anyway...when you're feeling better. To eliminate you as a suspect to a jury if it ever comes to that. I'm sorry."

"No. Oh no, deputy Tinsley. Please, it's me that should apologize. My sarcasm. I know there are many fine women here. It's just that I don't really know anyone, and the only ones I've heard about were...well, you already know all that."

"Then, your prints?"

"Sure. Anytime you want."

"Okay, here is the rest. Time of death has been set between midnight and 2:00 am last Friday night...Saturday morning, actually. Mr. Bradley had filed no complaints or had any filed on him recently with the Sheriff's office. He still had his wallet and there was over a hundred dollars in it, so...no robbery." He glanced at Mrs. Bradley.

"Go on, please," she said.

"According to the preliminary report from the coroner, Mr. Bradley had...he had been with someone 'recently.' I don't know what 'recently' means yet."

"When you say he had been with someone, are you talking about, like with a woman? Intimately?"

"Yes. With a woman."

"Again, not me," she responded, unblinking.

"We don't know who, yet. I've been around to some of the places where I used to see his truck. But right now I'm at zero."

"Why is it important to find her? Do you think a woman..."

"Find her, find a husband. Maybe a boyfriend, or a father. Someone with a motive."

"I see."

"Can you think of anyone else, specifically, who might have a motive?" he asked.

She closed her eyes a moment, thinking. It gave Wayne an opportunity to steal a closer look at her. He had always thought Faye Cowen was the prettiest woman he knew. And she was, in her own way. Her beauty was different, however. Strong facial features, piercing eyes, and a no-nonsense jaw enveloped an almost non-descript beauty.

Before him, however, lay another beautiful woman. But how different she was! She was so soft, her skin—untarnished by years—he knew would feel just like a peach. She had a movie star look. He remembered Ingred Bergman in Casa Blanca—how she looked with the camera slightly filtered. But mostly it was her eyes...her eyes!

They were staring back at him! He stammered, "You alright, ma'am?"

"Are you?" she responded.

"Sure. Okay, you were about to..."

"I was going to say 'no,' I don't know anyone who, recently, has more reason to want Bill dead than anybody else...then I remembered..."

"Yes?"

"He kicked some of our Negro hands out of a house the other day. Do you think he...I don't know his name..."

"Isaac Wilson. It was his family he kicked out of their house. Isaac is still in jail though, on another deal. Couldn't a been him."

"Okay. Never mind. I was remembering how that colored boy came to the house that night looking for Bill…he seemed really upset. I just thought there might be a connection."

"What colored boy? When?"

"I…I don't know…Friday night, I think," she said, startled at the deputy's sudden abruptness. "He came to the house that night…I didn't let him in, of course…said he had to see Mr. Bradley."'

"What did he look like, then?"

"I'm sorry. It was dark, and I can't really tell them apart anyway. All I know is, he was young. Maybe seventeen or so."

"Have you ever seen him before? Try to remember."

"You know, now you mention it…but I'm not sure…"

"What?"

"I think…I **think** he's the boy Bill pointed out to me one day. He was helping an older hand work on a tractor."

"But he didn't say a name?" Wayne began to feel he was running out of juice.

"No. Bill said he knew the boy's mama. **Knew** her. And he said the boy's little sister had been run over by a bus."

Chapter 15

Deputy Tinsley killed the headlights as his patrol car crept through the darkness. Gravel skittered beneath slow turning tires as he eased closer to the railroad trestle. A half mile away he shifted into neutral and coasted to a halt without touching the brake pedal.

He saw the occasional flickering of a campfire as a soft glow shimmered, a reflection off large railroad timbers beneath the tracks. Wayne never doubted who was at the fire. After his conversation with Mrs. Bradley, and with the additional information from Jeff Cowen, he was sure the colored boy reported by the *Santa Fe* train conductor was Johnny Wilson.

Instead of calling for a backup deputy from Hoover, Wayne grabbed Allen Cowen as he left their place. Allen had been upset when he heard the boy had been hiding in his barn…and that Jeff knew it. Wayne figured they could visit while he drove, and it would give Allen a little time to cool down.

They hadn't talked about it though. He told Allen where they were going. Allen responded, "Okay," and that was it. The deputy liked Allen, but he wasn't really comfortable around him. And Wayne Tinsley was comfortable around almost everybody.

He slipped into the barrow ditch beside the *Santa Fe* maintained gravel road to make less noise as he walked. Without speaking, Allen did the same, slowly blending further into the darkness until he disappeared entirely.

Tinsley was aware of the Colt .38 caliber revolver on his hip, but didn't unsnap it. He felt no more emotion about the gun than he would over a socket wrench. It was a tool. As he neared the fire, small sounds occasionally broke through the darkness. Shuffling feet. A throat cleared. Another stick on the fire. One thing was sure. **Someone** was here.

He slid around a huge clump of sand and tumbleweeds to the left. Then he saw him. Johnny stood, his back to Tinsley, gazing into the fire, hands hung loosely at his sides. Wayne walked toward the tall boy quietly, quickly—when he spoke, he wanted it to be clear, quiet… conversational.

If this boy had rabbit blood in him, Wayne didn't want to give him a jump start.

"How 'ya doin', Johnny?" he said quietly.

The boy jumped, startled, but stood fast. "Doin' okay, I guess, sir." He didn't turn, and his hands remained at his sides.

"Folks around have been looking for you. Guess you knew that?" He continued walking, closing the gap.

"I weren't positive, but I thought, maybe."

"You want to turn around, son?" Tinsley was within five yards of him.

"Yes, sir. That all right?" The young man turned his head first, then followed slowly with his body. His stance and the tension in his body looked like he was bracing to be hit head-on by a *Mack* truck. "Sheriff?"

"Deputy," answered Wayne. "Deputy Tinsley. We met at the bus accident…with your sister. I need you to come with me for a bit. We need to talk about some things."

Wayne reached gingerly for the handcuffs which draped loosely over his belt in a loop. Johnny didn't miss the movement. His eyes began shifting from side to side, his nerves breaking down. Wayne relaxed and dropped his hand back to his side without the cuffs.

"Maybe you'd like to talk here a few minutes first?" he asked Johnny, trying to calm him.

Tinsley knew he could forcibly arrest this kid. But the boy looked strong, and he was scared...not a good combination, and Tinsley wasn't positive he could arrest the boy without hurting him.

"Okay. What you want with me, sir?"

"Some people think you might know something about Mr. Bradley."

"I didn't kill nobody!"

"I didn't say he was killed, Johnny. You did. Can't you see how we might need to talk this out?"

"Mr. Tinsley, I appreciate how you're being...talking to me like a man and all. I know I ain't real educated, but I ain't dumb, neither."

"'Course you're not."

"No, sir. I mean it. I know what talking about this means. You'll put me in jail. Then a bunch of white men acts like they're listening to a trial. Then they kill me in a 'lectric chair."

Tinsley thought the boy was probably right. "It's not like that, Johnny. I'll see you get treated fair."

Johnny stood several moments looking at the deputy...searching his face...searching for an indication of the truth.

"No, sir. I think I'll just stay right here for now. I didn't kill Mr. Bradley. He needed killing, but I didn't do it. No disrespect to you."

"Johnny, you really have no choice. I didn't want to have to do it out here like this, but I'm gonna' have to arrest you...for suspicion of murder."

Johnny stared at him, saying nothing.

Tinsley stepped forward, nearing the slight distance between them. "Turn around, son. Don't give me any trouble. It'll only make things harder for you." He touched Johnny's right arm and nudged him gently to turn around. The boy stood his ground, still silent, his eyes burrowing into the deputy.

"Okay, I guess we'll have to do it the hard way," Wayne said, grasping the right arm. He slid his hand down to Johnny's wrist and twisted it, causing the boys body to turn slightly, relieving the pressure on his arm.

Johnny tensed up, his muscles hardening under the long sleeved shirt. Wayne felt the tension and tried to calm him again. "Just take it easy. I don't want to have to hurt you." He increased the pressure and reached for the boy's left arm.

Johnny exploded suddenly in a frenzied struggle to escape Wayne's grasp. Pulling, jerking, he almost broke free when Tinsley regained control of his right arm and slammed him hard to the ground face-first. They landed with a loud thud, expulsions of breath emitting from both. They struggled fiercely, Johnny trying to escape, Tinsley trying to hold on to him…trying to get him handcuffed. Dust stormed around their bodies.

Suddenly Johnny was on top, as surprised as the deputy to find himself there. He was even more surprised when he saw the deputy's gun lying beside his head on the ground. Tinsley obviously did not know the gun was there, because he did nothing to stop Johnny as he reached quickly for it. Wayne was still using all his energy trying to reestablish dominance in the struggle.

He stopped when he saw the gun. The boy straddled Tinsley's waist, the .38 pointed at the deputy's forehead. The barrel wavered with each forced intake of breath as the boy gasped for air. Wayne was spent as well, but found himself holding his own breath, his chest aching.

"No," was all he could get out.

"I didn't kill him."

"Okay."

They both stared into the eyes of the other, each wondering, measuring the other. Wayne Tinsley, in an insane moment, wondered which deputy would work his murder. Killed by his own gun. Then he wondered how badly it would hurt, being shot in the head. Or would there just be nothing at all.

"Johnny. This is not the way to do it. You got a chance now…a chance to live. If you kill me…well, you know. If you kill a cop, there's no place on earth you could hide. And there won't be no trial. You know I'm right."

"I know. Wasn't gonna' shoot you no-how." But Johnny's finger remained inside the trigger guard, and Tinsley could see the wad-cutter bullet at the back of the barrel aimed directly at him.

"Good. That's good. Now, why don't you just set the gun aside and we'll talk this over…see what the right thing to do…"

"Can't I just go, Mr. Tinsley?"

Wayne wanted to say "yes" so badly he ached. "I can't let you do that, Johnny. I'm sorry. I really am. Now, go ahead…put the gun down."

Johnny looked long into the eyes of the deputy. And as quickly as he had exploded into violent resistance, his eyes glazed over, and the gun barrel slowly began to drop.

The impact slammed him to the ground. His flight through the air was joined by a simultaneous "crack." Allen Cowen took a second swing with the wooden club, although the boy was not moving. Wayne, stunned for a moment, looked frantically for his gun. It lay several feet from the prone boy, in the shadows of the firelight. He saw Allen raise the large club again, a dark shadow only, just outside the dim orange of the hot coals.

"Stop!" he yelled at Allen, but the club came down again, this time with a sickening thump. The boy's head was a mass of blood, as his body jerked with each blow. "Stop it, I said!" He grabbed the club as Allen raised it over his head again. Something sharp snagged his hand as he grabbed the club, but he held firmly.

Allen looked at Wayne. His eyes were wide, the whites showing even in darkness. Wayne pulled the club…a broken fence post…from his grasp, noting the sharp pain in his hand was from a barb attached to a wire still wrapped around the weapon.

"Sorry it took so long, Wayne. I almost never found something I could use." He was panting, adrenalin still pumping through his body.

"Thanks, Allen. I guess you were just in time." Wayne Tinsley looked at the still boy. He recovered the dropped gun, then knelt near Johnny's bludgeoned head. Feeling his neck for a pulse, the deputy discovered, to his surprise, that the carotid artery still pumped blood to the boy's brain.

"Get the car, Allen," he said. "Hurry. I don't know how long this kid can hang on."

"You think he might die?" Allen seemed surprised.

"I think he probably **will** die. And I know he will if you don't hurry!"

Tinsley heard Allen's feet crunching gravel along the road as he scurried back to the squad car. He rolled Johnny Wilson over onto his back, taking account of his injuries.

"Dear God," he whispered.

Chapter 16

Wayne Tinsley placed the pencil quietly on the desk. His long fingers comforted, relaxed his scalp as he swept them through mussed, thick hair. Coffee on the table was within reach but had cooled to room temperature. He took a long pull on it anyway. It was wet and tasted awful. He grimaced.

On his desk—which also served as his kitchen table—lay a blank sheet of paper. Several other pages were wadded up in assorted locations on the table and floor. He couldn't make it work. He could not make it come together where it made any sense.

People in town were slapping him on the back, buying him coffee and pie at the café. He was a hero. He tried to convince them he had done nothing but get out-fought by a kid, and almost killed in the process. Some hero. But they wouldn't have any part of it. They wanted a hero, and he was it…regardless. He had solved the big murder case, and "nearly beat the nigger to death" in the process. All was back to normal.

But every time Wayne wrote his report, the narrative left him unsatisfied. Bradley had come to the Johnson's house—actually Bradley's house—where the Johnson family had lived. He found Johnny trespassing there. He and Johnny got in to a fight. Some fight.

The location of the fight had been confirmed when Wayne went to the Johnson house. Blood was splattered all over the living room, compelling evidence it was the place of the beating. There was even enough blood to determine it was the same blood type as Bill Bradley's.

The front door was standing open when Tinsley arrived there, also indicative of the rapid departure by Johnny. Everything in the house confirmed what Johnny had told Jeff Cowen…at least regarding the assault which occurred there.

Then there was Mrs. Bradley's statement about the boy coming to their home the night Bill was killed. And neighbors—other Bradley hired hands—had admitted seeing Bill Bradley's pickup at the Johnson place on a couple of occasions when Isaac and the kids were away. That was when Mrs. Johnson was still alive. They saw it again on the afternoon before Bradley was killed.

Johnny certainly had motive. If he knew Bradley was slipping around with his mother…if he was afraid Bradley was going to have him jailed for trespassing…if he knew anything about the old devil at all…he had motive.

What Deputy Tinsley had not put together was why Johnny would run away, then come right up to Bradley's house, know he had been seen by Ivy…Mrs. Bradley, then kill her husband. Maybe he was just that angry. Angry enough he didn't care whether he got caught or not. Tinsley didn't buy his own theory.

The way Bradley was murdered did not look to him like case of extraordinary passion…he would have been stabbed numerous times if that were the case. And whoever had done it had forced him to go to the barn…or had laid in wait for him.

It was like two pieces of a puzzle that almost fit together…all except for that little gap. Like two pieces that, if forcefully pressed together hard enough, could be made to look almost right. Wayne wished he could talk to the boy…Johnny. Maybe he could supply answers to those questions.

He hadn't regained consciousness. He had a concussion, perhaps brain damage, and was lying in a hospital bed in Hoover with a deputy guarding the room. It had been two days since the arrest. Wayne knew he would have been in terrible trouble with the Sheriff for taking Allen along…the way things turned out. Except for the fact Johnny was colored. There was even a remote chance the arrest might help Sheriff Hand win the election.

Mrs. Bradley had been released from the Cash Hospital. She found insurance papers along with other legal documents in her deceased husband's desk, she told Wayne by phone. She asked him to come look over the papers with her.

"I'm not very good at this sort of thing," she said.

Wayne wasn't too good at that sort of thing, either, but he agreed to look over the papers with her. She met him at the door wearing a simple black dress that highlighted her features. She wore stockings, but was barefoot.

He studied the papers at length, making sure he was accurate in what he told her. "You know, Mrs. Bradley…"

"Ivy, please. My name is Ivy."

"Yes ma'am. You know, you should really call a lawyer. Some of these papers are pretty complicated."

She nodded, "I will. What is your opinion, though?"

"My opinion is that, unless a more recent will is found, Bill left you in pretty good shape…financially, I mean."

"That's what it looked like to me."

"Actually, to be more specific, it looks like…in addition to several properties—your home, farm, outbuildings, six houses in the area—and all the farm equipment that doesn't have liens on them…in addition to all that, it appears there is an insurance policy for five hundred thousand dollars."

"It's more than I would have thought. Actually, **anything** at all is more than I would have thought." Her tone changed no more than if she were discussing a new recipe.

"Mrs. Brad…Ivy. This policy has a rider on it, also. Because of the nature of his death, I'm not positive, but I believe this would pay a double indemnity."

"What does that mean, Wayne?"

"It means if I'm right…and I repeat, **if** I'm right, you'll be a millionaire."

She stared vacantly at him for a moment. "What if I don't claim the money? Do I have to take it?"

It was his time to stare. Her dark eyes bored holes in him. Her apparent total confidence in him was unnerving. "I don't really know the answer to that. I'm sure the insurance company wouldn't mind if you let them keep the money. The truth of the matter is, I don't know of anybody not wanting insurance money before."

"I don't know what to do," she lowered her eyes, thoughtfully. "You know more about Bill than anybody else in this world except me. Anything he touched would be dirty. I have enough money to get by…from my family on the east coast…and from the farm; I could lease it out for part of the crop profits."

"I guess so. Maybe you might want to give the money to a charity or something…turn his dirty money into something good."

"Perhaps. Thank you."

"No problem, Mrs. Bradley."

Later that evening, lost in reverie about his conversation with Ivy, Wayne didn't hear the '51 Ford pull into his driveway. The "driveway" consisted of two strips of dirt worn into a thick thatch of grass, terminating at the corner of his two bedroom house. He did, however, hear the car door slam shut.

Easing himself to the kitchen window, he pulled back the cotton curtain. The driver was already out of sight, apparently approaching the front door. Wayne didn't see the driver, but he knew the car. It belonged to the Cowens.

Wayne's heart sped noticeably, but the strong, sharp knock on the door told him his visitor was probably Allen. He sighed as he tugged the door open.

"H'lo, Allen," he said.

"Wayne, can I come in?"

Tinsley pushed open the screen door without answering. "Want some coffee?"

"Yeah, thanks." He followed the deputy through the living room and into the kitchen. He saw Wayne's coffee already poured and sat across the table from it.

"Sugar?"

"No. Thanks, anyway. Lots of books in there." He nodded toward the living room.

"I read a lot."

"Guess there's not much for a single man to do in Cash."

Wayne hesitated an instant, wandering if there was a hidden accusation in the question. "No. Not usually. Least wise, not until this Bradley business came up."

"Yeah."

"What's on your mind, Allen?"

Allen looked deeply into his coffee cup. He didn't look up. "I didn't hurt that boy on purpose. Not bad like that, I mean."

"Never thought you did."

"Some people in town think I did. Ralph at the pool hall slapped me on the back today; said 'I guess you showed them niggers not to mess with a white man.' Then he laughed."

"He's an idiot. You know that. Who cares what he thinks?"

"I know. But the place was full of men, and they all laughed with him. I don't need that kind of thing going around."

Wayne shook his head and sipped at the cold coffee. When he set it down, Allen was staring at him, waiting.

"Okay, there's **lots** of idiots around here. Most of them hang out in the pool hall while their hundred-dollar-a-month hired hands work their land so they can come to town and complain how the government mistreats them."

"Wayne, I hit that kid 'cause I thought he was going to shoot you. I would'a done the same thing if he was white or Mexican...I think I would. I sure do."

Tinsley wasn't sure what Allen had in mind. He had never known the man to be particularly introspective.

"Can I get into trouble over this?" Allen asked finally. "I mean, you **did** ask me to go. Isn't that sort of like being deputized?"

"You won't get into trouble. Who would complain around here about a colored boy getting beat up?"

"Probably nobody. You're right, I guess." There was no conviction in Allen's voice.

"What have you heard?"

"I got a call. Wouldn't give his name. He said the nigger school teacher was nosing around asking questions…about what happened."

"So?"

"So, maybe he's got connections…up north."

"What are you talking about?"

"All this integration talk, Negroes around the country demanding to be treated equal…water fountains…buses…all that stuff. It's unsettling. Bunch of uppity niggers stirring up the natural order of things."

Wayne didn't respond.

"I just don't want to be in the middle. You know? I don't want my family bothered."

"Don't worry about it, Allen. Nobody cares."

"I'm sorry, Wayne. It's just that…I don't know…things seem to be unraveling on me lately.'"

Wayne's expression was an inquiry, but he held silent.

"I was so surprised at Jeff, hiding that murderer in my barn. Disappointed, I guess. You know, when Faye wanted that boy to stay with us, Jeff was against it as much as me."

"Faye wanted Johnny to stay with you?"

"Yeah, after his dad got locked up…like at the barn, though. Not in the house. I said 'no,' of course. Didn't need that kind of trouble. And it was your sheriff that brought it up in the first place."

"Why would she do that? Faye, I mean."

"She's always thought she was a pretty good judge of people. And she usually is. But she was sure off on this one."

"Maybe."

"Maybe? How can you say that? He killed Bill, didn't he?"

"I think so. Maybe. It's just…I don't know…" Wayne ran slender fingers through his hair again. "I guess I'm a little like Faye. I've always considered myself a good judge of character, too. And I just don't see this kid as a cold-blooded murderer."

"He tried to kill you!"

"He **could** have killed me."

"Then who…?"

"I don't know! I don't know. Maybe it **is** him." He poured the cold coffee down the sink drain and tilted the percolator spout at his cup. A thick black liquid burped out, full of coffee grounds. He put the cup on the cabinet with disgust and turned off the flame at the stove.

"I need to talk to the boy. Interrogate him. Then, I think, I would know for sure."

"Is he still unconscious?"

"Yeah, as of this morning, anyway." Then, as if on cue, the telephone rang.

Tinsley picked up the heavy black receiver and bent over slightly to accommodate the thick, short cord.

"Hello."

"Deputy Tinsley?" The voice was effeminate, but male. At least Tinsley was fairly certain it was a man's voice.

"Yes. This is Tinsley."

"I am Mr. McCallister. I am the administrative assistant at Saint Paul's Hospital in

Hoover."

"Yes, sir?"

"I am calling to inquire as to when someone will be picking up this boy. I talked to Deputy Lightsey here at the hospital. He told me to call you."

"I don't understand, Mr., uh…Mr. McCallister. I'm no doctor. Do what you do with people in his condition." Tinsley looked at Allen and shrugged.

"Deputy, please understand. The boy has no insurance, I'm sure. In the past, also, your Sheriff Hand has not been very forthcoming about paying prisoner's bills either."

"I see."

"Anyway, he's awake now…"

"How long?" Tinsley interrupted.

"Fifteen, twenty minutes. Anyway, he's awake. You people can take him off to jail or whatever you do."

"Isn't this a little soon?"

"No. It's a little late. We've tried to maintain security...privacy...but you know those nurses."

"What?"

"Word is out. Many of our paying customers...patients, and their families, are not at all happy knowing there is a Negro murderer in our hospital."

"Okay, Mr. McCallister, tell Deputy Lightsey to call me. We'll work something out." He slammed the phone onto its cradle.

"Fruitcake."

Chapter 17

Jeff hesitated a moment before knocking on the front door. It had been exactly one week since he found Mr. Bradley in the barn. Today he went to the house first, not sure what he should do. The Thoroughbreds still needed the kinks worked out of their backs, but he wasn't sure Mrs. Bradley would care one way or the other.

"Hello Jeff," she said, smiling. He hadn't seen her smile often. The day at the corral when she caught herself laughing with him and his friends was the only levity he had ever witnessed in her. But that laugh, on that day, did not compare with the breathtaking smile.

"Mrs. Bradley," he nodded, then—embarrassed—removed his straw hat. "I was just wondering if you wanted me—us—to keep working the horses."

"You know, I hadn't even thought of that."

"Yes, ma'am. I didn't know if it was the right time for me to ask about it. It's not the money," he added rapidly. "I'll break them for you for free."

She cocked her head slightly to one side. "Why on earth would you do that?"

Jeff felt his face burn. He cleared his throat. "I just hate to see all the work we've done go to waste. And the horses won't bring you anything at auction if they aren't broke."

"Oh, Jeff, I'm so sorry. I'm really out of practice having company." She pushed open the screen door. "Please, come in. I have coffee brewing now. Would you like some?" She wore the same bright white terry cloth robe she had worn that morning a week ago.

"That sounds great," he answered. He followed her through the living room into the kitchen, trying to not stare, then to a small room off the kitchen that was mostly windows. There was a small round table in the center of the room surrounded by three small chairs.

"Take any seat, Jeff. How do you like your coffee?"

"Black, I guess."

"Are you sure you wouldn't like some sugar or cream? Cream's fresh."

"If that wouldn't be too much trouble, thank you ma'am." Jeff sat on the nearest chair. It was not very comfortable, but the entire room had a good, cozy feel to it. Early morning sun beamed through the glass warming the entire area. As he pulled the chair back, he glanced a small piece of paper lying in the floor near the table leg. He knelt to pick it up and was nearly upright when she grasped his hand. She held his wrist with one hand and slipped the paper from his fingers with the other.

"I am terrible, Jeff. If I had known you were coming I would have cleaned up better."

He saw four numbers on the paper before she took it from him. They were easy to remember…three nines and a four. A telephone number? Probably, he thought.

"Oh, it's nothing. I wasn't…I wasn't bothered by it. Just thought I'd give you a hand."

She sat next to him after placing their coffee on the table. "Jeff, I have a confession to make to you." She sipped from her cup, quietly, eyes lowered. Jeff noticed she already wore makeup…lipstick; and her hair was…

"That paper you saw has a telephone number on it. I didn't want you to see it. You have become a real friend, and I just didn't want you to think less of me."

"I could never do that. I think you're…I mean, I could never think less of you."

"Wait till I tell you." She took a deep breath. "This past week I made an appointment in the city to talk to a, well, someone who can help me. Do you know what I mean?"

"You mean like a lawyer?"

"No. I'm having to deal with a lot of things now…for quite some time, actually. I don't know how else to say it except just to say it. I'm seeing a psychiatrist."

She seemed to be waiting for a reply. Jeff just looked at her.

"Does that bother you, Jeff? Say something, please."

"No. Is that all? No, it doesn't bother me. It's no big deal."

"It is to a lot of people. A lot of people feel like the only people who need that kind of help are, well, crazy."

"I don't."

"I can see that now. But, as a favor to me…would you mind letting this be our little secret?"

"Sure."

"Thank you. Now, tell me a little about yourself."

"Not much to tell. High school senior. I like cowboy work, but you already knew that. I played football all four years. Guess I'll go to college next year, maybe be on their rodeo team."

"I didn't even know they had college rodeo teams. Will you come back to Cash, after college?"

"I don't know. Hope not."

"Why?"

"Nothing much to do here, I guess."

"And I suppose you have some pretty bad memories of this place now?"

"Yeah. Good and bad. People say the town is changing. The week before Mr. Bradley…well, the week before that…someone messed with a little colored girl…you know, molested her."

"My goodness."

"Yeah. It's all around school."

"Who did it?"

"They don't really know. People around town are real concerned. Next time, it could just as easily be a white girl."

"How awful. I don't know many people around here."

"Most are good people. There are a few trouble-makers. Like this guy...the one who..."

"You know, I believe that kind of person instinctively knows who they can push around. It's like...well, a person who is mean knows who he can hurt. How he can hurt others."

"I guess I agree with that."

"I've seen it, Jeff. I've seen it up close. Some of those people... people who like to hurt others, I think they just have an evil soul. It's...I don't know, it's really hard to explain."

"Girls aren't usually picked on in school, are they?" he asked suddenly.

"Sure. I saw plenty of it. Girls can be every bit as mean as boys...or men. They are just sneakier about it."

"Were you picked on in school?"

"No. Not in school. More coffee?" She nodded at his cup, almost empty.

He didn't care about the coffee. Through the glass table he saw her crossed legs beneath the robe. Her bare foot swung loosely, the slightly darker toes of the stockings evident and, somehow, elegant. The robe exposed her legs from mid-thigh down. The last thing in the world he wanted to do was leave.

"No thank you. I guess I'd better get to work." He spoke the words, but made no motion to rise. He was hypnotized. She smiled at him again.

"What did my husband pay you...you and the other boys?"

He hated her calling him a boy. "He paid us five dollars for each horse, rough-broke, to run in harness."

"That's not very much, is it...considering the danger and all?"

"I won't lie. We all needed the money he paid us, but we weren't doing it for the money."

"Then why?"

"Excitement. Experience. Being cowboys. Stuff like that."

"Okay, I do want you to continue working with the horses. I'll pay you seven-fifty per horse."

"That's not necessary…"

She held up her hand. "Not for discussion. You take care of the entire operation. I've heard you and the other boys talking, and you are the obvious leader. So lead. Set your hours, and the order of the horses to be broken. Turn in your work at the end of the month. The extra two-fifty for you is to supervise and coordinate."

Jeff's chest swelled. He was going to be a foreman. He was going to be **her** foreman! What could be better than that?

"Jeff, I expect a good return on my investment. I want those horses bringing top price.

Can I depend on you?"

"You can depend on me." Jeff saw no change in the shape of Ivy's mouth, but in his thoughts later, he would swear she smiled with her eyes.

Chapter 18

At 9:00 am, the Texas sun was already punishing Deputy Tinsley. The slick vinyl seat of the squad car was tacky against the underside of his legs, burning, unyielding. He pulled over against the edge of the street to reach across to the front passengers side window. He cranked it down and felt a slight breeze flow through the car.

It wasn't significantly better than before, but at least the air movement gave the impression of being cooler. He had already pulled out the vent knob, but the air coming in around his legs was also hot.

He eased up to the stop sign at Main Street. He stopped because he was in a marked sheriff's department car. No one else stopped there or at any of the other three stop signs in town. He had plenty of time to pull onto Main, but elected instead to let the big John Deere tractor pass ahead of him.

He waved at the driver, an unknown Mexican field hand. The loud pop-popping of the single-cylinder tractor was a melody in cotton country. Wayne sat looking at the machine as it grew ever smaller in departure. He didn't realize he was staring till a loud horn blasted at him from behind.

He looked into the rear view mirror and waved apologetically at the driver in his rearview mirror. Wayne started onto the street when another horn honk startled him. He slammed on the brakes as a pickup truck headed north on main veered to miss him. Three feet separated their vehicles as the young male driver laughed, shaking his head as he proceeded on down the street.

"Two other cars in this entire town are moving right now. And I try to run over half of them," he muttered. This time he looked both ways before continuing into the intersection and south bound in the direction of the downtown stores.

The big Ford slid easily against the curb in front of the drug store. There were only two other cars on the block. One belonged to a troublemaker in town—Earl Smith. The other car he didn't recognize. Store owners and clerks always parked in back.

Mrs. Griffen swept dust from the concrete steps in front of her variety store. She spoke and smiled broadly. Her silver hair was swept back into a tight bun. Tinsley couldn't remember her looking any other way. In his mind, she looked exactly the same the day his mother took him into her store to purchase his first school tablet.

"'Lo, Mrs. Griffen. Little warm today, huh?"

"Sure 'nuff, Wayne. Might as well get used to it, though. The almanac says it's going to be a hot summer this year."

"I believe it, then," he said, smiling back at her. They had a running joke about the *Farmers' Almanac*. People around there had sworn by it for years...especially those in the agriculture industry. Farmers were almost as superstitious as baseball players, he reckoned.

The nine feet tall oak door panes were laced with intricate etched glass on the top half. The heavy brass latch was almost rust colored from weather and long use. Wayne pulled on it and immediately felt a rush of cool air hit his face.

The drug store was one place he could count on...its swamp cooler was always churning away. Brass fans hung five feet from the ceiling and chopped air downward three feet above Wayne's head, also.

The bronze colored ceiling was of molded metal, formed into ornate patterns in thirty-six inch squares.

A large bar, twenty-two feet long, stretched alongside the left of the room front. A few medicinal supplies and trinkets held down the glass shelves on the right side. Metal stools with red padded vinyl seats were bolted to the floor at the bar, and a twenty-two feet long brass footrest gave an additional degree of comfort to those who sat there.

Four booths huddled comfortably in the rear, their deep dark wood and tall straight backs evidenced far more elegance and dignity than comfort. Wayne saw the tops of two men's heads at the most distant booth.

Billy Fred Williams, wearing a stark-white bib apron, washed glasses behind the bar. From somewhere in the back the smell of sausage drifted faintly into Wayne's consciousness.

"Morning. Still doing breakfast?" he asked.

"Sure, Wayne. What'll it be?" Billy Fred was short and stout, a man of about forty, Wayne guessed. He had bought the drug store and moved to town six years before, making him a newcomer.

"What's on special?"

"Same as always. Whatever you order will be special."

Wayne slid onto a near stool and propped his arms on the smooth round bar edge. He tapped his fingers a couple of times on the wood as if in deep concentration.

"Billy Fred, if you're ready to take my order…"

The man picked up a paper pad and held it at the ready. "Go ahead."

"Today I believe I'll have three fried eggs—sunny side up with extra pepper, four slices of bacon—cooked crisp, two pieces of thick toast with strawberry preserves…"

"Anything to drink with that?"

"Coffee…black, and a small orange juice."

Billy Fred stepped to the door behind him, cracking it open slightly. He hadn't written a word. "Honey. Wayne's here for breakfast." He closed the door and returned to his glasses. "Virginia said 'morning.'"

Wayne smiled and nodded. Then he tilted his head slightly to the right. "Who's your company? Earl?"

Billy Fred frowned. "Yeah, him and one of the Patterson twins—can't tell one from the other. Lord knows I need all the business I can get…" he lowered his voice even more. "But I'd as soon these two went elsewhere."

"Why? Have they caused problems?"

"It's not that exactly. They're surly, alright. But so are some other customers. Those two just seem to intimidate people. Makes 'em uncomfortable."

"I see."

"And that's bad for business. People don't go where they're uncomfortable."

"You want me to tell them to stay out?"

"No. They'd just throw a rock through my window or something. Just leave it alone, I guess. Maybe they'll get bored and start hanging out somewhere else."

"Aren't they supposed to be in high school?"

"They don't go half the time. I think the teachers are afraid of them. Not that I would blame them."

"I heard they got into a fight not too long ago   between themselves, I mean."

"They did. You should have seen them the next day. Looked like they had been beaten with baseball bats."

Virginia brought out coffee and orange juice and set them before Wayne. "Breakfast will be right out."

"Thank you, ma'am." Tinsley sipped at the hot coffee. "Kids. You ever hear what it was about? Their fight."

"No, they don't talk to me. I heard bits and pieces the day before, though, but none of it made sense. I was afraid they were going to get in to it here in the store."

"Really?"

"That's the way I heard those bits and pieces. Their voices were raised—angry. But with that air conditioner blowing," he pointed at the cooler in a rear window, "you can hardly hear anything going on back there."

"What were the bits and..." Tinsley stopped mid-sentence.

Virginia entered with his breakfast, placing plate and saucer exactly the same as always. "What you need, young man," she began, "is a wife. I'm not always going to be around to cook breakfast for you."

"Why is it married women hate to see a happy, single man?"

She placed clenched hands on broad hips in mock exasperation. "Ain't no such thing as a happy single man. If you was happy, you'd have more meat on those bones."

"Guess you got me there."

Billy Fred placed an arm around her shoulders. "Honey, leave a man to enjoy his breakfast before sermonizing him."

She huffed, smiled, and turned back to her work area. "I'll finish this later, Mr. Wayne Tinsley."

"Yes, ma'am. I know you will." They both chuckled and he dug into the hot food.

When Earl Smith and Ronnie Patterson paid their tab at the cash register, no words were exchanged. They tossed down their money with the bill and gathered up the change Billy Fred counted back to them. Neither acknowledged the presence of Deputy Tinsley, although he was watching them.

As the front door closed behind the boys, Wayne glanced up at Billy Fred. He placed the last bite of toast in his mouth, following it with warm coffee. He shrugged, "Friendly, huh?"

Wayne paid for his breakfast and called into the kitchen, "See you tomorrow!" He heard a muffled return that may have been "bye."

"See ya' later," he said.

Billy Fred smiled and waved.

Virginia came back almost immediately. Humming a Pat Boone song, she carried a cleaning rag which she began using to eliminate anything around the bar not shining.

"Oh, man!" said her husband.

"What?"

"I never got to finish telling him."

"You really don't know anything, Billy. Just a word or two. A name. And it was just a kid fight anyway."

"I know. I just thought he might want to know **who** they were discussing, anyway."

"Why? It's not even our business."

"I agree. And I wouldn't have thought anything about it at all…"

"But…"

"I don't know. Her husband **did** get murdered last week."

"Yeah, and they caught his killer. That colored boy."

"I guess you're right, honey. Say, did you know they say that boy stuck an ice…"

"Stop it!" She held her hands over her ears. "I know what I heard and I don't want to hear it again."

"I'll never understand how they can do something like that…so…so violent. Cruel."

"I know," she answered. "They're not like us. Their tempers just get them out of control. It's not really even their fault."

"What do you mean?"

"It's just how they are. They can't help it. Besides, it's a scientific fact their blood is several degrees hotter than white peoples'…I guess something to do with all that heat in Africa."

"Yeah, I've heard that."

Chapter 19

The Hensley County Courthouse was the premier building in the area, at three stories high the tallest building in the county. It housed the Sheriff's Department, County Tax Assessor, County Clerk, other local government agencies, including a small office for the district Department of Public Safety Trooper.

The building interior was all deep dark mahogany aged like an old briar pipe. The exterior was drab beige brick fascia with no outstanding characteristics. Tinsley occasionally felt on the outside fringes of the sheriff's office, since all the other deputies worked out of the court house. They had desks, lockers, gun cases…and the jail was on the third floor.

When he first went to work for the sheriff, Wayne had to do a three month stint in the jail booking and tending prisoners. He hated it. And those occasional feelings of not belonging had grown farther and farther apart as he grew to cherish his independence more than a desk.

His boot heels sounded loud on the slick marble floor. He spoke to a young couple leaving the building. They were giggly and exhumed an effervescence that could only mean a new marriage license. He remembered that day when he and Linda were in those shoes.

It all seemed so long ago now. He checked his watch, only to find its second hand not moving. He held it to his ear and heard silence. In his haste getting his uniform pressed and boots shined, he had forgotten to wind the thing.

He quickly located the lobby wall clock. He wasn't late. The arraignment was set for 9:00 am, and he still had a few minutes to spare.

Two sets of stairs were available from the lobby. They joined half way up the floor to a half floor which led to a single staircase in the middle. That one led to the second floor. Between the two lower stairways were the water fountains. He paused at the one with the sign "Whites" above it, and took a long drink.

His thirst sated, he climbed the stairs to the second floor which housed the District Court. Judge Henessee would oversee the proceedings. Wayne was impressed with the magnitude of the room— and of those things which transpired in it. District Court handled only felony criminal cases. Cases where people went to prison...or to the electric chair.

He saw Deputy Bill Lightsey sitting in an aisle seat near the back of the room. He stepped past his friend, skipped the seat beside him, and lowered himself into the next.

"Hey, hero," Bill said.

"Yeah, right." Wayne wiggled his holster and handcuffs so they would fit between the arms of the hard wooden fold-up seats. "I expected that from the other guys, Bill, but not from my old hunting partner."

"Hey, I mean it, buddy. You solved a cold murder and got the spook in jail before the sheriff got home."

"I didn't do anything, Bill. People told me everything, including where he was hiding."

"Well, you go on and play the humble servant. Me, I'd ride that horse till he was good and lathered up."

"What are you talking about?"

"Equipment. Better car. Maybe a shotgun. The sheriff, he likes good press. Especially now at election time. Take advantage of it."

"Bill, listen. I almost got myself killed arresting that boy. And because I didn't do it right, I almost got him killed, too."

Bill frowned and leaned toward Tinsley. "This is just you and me talking," he whispered. "The only thing I see you did wrong was not killing him out there."

"Bill…"

"No! I mean it. When one of these people tries to get your gun, you kill them. That's the way it is…always has been. It **has** to be. They have to know that's what's going to happen to 'em if they…"

"All rise!" The bailiff's voice boomed surprisingly through the court room. They stood—shuffling dangling belt equipment out of the seats—just in time to sit back down. The judge sat, glaring at the bailiff.

"John, why am I sitting here looking at an empty defendant's chair?"

"I'm sorry, your Honor. I…" he stopped when the Judge waved his forefinger at him, then curled it backwards. John shuffled to the bench and held his ear close to the judge, who leaned far forward. John was, in Wayne's estimation, somewhere between eighty-five and two hundred years old.

The bailiff nodded several times, then creaked to the door at the front corner of the room. Just as he pulled on it, someone pushed from the other side, banging his shoe sole. The young deputy and John danced a moment trying to establish a semblance of decorum as they brought in the prisoner in belly-chains and leg-irons.

Johnny had limited mobility, able to scoot his feet about eight inches before pinching his legs in the ankle cuffs. He was bent slightly at the waist, giving to the short belly chain.

Tinsley stopped himself short of a gasp. Only a few days since the arrest, he could not believe the damage still evident on the face of the prisoner. Johnny's eyes were swollen almost completely shut. The bridge of his nose, obviously broken, was at odd angles with the rest of his face. His left cheek looked like he had been bitten by a rattle snake, swollen horrifically.

Wayne felt a sour gas in his stomach. The boy's appearance bothered him—and it shouldn't. Bill Bradley would probably be alive today if this kid hadn't murdered him. And what if Ivy had showed up then? What would Johnny Wilson have done to her? The boy was lucky to be alive. Everyone said so.

"John…Mr. Witcher?" Judge Henessee said to the old bailiff.

"Honest Judge, he's on his way…here he is!"

The rear door swept open and a young man in a *Sear sucker* suit hurried down the aisle, leather briefcase swinging. His blond hair was in a crew cut and it was almost apparent he was working on a growth over his upper lip. Almost.

"I'm sorry, your Honor." He sat quickly beside Johnny Wilson and whispered something to him.

Johnny shook his head and said something back. The young attorney raised both hands, as if in despair, and seemed to argue with his client. Tinsley strained to hear, but they were too far away.

"Mr. Witcher!"

"Yes, sir…your Honor."

"When were you appointed by this court to represent this client?"

"Uh, Tuesday, sir. This Tuesday."

"And what is today?"

"Thursday?"

"Yes, I believe you're right. So why are you having this conversation with this boy now…on my time?"

"Your Honor, I haven't had time to talk to him, and from what I've heard, I assumed he was going to plead…well, I wasn't sure."

"You haven't met your client until now?"

Witcher lowered his head. Barely perceptible were the words "No, your Honor."

Judge Henessee put his head in his hands. "John."

"Sir?"

"Water."

"Yes, sir."

"Mr. Witcher."

"Sir?"

"Your daddy is going to be very disappointed…" he raised his head and his voice, "if you don't stop doing stupid stuff in my court!"

John placed a glass on the bench. Witcher sat frozen in place.

"Counselor, is your client ready to make his plea?"

"Yes, your Honor." He stood and motioned for Johnny to do the same. Chair legs screeched against the hardwood floor as he lifted himself to almost upright.

Judge Henessee read the charge against Johnny Wilson. First degree murder.

"Mr. Wilson," continued the judge, "have you seen the charging document, and if so, is your name spelled correctly?"

Johnny stood silently, a confused look on his face. Witcher nudged him with his elbow, "Say yes, sir."

"Yes, sir," echoed Johnny.

"And do you understand the indictment as read?"

"Say yes, sir," from Witcher.

"Yes, sir," said Johnny.

"And how do you plea to the charge of first degree murder?"

Johnny stood still, looking at his lawyer. Witcher faced forward, not speaking.

"Mr. Wilson! Did you hear my question?"

Johnny snapped his head forward, facing the judge. "Yes, sir. I heard your question, but there's been a mistake."

"Mr. Wilson, all I want out of your mouth is an answer to my question. We are not going to discuss this case like we're at a back yard bar-b-que."

"Yes, sir."

"I'm waiting for your answer!" stormed Henessee. "Don't try me, boy. This has not been a good day for me."

"Guilty." The word was spoken so softly no one knew positively he had said it.

"Did you say 'guilty,' Mr. Wilson?"

"My lawyer said 'say guilty,' so I did."

"Mr. Wilson, I don't know what shenanigans you and Mr. Witcher are up to, but I am accepting your plea of guilty. From what I hear, you're lucky to be standing here at all. Most officers would have shot you when you resisted arrest."

"Yes, sir."

Chapter 20

Faye Cowen had wondered how she could meet with Wayne Tinsley without drawing attention, so she was especially pleased when they almost collided at the post office door. He was exiting the narrow building, looking down at his mail as she reached for the door. He shoved it harder than intended and knocked her back on her heels.

"Oh, my...Faye! I'm sorry. Are you alright?"

"Just startled. I'm okay." She looked at the back of her forearm and found a small abrasion where the edge of the door struck her.

"You're hurt," he said, almost frantic.

"Wayne, look. It's a tiny scratch." She showed him her arm again.

"I feel awful, Faye. How stupid I am."

"No, don't. It's good fortune, actually."

"Why do you say that?"

"I need to talk to you. I know something that may be important to you...to your investigation about Mr. Bradley."

She wasn't particularly short for a woman, but she still had to look up at Wayne. He looked into her chestnut eyes, and glanced away quickly. Had she noticed, he wondered. "Sure. Here?"

"I would rather not, if you don't mind."

"Okay. We can't go to my house...wouldn't look right. Too many gossips around." Wayne also had two other reasons he did not want to go to his house. For one, it was a mess.

"How about the cemetery?" she offered.

"The cemetery? Sure, okay. Why not."

"It's a semi-public place. It wouldn't look out of place for us to accidentally meet there. And, during the week, there is hardly ever anyone there anyway."

"Now?" he asked.

"Yes. I'll be right along. As soon as I get my mail and drop by the emergency room."

"Emergency room?"

She pointed at the scratch on her arm and laughed. Her laugh was the most real thing he had ever heard. It made him happy just hearing it. He laughed back and waved, "See you there."

By the time Faye pulled into the cemetery, Wayne was beginning to think she really did stop by the emergency room. It had been almost half an hour. Leaving was never a consideration, however. He would have waited till he starved.

She stepped from the car without looking up. There was a look in her eyes, on her face, with which he was unfamiliar. He had seen her happy, and he had seen her in grief. She looked different; worried, obviously. Afraid? Maybe. Deeply…emotional. But quietly so.

He slid out of his car and met her half-way.

"Walk with me," she said quietly.

Without speaking, he kept pace beside her. She looked down at the green, patchy Bermuda grass as they walked. Her steps were slow, deliberate. Neither of them spoke as they drew nearer to a grave Tinsley knew well. He had led the funeral procession that day, and stayed, of course, for the graveside service.

Nearby squatted a concrete bench, barely large enough for two adults. She sat, patting the bench beside her, and he followed her lead. They remained silent a moment longer, hearing only the distant moan of the Texas wind and the rustle of leaves from one of the three elm trees there.

Wayne was intensely aware of her nearness. He smelled her

inexpensive, elegant perfume; the clean scent of her hair. It was impossible to not touch her. To brush an elbow against hers; to glance against her shoulder with the slightest unintentional movement. He sat as near the edge of the small bench as possible, but the nearness was inescapable.

Wayne hated how she made him feel. And he loved it. His heart pounded, breath too hard to come by. He could not think straight. She had never done a thing to encourage his feelings for her. And there had never been a word spoken of it between them. He wasn't sure she even knew. She was always so solid. So strong.

And, she was married. He hated how she made him feel.

"He would have been five in September," she said finally, looking at the small metal grave marker. He didn't respond, but sat silently. Being with her.

"It was my fault, Wayne."

"No, Faye…"

"That's the first time I've said it aloud to another person."

He stopped, not knowing what to say. He waited for her to continue.

"I've thought it a million times, but I've never said it out loud." Her eyes were dry, looking somewhere Wayne couldn't see. He would wait for her. He would be here when she returned.

They sat for several minutes, silently experiencing strange, unfamiliar territory to them.

He knew she had something to tell him…something not related to these moments at all. He wondered if what she had to say was so terrible she was just putting it off. He didn't really believe that was the case, though. He had seen her car here often in times past. Times when he kept his distance, watching, wishing Allen was there with her…someone; anyone to help take away her pain. To experience it with her. To shield her.

"Thank you, Wayne," she said finally. "You're a good friend. I didn't have this in mind when I asked to meet you here. I just…I don't know."

"It's okay. I'm…I'm very happy you feel comfortable enough to allow me to be here," he nodded toward the grave.

"Your time is important, I know, so shall we get to it?"

"Anytime you're ready."

Faye sighed deeply. "What I'm going to tell you...well, you decide what to do with it."

He nodded.

"I have a ledger at home. It has some things in it that could, potentially, ruin a lot of lives." She took a deep breath. "In the ledger— it's really a diary..."

"Who's?"

"Mrs. Wilson's. It's her diary?"

"How did you..."

"I'll get to that. But for now, just listen."

"Sorry."

"In her ledger she says Mr. Bradley came to her, when Mr. Wilson was away at work."

"He ran around with a lot of women, Faye."

"She also wrote he had threatened to kick them out of his house unless she," Faye lowered her head, embarrassed at the topic, "unless she, you know, cooperated with him."

"That sorry..."

"Yes, he was. Sorry. But I thought you should know. If Johnny found that diary before I did..."

"Sure. Even more motive. As if he needed more. I already knew he was seeing her." He answered the questioning look on Faye's face. "Some of the other hired hands had seen his pickup over at the Wilsons' house a few times. But the ledger will solidify their statements. They really don't want to testify against the boy."

"They wouldn't have to, would they?"

"They're supposed to, if we subpoena them. But they won't. They'll just dummy up and say they don't remember."

"I don't know that I blame them."

"But with that ledger, all those problems go away. It doesn't get much better than the actual words of the woman involved...just before she hung herself."

"She what?"

"I'm sorry, Faye. I forgot; most people don't know…think it was natural causes."

"But, why? Why would she do that? Why would you hide it?"

"I promised Mr. Wilson. The kids were at school. He came home for lunch and found her. There was a note, obviously a suicide. I just didn't see any reason to hurt those kids more. And Mr. Wilson…lost his wife and daughter within six months of each other."

"And now, probably a son," she added.

"Pretty lousy deal, huh?"

"It's terrible, Wayne. And with him in jail, too…"

"I know. I've wrestled with this whole thing. Mulled it over and over in my mind. I don't want the boy to be guilty. But facts are what they are, and the case looks pretty strong against him. And with the ledger…"

"You can't have the ledger, Wayne."

He stared. "What? What do you mean?"

"You can't have the actual ledger. I'll testify what it says, if I must. I'll make exact notes from her writing. Anything you want. Anything but the ledger."

"But, why? Faye, it's important. I don't understand."

"I can't tell you."

"Can't tell me? Faye, this is a murder investigation. We **must** have any available evidence. They can make you give it to them."

"To you, you mean?"

"Yeah, to me."

"I can't, Wayne. You must believe me. I can't. You cannot believe…you can't possibly know how important it is that no one else sees that ledger…ever!"

"What is it? What is it you're afraid of? What could Mrs. Wilson possibly write that could have that much affect on you?"

"I've told you what I can, Wayne. Please believe me."

"We can get a search warrant for it, Faye." The moment he said the words he regretted them, but he knew that's what would happen if she continued to refuse cooperation.

"A search warrant? You would come to my house with a search

warrant?" She looked directly into the eyes of the deputy, searching. And in her eyes he saw the unmistakable welling of tears, building…until they spilled quietly down her cheeks. He knew he would explode. Why didn't he just find a litter of puppies and stomp them to death?

"Faye…"

"No. Stop it Wayne." She sniffed, and he handed her a handkerchief.

She took it momentarily, then returned it without touching it to her face. "I thought I knew you. I thought I could tell you this in private. You would do the right thing with the information…"

"I will…I'll…"

"You bring your search warrant, Wayne. You and your police friends come to my house…where my husband and boys live. Things will never be the same. You have no idea…"

She arose quickly and rushed back to her car. Wayne saw her wiping at tears with her bare hands as she walked. He looked away and heard the car door slam shut. The motor roared to life, and she sped away.

Tinsley looked down at the white handkerchief in his hand. He leaned forward, elbows on his knees…looked back up at Oma's grave, then touched the cloth in his hand to his own eyes.

Chapter 21

The telephone book was a quarter of an inch thick and had phone listings from six other towns in the area besides Cash, Texas. Five pages listed Cash residents. It still took Jeff a few minutes to find the number he sought.

"Here it is," he whispered to himself. "Nine-nine-nine-four." His right forefinger traced backward to the names Herman and Jenye Smith. Herman and Jenye Smith? There was no address beside the names, but there didn't need to be. In Cash, it wasn't necessary.

Herman—a known alcoholic—and Jenye, were the parents of Earl Smith. Their other three boys had already gone away from home, one to the Army, one to prison, and the other just gone...no one knew where.

What would Ivy have to do with them, Jeff wondered. But the bigger, more aggravating question remained. Why had she lied to him? Jeff knew it took six numbers to call long distance into the city. Only local calls could be made using four.

He had enjoyed being with her so much that day, he didn't want to spoil the moment by questioning her word. Besides, she **was** an adult, and it wasn't in his nature to challenge her story.

She hurt his feelings with her lie. Maybe it was just a mistake, he thought. Perhaps she thought the paper he picked up was actually another one…one with the psychiatrist's telephone number on it. An honest mistake.

Still, she **did** have Smith's telephone number. And Jeff didn't think she had business with Herman or Jenye. He wished he had never even seen the paper…that he had never looked up the number. Just her knowing anyone in that family…that fact alone…was troublesome.

Hers was still the face he saw when he closed his eyes at night. The memory of holding her in his arms that Saturday morning still caused his body to warm, his mind to cloud.

He slammed the telephone book down on the kitchen table just as Faye walked in. Embarrassed at his brief fit of temper, he inclined to turn away…until he saw her face. Her eyes were red and puffy, her cheeks flushed. She was as surprised to see him as he was her.

It was Faye who turned her eyes away, walking quickly toward her bedroom.

"Mama?"

"Not now, Jeff."

He heard the door to her room close, and the coil springs of her bed squeaked in protest as she put weight on it. Jeff sat still, not knowing what to do.

He had seen his mother cry a couple of times, and had heard her other times when she didn't know. Her tears never failed to impale his spirit. Jeff had never seen his dad cry, however. Not even when Oma died. He was obviously deeply hurt, but he never cried. Even as a young boy, Jeff had tried to hold back his own tears at the funeral, but failed. He would never be as strong as his dad.

The only telephone in the house was in the living room, and he strode to it when the idea came to him. He quickly dialed 9-9-9-4, snapping each number to the finger stop as quickly as the dial rotated back from the previous number.

"Hello." A woman's voice.

"Mrs. Jones?"

"No. You must have the wrong number. This is the Smith residence."

"Sorry." He placed the receiver quietly back on its cradle. It was just an idea, he thought.

Closer to his parents bedroom now, Jeff listened intently for his mother. He heard no crying. What he **did** hear was the distinct sound of her old cedar chest being opened, then closed again.

Faye lifted the book out of the chest and let the lid back down. She held it closely against her body, her arms crossed over it like a gentle wrestling hold. She sat back on the edge of the bed, her heart racing.

She should just burn it...destroy the thing along with its evil secrets, Faye thought. And as she thought of destroying it—in the same instant—her heart demanded a better ending for Mrs. Wilson. No doubt buried in a pauper's grave at the colored cemetery, the ledger might be the only real evidence the woman ever lived.

The conflict between mind and spirit drained Faye, made her weak. Wouldn't Mr. Wilson want the ledger when he got out of jail? Recalling his wife's last entry—about Bill Bradley—Faye thought it might really be the kinder thing to just leave the man with his memories. He didn't need that memory, too.

Her quandary was not, however, just over the Wilson family. What about Allen? What should she tell him? Anything? She had to tell him, didn't she? He had a right to know, surely. Was it more cruel to tell him, or to leave him in his world of ignorance?

And the boys...there was no end to it. In a few years, Jeff could easily be a father. And then Randy. What if they fathered a child who looked Negro? They should be warned. But if they knew their ancestry, and told others, what girl would even go with them? What father would permit it?

The never-ending ripples were staggering. How many generations could this affect?

Faye also fought her own demons. What if she had known about Allen before they married? Would she still have gone through with it? She loved him, so—certainly she would. Except...if she knew before they dated and fell in love, would she have gone out with him the first time? Faye realized she likely would not have agreed to go out with him—with Allen Cowen the stranger, the mulatto. And that realization caused her shame.

She tried to act normally, but Allen—even Allen—had noticed something different between them. She knew she had been more distant emotionally. After all, she did not like keeping a secret from him. She knew she had also withdrawn from his touches, however involuntarily. As much as she wanted another child—a baby—Faye was afraid...terrified of what their fourth child might look like.

An innocent, sweet baby...born with the wrong features—the wrong color—could destroy their entire family. No, she corrected, the baby wouldn't destroy...peoples' reactions would destroy. But it would still be destroyed.

That was the reason, she determined, that she had separated herself physically and emotionally from her husband. It had nothing to do with the fact he was half colored. It couldn't be that. He was the same man now as he was before she knew the truth. Exactly the same man. So, it couldn't be that. She was sure it wasn't. She prayed that was not the case. It couldn't be.

But she feared it was.

Ordinarily Wayne Tinsley would give a day's pay for an excuse to stop at the Cowens' house. Ordinarily. But this evening, with Bill Lightsey beside him, he would have given everything he owned to be elsewhere.

He had reported to Sheriff Hand what Faye said was in the ledger. He tried to minimize its importance, citing several colored families who could testify to the same information. In spite of his pleadings and disagreement with his boss, Wayne found himself in possession of a search warrant—brought to him by Lightsey—for the Cowens' home...a search for "A ledger, the property of the late Mrs. Wilson of Cash, Texas." They don't even know her first name, thought Wayne.

If possible, his spirits dropped even lower when he saw the Cowens' Ford in the driveway. He could not erase from his memory the way she looked at him at the cemetery, her liquid brown eyes...the look of one betrayed.

"What's the matter, pard?" asked Bill Lightsey.

"Nothing."

"Yeah, I can see that."

"Let's just get this done."

They both reached for the car door handles as Wayne put on the parking brake.

"Wait," said Bill. "Listen, I know you are friends with a lot of folks over here. Want me to handle this?"

"You know the sheriff's policy. Search warrants call for at least two deputies."

"That's just a safety thing. You and I know these are decent people. The sheriff will never know."

Wayne sighed as he opened the car door. "I can't do that, Bill."

The evening shadows were long, but spring warmth lingered in the air. The front door of the house stood fully open, with only a wood-framed screen door separating the outside from the inside. Before the deputies stepped onto the porch, Allen was at the door. "Wayne," he said, nodding. He stepped outside, looking at Bill.

"Bill. Bill Lightsey," the deputy introduced himself and held out a hand which Allen shook.

"'Lo, Allen," offered Wayne.

"What's up boys?" Allen took the lead. A look of concern was apparent on his strong facial features. "Jeff's not in any trouble, is he?"

"No. No, nothing like that," answered Wayne.

"And the Negra boy...he's still kicking?"

"Better every day," said Bill.

"Then y'all must'a found out about my moonshine still in the back yard...I knew I couldn't trust those dope fiends to keep a secret." He laughed nervously.

Bill laughed with him, politely, but Wayne didn't have it in him. Allen noticed.

"Okay, Wayne. What's going on?"

"We...the sheriffs' department...believe there is a book in your house. It may be evidence in a case we're...I'm working on."

"A book?"

"Yes…more like a ledger. If you know where it is, we could just take it and get out of here quick…without bothering your family."

"A ledger? I'd be happy to help you out, boys, but I swear, I don't have the slightest idea what you're talking about."

"It belonged to the colored folks across the street. Some of its writings might have to do with Bill Bradley's murder," Wayne said.

"But why here? Why do you think it would be here? We didn't hardly know those people."

"It's complicated, Allen."

"Complicated? Doesn't sound complicated to me. You think one of my boys stole a worthless old ledger-book from over there." He nodded in the direction of the Wilsons' former home, his aggravation beginning to surface.

"No, I don't. I don't think that at all. It's just, we heard the book might be here. I wouldn't be doing my job if I didn't check."

"You want to search my house? Is that it?"

"Yes, I'm sorry, but that's what I have to do."

"And if I say no?"

"We have a search warrant, Mr. Cowen." Bill held up the folded document for Allen to see. Allen looked back at Wayne.

"Why didn't you tell me that?"

"I'd rather do this with your permission…I don't like coming into a man's home against his wishes."

"Allen!" He turned at the sound of Faye's voice. "Let them in." She stood in the middle of the living room, her cotton dress protected from the waist down by a plain white apron. She finished drying her hands on it and let it fall before smoothing out imaginary wrinkles.

Without speaking, Allen swung open the screen door and motioned the deputies inside.

He followed behind.

"Don't worry, Faye. Wayne just needs to see if he can find a book, or something. He won't, and they'll be gone."

"No, he won't," she answered without emotion. Something in her voice gave Wayne pause. Allen was standing by Faye now, but Tinsley watched her.

"I'm sorry, F…Mrs. Cowen."

"You won't find what you're looking for," she repeated.

"What are you saying? Is it…gone?"

"Gone? Yes, gone, I guess. Destroyed."

Wayne looked at her, surprised. He heard her words, but her face…her eyes were speaking something else. A plea?

Allen stared at her, bewildered. "You know about this? You know about this book?"

"Yes, Allen. I do." Her eyes remained fixed on Tinsley.

"Well, when was **I** going to hear about it? Looks to me like everybody in town knows what's going on but me."

"Later, Allen." She turned her head to face her husband. "Please."

"I don't like this, Faye. I don't like being on the outside of things in my own home. Later will be fine, when these boys leave."

"Thank you. I'll tell you whatever you want to know." Throughout the entire exchange Wayne could not detect the slightest change in Faye's voice. It was as though she were in a trance. Then he heard her add, to Allen, "More than you want to know." She turned back to Wayne. "Are you finished here, then?"

"You heard her, Wayne. There's nothing here to find," said Allen.

Faye watched him; the only emotion visible was so deeply hidden in her eyes it pained him to see.

"Yeah, I heard." He paused, knowing somehow the book was still there. "Let's go Bill."

"Are you sure?" the deputy asked.

Was there a "thank you" in those eternally deep eyes? Or was Wayne misreading them entirely? Was the real message one of conquest over a naïve deputy?

"I'm sure." Wayne nodded to the Cowens. "Sorry to have disturbed you." He let himself out without looking back.

In the car, half way back to town, Lightsey finally spoke. "I'm sorry, pard, but she didn't sound all that convincing to me. Maybe we should have searched."

"Probably."

"Did you believe her?"

"Not her words."

"What? I don't get it."

"Neither do I, Bill. Let's drop it though, if you don't mind."

"Wayne, you're a good man. A good deputy. And I ain't saying this against you, but I caught some serious vibrations back there. Do you think maybe you're too close to the people in this deal?"

"Yeah, I do."

Chapter 22

Every minute of every day Johnny Wilson remained locked in the same concrete cubicle, about the size of an indoor bathroom. He was given a cup of water with his meals three times daily, and his chamber pot picked up and emptied each morning by an old Negro trustee who had the run of the jail.

Johnny waited as long as possible before using the chamber pot. In the close quarters of his cell, the smell was overwhelming.

His head hurt. It seemed most excruciating when he bent over, but pained him some almost all the time. He breathed through his mouth mostly, since his nose passages weren't functioning properly. Slowly, day by day, he could finally feel slight improvement in his condition.

He didn't know how long he had been locked up, but he did know it had been two days since he had gone to court. He was told he would get an attorney for free who was on his side, but he couldn't figure how telling the judge he was guilty would help...maybe some sneaky lawyer trick to get him off. He would ask the lawyer when he saw him again.

He had grown accustomed to the twenty-four hours each day of clanging cell doors and boots shuffling across the concrete floor, so when he heard that same sound on this day, it didn't even register with him. He had already had his beans for supper, and was expecting no one.

When the sounds of foot falls stopped outside his cell, the unmistakable clunk of a large brass key into the locking mechanism on his cell door caused him to look up quickly, frightened.

He didn't recognize the white man at the door. He wore Sunday meeting clothes and was overweight, mostly in the stomach. The suit coat lacked several inches from coming together in front, and his white shirt stretched against its buttons, leaving gaps large enough to see his undershirt in two places.

The voice startled Johnny. After the long silence of his cell, the harsh, booming voice of the man seemed even more intense.

"You believe in God and Jesus, boy?"

"Yes, sir. My mama, she…"

"Well that's good. That's good. 'Cause you and me are going to go down this here hall and have a little prayer meeting. I call it my getting right with God room."

Johnny raised himself from the concrete floor, cautiously watching the man. The words seemed harmless enough, but the tone of the big man's voice seemed ominous.

"Yes, sir. You a police?"

"Would I be standing here with this key in my hand if I wasn't?"

"Yes, sir…I mean, no, sir," he stammered.

"Let's get a move on, boy. It's less than a hour 'till going home time for me."

Johnny eased toward the opening, head lowered slightly. "Is Mr. Tinsley here, sir?"

"You mean **Deputy** Tinsley? No. As far as I know he's still over in Trash…I mean **Cash.**" He laughed at his joke. Then he stopped laughing and glowered at the prisoner. "Are you planning on giving me any trouble, boy? 'Cause if you are, I'm telling you…that little bump on your head will feel like a hangnail when I'm through with you."

"No. No trouble, sir."

"I heard you jumped Deputy Tinsley."

"I guess so, sir."

"You **guess**? Weren't you there?"

"Yes, sir, but..."

"That's just what I'm talking about! You making excuses for your bad deeds...trying to live on those half-truths which are nothing but whole lies."

The big detective opened a standard wooden door into a small room. There were two facing chairs inside. The walls were drab gray and the floor of tile squares, several of which curled at the edges.

"Sit down," ordered the detective.

Johnny chose a chair and started to sit.

"Stop! What do you think you're doing, boy?"

"You said..."

"Don't tell me what I said. You think I'm stupid, boy?"

"Nah, sir. I just, uh..."

"Did I tell you to sit in **that** chair?"

"No, sir." Johnny's eyes darted about the room like a cornered cat, searching for...what?

"You're right, I didn't. This is what you gotta' learn right up front. You listen to me, and you answer right. You do what you're told. That way, you get to walk right outta' here the same way you walked in. Otherwise..." he left the thought hanging heavily in the air. Johnny was still standing, and the detective pointed at the chair nearest him. "Okay, now sit down in that chair."

Johnny said nothing and seated himself in the assigned chair, the same one he had started to sit in to begin with. He watched the big man, but avoided direct eye contact.

"You want to know the trouble with you people?" the detective asked. He twirled the second chair around, straddling the seat and crossing his arms over the backrest. He was less than two feet from Johnny's face. When Johnny said nothing, he continued.

"'Course you don't know. That's because you're dumb...all of you. And I'm going to prove it to you." There was no response, and the man continued. "All you people are poor, right?"

"Guess so."

"That's 'cause you're all dumb. And even though you're all poor, you keep sproutin' little nigger babies like they was onions. Dumb. And that brings us to you."

Johnny caught the man's eyes for a moment, trying to hide his anger, but looked away quickly.

"Didn't like that, huh? Okay, we've already proved you're dumb. Now, here's how I know you're even dumber than most." He held up his beefy hand and lifted an additional finger for emphasis with each point.

"One, you beat up a white farmer. Two, you **killed** a white farmer. Three, you resisted arrest. Four, you pointed a gun at a county deputy. And, five, I know you're dumb because you didn't kill yourself years ago before you got hair under your arms." He sat, glaring at the youth.

Johnny held the arms of the metal chair he sat on. His hands began to cramp.

"Now, **Mr.** Wilson. Now that the pleasantries are over, you're going to tell me what I want to know. Then I'll write it down and you can sign it, or put your mark down."

"I can write."

"Well, aren't you the educated spook?"

"A little."

"Good. Then you can understand my questions. Tell me…true now…tell me about killing Bradley."

"Didn't kill nobody," Johnny answered, looking at the floor.

The detective lowered his voice to a whisper and inched even closer. "Now, see. That's what I've been talking about. Dumb. You are going to die for what you did. That's already settled. Out of your control. Here's the good part…what you **can** control. You are in control of what happens to you between now—this minute—and when you die. You can be treated pretty good and feel good, or you can be in horrible pain and hungry from now till they pull the switch on your little murdering…"

"I didn't! I didn't kill…" Johnny's words were violently severed with the explosive slap to his head. Johnny's peripheral vision began to narrow, and he was sure he would pass out. His head pounded. He slowly became aware the detective was still talking, but no longer in a whisper—he was screaming.

"…and another thing, you little son…"

"Excuse me! Hey! Excuse me." Tinsley's voice was raised to penetrate the volume of the detective's.

"Tinsley. I'm a little busy, here. Can't it wait?"

"No. No, it can't. The sheriff wants you to wait for him outside his office. He's on his way in. Said it's important."

"Agghh! Okay. Rats. Just a second. I got to put this boy back…"

"No, leave him. I'll put him up. You better get along."

"Yeah, sure. Okay." He looked at Johnny Wilson. "Later." The door slammed loudly behind him.

Tinsley turned the chair back around and sat, facing the younger man.

"Looks like you're hurting some," he said.

"Some," he acknowledged.

Wayne took a small bottle of *Saint Joseph's* aspirins from his shirt pocket. He twisted the metal cap as he spoke. "Brought these from home—just in case you might need one." He poured three pills into his hand and offered them to Johnny. "Can you get these down without water?"

"Yes, sir." He took the pills and held them in his hand.

"They taste just awful. You sure?"

He tossed all three in his mouth, chewed them up, and swallowed. His face involuntarily screwed up.

"Yes, sir. They sure do taste awful."

"You know what, Johnny?"

"What?"

"If you was a door, you'd be closed." Johnny didn't answer. "I mean, look at you. Shoulders are all bunched up, hands clasped tight, knees squeezed together. It just struck me…you look like a closed door."

"Feel like a door, too."

"How's that?"

"Slammed plumb to death."

Wayne chuckled. "That's a pretty good one. I never thought of you as having a sense of humor."

"Why not?"

"I don't know, really. Maybe because every time we've been around each other it has been under bad circumstances."

"Yes, sir. Sure has."

Tinsley's face turned serious. "Johnny, we have to talk about why you're here."

"That murder?"

"Yeah, Mr. Bradley."

"Are you going to talk to me like that fat guy?"

"Detective Benningfield? No, I'm not."

"Why does he be that way? Why does he hate me?"

"He doesn't hate you, Johnny. He's just…"

"Yes, sir…no disrespect meaning, but I'm pretty sure he does."

Tinsley remained quiet a moment. "Johnny, can we just talk? Me and you? What we say be just between us?"

"I guess so, Mr. Tinsley."

"Wayne."

"What?"

"Wayne. That's my first name. You can call me that if you like."

"Thank you, sir, but no, sir. I can't. I don't believe I can do that."

"Okay. Up to you. About your question…yeah, Benningfield hates you."

"Why? He don't even know me."

"He hates everybody. He's mean to white prisoners, too."

"Bet he don't call them no nigger, though."

"No. But he does call them some pretty awful stuff, just the same."

"What makes people like that?"

"I don't know. Some folks have troubles at home and take it out on others. Some people are afraid of others, so they yell loud and act aggressive to hide their own fears…"

"I don't think that fat man is afraid of me."

"Probably not." Wayne hesitated a moment, then continued.

"There's another group of people…people who are just plain old mean. They're born mean, and they die mean."

"I think the fat guy is like that."

"You know who else is like that?"

"Who?"

"Mr. Bradley. He was like that."

"Oh."

"He was a mean, selfish, evil little man. The world is better off with him dead."

"Really. You really think that?"

"Between you and me? Yeah, I do."

"And you wouldn't be mad at who killed him?"

"Mad? It's not about mad, Johnny. No matter how bad Bradley was, nobody…nobody had a right to kill him. I work for the law, so I have to make sure his killer stands trial with a jury."

"How do they figure who's on a jury, anyhow?"

"Well, they draw names from people who are registered to vote, so a man can be tried by his peers."

"Peers?"

"Yes, other people. Just plain people. People like the accused."

"Will there be other people like me on my jury?"

Tinsley thought a moment, frowning slightly. "I don't think so."

"So there won't be none of my peers?"

"There may be a couple of Mexicans."

Johnny gave him a curious look. "Mexicans don't like us any more than y'all do."

"Look, I don't know a lot about juries. But if you're not guilty, your defense attorney should get you off. That's how our system works." He thought he saw Johnny's head shake slightly. "Okay, Johnny, maybe not **your** lawyer."

"Can I ask you another question, Mr. Tinsley?"

"Shoot."

"What?"

"Shoot. It just means go ahead."

"Okay. Mr. Tinsley, I don't think you are sure in your head that I did that killing on Mr. Bradley."

"That wasn't a question, son."

"No, sir. Here's the question: If I'm right, and you think maybe I didn't do it, how come you put me in here?"

"I don't know you **didn't** do it either. Lots of evidence says you did."

"I said I didn't. Don't that count at all?"

"No, it doesn't. Everybody says they don't do what they do."

"I don't."

"You said you killed him."

"I never did!"

"Yes, in court. You plead guilty."

"My lawyer told me to."

"Do you always do what you're told?" Johnny started to answer when Tinsley stopped him. "If you didn't do it, just tell me what you do know. Tell me everything you did…all you know. Give me something to help you. Start to finish."

Johnny Wilson looked at the deputy, trying to read the man. "Okay. I'll start when Mr. Bradley came in my house…that okay?" His rendition of that day's events were nothing Tinsley hadn't already heard, or didn't already know.

"So, after you ran out of your house, you hid in a field out by the lake till dark, then hid in the Cowens' barn? Is that what you're telling me?"

"That's what there is to tell."

"You're leaving out one part. One really important part. You went to Bradley's house that night, looking for him."

"No, I never."

"Johnny, there's an eye witness. I know you were there."

"I wasn't, Mr. Tinsley. I swear I wasn't."

"Have you ever seen Mrs. Bradley?"

"No, sir. I don't think so."

"Be sure, Johnny. I can't do a thing for you if you lie to me."

"I'm not lying, Mr…wait…I did see her, one time." Tinsley waited. "Me and my daddy, we was working on Mr. Bradley's tractor—his old

John Deere, not the new one. We was out back by the barn. The hydraulics was leaking and we had some…"

"Johnny…Mrs. Bradley?"

"Okay, yeah. She came out the back and walked around to the side of the house. I was watching her, but you couldn't hardly see her face—she had on a big old hat. Anyway, I guess I was staring, 'cause Mr. Wilson said to stop or we'd be in big trouble."

"That was it?"

"Mostly. But I kept kinda' watching her—like out of the side of my eye—I couldn't see her good, but she dressed real pretty."

"Uh, huh."

"So then this car comes down the road and starts slowing down like it's going to turn in.

She was looking at it. Just then Mr. Bradley comes speeding in from the pasture like his tail was on fire."

"So…"

"The car just sped up and went down the road. Mrs. Bradley turned and ducked her head and headed straight back to the door."

"So you never saw her face?"

"For a second. When she was about to the house, she looked up—quick like—and looked right at me. I turned away, but it was too late. She saw me looking."

"Did Mr. Bradley ever say anything to you about watching his wife?"

"No, sir. He never did. I guess she didn't even tell him."

"About that car…can you describe it?"

"Sure. It's a brown 1950 Studebaker."

Tinsley smiled. "You're not so dumb, are you?"

"The fat man thinks I am."

"The fat man is an idiot…uh, between you and me."

"Yes, sir."

Wayne locked Johnny in his cell and brought a cup of water to dispel some of the aspirin taste. Walking past the sheriff's office on his way out, Wayne saw a red-faced Detective Benningfield pacing the floor.

"Tinsley!" he stormed, "I thought you said the sheriff wanted to see me here now. The dispatcher finally found him. He's at a school play with his wife."

"Oh, is that what you thought I said?"

"That **is** what you said!" he fumed.

Wayne spoke very softly into the larger man's ear. "No. What I said was, if you ever treat another one of my prisoners like you did that boy, I'll beat you so bad even God won't recognize you."

Chapter 23

She leaned heavily against the sink, the cool porcelain absorbing some of the heat in her body. Faye's head bowed completely forward, her dark hair falling past the edges of her face. There was not a muscle in her neck...impossible to lift her head. Thoughts...images, raced through her mind faster than she could put them into any order.

Then, with a power beyond her, she did lift her head. The medicine cabinet mirror before her showed what she didn't want to see. It **was** her. This was happening to her...to her family. And, for the first time since they buried Oma, Faye **looked** at herself in the mirror.

She went through the mechanisms of keeping herself presentable before this same piece of glass every day...but she never **looked.** She would focus on an eye as a little shadow was applied, or on her lips at the application of lipstick. She saw the parts that made up her face, but not since that afternoon—just after the funeral, had she looked herself in the eyes and took stock of who she saw there.

On that day she saw an unworthy mother. On that day, for the first time, she allowed her thoughts to become part of her soul. She looked at the woman in the reflection and thought, It's your fault. For the rest of your life, no matter what else happens, you will have been responsible for the death of your baby...the baby God gave to your care. Nothing bad enough can happen to you to erase that fact, or to make up for it.

This time the circumstances were certainly different, but there was something frightfully familiar about the emotions.

Faye had walked directly into the bathroom before Wayne and the other deputy were well out the front door. She needed a moment. She needed to brace herself. Locking the door behind her, she could get no further than the sink. Her altar of retribution; a bathroom sink and an old, darkly spotted mirror. Appropriate, she thought.

Allen had been so pleased with himself when he completed the bathroom. It cut several feet out of what had been the living room, but they finally had an indoor toilet. He was proud he had been able to build the small room using other peoples' throw away lumber and used facilities. She was proud of it, too. That long walk to the outhouse was awful in the winter.

She was diverting herself, she knew, from the present…but the thoughts she fought against kept banging at the door of her consciousness. They would not be silenced. She peered deeply into the eyes that looked back at her, accusing. You've caused all this. You betrayed your husband with your secret. You lied to your friend. You. You are about to tell your husband things which will hurt him more than he can imagine. Your words will ultimately change the lives of your sons. All you had to do was mind your own business. All you had to do was burn the book. If you had burned the book and told one lie, this moment wouldn't exist. We could all still be ignorant of all this…this what? Ignorant of the truth about us?

An attractive woman looked back at Faye, but she didn't see her. She never had seen that woman. Faye was a mother, a wife, a homemaker, a gardener, and a field hand. That was who she was. That's all she saw. Pretty was not a characteristic necessary for any of those things. Not an ounce of fat clung to her. She could pull more cotton in one day than any two men Allen knew…that is what he said.

Her body was hard as a rock, her hands rough. Her face was weathered like ancient and well polished maple furniture. Smooth, but richly deep in texture. There were things about her other people saw and admired. She saw none of it.

Faye saw a failure. A plain, rough-edged failure. She saw a lonely woman with only family to hold her up. And she was about to crumble that very family. It didn't matter what happened to her. Nothing could ever be bad enough...that had been her promise to the mirror years ago. But how about Allen and the boys. They had made no such promise. They didn't let Oma die. They didn't steal a book from neighbors. They didn't hide it and lie to Wayne. They didn't know what she knew. But they would soon. She was about to stick a spear right through the heart of her husband.

Closing her eyes tightly, she hid from the image before her, turned, and unlocked the door. Allen sat at the kitchen table, in his spot, gazing across the room at nothing in particular. She wondered where his thoughts had taken him. Allen was not usually an introspective man, she knew. Was he now, finally, catching a glimpse of himself? Or was he wondering how to fix the well pump?

The kitchen table was where family business was handled. It was where the two of them sat after the cotton crop money came in, looking through the Sears Roebuck catalogue for that year's Christmas presents for the boys. There were never many, but Faye and Allen attacked the process with energy and a serious attention to balancing what the boys wanted against what they needed.

The table is where they scattered out bills, also, determining which would be paid that month and who would get an apology with a promise for next month. Decisions were made there. It was an appropriate place for them to have this talk. Faye prayed silently he would let it go, knowing full well Allen Cowen was not that kind of man.

He pushed back a chair for her when she entered the kitchen, but didn't speak. His face was stone, and he avoided eye contact with her. Hurt and embarrassed, he would have to know.

"Okay, Allen. What do you want me to say?"

"There were two cops here a few minutes ago. Maybe you noticed?"

"You don't need to be sarcastic, Allen. I told you…whatever you want to know…"

"I want to know what's going on, Faye. Can you imagine how it makes a man feel to have all this happen in his own house…to not know anything? It's almost like you cheated on me."

"No, I guess I didn't know. I had no idea you would see it that way. I'm sorry."

"I don't know. Maybe I'm over reacting. That's just how I feel, though."

"I understand. You should know, Allen, I haven't betrayed you. Except for going into the Wilsons' house, I don't think I've done anything you would be ashamed of me for."

"I needed to hear that. Why **did** you go in that house?"

"I don't even know now. It all seemed so plain to me then. So right. I just needed to be in their house. Maybe because of the little girl getting killed. Maybe because Mrs. Wilson had died at that same house only shortly before that…did you know she committed suicide?"

"Yeah, I'd heard something about it in town."

"Why didn't you tell me? And who told you?"

"Old man Payne at the funeral home told the guy that runs the Phillips 66 station. He told me. I didn't say anything 'cause I figured it would just upset you. Besides, wasn't anything we could do about it."

"It was just that Wayne was trying to keep it secret, for the sake of the family."

Wayne? Why did he tell you? Is there something I need to know about Wayne?"

"What do you mean? Me and Wayne?"

"Yeah."

"No. Of course not. Wayne is a friend…**our** friend. I've known him since high school. I'm surprised you would even think such a thing."

"Well, I didn't really think it. So, why did he tell you?"

"It just slipped out, accidentally, when we were talking. He didn't intend to tell me." Faye was relieved they were only talking about whether or not she was having a love affair. It was a safer topic than the alternative, but her relief was short-lived. Allen couldn't help but pick at the most painful wound.

"What's the big deal about the book? You were shaking when they came to the house. Why do they want it? Why do you have it? Why did you burn it?"

"That's a lot of 'whys,' Allen."

"There's more."

"The book. I stole the book from the Wilsons' house." She looked at Allen for a surprised reaction, but he simply sat, looking at her…waiting. "I went over there one morning after you went to work."

"Why? I just don't understand why."

"Like I said before, I'm not sure why. I wish I could give you a good answer, something noble. But I can't. I don't understand it myself."

"Go on."

"When I was over there, I found a ledger in the sofa…"

"You were searching through their sofa?"

"Allen!"

"I'm sorry. Go ahead."

"I found the book, and started thumbing through the pages." Allen shook his head in disbelief, but remained silent.

"What I read in the ledger interested me…intrigued me, so I brought it back home. I was getting uneasy about being in there so long."

"Faye, they have a name for what you did. Theft…robbery… burglary…take your pick."

"I know. I didn't think of it like that. I always intended to return it to someone in their family." She paused, not wanting to continue.

"So you read everything in the book? You know why the cops want it?"

"Yes, I read it all. There was an entry in there about Mr. Bradley… how he had blackmailed Mrs. Wilson into having…into going to bed with him."

"I never could stand that guy."

"Wayne thinks the book might be good for a jury to see to show why Johnny would have a motive to kill Mr. Bradley."

"Well, 'course it would. Who could blame him, if he knew."

"So that's it. That's why they wanted the book."

"Well, that wasn't so painful, was it?" he said, smiling for the first time.

"No, not so painful. I'm sorry I didn't tell you sooner, Allen. I was ashamed, I guess.

Thanks for understanding." Relieved at the apparent conclusion of the discussion, she started to rise, but he grabbed her wrist.

"Just a minute." She lowered back into the chair. "I understand why the police wanted the book. What I don't understand is why you wouldn't let them have it."

Faye looked down at the table, making tiny circles with her forefinger, deep in thought. So, here it is. She looked up, directly at her husband. "Allen, please don't make me answer that question."

"I need to know."

"No, Allen. You don't need to know. There is nothing I can tell you that can turn out good for us. There is only trouble and pain in a truthful answer…and I promised myself I wouldn't lie to you. So, please…"

Surprisingly, Allen seemed hurt…not angry. "Faye, do you think I'm that weak? There is something, obviously something bad, that you're carrying alone. And if my guess is right, whatever is in there has something to do with the way you've been the past couple of weeks…you know, different with me."

Faye was surprised at her husband's insight. He was more accurate than she would have ever imagined. He continued. "I thought at first there was another man…"

"Allen!"

"I know. I know. But things go through a man's mind when things start to happen—or not happen—between him and his wife. Anyway, that's what I was thinking…so can't you see how anything you know out of that book will be an improvement?"

"I see what you mean." Faye shook her head. After all these years, she would have bet the farm Allen didn't have a jealous bone in his body. Shamefully, she felt some comfort in the fact she had been wrong.

"So just bite the bullet, as they say. What is so terrible you didn't think you could tell me?"

The roller coaster of emotions running through Faye had her exhausted. She sighed deeply, the expulsion of breath loud in the otherwise silent house. "Where are the boys?"

"I told them to wait in their room till I called them out."

"Okay." She sighed again. "When the Wilsons first moved in here, and found out the names of the people across the highway…"

"Us?"

"Yes. When she found out our…your name was Cowen, she was…I don't know, interested I guess…just because of the name."

"Why?"

"They had known a Cowen family where she grew up in Virginia. Well, they knew **about** some Cowens."

"That's not so odd. There are lots of us Cowens around the country. My folks were from there…got married in Virginia, as a matter of fact."

"I know. You see, Mrs. Wilson's mother, at a very young age, did the unthinkable. She fell in love with a white man."

"No kidding?"

"No, I'm not. And—at least as far as Mrs. Wilson was concerned—the young white man was in love with her mother, too."

"I seriously doubt that. He probably said so, though…just to get her to go along."

"Why do you say that? Why couldn't he be in love with her?"

"She's colored. White men don't fall in love with Negroes. And that would have been, what, the early thirties? Tell me one time you've ever seen that happen."

"Allen, please. You're just making this harder. Let me finish."

"Sorry. Go."

"Anyway, this young couple…the girl gets—she looked around, assuring herself the boys couldn't hear—she got pregnant."

"Oh, man."

"Yeah. Anyway, the boy went away, I guess. There wasn't any more about him in the ledger."

"Naturally. Told you."

"But when the baby was born...their baby—Mrs. Wilson's little brother—the family couldn't believe what they saw."

"What? What was wrong with him?"

"Nothing was wrong with him, Allen. He was perfect. He was a sweet little baby who grew into a wonderful man."

"So what..."

"He was white. He was as white as his daddy."

"Mercy. I'll bet that made a stir."

"Only in the family. No-one else knew."

"When you say 'white,' you mean he was really light colored?"

"No. I mean he could have been the baby of the grand dragon of the KKK. White. Not a feature...not a single feature that would suggest he had any other blood in him." Faye watched her husband's face for any sign of how he was being affected. All she saw was a man interested in an unusual story.

"So what does that have to do with us?"

"Soon after the baby was born, a couple came and took him away. I don't know how they knew about him, or what kind of arrangements were made...Mrs. Wilson didn't go into any of that in the ledger." Allen merely looked at her, waiting.

"Allen, the couple who picked up the baby were a nice white couple. They took him and raised him as their own son. They never told him who his real mother was."

"I can understand that. No need, I guess."

"No. I guess not."

"So, where do we come in, Faye?" He smiled slightly, but there was the beginning of a furrow on his brow.

"The couple who took the little baby...their names...God, Allen...don't make me do this..."

"Faye, what is it?" She could see serious concern in his face for the first time. Was he beginning to get a glimmer of the truth?

"The couple who raised that baby...their last name is Cowen."

Allen stared at her, his face melting from the original small smile to a complete lack of understanding, to a dawning of understanding. "No. No. I see what you're saying. There's been a mistake."

"No mistake. You were that baby."

Whatever Faye expected of her husband, it was not what happened. He sat, thinking, looking at her like she was a stranger. His face went through more changes than she had seen the entire time she had known him. One of those unfamiliar faces was one of fear.

"Allen? Are you alright?"

"How would she know it was me? There are lots of Cowens, like I said. It's impossible. The Wilsons moving in right across the street…and me being, well, like you said. The odds are just too great."

Faye didn't speak. He was trying to work this out, and she had no idea what he needed at this moment from her…except space to think.

"Besides," he looked at her, a false excitement in his voice. "I would know something like that. Wouldn't I know something like that? You can't be half Negro and just not know it."

"She saw you. In town, I believe. She saw you up close. You looked so much like your…like the man in Virginia…she thought you were him at first."

He lowered his head, defeated, stunned. "How can this be, Faye? What does all this mean? It's more than I can take in."

"You have to know, Allen…you have to know a few things. Your parents, the Cowens, love you. You are their son. They may not be the people who gave you birth, but they gave you a life. And I love you. And the boys love you…they adore you…"

"The boys! They are, what, a fourth Negro?"

"Yes. And that doesn't make you think less of them, does it."

"They don't look Negro either."

"I know. From what little I know of such things, that is pretty strange in itself.

Statistically, we are way over our number on white kids. I've been doing some reading about genes since I found out."

"Faye?" His face had a sudden look of horror.

"What is it, Allen?"

"That's why! That's why you've been…why you haven't been the same with me. Now you know I'm half…now you know, I disgust you!"

136

"No, Allen. That's not true. I fell in love with you long ago. I still love you. Nothing has changed between us. You are the same man you were the day I married you."

"You're wrong. Nothing is the same. Not since you took that book. Why couldn't you just leave things alone…the way they were?"

"How I wish I had," she moaned.

"See. It does matter to you. You can never be with me the same again. You've ruined everything."

"It doesn't have to be that way. Allen, listen to me…" she grasped his face in her hands. "It doesn't have to be that way! Don't let it."

"All right, Faye. Come to the bedroom with me. Right now. Let's just see if everything is still the same…if you still see me the same way."

"Not now. The boys…"

"See! Just as I thought. Faye, how could you…" and for an instant she thought he would burst into tears. "I don't even know how I feel. I don't know **how** to feel. I have to go somewhere. I have to think."

"Let's talk it out, Allen. Let's get through this together."

"No. I don't want to be with you right now, and I can't be sure you really want to be with me."

"Allen…"

"No." He held up his hand to her face, jumped up, and stormed out the front door. She heard the car door slam shut and the engine roar. He sprayed gravel as he sped from their home…away from his life.

Faye didn't hear another sound for a moment. She held her head in cupped hands, elbows resting on the table. Huge tears streamed over her cheeks and splashed puddles on the table top. She heard beyond her own thoughts what sounded like a small sob.

Fearfully, she turned and looked toward the door. Her horror was reality. The boys stood together, staring at her. Their eyes…those precious eyes…she couldn't bear to look at them.

Chapter 24

Consciousness hovered softly over Tinsley's immobile body. He could almost feel its presence, as the cool breeze of the south plains Texas morning rushed through the window and brushed gently against his bare shoulders. Somewhere between the nether lands where dreams hide and the world where wives die, he found himself floating in a place he loved.

He stretched involuntarily as he became fully awake, but his eyes remained closed. He tried to will himself back to that place of cool, sweet comfort…back into the darkness. He knew he would fail. He always did. His mind, at the exact instant of its release from sleep, began giving Wayne his morning instructions.

Sometimes those instructions were in the form of ridiculous notions bordering on fantasy. Occasionally, they seemed brilliant, those early morning gifts from his mind. But there was one thought he could always rely on. His brain always remembered its request for strong, hot coffee. His eyes remained closed as he absorbed the deliciously cool breeze, It was still early.

He reached for the bedside lamp in the darkness, finding and pulling the beaded chain. The bright light bulb hurt his freshly opened eyes, but the clock beside the lamp had a large, easy to read face, and it told him it was only a few minutes after 5:00 am. There was no need to check the clock…he could hear its loud, clunky ticks from two feet away.

It was useless trying to return to sleep. Once awake, he was up for the day. He also enjoyed reading early in the morning, and he was more than half-way through a *Perry Mason* novel. It didn't matter to him the outcome was obvious before he finished the first page. If only criminal cases were really that simple, he thought. He had no time to dwell on that now. First, coffee.

His fourth cup of the black liquid sat tepid and ignored as he delved into the final chapter of the book. Dawn had introduced itself to Cash, Texas, but hadn't blossomed into full-fledged day. The loud ring of the phone startled him. He lifted the receiver with some trepidation. Night time and early morning calls—in his business—were never good news.

"Hello."

"Wayne?" The voice was soft, strained.

"Yes. Faye?"

"Uh, huh. Did I wake you? I can call back."

"No, of course not. What's wrong?"

"I'm just tired. I've been up most of the night with Randy…"

"Is he sick?"

She paused. "No. Wayne, I won't keep you…there is just something…something I need to tell you."

"Sure." His brow furrowed. Where was the strength—the energy he always felt from her?

"I lied to you last night. I've always respected you…you are a good friend. I don't want that lie between us."

"There is no lie between us."

"There is. I still have the book."

"I know. You told me last night." The silence on the other end of the line persuaded

Wayne to continue. "I know what your words said, but I also know your face, your expressions…your eyes…they said something else."

"Thank you. I didn't know if you…"

"It's okay, Faye. I'll admit, I don't understand what you're doing, or why. But I believe in you…in you doing the right thing."

"Oh, Wayne!" she cried. "I think I've done something terribly wrong."

"Easy…easy, girl. It's just a book." Then he added, "Or is it something else?"

She sniffed, sighed, and continued. "I'm sorry. It's very personal. I shouldn't have said anything."

"It's okay. Really."

"You can pick up the book whenever you want."

"Are you sure? We've already run a search warrant and—as far as the sheriff knows—we came up empty. No one has to know."

"You would know, Wayne. And that would bother you."

She was right. "I don't want to hurt you any more," he added.

"You won't. I would really just as soon you have it. I would like it out of my house."

"All right, then. Would later today be okay?"

"Yes. Anytime. You might call first, if you don't mind."

"Of course. Faye?"

"Yes?"

"Are you okay?"

"No. No, I'm not."

"Why don't you try to get some sleep. You sound really tired."

"I will. But it really doesn't matter. Bye, Wayne." The phone went dead in his hand.

It matters to me, he thought.

At 8:00 a.m., Tinsley called the sheriff's department. It was a habit he developed his first week on the job. Shifts changed at 7:00 am in Hoover, and Wayne could get the latest information about any criminal activity he might need to know about from the day before.

The dispatcher answered, a sleepy-hoarse voice, "Hensley County Sheriff's Office."

"Morning. This is Tinsley."

"Morning, deputy. How are things in Cash?"

"About as well as can be expected, I guess. Got anything for me?"

"Actually…" he heard papers rustle. "It was a pretty slow night."

"Good."

"Oh, here's one thing...two of your locals got picked up last night."

"What happened?"

"Let me see...traffic stop out on farm to market road...driver, D.W.I...that would be one Earl G. Smith. Looks like deputy Raines discovered some unusual stuff in the back of the car, a 1950 Studebaker..."

"What kind of stuff?"

"Well, there's a list, here. A record player, a set of flippers off 15 inch wheels, women's assorted jewelry, some horse tack, a jar of pennies..."

"Sounds like a residential burglary."

"That's what Raines thought, too. He also found a pry bar in the trunk. He charged both of them with being in possession of burglary tools and suspicion of burglary."

"Do we know where they hit yet?"

"No. Someone will be calling in pretty soon, I imagine, madder than a wet hen."

"I suspect so...say, who was the passenger?"

"A, uh...Patterson. Burl Patterson."

"That figures."

The instant the receiver touched its cradle, Tinsley's telephone rang. He was surprised to hear the earthy voice of Ivy Bradley, like dried corn husks in a gentle breeze, he thought.

"Deputy Tinsley, I'm sorry to bother you at home. I didn't know if I should call you or the sheriff's office."

"My home is also my office, Mrs. Bradley. Is there something I can do for you?"

"I do hope so. Someone has broken into my house."

"While you were there?"

"Yes. During the night last night. I slept right through it."

"How long have you been awake?" he asked, concerned. "I mean, are you certain there is no one there, now?"

"I, uh...I just noticed the break-in. I've been up a few minutes."

"Leave the house, Mrs. Bradley. Take your car keys...check the car first, then get in and drive away."

"But my house."

"Leave it. Just drive down the road. Keep it in sight if you like, but get out of the house now. Nothing in there is worth you getting hurt."

"Okay." She hung up the telephone.

Wayne was sure the burglary had been the work of the two boys locked up already in Hoover, but better safe than sorry. If it was them, she'd be glad to know her property was already recovered. He dressed quickly and—on the way to Mrs. Bradley's—radioed the dispatcher where he was going, and why.

No, he didn't need a backup. Yes, he thought this would be the burglary report they were waiting to hear about concerning the two in lock-up. Within five minutes he passed Ivy in Bill's black pickup sitting beside the road. He waved as he passed on by and stopped at her home. He took a slow walk around the house, watching...listening.

At the rear door which entered into the kitchen, Tinsley discovered the glass broken out. It lay shattered on the porch, and his boots crunched on the smallest of the pieces as he walked past it and inside the house. None of the pieces of glass were large enough to get a footprint. Perhaps a fingerprint was possible, he thought.

Just inside the doorway he paused, listening. The house was quiet, no squeaking boards to give away the presence of a lurking criminal, no pleas for him to not shoot. Nothing. Not that he expected any of those things. His expectations were exactly what he was experiencing.

Although confident of what he would find, Wayne did not entirely let down his guard until he had made a thorough search of the house. After investigating the interior, he went back out the front door. Standing in the front yard, he waved largely, trying to get Mrs. Bradley's attention.

The pickup proceeded forward immediately, her expression one of concern as she pulled back into her driveway behind Tinsley's car.

"They're gone," he offered. "I thought they would be, but you can't be too careful."

"Of course. I can't believe it never crossed my mind. I could have been killed...thank you. It's a real comfort knowing you know what you're doing."

"Well, they **were** already gone. As it turns out, your leaving wasn't really necessary."

"But we didn't know that…not until you checked. That's all I mean."

"Would you mind coming back in with me now? I've checked it for people, but we need to look more closely…see if you can tell me what might be missing."

"Sure." She started for the front door, then stopped. "Deputy Tinsley, how many times have we seen each other?'"

"I'm not sure…a number of times I was with you when you didn't know it. A few, I guess. Why?" He smiled.

Ivy looked down at her robe. "I was wondering if you've ever seen me dressed…in regular clothes."

Tinsley felt a heat rising in his face. "From the road a few times."

"That was you? I just knew police cars came by occasionally. You always waved. I thought that was so…nice."

"Everyone around here waves at people all the time."

"Not at me. I wonder why?"

"I don't know. I guess they can't see whether you're looking at them or not…your big straw hats, you know."

She nodded. "It wasn't really important. I just realized a minute ago that I couldn't remember ever seeing you when I wasn't wearing this same old robe." It was the white, terry-cloth she had been wearing the day they found her husband. It was very thick, of modest length and cut, but somehow very personal. Today she also had a terry towel wrapped around her head.

It, too, was white. And even though she did not appear to be wearing makeup, her huge, dark eyes would have been the envy of any model in the country.

Inside the house they began a room-by-room check of her personal property. "I noticed the glass broken in the back door when I went out," she said.

"Yes, I saw it." He frowned, involuntarily.

She didn't miss the expression. "What is it, Wayne?"

"Nothing. Please, go on. I'll list the things as we go through. I'm sure you'll find other items missing later. That's normal. People often realize they are missing articles for days after a residential burglary."

"Okay. I called you from my bedroom, of course. That's where I noticed things weren't normal."

"Not normal?"

"A drawer pulled out…my jewelry box open. Things like that." Tinsley noticed a slight change in her voice when she mentioned the jewelry box…a prelude to tears, perhaps.

"Let's begin there, then, if you don't mind."

"Of course. I'm sorry, please excuse the mess. I called you right away…and, you know, ran like you told me to. I haven't even made the bed."

"Don't think a thing about it. I've seen lots more unmade beds in this business than otherwise…and with much less excuse than you have." Nodding at her feet, he smiled.

"What? What's the matter?"

"Do you even **own** a pair of shoes?" They both laughed at her bare feet. Her toenails were red and trimmed, as he would have expected.

"I **was** in a hurry. You should have seen me running out of here."

"I guess that was a sight, all right."

"But, I can't blame my criminals for this," she pointed at her feet. "You're right. I almost never wear shoes when I'm home. I like padding around in my bare feet. I'm awful, I know. Wash my feet about forty times a day."

He smiled again.

"Wayne. Why is this happening?" Her radiant smile was suddenly replaced with an expression of concern.

"What? This burglary?"

"All of it. Bill hasn't been gone two weeks, then this. Why is this happening to me?"

"I should have warned you, Mrs. Bradley. It's not that uncommon. Thieves often read the newspapers to see who has died. They are more likely to hit a house during the funeral…the time is listed in the paper, of course, or when the family is away for a burial out of town."

"But I was home. Isn't that odd."

"It is more rare. Burglars usually try to avoid places where people are at home…they are normally not confrontational. But those who do should be considered very dangerous if cornered. I'm really glad you didn't wake up."

"Me, too. Dr. Mack has me on some medicine to help me sleep. I guess it really works."

"Apparently."

"But to tell you the truth," she paused, appearing to decide whether to complete her sentence. She did. "Even though it may have helped me—from a safety standpoint—it really bothers me…more than you might imagine. I mean, knowing a man—or men—stood in this room…in my home, in my bedroom…it bothers me a lot."

"I can see where it would."

"I never really thought about it before. I would read about someone's house getting broken into. I would think, gee, that's too bad. They stole those people's stuff…their money…whatever it was."

"Yes, it is awful."

"But that's not the worst, Wayne. I don't think I can explain it. I feel…like it was a personal violation…like I have been violated. Do you know what I mean?"

"I think so. Ivy, is there more? Is there something they did? Something you don't feel comfortable talking to me about?"

"Oh, no. It's nothing like that. It's just a burglary, I guess. But I don't know how I will sleep here tonight. I don't know if I can feel safe here again. For the first time in my adult life…these past weeks since Bill's death…I have felt really safe. Safe in my own home. And now, this."

"I guess I really didn't understand, Ivy. I didn't realize."

"I don't know what to do."

"Well, let's finish this list…let me complete my investigation. Then I'll run up to the lumber yard. They have sheets of glass there. I'll measure your door window and cut a piece for you. We'll get this place in better shape than before."

"That is sweet. Thank you."

"Then we'll find the best door locks in Hoover, and I'll install them for you."

"I like that."

"Then…"

"Then? You mean there's more?"

"I'll pull a few night shifts for awhile. I'll be patrolling your highway practically non-stop for…at least until you feel comfortable again."

"You would do all that for me?"

"You pay my salary, as they say…tax payers." He smiled.

"I just can't believe you would do all that. I'm…I don't know what to say."

"I'm glad to do it, and I enjoy working night shifts occasionally. Besides, I can't have you afraid in your own home. My job is to help you feel secure."

"You're very good at your job. Thank you, Wayne."

"No problem."

"But, if you're going to do all that, the least I can do is cook you some breakfast. How do you like your eggs?"

"That's not necessary, really."

"It's not up for discussion, deputy…your eggs?"

"I like 'em sunny-side up. Thanks. Let's finish this list first, though."

"Okay. Then I'll get dressed and fix my hair while you go to the lumber yard."

"That sounds fine."

"It's about time you see me with my clothes on," she added.

He shook his head slightly. Ivy was either the sweetest, most naïve woman he had ever met…or she was the slyest flirt. Either way, her unusually delicate and—at the same time—brutally blunt approach to things…to herself, had a way of exciting a man's imagination. For the second time in a moment he shook his head. Get back to work, he told himself. This lady is a recent widow. She is lonely. And you may not even have her husband's murderer in jail.

Chapter 25

Allen twisted the bottle cap open, fumbled, and watched it spiral onto the cold tile floor with a hollow clack. He looked at the cap, upside down and chuckled to himself. The bottle only held a pint of whiskey, and there were still two inches of the liquid at the bottom. He had never been a drinker and wasn't drunk now.

He wanted to be drunk. He wanted to be somewhere else...someone else. He wanted his wife, his boys. He wanted his dead little boy. He wanted to understand. He wanted his life. **His** life...not the life of this person to whom he was introduced three days ago.

He used all his energy just to stand up from the edge of the sweat-stained mattress. The bed spread lay wadded up into a formless, comfortless clump of bothersome material. Another reason he couldn't sleep.

Edging his way across the small, dark motel room, he reached for the old brown curtain, pulling it back...not so much to let in light, as an impotent effort to let the darkness out. The musty smell of old dust filled his nostrils. Another odor was present, and he stumbled slightly as he turned to seek its source.

This time he didn't chuckle. He laughed aloud. The odor was Allen Cowen...unwashed...a sweaty, nervous, tension-based stink. He felt the prickly surface where his smooth chin used to be. A bitter sour acid scorched his stomach relentlessly.

He came here to think, didn't he? So why was it so difficult to use his mind? He had to get a grip. He was a strong man; always had been. His sons had never seen him shed a single tear. He had always been a man's man...a person others came to when they needed to know what to do—how to fix—who to go to for the best work.

He was a good father. His boys were good boys. He was a good husband, too. He should have been better. Faye deserved better. She was the strongest woman he had ever known...and the kindest. Why did she have to...? No. He had promised himself he wouldn't do that. She **did** take that cursed book. No sense beating that same old dead horse.

He wasn't a prejudiced man. They had fed lots of colored people who came to their back door looking for handouts, him and Faye. And, living near the railroad tracks, they also fed many white hobos in the same manner. The food was usually a couple of biscuits left over from breakfast...perhaps some sausage or bacon. Whatever was available.

He didn't hate those people. Not a single one of them, white or colored. He tried, but could not remember even one Negro he hated.

There had been a revelation within himself, though...it had been yesterday, he thought. Time was so hard to keep up with in the dark room. On his second day there Allen had discovered an amazing fact. He discovered a secret...a trigger word, that changed everything. The word was **they.** Sneaky little word, **they.** Slips right into conversations.

And now, with Allen's new-found insight...something absent his entire life before, he realized it was much easier to falsely categorize a **they** than a person. **They** are all thieves; that came easy. Mr. Wilson...Mr. Wilson is a thief; that was harder. Even though Wilson was in jail for just that crime...theft.

But Allen had watched Mr. Wilson for two years, coming and going to work and back every day, often bent from hard, grueling work. He had watched Mr. Wilson and Johnny tinker with the old farm pickup Bradley let him drive. He couldn't hear the words, but occasionally Allen heard laughter from them, or a sudden "Ouch!" when a knuckle busted itself on metal at the slip of a wrench. Somewhere during those two years, Mr. Wilson had slipped out of the **they** column.

Allen knew the real reason he was unwilling to help them with Johnny when asked. It was because of Allen's friends. What would they think? He leaned his head back against the bare wall. There was no head-board.

They? What were some other **theys? They** all like watermelon. Do they, really? What else? **They** can really dance. Can they? He didn't remember ever having seen a Negro dance. **They** have an extra muscle in their backs…that's why they can run so fast. Can they? Can every single Negro run fast? He thought of Mrs. Carter who did cleaning in the Watsons' house. She must have weighed about 400 pounds. Was Mrs. Carter fast?

There were others. This was easy once he found the secret word. **They.** What **they** words applied to the white part of Allen? What **they** did white people use for their own race? They all…he couldn't think of a one.

Guess I'll have to ask my colored relatives about that one, he thought. I'll bet they've got some doozies about white people.

Allen remembered since childhood, things like "Watch 'em close, **they** will steal you blind. **They** like chitlins' better than steak…eat 'em all the time. **They** aren't smart enough to hold good jobs. **They** don't want an education. **They** are louder than us. **They** are violent."

He was growing weary of his **they** game. He knew it was the same for the Mexicans. **They** all like hot food…and carry knives…

Allen thought someone else should know the secret he had discovered on his trek for self analysis. Others should be aware. Anytime a person talks about an entire group of people and begins with the secret word, **they**, people would know a lie was about to follow.

It would not be an on-purpose lie. It just meant someone was about to perpetuate that lie of ignorance that someone else told him because they heard it from someone who heard it from someone, and on and on…

They, he thought, never did anything. **They** never felt this way, or liked this thing, or acted in a certain way. He had arrived at a place in his mind and in his heart where he never expected to be. Having hidden his feelings and thoughts from himself for his entire life, it felt like a dam had burst.

There were, in fact, loud-mouthed, thieving, watermelon loving, chitin' eating colored people with great rhythm. At least, he assumed that to be so. He also assumed there were white people with the same traits. Except maybe for the greasy chitlin' part.

He further assumed there were quiet, honest, hard-working Negro people who don't like watermelon, can't stand deep-fried guts, and who couldn't carry a tune in a bucket or dance any better than he. He was sure he was right. His theory seemed right. But he didn't know. He had never bothered to find out.

All this had been right in front of him, and he had been blind. It wasn't his overt feelings about Negroes that bothered Allen so much. It was his own lazy ignorance. He had seen things around him every day—things that were wrong. He had seen them, witnessed them first hand, even participated, and just didn't...he had just never given it enough thought to even wonder if things were right or wrong.

It wasn't that he had thought about it and decided things were okay as they were. He hadn't even spent the energy to wonder. He remembered Johnny that night of the arrest. Would he, Allen, have beaten that boy so badly if he had been white? Honestly? Johnny...that boy. His, what? His...his nephew! His half-nephew anyway. He could have killed him.

It was all too much. Allen hadn't had a great deal of whiskey to drink, but he hadn't slept in days. His mind sought more pleasant thoughts. Pleasant thoughts meant his family.

He smiled when he remembered their vacation to New Mexico several years before. They were going camping...sleeping on the ground. Their old car was so loaded it squatted badly in the rear. A state cop stopped them and demanded a search of the car. "Sorry folks," the officer said later. "Your car was sitting so low, I thought you were bootleggers."

Allen had been angry, but Faye laughed, and the boys began laughing with her. Before long, they were all laughing like a bunch of children, their voices of joy defeating the noise of the wind blowing through the open windows. Little Oma wasn't even walking yet. Allen and Jeff had a great time on that trip…a real mountain adventure. Faye, however, spent the entire week cooking over campfires, cleaning pots and pans and kids, and herself, and in her spare time kept Randy from falling into the fire at camp, or the river, not twenty yards away.

On their ride home, Allen wondered why Faye looked so tired. They had been on vacation, after all. But, true to her nature, she had never made a single complaint…and her smile lit up that camp better than any lantern.

Some of the radiance of that smile had died along with Oma. Allen didn't think she would ever get it back.

Now, Jeff…he was so much like her in many ways. People always said Jeff took after his dad, but that wasn't so. Not in the important ways. Faye's smile had been passed on to him…her indomitable spirit. Randy seemed more obviously like his mother at the surface, but actually his ways were more like Allen's. He was moody. He spoke out, often without thinking. And there was a shallowness about him…but, of course, he was only eight.

He missed them. He missed them all. Maybe he should write something down for them. A letter. He should tell them all the things he was discovering. But he was so tired.

A picture of Jeff appeared suddenly in his mind and he smiled, forgetting the letter. Allen remembered the day he was going to the barn when he saw Jeff…he was about…maybe nine years old…so, anyway, there was Jeff at the cow lot, hanging upside down on the fence, his face and shoulders pressed into the mud and cow manure.

Allen rushed over in a panic. Jeff was okay. He was in his jump-off-every-building-on-the-place phase. When he attempted to leap from the top rail of the fence, a nail caught his jeans leg, slamming him down and knocking the wind out of his lungs. Once he could breathe again, he held still, waiting for someone to come along. He looked and smelled awful. Faye's first response was, of course, concern. Once assured he was okay, she laughed at him and sent him back outside for a good hosing off.

There were so many times.

Allen had always known Faye was the life-blood of the family. As the man of the house, it was his responsibility to take care of the business of running the place. He hadn't been great at it, but not terrible either. But the mood of the home, the smell, the flavor...whatever things make a building into something far, far more...those things came from Faye.

He knew he didn't deserve her. Even before this colored thing came up, he knew it.

Divorce, of course, was never even a consideration. He just wished he had told her more...how he felt. He couldn't even remember the last time he told her he loved her, or brought her a flower...or anything else, for that matter. He was always going to do those things one day soon. Soon never came.

She had tried to keep their relationship close, but it seemed the harder she tried, the more he kept her at arms length. Why had he done that?

Finally, even Faye seemed to shrink back, determined this was her life—he supposed—and she would live it. He wasn't sure, since they talked little about such things.

Allen spent a lot of time thinking of his parents...both sets. It amazed him a white man, in 1919, would risk a relationship with a Negro woman. It amazed him so much he didn't believe it. Was she, like Mrs. Wilson, trying to keep him from taking something from her family? Their home? Their livelihood? Did she also pay him with the only thing in the world that was hers to give?

Or did he just force himself on her? Allen wasn't sure, but he didn't think that was even illegal in those days. Mrs. Wilson had believed it was love between his "parents," but she had been only a child herself when it happened. She would believe whatever her family told her. And the love story would have been the easiest one to tell a child.

Allen liked that story better, too, although he didn't believe it. Either Mr...whatever his name was—he didn't even know his name—either he was a worthless, selfish, immoral scoundrel, or she—his **mother,** was a sorry slut, selling her wares for money and trinkets. And he, Allen, was her punishment. Her little bundle of punishment.

Here you go, little lady. You want to play? Here's your present. Here's you a little white baby who looks just like one of your paying men friends. Raise him, and every time you look at him be reminded that you are the lowest trash on the face of the earth. Take him with you to town. Let everybody else see what you are. Here is your gift-wrapped sin.

But why **couldn't** it have been love? Why did he naturally assume otherwise? Maybe they were thrown together in some innocent circumstance and, in their day-to-day business, fell in love. What if the **they** word no longer applied to her for him? What if he felt about her like Allen felt about Faye? What if, when he looked at her, he saw a lovely person…a good woman—or girl, in this case. What if he could no longer see the color of her for the person he had grown to know?

He squeezed his eyes tightly, a surge of emotion pushed against his insides. Faye had been like that, seeing just Allen, the man. Could she possibly love him enough now to still see Allen, and not the half-Negro Allen? Maybe if she knew the secret of the **they** word. If only he had been a better husband…

But it **was** her who had acted differently. He wasn't prejudiced, so why did he care the color of blood flowing through him…it was red, wasn't it? He tried to laugh at his weak joke, but he could find no humor. As long as they know their place; that's what he used to say about Negroes.

He didn't particularly like watermelon. He had about as much rhythm as a three-legged mule. Why didn't he get any of those genes from his slut mother? Or was she the angel? What was she like? How could she have been so stupid? What did she think…that that stiff-lipped white stud was going to carry her off and marry her?

He had made himself promises throughout his life. He had promised to always treat others right. He had promised himself to be a man his parents—the people he thought were his parents—would always be proud of. He had never realized before, some promises are just too hard to keep.

They knew. All along, they knew. They knew he was half Negro. They knew his roots. They had always been cool towards him, he thought. Never demonstrative like some of his friend's parents. "We're just not huggers, honey. Doesn't mean we don't love you," they had said. They, in fact, were pretty frigid people…with everyone. But now he had to wonder; could they never put the thought out of their minds…what he really was.

How could he feel so cold…so calm…so dead inside, and his mind still race at a frantic, frightening speed? How was that possible, he wondered.

Lie down? Stand up? Breathe? Forgive? Cry? His emotional questions never really formed like words, but were a rush of tidal waves washing across and through his mind in no order…feelings only, but feelings smashed together in a nonsensical clutter of insanity. So tired.

A thought suddenly appeared. It actually seemed clear. He **was** prejudiced. I **am**, he corrected. All my life I have known Negroes were less important than me. All my life I've snickered at nigger jokes. I've watched them, in a lower social order than mine. I've seen their lousy lives without ever seeing. That's just the way it is. Always has been.

He had been hating himself all these years. He hated himself now. Now, because he was colored? Or was it because he was white? Was it because he knew how it felt to be white, but not how it felt to be…what did they call people like him? A mulatto.

Sounds like a disease, he thought. Sorry, I can't come to the domino hall today. I've got a really serious case of mulatto.

Allen slumped to the bed again, resting his elbows on the dirty, stained khaki trousers he wore out of his house way back…what day was that? His soiled undershirt was outside his pants and rumpled around his waist. None of it made sense. He glanced at the Gideons' Bible on the lamp table. He had tried to read it, but the words ran together, a clutter of things he could not follow. He was so tired.

What had Faye said to him? He was the same man he had been before they found out. What a silly thing to say. He had fathered two…three children. It was obvious he and Faye could never have more children. Children? He grunted. As if she would ever let him touch her again, anyway.

He sat for a long time, then, head held tightly in his hands. It really wasn't about colored or white. It wasn't about prejudice or whatever is the opposite of that. It was all just about a person. Thousands, maybe millions, of just one person at a time.

He was a child, his mother holding him in her lap as he cried. "Now. Now," she whispered. "Now, son…it's okay." Then, later…a football game. He had hurt a player from the other team with a particularly vicious block. Others stood around, looking concerned while Allen walked away.

Then there was Faye, their courtship. He had been so clumsy around her. She was so beautiful. Then the boys. Jeff, his first born…his pride. Strangely, however, it wasn't Jeff or little Randy that haunted his thoughts, which were now completely out of his control. Oma.

Their little boy. Their dead little boy. He hadn't been close to Oma. The little one seemed so timid, so shy. Allen had secretly feared he would grow up and be a sissy. No problem, Allen. He'll just die for you, then you won't have to worry what people think of **you**.

And now he was just a dust-covered mound somewhere in the Cash Cemetery. I should'a gone out to visit him there, he thought. Faye did. No matter what else I do, Oma will stay dead. I'll never see him again for as long as I…

He grabbed the gun from under the pillow. "Too bad Jeff can't see me now," he said aloud. "He could finally see his old man cry." And, as huge tears coursed their way down his whiskered cheeks, he put the gun in his mouth and pulled the trigger. The sound in the tiny room was deafening.

But not to Allen.

Chapter 26

Tinsley directed the spotlight on Ivy Bradley's house as he drove slowly past. He knew he would not see a criminal lurking in the bushes. The light was for Ivy to see, to know she was safe. He had done the same thing for others many times.

The presence of law enforcement watching out for them meant a great deal to crime victims. Ivy wasn't the first to express the feeling of having been violated...personally violated. He knew of people who had moved out of homes where they had lived for years, because they could never feel safe there again.

Wayne readily admitted to himself the investigations aspect of his job was his least favorite. He would never say those words to another officer again, but he actually became interested in law enforcement because he wanted to help people. He had confided that fact to a senior training officer years before and almost never lived it down. He was considered naïve and immature because of his statement.

Tinsley knew he was something of an outcast among his peers in many ways. Even the distance in miles between him and the others made for some difficulties, but—for him—it was worth it...he even preferred it. He could run his own shop mostly, and because he hardly ever received complaints, the sheriff was happy.

Wayne being responsible for a homicide investigation really wasn't all that unusual. It was usual for **him**, having never had that task before…but that type of thing happened frequently. In areas where sheriff's departments were the only law enforcement agencies available, it happened more often than not. One untrained, inexperienced deputy was as good as the next.

The Texas Highway Patrol Officers stayed true to their names. **Highway** Patrol. If it wasn't a traffic violation or car wreck, they didn't participate.

Wayne, therefore, didn't spend much time ruing his bad luck. He also didn't waste a lot of time being excited about leading a murder investigation. He was okay with the responsibility of it. He was not okay with his lack of knowledge of the process.

The bright lights of the car approaching him dimmed, and he responded in order, pressing down on the floor dimmer switch with his left foot. In the darkness, it was difficult for him to recognize the model car. It looked a little like the Ford Allen Cowen drove. Wayne was surprised the car looked so much like a *Studebaker* at a distance…at least, until he was close enough to see the lack of the long bullet-like headlights common to that model. He made it a habit to take notice of cars out late at…

Suddenly he swerved into the barrow ditch, killing his headlights and motor. He stared five seconds into the darkness, then began slamming his hands against the steering wheel, timing each strike with a self-deprecating, "Stupid! Stupid! Stupid!" he growled. Things hadn't felt right for Wayne all day. And now, in the still darkness of night, driving along the stretch of highway past Ivy's house, a couple of things began to tumble into place.

They weren't definitive, of course, his thoughts about the murder. He didn't have many of the answers, actually, but he was finally coming up with a whole hat full of new questions.

Earl Smith's car…a 1950 *Studebaker*…was the same type car described by Johnny Wilson that day in the jail…the car Ivy was going out to meet the day her husband spoiled things and apparently frightened them away.

How would Ivy even **know** the likes of Earl Smith? And what possible business could she have with him? He didn't like the answers that came to mind. And now, with Smith and Patterson in jail and her house broken into...

Broken **in** to. The glass was outside the door on the back porch. He had walked through it that morning. The glass had been broken from the inside of the house. He still had glass shards in his boot heels, and Ivy had said she ran out the back door in fear for her safety. She was barefoot, and there were no cuts on her feet!

Tinsley tried to get over the anger at himself for being so slow in realizing...he needed to think straight. One thing he knew already. He knew he didn't **want** Ivy to be guilty of...what?

Murder? Anything. He liked her, and he felt sorry for her.

The most obvious question that loomed over him was whether or not Ivy and Smith...and maybe Patterson...had something, in concert, to do with her husband's murder. She even told Wayne she was the perfect suspect. Was she incredibly honest or incredibly sly?

It did not seem possible to Wayne that Ivy would even **know** Smith...much less hatch some horrible scheme with him. And there was still the mystery of the "burglary"...if that is what it was. Why would they steal from their co-conspirator? Surely, if the worse case scenario was true, she would have offered them money to do the job. Why would they jeopardize that? Or had she promised them something else?

He had never been comfortable thinking Johnny stabbed Bradley with an ice pick. He knew Johnny had beaten Bill—beaten him badly— but the ice pick seemed such a cold, deliberate tool...so personal. Like something a wife would use against a cheating husband. Wayne didn't like the drift of his thoughts, but they could not be ignored. There were too many coincidences.

He slammed the steering wheel again. Had he been sniffing too much Ivy Bradley perfume? The autopsy report! The examiner had promised to call Tinsley when it was finished. That should have been days ago. He had expected no surprises...the man **did** have a sharp instrument in his eye. But he should have looked it over anyway.

Tinsley made a mental note to call the medical examiner the first thing in the morning. He then erased the mental note and decided to call him immediately. After all, the man was very delinquent with his report…and it **was** a murder investigation.

He roared back onto the highway, making a sweeping U-turn. There were no pay phones.

He would have to call from home. The telephone rang five times before Wayne heard it being wrestled clumsily from its cradle. A muffled voice finally answered.

"'Lo?"

"Dr. Christian, this is deputy Tinsley…in Cash."

"What's the matter, Tinsley?"

"I'm calling about the autopsy report on William Bradley."

"What? Do you know what time it is?"

"Yes. I also know I should have received a report four days ago. I'm trying to investigate a murder."

"You **did** get a report. And it was five days ago…not four."

"I never got anything from you, sir. You said you would call when you were finished with your report."

"I know what I said…" There was a muffled sound over the phone, and Wayne could hear the doctor away from the receiver. "It's nothing, Dear. Go back to sleep. No, really…it's okay. No, I'm not going out."

His voice came back strong on the phone. "Tinsley, you people need to get your act together. I called for you at the sheriff's department, and you were not there. I talked to Detective Benningfield."

"Benningfield? You gave the autopsy report to Benningfield?"

"Why, yes. He said he would pass the information on to you."

"I'm sorry, Doctor Christian. I'm really embarrassed. I'll talk to him first thing tomorrow…"

"Good idea. Good night."

"Wait! Doctor…while I've got you on the phone…and already messed up your sleep, would you mind giving me a brief recap? I know that's a lot to ask, but it may be really important."

"Okay, Tinsley. Briefly. Mr. Bradley died from an acute case of getting the back of his head caved in."

159

"What? Doctor, I'm talking about the man from Cash. The man with the ice pick in his eye…"

"Yeah, I'll bet that would have hurt too, if he had been alive."

"You mean…you're telling me he was already dead when the ice pick…?"

"Very good, deputy. It was what you professional police officers would call a post-mortem event."

Tinsley was stone silent. What could he say?.

"Don't feel too badly, deputy. I didn't know the cause of death at the scene, either. As you recall, he was lying in blood a half inch deep. His hair was so matted in the stuff…"

"Yes, sir."

"By the way, Tinsley, I do have a question for you, now that my night's sleep has officially been ruined…"

"I'm sorry…what question?"

"Did you close Mr. Bradley's eye lid…his right eye lid?"

"No. Why would I have done that?"

"You wouldn't if you knew what you were doing. I was just curious."

"Now I'm the one who's curious."

"Whoever stuck the ice pick in his eye ball…they held his eye lid open while they deliberately drove the thing in up to the hilt."

"My…"

"Yeah. Don't get much of that around here. Now, can I get back to sleep, officer?"

"Of course. Again, I'm sorry doctor for disturbing…"

The telephone clicked silent.

Wayne stared at the receiver still in his hand. This thing was even more out of control than he had thought. Who would do such a thing? What kind of distorted hatred could cause that response?

The kind of hatred of a young man who's mother had been raped? The kind that can be bought? The kind that is a result of years of torment behind the closed walls of a person's home?

Or just the plain old normal kind…the kind he felt for Detective Benningfield at that moment.

160

Chapter 27

There were three prisoners he needed to interview and a fourth with whom he **wanted** to talk. He took that one first, removing Isaac Wilson from his cell and directing him to the interview room.

Closing the door behind them, Wayne took a long look at the man. Isaac, he guessed, was in his middle to late thirties. He looked sixty. His dark hair, like Wayne's, was prematurely gray, his head speckled all over with ash-colored ringlets. He looked down at the desk top without speaking.

"Mr. Wilson, my name is Wayne Tinsley. I'm a deputy with the sheriff's office."

"Yes, sir, Mr. Tinsley. I know who you is."

"I didn't know if you would remember…our meetings have been under very terrible circumstances for you…"

"Yes, sir. I remembers. You came when I found Mrs. Wilson…like she was…"

Wayne could see the man bracing himself, holding his emotions at bay. His fingertips gripped the edge of the desk, the only real visible indication of the tension inside.

"I remember," Wayne said.

"Then with little Mattie-Mae…"

"Yes."

"You was real nice, Mr. Tinsley. You gave me your word you wasn't gonna' tell folks about my missus. About how she...the hanging, and all."

"Yes, I did give you my word."

"Ain't nobody never said nothing 'bout that neither. I thank you for that kindness to her. Mrs. Wilson wouldn't want people to know what she done."

"Yes, sir. I guess I can understand that." Tinsley sat across from Isaac as they spoke. A silence followed the man's last remarks. Tinsley waited, allowing Wilson to get anything else said that might be on his mind.

"Did you need me for something, Mr. Tinsley?"

"I just wanted to visit for a minute." Isaac Wilson only nodded, but the skepticism he tried to hide showed on his face. "I guess you know Johnny is in jail?"

"I heard. Ain't seen him though. He ain't my real boy, you know. Step-son."

"Seems like I did know that. Maybe you mentioned it before. How do you feel about that?"

"Him not being my real boy?"

Tinsley nodded.

"At first, it was kinda' hard. He was real young, but he was the man of the house before I showed up. He didn't much cotton to me."

"How did he respond? Angry?"

"No, not so you'd know. He'd just sort of swell up—like kids do, when their feelings is hurt."

"How long did that last?"

"Don't rightly know. We just gave each other some space between us. Then, one day...maybe a year or so...I noticed I was thinking on him like he **was** my boy. And he acted like I was his daddy. It just sort of happened, gradual-like."

"Guess that's good, huh?"

"Guess so. His daddy was a sorry man...that's what I hear. No telling how that boy woulda' turned out if that old devil hadn't took off."

"Do you know why Johnny's in jail?"

"Old darkie in here that mops floors, he told me for a killing."

"How do you feel about that?"

"'bout him killing somebody?"

"Yes, sir."

"Does it matter? What I say, I mean.."

"It matters to me."

Isaac smiled a little for the first time. "You're a pretty slick one, Mr. Tinsley...for a white man."

"What do you mean?"

"No matter. Okay, what do I think about that? I think Johnny could kill a man, if he had reason enough."

"Like what?"

"Doesn't matter. Both his reasons is dead."

"Are you pulling me in circles, Mr. Wilson?"

"I guess, a little. Okay, here is what I think. Johnny didn't kill nobody."

"You sound pretty sure. How..."

"Hang on there, boss. Reason I **know** he didn't do it is 'cause he told that old mopper-man to get the word to Mr. Wilson he didn't do what they're saying."

"And because he **said** it..."

"Yeah. That's how I know. Long as I been knowing that boy, I can't remember him ever telling me no lie. Not even one. And a few times things woulda' gone a lot easier on him if he **did** lie."

"That's not very hard evidence, Mr. Wilson."

"I thought we was just having a visit, deputy."

This time it was Wayne's turn to smile. "I guess you're a pretty slick one, too...for a colored man." They both chuckled quietly.

"Not too slick. Look where I'm sitting."

"How's your case going, anyway?"

"I told 'em guilty, 'cause I am. They're going to write me up for ten years down in Huntsville."

"Ouch."

"Ain't so bad, I hear. Some other men in here done been to prison. They keep saying 'three hots and a cot.' That means I'll get fed and have a place to sleep."

"Then you're okay with that?" Wayne asked, surprised.

"No, sir. I ain't. I hate it. I even hate it in here, and this is just the county jail. But I did what they said."

"How about Johnny?"

"They goin' to 'lectrocute him." He shook his head wearily. "Doin' it or not doin' it makes no never mind. The white laws say he done it...that's all there is to it. No offense, Mr. Tinsley."

"Why did he plead guilty?"

"Didn't know he did. Lot's of reasons he mighta' done that, besides him actually **being** guilty." He looked directly into Tinsley's eyes, an uncommon thing for Isaac. "You don't think he done it either."

"It doesn't feel right. I'll give you that much...I've got a couple of ideas..."

"Ideas won't help Johnny, beggin' your pardon, Mr. Tinsley. Only thing can help him is for the one that did the killin' to turn hisself in...or for you to catch him. Savin' that, Johnny is going to die from electric."

"But why didn't he plead not guilty? I still don't understand."

"I guess he just ain't as slick as me and you is."

* * *

Earl Smith slumped heavily into the chair still warm from Isaac Wilson's body. His right tee-shirt sleeve was rolled up to the arm pit. The left had a pack of cigarettes rolled into it. Tinsley had to remind himself this guy was nineteen, and not the thirty or so he more closely resembled.

His right forearm bore a heart-shaped tattoo, once bright red, now faded. Inside the heart were a few letters, blurred from a poor job of printing. The letters may have been "Mom," Wayne thought. Earl Smith's arms were short compared to his body, and looked like tree trunks.

"Looks like you're in good shape," Wayne began without introductions. "You work out much?"

Earl scratched at something on the desk top with a grease-packed fingernail. "I work," he said, "but not at some homo gym. I do real work. That's why I'm in good shape." He looked Tinsley up and down. "Looks like you could use a little work yourself."

"I'm sure I could."

"So, what do you want with me? I done told the other cops I ain't sayin' nothing."

"Okay. So, you're afraid, then?"

Smith sat straighter in his chair for an instant, glaring at Tinsley. "I ain't afraid of nothing! Y'all got nothing on me. I don't know nothing about that stuff in my car. That's why I ain't talking. I know how y'all work."

"Okay, so if you're not afraid, you're saying you're just dumb. Is that it?"

Earl's nostrils flared like a young bull's. "Are you calling me dumb?"

"I didn't say that. I thought that was what you were telling me."

"I never said nothing like that." He rubbed a grimy hand over his mouse-colored crew-cut.

"Okay, maybe I'm confused."

"You **are** confused!"

"All right. Help me out then. Correct me if I get something wrong." Earl stared blankly at him.

"First," began Wayne, "you and Burl got yourselves arrested last night..." He looked at Smith, a quizzed look on his face.

"Yeah."

"Okay, now we're getting somewhere. You were driving drunk...D.W.I. That tells me you're dumb because **nobody** gets drunk, then drives around just asking to get stopped by the cops...with stolen stuff in their car. That's dumb!"

"I said I'm not dumb. I didn't even know that stuff was in there."

"Okay. We're just going through this. You don't know what's in your own car. I can see how that could happen. It must be Burl, then, that did the burglary and sneaked the stuff in your car without you knowing."

Earl's breathing increased slightly. When Wayne saw him lick his lips the second time in a few seconds, he knew he was getting to him.

Tinsley continued. "I keep coming back to the same result though, Earl. Burl sneaked that stuff into your car and you didn't even know it. That's even dumber than before. Especially since you're still in jail. Are you too dumb to tell the truth and go home?"

"I ain't no rat!"

"Yeah you are, Earl. You're the worst kind of rat. And do you know what? I don't care one single bit about your burglary charge."

"You don't?" Earl was obviously dubious.

"No. I have much bigger fish to fry…how much you weigh, Earl?"

"Not sure."

"Guess."

"Two hundred and twenty pounds."

"Two-twenty. Yeah, I've got a two hundred and twenty pound fish to fry…in the electric chair."

"You can't use that on me. They don't execute people for stealing."

"They can, and they do, when it's stealing out of somebody's house. Breaking and entering…sure they can."

"They **can**. But they don't. Besides, like I said, I don't know nothing."

"And like I said, I don't care."

"Huh?"

"I don't care about that. I'm going to have them light you up, boy, for murdering Bill Bradley!"

Earl Smith couldn't stop his jaw from dropping. He looked as though he had been kicked in the stomach. He slowly closed his mouth and took a deep, dry swallow. "I don't know what you're…"

"Shut up!" Wayne knocked his own chair over and rushed across the desk to close space on Earl. "Don't lie to me, you coward!" He grabbed the back of Earl's tee-shirt and wadded it into a ball, squeezed tightly in his powerful grip.

"You and Burl…your deal with Ivy Bradley…I know all about it!" At the sound of Ivy's name, Wayne felt Earl's body shrink, closing in on itself. "You and Burl made a deal with Ivy…to kill Bill…that's called a conspiracy. But then you did it, and that's called murder."

In some indefinable way, Tinsley felt his last statement cost him ground…that he had lost some of his edge. Smith seemed, though infinitesimally so, to regain a degree of confidence. Wayne had to keep pushing him.

"Murder gets you dead in Texas, boy."

"I didn't kill nobody!" Earl yelled back.

"Then who did? I know you know. Who did it? Burl? Mrs. Bradley?"

"I'm leaving!" Smith started to rise quickly from his chair, and Tinsley slammed him back down, harder than he intended. Smith's forehead bounced off the table with a crack. When he started to bring his head back up, Tinsley slammed him back into the desk.

"Talk to me, you cowardly…!"

"No! Stop! Please, stop!" Tinsley regained his hold on the shirt and allowed Smith to sit erect. The deputy leaned over next to his ear.

"You've got thirty seconds to make me happy. After that, I'll use your head for basketball practice."

"Honest, Tinsley, we didn't kill him!"

"Then who did?"

Smith paused. Tears welled in his eyes. "Are you going to talk to Burl, too?"

"You have ten seconds left. Are you sure you want to spend it asking **me** questions? Who killed Bill Bradley?"

"Honest, I don't know. Me and Burl said we would, but we didn't."

"Who…"

"I don't know for sure. Maybe her?"

"Her?"

"Mrs. Bradley."

Wayne felt a pang in his stomach. He had known what he heard was a possibility. He did not want it to be true, however. He went back across the desk, picked up his chair, and sat down, facing Earl Smith. The boy's eyes were watery and looked like liquid glass. A red spot had appeared in the center of his forehead. He could not look Tinsley in the eyes.

"All right, Earl. Maybe you are getting less dumb. Why Mrs. Bradley?"

"She hired me to do it. She was going to pay me a thousand dollars when her insurance money came in…"

Tinsley sat, not speaking, knowing the uncomfortable silence would generate a continued response from Smith. It did.

"So I told Burl…said I'd pay him some of the money to help me."

"And he agreed?"

"At the time."

"Go on."

"We planned to get him out away from his house…she didn't want to **see** us do it. We had a couple of chances, but we couldn't…we couldn't do it. I thought I could. A **thousand** dollars…and I couldn't do it."

"It's a lot of money."

"Yeah. Anyway, one morning we heard in town Mr. Bradley had been murdered."

"And you assumed **Mrs.** Bradley did it?"

"Sure. Of course. Either that, or she hired somebody else…'cause we were taking so long."

"Earl, tell me about that night you and Burl went over to Mrs. Bradley's house after the murder…the night you faked the burglary."

"You knew? I mean, how could…have you already talked to Burl?" Wayne merely shrugged.

"Do you want me to tell the judge you cooperated with the authorities, or do you want to take the fall?"

"I thought we could get some money from her…since we knew."

"You were going to blackmail her?"

"No! Yes, sort of. We didn't do anything wrong…she did. We didn't kill him!"

"What happened that night?"

"I came in like I was really mad…how she cheated us out of a thousand dollars, and all. She was crying and said she tried to reach us to call it off…"

"Did she?"

"Well, no. I mean, she did call one day and asked me to come by her house right then...said she had to tell me something important. I started out there, but Mr. Bradley came driving up...I mean right before I turned in to the driveway."

"So you don't know what she wanted to talk about?"

"No. Next time I talked to her was that night we faked her house break-in."

"What was that about?"

"She kept saying she didn't do it. She thought I had killed him, she said. Anyway, she didn't have but seventeen dollars at the house, so we just went through, kinda' picking out things we wanted. She didn't want us to take the jewelry...said some of it was valuable. I told her to put in a claim with her insurance company...then she could get new stuff."

"What did she say?"

"Nothing, she just sat in that chair in the living room and cried. I told her I'd make it easy on her, so I kicked out the glass in the back door...told her now she really had a break-in."

"Then what?"

"We left."

"She didn't say anything else?"

"Nah...well, yeah. She asked if she still owed me the thousand."

"What did you make of that?"

"I think the lady done went crazy."

"Can you think of anything else, Earl?"

"Huh, uh. Say, since we really didn't break into her house, and she knew the stuff we were taking out...that's not breaking and entering anymore. Is it? I mean, it's not even a real theft."

"I guess one could argue that point," Wayne answered.

"Then will we be able to get out soon? I told you everything. We didn't kill nobody, and we didn't steal nothing. Nothing but that set of flippers, and that was just from some kid. Are they gonna' let us go now?"

"Shoot, Earl...I don't know. The stuff you're charged with is not even my case."

Chapter 28

Tinsley's talk with Burl Patterson went even easier than with Smith. He told the same story from his own perspective and, against Wayne's own personal preference, he believed them both.

He then took Johnny Wilson to the interview room. He wanted to boost the boy's spirits without giving him false hope. Johnny had heard talk outside his cell about what happens to a human body when it is electrocuted. Other inmates, no doubt knowing Johnny's offense, had obviously made the frightening descriptions for his benefit.

Tinsley corrected a few of the falsehoods, but most of the things they said he knew to be true. In the end, all he could do was tell Johnny he had seen Isaac Wilson, and he was okay. Yes, he was working some leads and—more important—he didn't believe Johnny killed Mr. Bradley. Of course, Wayne's thinking him not guilty was a long way from him walking away a free man.

On his way out, a rough looking receptionist called down the hall to him. Her straight hair was the color of wet sand, her pock-marked face indicative of serious skin problems in her youth. Her cotton dress looked like it might explode from the pressure inside.

"Wayne!"

"Yes, ma'am."

"Phone."

"Okay. I'll be right there." It wasn't common for him to receive calls at the sheriff's office, since he was rarely there. Someone wanted him badly enough to track him down.

"Hello."

"Wayne?" A woman's voice. Faye, he believed, although he couldn't be certain.

"Yes, it is. May I help you?"

"It's Faye Cowen. I'm sorry to bother you at work. It's just that…"

"Don't think a thing about it. That's what I get paid for." He tried to sound up-beat. She still seemed depressed…her voice tone was low and lacked vitality. He really needed to be going to Ivy Bradley's place, to follow up on what he had just learned, but it was not in him to be rude to Faye.

"Thanks. I never got to talk to you again the other day. I thought you were coming by for the ledger."

"I'm sorry, Faye. I really didn't forget. It's just I've been so covered up with this murder investigation…"

"No, Wayne…it's all right. I just wanted to apologize in person… for the way I…"

"You don't owe me an apology, Faye. But I will pick up the ledger very soon. I'm not so sure it will be important to the case now, but I'll take it just in case…"

"Not important?" Her tone was that of a child just told there is no Santa Claus.

"Maybe not. The boy may not be guilty."

"That's good. I hope he's not. So, you never actually **needed** the ledger after all…there was no reason…" her voice trailed off into silence.

"Faye? Are you there?"

A moment passed. She answered. "Wayne, the reason I called is, I need a personal favor."

"Of course. What is it?" He glanced at his watch, wondering how long it would take with Ivy. It was already almost 4:00 pm. If she confessed, he would be working late into the night.

"It's Allen. I need to know if he's okay."

"I don't understand."

"He hasn't been home for…since that evening you came with the search warrant. When he left he was really angry."

"And he hasn't been in touch since? Not even by telephone?"

"No. I haven't left the house. He's in the car. At first I thought he just needed time to think…to sort things out. But now…I'm worried."

"Did we make him that mad?"

"No. It wasn't you."

"So, do you want me to see if I can find him…have him check in with you?"

"No. I know where he is. Mrs. Wilson just called and told me our car is parked at the Half Moon Motel on the east side of Hoover."

"That was nice of her."

"She's a gossip. I'm sure it's all over town Allen is meeting some woman while I sit at home."

"Oh."

"I don't really care about that, Wayne. I don't care what they say. I'm afraid. I need to know he's okay. This is not like him."

"No, it's not, but I'm sure there's a reasonable explanation." He glanced at his watch again, and sighed deeply. "Tell you what…I'll run over there right now and check on him. I'm sure he's okay."

"Just ask him to call me. Okay?"

"Sure."

"He doesn't even have to come home. Just call."

"I understand."

"Wayne?"

"Yes?"

"If he won't call…or if he can't—for some reason—will you…?"

"I'll call you myself."

"Thank you. I'm sorry to ask. I know how busy…"

"Shush, now. None of that. It won't take more than a few minutes. Don't worry."

"I'll be waiting for a call."

"You'll get it."

"Bye." She hung up.

He really didn't need this diversion. He felt he was really close to pulling the murder case together. On the other hand, it wasn't characteristic of Faye to ask favors, or to overreact. There had better be something wrong with you, Allen, he thought. 'Cause if there's not, I'll put a knot on your head myself for scaring Faye half to death...and for wasting my time.

He arrived at the motel twelve minutes later, not in a good mood. He saw the Ford immediately and pulled in beside it on the left side. The weather was warm for spring, and without the slightest stir of a breeze...also very unusual for spring. It had been the same the day before, as well. Tinsley thought that fact noteworthy because sand, leaves, and debris were blown around the tires of the car. It hadn't been moved in at least two days.

Wayne filed that information away in his "I don't like the looks of this" bin. He looked inside the car and pushed the door handle button on the passenger side. It was locked. A glance told him all four doors were locked. Nothing inside the car looked amiss.

He didn't get a room number from Faye...she probably didn't know it. He walked to the door immediately in front of the car, saw the number "11" on it, and knocked. After a moment, he knocked louder and called out to Allen. There were no other cars in the motel parking lot, and no response from the room.

He felt that familiar emotion of dread that appeared in his stomach occasionally. It began, always, as a small stirring...of a tiny living something that didn't belong there. He knew he did not want to go into that room. What if Allen had become ill and needed medical aid? It was possible. Wayne didn't buy that theory, but he had not allowed another to take its place yet.

Maybe Allen was just being Allen...stubborn and hard headed, refusing to answer the door. That could be it. He walked to the motel office and found it empty.

"Hello!" No response. "Anybody here?" he called out, louder. Silence. He glanced at the peg-board behind the counter. Under the number "11" was a key, just like all the other rooms. He looked around again, certain no-one was nearby, then removed the key from the board, certain they'd rather he borrow a key than smash down their door.

The key fit perfectly into the knob, and he twisted it open, pushing lightly on the door.

"Allen!" He opened the door a little more and felt inside for a light switch. Before his fingers found the switch, the odor hit him. It came rushing out of the confined space and through the small opening of the door. Wayne flinched, repulsed. He had smelled that smell before... one a man never forgets. He groaned and pushed the door wide open, flipping on the light. The small knot of dread in his stomach had turned to a bowling ball.

Allen's feet were flat on the floor, his torso bent back to the side and backwards...as though he had lain back to rest. His face was swollen and bruised, but otherwise unmarked. The spray of blood and chunks of body materials on the wall behind Allen told Wayne the story before he even checked the back of his head. A revolver lay on the floor between Allen's feet, the grips tilted slightly against his left big toe.

"Oh, Allen." Wayne shuffled to a vinyl arm-chair and slumped heavily into it. "Allen," he said again, softly. He shook his head, not wanting to believe, unable to understand. "I would have walked barefoot through Hell to have what you have...what you had," he whispered. He sat a few moments, taking in the room, the whiskey bottle, the gun, the body...

"Oh, Dear Lord!" cried the woman in the doorway. "I saw the police car...oh, dear Lord!"

"Shut the door, please, ma'am. And call the sheriff's department. Tell them there's been a suicide here."

"Suicide? Are you sure he's dead?" she stammered, frantically.

Wayne tensed, trying to be calm with the distressed woman...the proprietor, he assumed.

"I'm as sure about that as I'm sure I'll throw you in jail if you don't shut...that...door!" Then, more to himself, "I don't want a bunch of blood suckers standing around gawking at him."

She slammed the door, and he heard the rapid clicking of her hard shoe heels snapping against the concrete sidewalk. They quickly dissipated, and he was alone again with Allen.

174

Occasionally a long expulsion from Wayne's lungs filled the room. He had seen several bodies before. There was no excitement in seeing them, for him. He had lived too long and had seen too much death to not realize the terrible affects it had on families and friends…especially a suicide.

He pulled in breath after breath of the stench-filled air, knowing what would come later would be infinitely worse than anything he could experience in that lonely motel room. Allen's problems on this earth were over. But what of his family? How could he do this to them?

Wayne was not surprised to discover he was angry with Allen. It was a common experience among those left behind. He looked again at the body, knowing it was not Allen Cowen lying there, but only the house in which he used to live.

He made no notes, no diagrams…nor did he look closer at the body. He knew rigor mortis would have already set in and gone…the odor told him Allen had been dead for quite some time. Those things, along with others, were mere passing acknowledgements of the obvious. He had no intention of working this incident. He hoped Lightsey would get the call.

Wayne had promised Faye a telephone call. He wouldn't call her, of course. This was not the sort of thing one announces by telephone.

He thought of how she looked the day they buried Oma. Linda was still alive then, and she mentioned to Wayne how strong Faye was…how well she was holding up. But Tinsley knew Faye…he knew her every expression…the fire that flashed behind those dark brown eyes.

He remembered as a boy seeing a powerful, willful stallion broken hard by rough handlers until his spirit was broken. The beauty of the horse on the outside, his rippling muscles, the internal strength, and his heart of pure energy, still existed. But in the stallion's eyes, in the way he held his head, another picture of him emerged. He was defeated. Broken, he would never feel the freedom of his own raw emotions again.

It was that same look Tinsley saw in Faye's eyes that day. Had she buried her spirit along with her little son?

Bill Lightsey was not the responding officer. He did show up momentarily, however, and assured Wayne he would keep an eye on things…make sure everything was handled properly.

On the bleak, lonely road back to Cash, a thousand thoughts hammered at Wayne's consciousness. How could he tell her? The one thing he **hated** about his job was delivering death messages. They never got easier. But **this** death message…to Faye! He groaned, not for the first time that evening.

It had taken longer at the motel than Wayne wanted. Faye's call had come in around 4:00 p.m. It was now almost 7:00 p.m. Darkness was closing in as he turned into the gravel drive. He sat for a moment staring at the steering wheel. What possible thing could he say to make this easier for her. He knew the truth already. There is no good way to say "Sorry, your husband blew his brains out and is dead." He frowned at the thought and opened the car door. His feet and legs would barely move. They felt so heavy…he, so tired.

Stepping onto the porch, the door opened slowly, with only the screen door remaining to separate them. Her eyes searched his immediately. He noticed how erect she stood, her back arched proudly, chin up. Her eyes held the truth of the fear in her.

"Faye, can I come in?"

She pushed the screen open, and he stepped inside. Her eyes never left his. "You said you'd call."

"I couldn't, Faye. I'm so sorry…I…"

"No…No!" She clutched the neck of her dress with both hands, squeezing her knuckles white.

"Faye," he reached out a tentative hand to her forearm. "I'm so sorry."

"No. Please, God, no. Don't let this be…" she burst into a racking, sobbing blur of words and guttural sounds Wayne couldn't understand. Her heart, her soul, her life, her hopes, her love…all poured out in gushes of tears that fell to her bosom and onto the floor. She emptied herself so completely, all strength began to wane, and Tinsley managed to grab her just as her knees buckled.

With his arm around her waist, and the other supporting an elbow, he guided her gently to the sofa. He helped her sit, and sat beside her.

Her sobbing had quieted somewhat, and he moved his arm from her waist up around her shoulders. Bitter bile hung close in his own throat. He had to be strong for her. This was not his occasion to fall apart.

Her crying became calmer for a moment, and Wayne thought the worse might be over. She managed to look up at him then. He would have cut off both his arms to take away the look of hurt in her eyes.

"Wayne…how…why…?"

He could only shake his head. "It'll be okay," was all he could get out. He involuntarily pulled her against him, nestling her head on his shoulder, against his neck, holding tightly to her hands…both her small hands squeezed by his one free hand.

She cried intermittently then for almost an hour. They were still sitting on the edge of the sofa, and Tinsley's back—oddly twisted to accommodate Faye—was beginning to cramp. He held fast, knowing he would sit in that exact position till the end of time if that was what Faye needed.

After a time of silence, Wayne asked her what he had been afraid to ask earlier, not knowing how she would react. But he needed to know. "Faye, where are the boys?"

"Spending the night with friends. I was afraid…didn't want them to be here…just in case."

"Okay, I just wanted to make sure I didn't need to get them or anything."

"No. Let them sleep tonight," she sniffed, and dabbed at her nose with the blue handkerchief Wayne gave her earlier. "It may be the last good night sleep they have for…for awhile."

"Okay." He squeezed her shoulder, sensing her emotions welling up again. She sighed deeply, a sign she was wearing down, physically and emotionally spent.

"Do you need to go, Wayne? I've kept you for a long time."

"No." He thought of the meeting he had intended with Ivy…perhaps breaking open the murder case. "No. There is no place I need to be…except here…as long as you need me."

"Seriously?"

"Of course."

"Then stay with me tonight."

Wayne stared at her, stunned. Like Earl Smith earlier that day, he had a jaw to re-set. She almost laughed at him.

"That sounded awful, didn't it?"

He didn't answer.

"All I meant was, I don't think I can stay here alone tonight. I'm frightened."

"Of what, Faye?"

"I don't know. Frightened...maybe of just being alone. I don't know. Forget it, Wayne. It was thoughtless of me to ask."

"No. I'd be happy to stay," he said, "I was just wondering what people would say...your reputation."

"I didn't think, Wayne."

"It's okay. I'll stay."

"You know, I don't care at this moment what people think of me. But you are another matter. You could lose your job. I'll be fine. Really."

"No arguments. I'm staying. We'll leave the door open and the lights on. Anybody passing by can see us in the living room through the picture window. Maybe you can get some sleep." She shook her head. "I know," he said, "You probably can't...but at least you can rest."

"Thank you."

"I'm glad to do it. I care about you...you and your family. I'll take you to pick up Jeff and Randy in the morning."

"I can't even think of that right now." Her voice still sounded stuffy, nasal.

"Okay."

"I'll make some coffee. Maybe we can talk a while about unimportant things."

"That sounds fine," he said.

"Then, if I...when I get up the courage, I'll need you to tell me about Allen."

Chapter 29

Ivory Blankenship insisted his wife talk to their daughter, Shirley. There was a marked change in her behavior of late, and he wanted to know why. Mostly he wanted it fixed. Mrs. Blankenship could not argue his point. She had also noticed the changes, and hoped it was only her daughter "going through the changes."

Shirley was faking illness frequently in the mornings, avoiding school. That alone was unusual since she loved it so much her first two years. Missing school was not, however, really the primary issue with Ivory. They could **make** her go to school. Besides, most of the older kids dropped out of school entirely in the fall when the harvest was on.

Shirley was also acting peculiar in his opinion. She had "taken to" sleeping with the light on. When they made her turn it out, they would discover in the morning where she had managed to get it back on during the night. Fortunately, the three older children who shared the bedroom with her were sound sleepers and didn't complain.

And she had become so shy. Was that even the right word? She slept in her clothes! There were so many things. And Ivory knew it was his wife's place to handle it.

"Just straighten it out, that's all," he said.

"How am I supposed to do that, Mr. Know-it-all?"

"She's just spoiled. That's my thinking. Spank her."

Mrs. Ruth Blankenship shook her head. "Men," she whispered, but not so quietly her husband couldn't hear.

"Are you going to handle it, or you want me to?" He began unbuckling his belt.

"No, you go on to work. I'll take care of it this morning. She's got a sick stomach again."

"Hmmph!" he grunted, walking to the door. He stopped. "Boss, he says I can come in for dinner today. He's got to go to the blacksmith shop and get a plow welded."

"Okay. About 12:00?"

"Probably."

"Okay. Bye."

As the door closed, Ruth looked toward the room where Shirley slept. She is probably awake, Ruth thought, and I bet she heard every word. Wiping residual flour from her hands on the cotton apron, she stood and walked into the bedroom. There was no door to open.

She sat on the edge of the bed beside her daughter, a sudden sense of foreboding closing in on her. Shirley had turned nine only a few months before. The girl lay face down, her face turned away from Ruth. She was covered to the neck with a hand-stitched patch quilt. Curly hair sprang in all directions from her head. Ruth put her large hand on Shirley's head, patting it. "Quite a rat's nest you got here, baby girl."

There was no response, but Shirley's erratic breathing was all the evidence her mother needed.

"Didn't nobody ever tell you? You can't fool a mama. Turn over and talk to me."

There was a very brief hesitation, followed by slow movement under the quilt. Shirley rolled onto her back, the bed cover tucked under her chin. Large brown eyes looked up at her mother. Dark pupils surrounded by the color pearl.

"Are you gonna' spank me, mama?" she asked fearfully.

"Do you think you deserve a spanking?" Ruth smiled down at her.

"Maybe."

"And why would that be?"

"School and stuff…"

"Like your daddy was just talking about?"

"Yes, ma'am. I guess so."

"Forget what you heard, sweet baby. I want to talk to you about grown up things."

Shirley turned her head away immediately, looking away from her mother. "Don't know grown up stuff." Her voice was so small, Ruth could hardly hear.

"Baby, look at me. Look at your mama." She spoke kindly, but firmly.

Slowly Shirley's head turned, revealing tear-choked eyes and a lip that would not stop quivering. Ruth saw her face, and her own eyes began to water. She dabbed at them with her apron. She stroked her daughter's forehead and cheek with a gentle hand.

"Oh, my poor, poor, little thing." She stopped herself and paid close attention to her own words. "Shirley, I need you to listen to me real close. I know you think I don't know about some things, but I do." No, she thought, I'm thinking too much…this is my daughter…talk to her. "Let me start over. Okay?" Shirley nodded. "All men are stupid, including your daddy." Ruth laughed at her own remark, and Shirley joined in with the tiniest beginning of a smile.

"We agree on that, then?" Her daughter nodded again. "Okay, so they're all stupid. That's why your daddy was carrying on so this morning. He doesn't understand…'cause he's stupid!" This time they both laughed a little. Ruth could see her daughter's defenses breaking down slightly.

"It's okay for 'em to be stupid, though…makes it easier for us girls to get our way." She paused a moment. "But there is also **bad** men. Stupid, **bad** men. That's **not** okay." Shirley's tears were dried, but her eyes bored holes in her mother. "Can we agree on that, too…that it's not okay for men to do bad things to little girls?"

Shirley nodded again. "Okay."

"I know about things bad men do to little girls…"

The remark struck the little girl like a knife in the stomach. Fear flashed on her face. Ruth knew then she had guessed right. She did not want to be right.

"Shhh. Quiet, little baby girl. You must listen careful now. You're afraid, I know. And, I know you're afraid for a reason. Want to tell me why?"

Her daughter shook her head, without speaking.

"Okay. Here's what we'll do. I'm going to guess why you're afraid. You'll be surprised how smart I am. Let's see…" she looked toward the ceiling as if in deep thought, and began pointing to her fingertips one by one as she went through her list. "When I get the right one, you just give me a big wink.

"Number one…you're afraid you did something bad, nasty even, and you're afraid you'll be in trouble." She looked down at Shirley, seeing no response.

"Alright, number two…the bad man said he would hurt you…or even worse…if you tell." Nothing.

"Number three…the bad man said he would hurt somebody else—like me or daddy—if you say what he done." No response, but she was listening intently.

"Number four…uh. Well, let's see…maybe I'm not as smart as I thought I was. I don't know what number four is. Can you help me, maybe, come up with a number four…you know, something like a bad man might say?"

Ruth didn't look directly at Shirley, giving her a little space. It was quiet in the room when she heard her daughter's very soft voice. "Maybe divorce?"

"Why, yes," said Ruth, "Divorce. That's a good number four. How would a bad man say it?"

"Maybe like, if you tell your mama and daddy they'll be ashamed and get a divorce and give you to a orphans' home. Maybe like that."

The thoughts that rushed immediately to Ruth's consciousness were not Christian, and surely nothing she would let her daughter hear. She hadn't even **thought** of such horrible words in years.

"Yes, baby. That's a real good number four. That would be real scary for a girl…to think that would happen."

"Would it?"

"Goodness, no. Parents would just hug and kiss that girl 'cause she's safe now. They would be real, real sorry they didn't know what happened, so they could stop it. They wouldn't get no divorce. And there ain't enough people in the whole wide world that could ever get them to take their little girl to no orphans' home. They would just keep right on loving and loving and loving and loving her."

Shirley smiled slightly. "You'd keep on loving me?"

"Sure, we would. Honey, I know it's hard to say the words, but I need to know who the man was, and what he did."

"No, mama! Why?"

"It's real important. We need to make sure he don't do nothing like that again to you or somebody else."

"I don't know his name. But he won't hurt me no more."

"We can't know that for sure, baby. Tell me what he did…I've heard all the words before…and this time it will be okay for you to say them. God understands you ain't being ugly."

Slowly, quietly, almost as though she were in a trance, Shirley described a painfully brutal rape…when, how…how he smelled…the blood…her blood…the pain…afraid she was dying. Nasty. The fear.

Ruth wanted to throw up. She also wanted to grab her baby girl close to her…to cry and scream and go crazy with hatred…to murder. But the calm, deliberate manner of talking with Shirley seemed to work best. Ruth **had** heard the words before…but not from her innocent daughter. Not expressed as a true event with her daughter the victim. The words had never been more evil.

"Well, honey, you did real good. That was hard for you, I know…but see…you've told me, and things are still the same with us. Don't you feel a little relieved…a little bit better."

"I think so."

"What is it, baby? Your words say something, but your voice tells mama something else is bothering you."

"You gonna' ask about the man, now?"

"Does that bother you?"

"I don't know what to say. I'm…uh, complicated."

STAN SIMMONS

In spite of her dark mood, Ruth stifled a smile. "I can see that. Is it also complicated about the man?"

"Uh, huh."

"Why is it complicated, dear?" She pulled the quilt back a little and took Shirley's hand in her own. "Let's get this done. We'll be through with it in no time, then let's bake some sugar cookies together...just us girls. Okay?"

"Can I eat some dough?"

"All of it, if you want."

Shirley put on a serious face. She looked very thoughtful, then began. "The bad man that did...what I said?"

"Yes?"

"He's won't do it no more."

"Okay, baby. So you're saying the man who...who hurt you, and told you to not tell...he won't do it no more? How can you be sure?"

"No, not both."

"What? I'm sorry baby. I don't understand what you're saying. I guess you really **are** complicated." She tried to smile, but it didn't work well.

Shirley seemed frustrated. "Okay...see, the man who hurt me didn't say nothing but that nasty stuff I told you." She checked her mother's expression and saw her nod. "Then the **other** man told me don't tell...and about the orphans' home."

"The **other**...! **What** other man?" Ruth sounded sharper than she intended. Shirley drew deeper into the covers. "I'm sorry, honey...I'm not mad at you. I was just surprised. Why did the other man threaten you? Was he there when it happened?"

"No, he's my friend."

"He's your friend? Why would he tell you not to say anything to us?"

"He told me so I wouldn't be a orphan."

"But you know now that's not true?"

"I guess so."

"And now you know this friend was not telling you the truth...do you see that? He was wrong?"

184

"Okay."

"What's his name, baby?"

She didn't answer.

"Honey, do you know your friend's name?" Shirley shook her head, yes. "How old is he?"

"I don't know."

"Can you guess?"

"I don't know. Real old."

"Is he a white man, too, like the one who hurt you?"

"No."

"So, he's colored." Shirley offered no response.

"Shirley, please. Why won't you tell me his name?"

"He made me swear."

"He made you swear not to tell his name? Why?"

She shrugged tiny little shoulders. "He loves me like you and daddy, he said. That's why he takes special care of me."

"Special care?"

"He says 'special care.' He pats me and does love touches."

Ruth turned away from her daughter, regaining composure…trying to remove the pain and hatred from her face. "How do you feel about the love touches?"

Shirley looked down. "They make me feel sad. Bad. I wish he didn't love me so much."

For the first time Ruth was speechless. Shirley, however, was not. "He made that white man stop hurting me."

"I thought you said he wasn't there."

"He wasn't. But he saw the blood…he saw the white man leaving the bus shed at school…he saw me. He cried."

"What did he do?"

"He said, I'll talk to that white man and ask him don't hurt that little precious girl no more. He knew who the white man was."

"Dear Jesus…" Ruth whispered. This was going to take a whole lot of praying.

"Mama?"

"Yes, baby. What is it?"

"How come you know so much?"

Ruth looked away again, staring into a distant place. "That's another story, honey, but not for today. Maybe when you're older."

"Okay. Can we make cookies now?"

Chapter 30

Ivy Bradley slept late again. All her married years—all her adult life—she had made breakfast for her husband. Bill was an early riser and expected the morning meal on the table the moment he was dressed.

Getting up at 5:15 am allowed her sufficient time to make his breakfast, which never varied. He required two brown-shell eggs fried sunny-side-up, two slices of dry whole wheat toast, two pieces of bacon pressed flat and dabbed of any excess grease, a half glass of orange juice strained of its pulp, and three pancakes with a pat of butter and real maple syrup. His coffee was always black with two heaping teaspoons of sugar.

It wasn't a breakfast that took long to prepare, but she got up a little earlier than necessary in the event she overcooked the bacon or eggs. When that did happen—very infrequently—she hid the imperfect product and started over.

Most days he shuffled in without speaking, sour and unsociable. He would be hung over or just tired from carousing most of the night. When he sat at the table, Ivy remained standing. His ritual included moving the eggs around with his fork, inspecting them, before eating anything. He often left one or two of the required food items without having taken a bite of them.

She never understood why he did that, but forgot to wonder or even care years ago. Early in their marriage she wondered what she had done wrong with the food that day. Occasionally, during his particularly foul moments, he would just stand over his food looking down at it like some brooding ogre. He then picked up everything and threw it in the trash, untouched, storming out the door in a silent, undefined rage.

She ate after he left. Now, however, Ivy enjoyed sleeping late, not leaving the bed until after 8:00 a.m. often. And she ate whatever she wanted for breakfast. Wednesday she made herself fudge brownies and had them with sweet milk. She hadn't enjoyed a breakfast so much in her life. Ivy knew those things were a wasteful luxury, and she didn't stay in bed because she was sleeping well. She did it because she **could**.

Nightmares came frequently. Usually they were about Bill. Not the dead Bill, however, but of the Bill who came back...who was somehow alive again. Two or three times she dreamed about the colored boy, too...the one in jail, charged with killing her husband. He had no face in her dreams, just a boy about to be executed for something he didn't do.

She sat up and stretched, reaching firm, slender arms over her head, then out to the sides, fists clenched. She added a terrific yawn to complete the pleasure of the moment. The new silk slip was loose enough to allow her freedom of movement, and tight enough against her skin to remind her she was a woman.

The two-piece pajama set she wore in the past was now ashes in the 55-gallon barrel out back where she burned trash. She would never again wear long-sleeved pajamas buttoned all the way to her neck.

Ivy was having trouble re-identifying herself. She had been told what to do for so long...had been demoralized, shamed, ridiculed, emotionally and physically tortured for so long...who **was** she anyway?

She didn't know how to feel like a woman. Two paperback novels lay on the table by her bed, their edges curled slightly. They were romance novels, and she enjoyed the stories, but she could not imagine herself in the role of either of the women in them. Their worlds were so strange.

Engaged in the relief of living in a world without Bill Bradley, Ivy still could not attach herself to the elusive goal of happiness. She didn't deserve to be happy, she knew. No matter how bad Bill had been to her, she married him of her own free will…sure, she was only a child at the time…but…it was her choice.

He seemed so dashing then. Like all young girls, at that time in her life she actually thought she knew what love was…what it felt like. She knew lust. She knew intimidation. She knew fear, and disgust, and pain. But love? The word was meaningless, an unknown thing to be sought and desired.

Maybe she would never know. But she knew how she felt to be around men, now…it was so different. When Bill was alive she only felt fear…that he would see her talking to a man, crossing a man's path in town, even waving at a passing car. When Jeff visited her Saturday—even at his youthful age—she was amused, but also intrigued, with the impact her presence had on him.

And deputy Tinsley—she liked his looks—he seemed like a man etched in granite. But, more than that, she liked the way he treated her. He was a gentleman, and he treated her like a lady. It wasn't a formal kind of polite behavior like the man at the funeral home or the clerk at the grocery store. Mr. Tinsley was warm. He looked right into a person's eyes without being too familiar. She had never been uncomfortable in his presence. She liked the way she felt when he was there.

Ivy shuttered slightly, then smiled to herself. Maybe that's how other women feel all the time.

Real, normal women. She stepped onto the floor and padded, bare feet, to the bathroom, absently grateful for whatever crop it was that finally allowed them to purchase a house with an indoor bathroom.

Ivy had avoided looking into the mirror for years. She now made a habit of doing it every morning. She put on makeup and took stock of the physical presence before her. In spite of what Bill said all those years, she **was** pretty. She **did** look good in the mirror.

And although she liked the shape of her eyes, and the color, she could not penetrate their depths…it was the one place she could not go. Looking too deeply exposed her soul, and it overpowered her.

How could she even think of hiring those awful boys to kill her husband? But then, the other question…how could she **not**?

She brushed her teeth with baking soda and began slowly, methodically brushing her long, black hair. Just as she was satisfied with that job, she heard the car pull into her driveway and stop just outside the front door.

Life-long experiences fade slowly, and her first emotion was of panic…dread. But, no. He's dead. She hurried to the nearest window in the living room and peeked out. She smiled. I was just thinking of you, she thought. As he approached the door, she suddenly panicked again—this time without the dread.

She ran for her bedroom, and reached into her closet for the familiar white terry-cloth robe. She looped the waist tie just as he knocked. She took two deep gulps of air, trying to catch her breath. "Coming!"

As she pulled the door open, Ivy was still a little winded. "Hello, Deputy Tinsley. How are you?"

"I'm fine, thanks. Are you okay?" He looked concerned.

"Yes, why?"

"You seem flushed, out of breath. Are you sure you're all right?"

She laughed, child-like. "I'm fine. You caught me in the bathroom."

"Oh, I'm sorry. I shouldn't have…"

"No, it's okay. I was brushing my hair. But I wasn't decent yet, and my run to the bedroom…guess I'm not in very good running shape."

"I am sorry. I should have called first."

"Don't be silly. You're welcome here anytime."

"We'll see," he whispered to himself.

"Excuse me…I didn't hear what you…"

"Mrs. Bradley, I need to talk to you. Is this a convenient time?"

"Of course. I don't exactly have to check my appointment book."

He looked around, "Where would you like to…?"

"Oh, come on in here." She pivoted on the ball of one foot and headed away from him, motioning for him to follow.

Behind her, Wayne absently wondered how it was possible for so much bright light to shine from black hair.

"Have a seat in there," she pointed to the small, glassed-in room with the round table, just off the kitchen. "I'll put on some coffee."

"Thanks." Wayne went into the room and stood, uncomfortable in his mission. He watched her quickly measuring out coffee and pouring it into the catch-cup at the top of the percolator. She filled the bottom of the pot with water and set it on the stove. She looked up at him.

"Deputy, please. Go ahead and sit down. That's very sweet, though."

He put his hat upside down on an unencumbered flower stand, and seated himself, his back to the wall. Ivy came in and sat across from him, crossing her legs. Unconsciously, she began rocking her right foot as it hung suspended just under the glass-topped table. "It'll be ready in a few minutes," she said smiling.

I shouldn't be doing this here, thought Wayne. I should have met her in an environment less comfortable for her. Or maybe one more comfortable for me. She continued watching his face, waiting. Her expression was one of complete innocence…not just an innocence of criminal activity, but of life. He knew that could not be true…not with what she had experienced with Bill.

"I need to visit with you…" he began.

"You said."

"It's about your husband…his death."

"I hope you're here to tell me they brought the insurance money in cash, and it's more than you could carry." She smiled again.

"So you did put in for the insurance?"

"Sure did. I think I can get over hating him easier if I'm rich on his insurance money." She expected a laugh from him but it was not forthcoming. He only nodded.

"Mrs. Bradley, in every murder investigation, officers must eliminate possible suspects…"

"Okay. Is that what you're doing?"

"I don't want you to think I'm accusing you or anything like that...exactly. I do need to put some pieces together on this puzzle, though."

"I see." She was no longer smiling; her small bare foot slowed its rocking motion until it stopped altogether. She leaned forward slightly. In the kitchen, hot water pumped furiously against the glass cap of the percolator, the aroma of coffee growing stronger. Neither of them noticed.

"Tell me about your relationship with Earl Smith." Wayne put his note pad on the table, unopened.

"My relationship?"

"Yes. How you know him. What your dealings with him have been?"

"I don't...," she began.

"Stop, Ivy." he held the palm of his hand toward her. "Don't. Before you say anything...I've already talked to Earl. I know the answer to most of the questions I'm going to ask you already."

"Then why ask me?"

"I don't want you to talk yourself into a box...a story you feel you have to stick to..."

"Why would you care?"

"I feel bad for you. I don't know how to put it...I just hate what you've been through. Maybe you deserve a break, if one is to be had." She didn't respond. "Things look bad for you now. I wanted to hear your side."

"Wayne..." she whispered the name through strained vocal chords. Her eyes filled immediately, and she looked down. Wayne's jaw locked, muscles rippling near his left ear.

"Please," he said. "Try to hold it together...we need...we **have** to get through this." She put her elbows on the table and lowered her head into her hands. Wayne stood up, towering over her for a moment. He placed his hand on her quaking shoulder, and even through the thick robe he felt her quiver. His hand remained there a brief moment, then he removed it, walking quietly into the kitchen. He found two cups and poured hot coffee into them. Into hers he added a little cool water.

"Have a sip," he said, placing the cup before her. He patted her shoulder and sat down. "Let me know when you're ready."

She took a long drink from the cup, her eyes lowered, hands shaking. When she finished, she continued holding the cup in both hands, watching it intently. "Okay…Earl Smith."

"Yes?"

"Bill knew him. He fixed Bill's work truck a couple of times…the one the hired men drive. Mostly, though, Bill bought things from him."

"What kind of things?"

"Oh, farm implements, parts, tools, tires…things like that."

"Stolen?"

"Probably. I don't know for sure."

"So you met him out here, at the house?"

"Yes. He came to see Bill, but he was out looking at some horses that day with a buyer in the other man's truck. Bill's pickup was here at the house."

"Earl thought Bill was home?"

"Yes. I heard Bill several times talking to other people on the phone about this bad man Earl Smith…how tough he is…how mean…would do anything for a dollar…that sort of thing."

"Is that the day you asked him to kill Bill?"

She studied the coffee cup, her brow furrowed in thought and consternation. "No. I told him I might have some work for him later, and he left me his telephone number."

"Weren't you concerned he might tell Bill what you said?"

"Of course, at that time he didn't know what the job would be."

"Did you know, then, what you were going to do?"

"No. When I met him—Earl—I remember the instant…it was more like a feeling than a thought. My heart just jumped in my chest. It was like freedom…an instant of freedom. I loved how it felt. I think the seed was planted at that exact moment."

"To have Bill killed?" She nodded ascent. "How long was it 'till you called him…till you asked him to kill your husband?"

"I'm not certain. Maybe two weeks. It was a morning after a

particularly horrible night. He was really on a roll that night." She set the cup gently, quietly on the table, but still could not look at Tinsley.

"And what did you ask him to do? Exactly?"

"I asked him if he could kill someone for a thousand dollars. He said 'anybody but Ike,' and laughed…like it was nothing."

"But he **did** eventually come to know you were serious, and that you were talking about Bill. Is that right?"

"Yes. He said he would do it."

"Did he say how he would do it? Or when?"

"No. He said it would be soon, but I didn't want to know when or how."

"Did you give him any specific directions?"

"No, not really. Only that I didn't want him to suffer."

It was Wayne's turn to inspect his coffee. The room lay ghostly silent around them. When she broke the silence, he would have sworn he heard a child's voice, so meek and small.

"What will they do to me, Wayne?"

"I don't know," he admitted. "I wish I could tell you, but I really don't have any idea. There are still things I have to know."

"What?"

"Do you know if Earl killed your…Bill?"

"Of course."

"Then he **did** kill him?"

"He's the only person I ever talked to about it…he and his friend. Who else **could** it be?"

"You?" He did look at her then, looking for a reaction…some sign so he might know. Her eyes grew enormous, her lips parted slightly and began to tremble.

"Me? You think I…?"

"I have to ask, Ivy."

She ran her tongue over parched lips. Retrieving the coffee, she took a long drink of the liquid, revealing a light pulse in her long neck. When she was finished, she replaced the cup and took a deep breath.

"Wayne," she said, "look at me." Her eyes captured his. "I did a terrible thing. I **did** try to correct it—I swear I did. I tried to stop Smith, but I was too late." She hesitated, taking another deep breath, making a concerted effort to maintain control. "I know none of that matters. I asked him to kill Bill, and he's dead. It's my fault. But I did not kill Bill. I'm not sorry he's dead, but I didn't do it. Please, Wayne…it's very important to me you believe me."

Tinsley watched her silently, thinking she might have more to say. She did, and as an apparent afterthought, added, "You know, from the beginning I always thought I would get caught. I know you can't trust people like that Smith boy to keep quiet."

"Then why, Ivy?"

"I thought, if I could just have one month…one month without him in my life, it would be worth it."

"Worth going to prison? Maybe worse?"

"Yes."

"It's only been a little over a week, though. I'm afraid you're not going to get your month."

He thought he saw the slightest indication of a smile. "You know what, Wayne?"

"What?"

"It was worth it anyway."

Chapter 31

When Tinsley left Ivy Bradley that morning she stood solemnly on the front porch, both hands pressed deeply into the huge pockets of her plush robe. She tried a smile as he drove off, but it was strained.

He told her she was under house arrest. She was not allowed to leave without telling him first. Tinsley had no idea if that was a legal order…or even if such a thing existed. Ivy believed it, though, and vowed to obey, relieved she was not on her way to jail.

Wayne found himself in a quandary unlike any he had ever experienced. He believed Ivy Bradley. The problem was that—as much as he disliked the man—he also believed Smith. Had he missed something? Both of them couldn't be telling the truth. **Somebody** murdered Bradley. Ivy said it was Smith. Smith said it was her…or someone else she hired.

Ivy had broken down very easily under his questioning. Too easily? No, he had the very specific impression she was almost relieved to have her burden exposed. She had been very ashamed, but relieved.

He believed her, but he reminded himself of her power. Ivy could look…smile at a man, and two hours later—without warning—there she was again…in his mind without notice, as clear as before. Her memory did not leave a man easily. Hers was a haunting presence, a surreal experience.

Was that the real reason she was still in the comfort of her home? She hired men to murder her husband, after all. Wayne wasn't sure of the legal specifics, but his feeling was she was in violation of law, even if she **could** prove she tried to stop it from happening later. Maybe he should have taken her in.

"Sixteen-thirty-seven," the *Motorola* crackled over the wind noise in the car. It was the second call for him from the dispatcher. Lost in thought, the first call had not registered in his mind.

"Go ahead, base," he answered into the heavy microphone.

"Are you familiar with the Holland farm?"

"Ten-four, I am."

"Mrs. Holland needs you to come by."

"Do you know why?"

"Actually…stand by…" there was silence on the radio as Wayne sped up the squad car. He was already going the right direction. "Sixteen-thirty-seven?"

"Go ahead."

"You won't be going to the Holland house. Mrs. Holland made the call for one of their workers."

"Okay. Where **do** I go?"

"Go past the Holland house one half mile and turn right on the dirt road. Go two miles up that road. The house will be the stucco on the left."

"Ten-four, do you have their name?"

"Negative."

Wayne replaced the "mike" to its forked hook which he had screwed onto the metal dash. He would be there quickly. The Holland farm house was less than a mile out of Cash. Their farm sprawled north and west, covering more than twenty sections. Twenty square miles of cotton.

The hired man's house was typical of many others scattered about the county. This one, Wayne noted, seemed to be a bit larger, maybe nicer on the outside. He had seen the house many times, but had never had occasion to stop there.

As he pulled off the road and on to the hard-packed dirt in front of the dwelling, a Negro woman stepped out onto the top of a three step porch. She looked perhaps thirty and—he thought—might have a pretty face if her expression was less severe. He wondered if she was angry, or just upset. He stepped out of his car.

"Hello. How're you, ma'am?"

"Are you Deputy Tinsley? They told me Deputy Tinsley would come."

"I guess I have to plead guilty to that one." He pointed to the name tag over his right shirt pocket. He smiled, but she was all business. "What can I do for you?" he added.

"I was told you was the one I should talk to."

"What seems to be the problem?"

"This is going to take a bit. Do you want to come in the house?"

He couldn't tell if her question was a question, a challenge, or a test. Did she wonder if he would come into her house, or did she really not want him to? "Sure." He started for the door as she turned and opened it. She hesitated. He motioned with his hand, "After you, ma'am."

His eyes adjusted quickly to the dark interior, and he was impressed with the simple, starkly clean and detailed items that filled the living room and kitchen.

"You want to sit at the table?"

"My favorite place." She remained stiff, in spite of his attempt at levity. Wayne took out his notebook and put it on the table. She sat across from him, erect...piercing him with dark eyes. Finally, she spoke again.

"This is very hard for me." He nodded, but didn't answer. "It's about my little girl."

"Is she okay?"

"Physically, I think so. But no, I don't think she's okay. She's with her daddy right now. I told him give me a hour at least—didn't know how long it would take you to get here."

As Wayne adjusted more to the dim light of the room he noticed her puffy, red eyes.

"What happened?"

"My name is Ruth Blankenship." She indicated the note pad. "Do you want to write that down?"

Wayne spent the entire hour with Mrs. Blankenship taking notes, clarifying questions, and listening. Finally, he flipped the notebook closed.

"I guess I'd better get out of here before Shirley gets back," he said. "I know I've already told you, but it would really help me if I could talk to her."

"I know."

"You would be present, of course."

"I'll have to think about it…talk to her some more. I just don't want her to be mortified."

"I do understand that. I just don't know how to proceed. Without the name of this **friend**—as he calls himself—I'm a little short of leads."

"I know. I don't really even know what I expected you to do. I just thought somebody ought to know."

"Don't you want that animal in jail?" he asked, harsher than intended.

"No! I want him strung up…I want him suffering and dying!" she snapped.

"Sure you do. I would, too."

"But I also don't want Shirley to have to go through all that, you know, in front of people." Silence filled the room, both lost in their thoughts. Finally Wayne spoke.

"I can't imagine what you're going through. What do you want me to do?"

"What **can** you do…with what you know now?"

He considered a moment. "Not much, I'm afraid. I can check around the bus barn…see if anyone else saw anything that day…whenever **that** day was."

"Is that it?"

"No, ma'am. I'll see if I can discreetly find out who Shirley hangs out with…what adult, I mean. Maybe I can find out…"

"She doesn't **hang out**, Mr. Tinsley."

"I'm sorry. Bad choice of words…but, when…what opportunities would she have to be around any men?"

"None. It's two miles to town, cross-country. I'm home most all the time. I just don't know. I wondered if, maybe some days, she goes to the school on the bus, but then goes somewhere else instead of school."

"Good point. Maybe you could talk to her a little more about that. Tell you what…I'll go by the school," he checked his watch, "tomorrow, and check with the teacher…he might have noticed something."

"Thank you."

"No problem." He stood, picking up his hat from the floor. "Mrs. Blankenship, I need to tell you something. Your daughter is not the first…and, truthfully, I'm almost out of time."

"Deputy?"

"Ma'am?"

"If you find out who he is, with Shirley not talking and all…what can you do?"

"Well, we probably can't get him into court. But if I know who he is, he will know I know…and he will soon learn I'm telling every human being in the country what he is. It's not enough, I know. But people around here have their own sense of justice…and all I can promise you is, as long as he stays in Texas, I'll make certain he's miserable every day for the rest of his life."

"That's something, isn't it?"

"Yes. Not much. Not enough."

"Will you really do what you say, Deputy Tinsley?" Her eyes bored into him, as when they first met.

"Of course."

"Why? Why would you do that for Shirley? For us?"

"Why wouldn't I?"

"The other girl, was she colored?"

"Yes ma'am. I'm going to find out who is doing these terrible things. I'm going to make him pay."

She peered deeply into his eyes. "I'll ask Mrs. Holland to call the teacher…let him know what's going on…so you won't scare him to death when you drive up. Now you'd better go."

On his way home, Wayne stopped at Sarge's Café in town for supper. He realized he hadn't eaten since the day before and was suddenly famished.

The chicken-fried steak and country gravy were excellent, but Wayne couldn't get the little girl out of his mind, and—half finished—he gave up and put his fork down. He sipped absently at his iced tea, trying to put some sense to the report. **Two** men? Bradley a rapist, **and** a child molester? Impossible.

In a town this size, it was impossible. All his life, Wayne had never heard of a child in the whole county being the victim of a sex crime. Not even one. And now he had two…but this little girl—a girl he had never even seen—was reporting all this to her mama. His information was all second-hand. The girl was about to get a spanking. What kid hadn't made up stories to get out of a spanking?

But not **this** kind of story. Kids didn't even know this kind of horrible thing happened in their world. However, Tinsley was about to decide he had probably been made a fool of. Mrs. Blankenship had been duped by her daughter. One fault with that thinking was that Ruth Blankenship struck Wayne as a very bright, no-nonsense woman. She would be hard to fool, he thought. She also seemed very aware…knowledgeable, about the offense suffered by her little girl. Not many parents would have picked up on the silent signals so quickly.

Well, he decided, even if he had been made a fool of, it was at least a diversion from the murder case. The details of that whole thing had taken so many turns, he knew he lost focus somewhere. He would free his mind from the whole affair for a few hours.

Then, tonight, in the quiet late-night hours at home, he would outline what he **knew**, emotions left out. He would get it all down where he could get a fresh look. He didn't want

Johnny Wilson to be guilty…and he surely didn't want him punished for something he didn't do. He didn't want Ivy to be guilty, but she already **was** a little, at least. He wanted Smith to be the murderer, but he didn't think he was.

He looked at his unfinished meal again, and smiled to himself; this is me not thinking about the case until later tonight, he thought.

"Something wrong?" asked Sarge.

"What?" Wayne looked up at the pot-bellied man in a greasy white apron.

Sarge pointed at the plate. "The food. Something wrong?"

"Oh, no. It's fine." Tinsley picked up his fork and poked at the steak. "I'm just not as hungry as I thought."

"Sure? 'Cause if it's not good, I'll make it right."

"No. Really, it's very good."

"But you're finished?"

"Yes."

Sarge picked up the plate and started to the back of the café without speaking. He walked past the garbage and dish-washing sink to the door. Curious, Wayne leaned far to his left. He heard the mumbling of quieted voices. Then, barely visible behind the bulk of Sarge, Wayne saw a hobo bolting down food as quickly as he could swallow. Sarge spoke to the man as he cleaned

Wayne's plate. When finished, the man nodded his thanks and disappeared into the darkening evening. The cook brought the plate back in and dumped it into the deep metal sink, half-filled with soapy water.

Shortly, Sarge came back to the front, wiping his hands on a dish towel. As he neared

Tinsley's table, the deputy smiled broadly.

"What!?" barked the cook.

"Nothing, Sarge. Nothing at all."

As the evening grew older, Wayne and Sarge argued politics and religion, cars and music, till past closing time. It had been a good repast for the deputy, and Sarge seemed to have enjoyed the company.

The few stores on Main Street had been closed two hours already, and a very light mist fell gently over Wayne. He looked up at a nearby streetlight, enjoying the cool spray on his face. All the tiny droplets appeared to be coming from the light, an obvious illusion, but interesting to watch.

In the car, Wayne turned the windshield wipers on briefly, then off again. He eased away from Sarge's, feeling some contentment in the time they shared, free from a world where the wrong people kill the right people and where grown men have souls so dark and evil, they prey on little children.

Moments later he pulled into his driveway. It was a perfect night to sleep. He would get back to work in the morning on the Bradley case. The night was so pleasant, Wayne didn't even feel guilty about putting that job off a few hours till morning.

The shotgun blast struck his face like a lightening bolt! His body slammed sideways onto the bench seat, blood immediately smearing against the vinyl. His body jerked involuntarily twice, then lay still. The fine mist slowly dampened his uniform, mixed with blood.

Chapter 32

Jeff swung the corral gate closed. He had already topped off three horses, and it was not yet 9:30 am. He could work three others before noon. Six head…they were almost finished out well enough to sell. Of course he, Ray, and Sam were starting others at the same time.

He had to keep the pipeline full, from untouchable rogues to finished *Thoroughbreds*. He no longer worked the Bradley job for the charm of doing cowboy work. Nor did he come just to be near Ivy Bradley. He hardly ever saw her.

He had to earn money. He had to make all he could to help support the family. He left school early most days to plow or to tend to other needs at the farm. There were only a couple of months remaining until high school graduation. Had it been much longer, he would have dropped out entirely.

Jeff and Faye Cowen had talked for hours around the kitchen table after Allen's funeral. There was only a graveside service, with a few friends and family present. That irritated some people in town, who wanted to see how good a job Palmer's Funeral Home did on Allen. And there were always those whose life assignment was to attend funerals and see how the "family held up," so they could make their report to anyone who would listen.

The meeting with his mother had surprised Jeff. She brought out all the paperwork—bills, receipts, projections—that she could find. She did not try to shield him from the truth, nor was she overly pessimistic. Three ledgers were brought to the table. One was for personal household expenses, debits and credits. The second for all farm-related items, to be used at income tax time. The third one he didn't recognize.

Faye was surgical in her approach as she explained the process of running the business of a household, and a farm. It was a quick lesson, some of which Jeff already knew. Much, he did not. His mother made it clear she was not dumping all the responsibility on him. She was making him a partner in the business of their lives. A full partner.

She was going to work at the school cafeteria. It had already been arranged. They would pool their incomes, and their energies, to keep the farm going. Whatever it took. They would go over the bills together and discuss which should be paid, and when. She had made an appointment with Mr. Reasnor at the bank for Jeff to come in and sign a signature card on her—their account, so he could write checks when necessary.

It was all business. They had cried and held each other, and cried more—for days. And now, life had to continue. They would continue to grieve on their own—in their own ways. But for the present, they had to survive.

Randy had not left his room except to pick at his food during meals. They went over what each of them could do to help the youngest member of their family get back to his life. They couldn't think of much beyond giving him a little time, and being supportive.

Jeff was impressed with how knowledgeable Faye was about things he always assumed his dad had handled alone. When they came across a copy of Allen's insurance policy, Jeff was suddenly uplifted. His mood was quickly dashed, however, when Faye unceremoniously threw the policy in the trash.

"What…?" he began.

"They don't pay on this type of death."

When all was boiled down at the end, there was one thing very clear to Jeff. They owed more money every month than they made. Even with Faye working in the cafeteria, their incoming numbers were too small. It boggled his mind, discovering the expenses of keeping up a home and a farm. Allen had used up most of their available credit. Jeff had to get a job…another job.

"Jeff!"

His head jerked up. He had not realized he was still holding the top rail of the corral gate with both gloved hands, his head bowed in thought. He looked toward the voice and saw her standing at the back door.

"Yes, ma'am?" he called back.

"Can you come to the house a minute, please?"

"Sure." He started toward the house. She used to come out to the barn. He wondered if it was hard for her to go out there now, after what happened to Mr. Bradley.

"I'm sorry, Jeff. I know you're busy."

"It's okay. I was taking a little break."

"I saw. You look tired."

"No, I'm fine. Did you need me to do something for you?" Jeff was immediately aware of the dress she wore. It was sleeveless, bright, and looked cool. He had never seen it before. He had never even seen her bare arms before, he realized. The dress made her look younger.

"I didn't need you to **do** anything. I wanted to talk to you, though." She motioned to her sun-room. "I've already poured you some iced tea."

"Thank you," he said, sitting in the nearest chair. She patted him on the back and sat across the table. Her legs crossed as automatically as the lids of her large eyes blinked.

"Jeff, I was just watching you out there. If you ever need to talk…?"

"I'm doing okay."

"Of course you are. I just never got a chance…I'm really sorry…for your loss." The expression in her deep brown eyes seemed genuine to Jeff. "I can't even pretend to know how you must feel."

"I don't even know myself, sometimes. I guess numb would be a way to say it. Like my brain is numb."

"You know I'm here for you, Jeff. Don't you?"

Actually, he didn't. He hadn't even considered the possibility. "Yes, ma'am. Thank you."

"You're welcome. Do you want to talk about it now? About your father?"

"No. If you don't mind. I'd really rather not."

"Of course, maybe later…some other time."

Jeff checked his *Timex* unconsciously. There was so much work…

"I suppose you're in a hurry." She pointed at his watch.

"Sorry. Didn't mean to be rude. I really like talking with you. It's just…?"

"I know. Time. There's never enough of it."

"I just need to finish up here, so I can be home by noon."

"Okay, I'll be brief. I've really been watching you the past couple of weeks." She smiled broadly.

"Really? Is something wrong?"

"No, of course not. I've been watching how you work the horses…from the window here. You have a really gentle touch."

"Oh. I'm almost through with three of them."

"I noticed." She uncrossed her legs and stood up. As she walked to the kitchen, Jeff noticed how tan her legs were. She had always seemed so pale and fragile, and the color looked good on her. She reached the cabinets and stretched as high as she could, groping the top shelves, her slender fingers working away at a small red tin can, until it tilted over into her grasp.

When she turned back around she met Jeff's gaze and smiled broadly at him before returning her attention to the can. Jeff identified the can as the kind baking soda came in. She wrestled the lid off and plucked some dollar bills from it.

She walked quickly back to the sun-room, counting the money. Her bare feet touched the floor lightly, without a sound, as she moved. Jeff thought he wasn't in a **real** big hurry to get back to work.

"Here," she said, handing him six one-dollar bills. He initiated an objection with the shake of his head, but Ivy cut him off.

"Take it. It's not a gift. This is just an advance on your work. You'll have more than that coming by next Saturday."

She took his hand in hers, opening his fingers to expose his palm. She placed the six dollars in it, then squeezed his fingers back down, cupping his hand between her own.

"It's your money, Jeff. You've earned it. Remember our agreement. We're partners."

"Yes, ma'am." He didn't pull away from her soft grip, and her touch was electrical. He could feel his neck, then face, flush warm. He supposed he could spare a few more minutes…

When he arrived home, Jeff found his mother at the kitchen table. She was deep in thought, poring over a ledger. He walked up behind her and placed his hands on her shoulders. They were tense, and he kneaded them a moment before speaking. "You okay, Mama?"

She reached a hand up and grasped Jeff's, still on her shoulder. She squeezed his hand gently, then patted it. "Sit down, son."

He obeyed, sitting in his usual place, arms folded on the table as he leaned forward slightly. He knew rushing his mother would do no good. Faye Cowen did things in her own time.

"Jeff, I've really come to appreciate your maturity. You've dealt with some really terrible things of late. I know it hasn't been fair to you, but you also know life isn't always fair." Her mind wandered for a moment.

"What is it, Mama?"

"I've been wrestling with something…about whether or not I should tell you…"

"About what?"

"I wasn't going to," she continued, as though he hadn't spoken, "but I think you have a right to know."

He didn't interrupt. His brow furrowed. He was not ready for more bad news, yet. And whatever his mother was leading up to didn't sound good.

"I've told you I don't know why your dad…why he did what he did."

He said nothing, so she continued.

"I still can't tell you **why**, but I can tell you what, I believe, brought him to that…crossroad."

"Okay."

"The problem is…what set him off…what caused him to run out of here that night…affects you, too."

"What could be that bad?" The first thought he had was he and Allen both had cancer. He felt sick in his stomach. Was he dying?

"That's just it, Jeff. It doesn't have to be that bad. With Allen, it came down to how he reacted to shocking news about himself."

"And I have the same shocking news?"

"Basically."

"Am I dying?"

"No. Oh, goodness no. Nothing like that."

"Then what is it?"

"First Jeff, I must have your word about something."

"What?"

"After I tell you…this," she pointed to the ledger, "you will stay here in the house. You'll stay with me…days if necessary…until you **know** you're okay. Until **I** know you're okay."

Jeff wished she would just say it. His stomach was in knots.

"But…"

"Promise me! Or I'll burn this book and never speak of it again."

"Okay. I promise."

She sighed heavily, opened the ledger, and turned it around in front of her son. "Read this, start to finish. It's written by Mrs. Wilson. You won't make any connection until near the end."

He looked at Faye, checking her eyes for sanity. She placed her hand over his, holding tightly to it.

"Read. When you're finished, we'll talk."

Chapter 33

His only emotion, only sensation, was of confusion. Darkness was total—not only difficult to penetrate—but a presence. An omniscient pall excluded everything else. As consciousness slowly returned, a blurry awareness crept closer, short of clarity.

Then came fear. Not terror, this fear—but the essence of foreboding…of not knowing, or feeling anything, save the darkness. As he tried to establish the parameters of his existence, even movement was a challenge.

He tried to lift his left arm, but something pulled back in opposition. He **could** move it, though. Although it wouldn't smoothly go where his muscles intended, it did move! It was a revelation for Wayne, the movement of his body, for until that moment he had not consciously acknowledged where he might be, who he was, or under what circumstances he existed.

There was no pain, but pressure compressed his entire head. He moved his legs tentatively, discovering they worked okay as far as he could tell. His right arm moved about easily.

"Well, hero! I was beginning to think you was gonna' siesta all day long."

"Bill?"

"No. It's your grandmother," came the deep masculine reply.

"Good. I was afraid they stuck me with this dumb deputy I know." The pressure on his head was even more severe when he tried to talk. His mouth moved only with exceptional effort, his tongue was thick and immobile.

"Glad to see they left your sarcastic sense of humor when they blew out the rest of your brains," said Bill. Wayne could hear a change in the direction from which the other man's voice came. Bill was standing over him. He felt the gentle touch of a rough hand on his left forearm.

"You okay, buddy?"

"I can't move that arm very well," mumbled Tinsley.

"Can't imagine why. There's not but about forty-five pieces of tubes and wires and tape and stuff stuck to it. Charles Atlas wouldn't 'a been able to move his, either."

"Bill?"

"Yeah?"

"What's going on? Where is this? What's wrong with me?"

"You don't remember nothing?"

"Nothing. No, wait…I ate at Sarge's, then came home. I remember that. Then…now, that's all."

"Too bad. I was kinda' hoping you could fill me in a little."

"You haven't answered a single question, Bill. What's…?" he sputtered. "Why can't I talk? I sound like I'm in a jar."

"Okay, I'll tell you whatever…"

"Wait!"

"What?"

"Bill, do me a favor."

"Sure Wayne. Anything."

"If that's your hand still on my arm, would you put it in your pocket or somewhere? What if a nurse walks in?"

"Wise guy," he muttered, but moved his hand. "I outta' call a nurse, and just as she walks in, plant a big old juicy kiss right on your forehead."

They both laughed lightly, although Wayne's facial muscles felt awkward doing so. A lengthy silence followed, then Wayne finally asked what he **really** wanted to know. "Am I going to be alright, Bill?"

"Sure you are!" he boomed.

"Bill…"

"Okay, here's the deal…oh, I guess you don't know…you got shot."

"Shot! Who…?"

"Don't know. Anyway, the thing is, you got shot—shoulder, neck, and face—with a shotgun."

Tinsley absorbed the information, then asked, "So why am I still alive? I **am** alive, right?"

"Yeah, you're alive. You're alive because whoever shot you doesn't hunt much."

"If he shot me in the face, I'd say he was pretty accurate."

"Didn't say he doesn't know how to shoot…I said he ain't no hunter."

"You're not gonna' make this easy for me, are you?"

"You see, the guy shot you with what I figure is about a number seven—maybe eight, shot. You'd a been in trouble if you was a quail."

"Bird shot? Somebody shot me with a load of bird shot?"

"I know, sort of embarrassing, huh?"

"That wasn't exactly what I was thinking. Bill?"

"Still here."

"Am I blind?" The three seconds it took Bill Lightsey to answer seemed more like hours to Wayne.

"They don't think so."

"Then why can't I see?" Wayne's voice showed signs of building irritation…fear.

"Hard to see through those five miles of rags they got wrapped all over your head."

"Rags?"

"Ace bandages. Sorry, Wayne. I was so excited when you woke up…I never thought how scary that might be…not knowing what's going on."

"Disconcerting."

"Do what?"

"Nothing. Why did you say they don't **think** I'm blind? Can't they tell?"

"The way I understand it is the pellets missed both your eyes…thank God."

"Really. So, what…?"

"You took the hardest hit on the left side of your face and temple."

"So?"

"Doc, he says there's this nerve that runs under the muscles in your temple…I guess a pretty important connector-nerve to your eyes."

"And if that nerve is damaged enough?"

"Well, then you could be blind, but they don't think you are."

"Why?"

"Before they wrapped you up like a mummy, the doc shined a light in your eyes. He said your eyes responded to it."

"Then I'm **not** blind."

"Well, probably not. Doc also said that light in the eyes thing isn't very conclusive. They won't know till they unwrap you. I guess you and the doc will know at the same time."

"Go get him. Let's do it."

"He's gone to get something for dinner. Said he'd be back around one o'clock."

Wayne sighed, resolute in the knowledge nobody in the hospital had the courage to call Doctor Mack away from a meal.

"Tell me about the shooting, Bill."

"Okay, your shooter was hiding behind your house. Apparently, when you pulled up, he stepped to the corner and blasted you."

"Foot prints?"

"Naw, it was raining. Nothing but dimples in the sand. Nothing distinguishable."

"What else?"

"The bird shot hit the left front corner post of your car and shattered the driver-side window and the windshield."

"Go on."

"I figure it was a long barrel shot gun…the pattern was too tight for a sawed-off at that range. Anyway, you took a few pellets, and a pot-load of glass, mostly in the face. They picked and plucked stuff outta' your head for about two hours."

"Sounds fun."

"Yeah. They pulled one little rotten-looking thing out, but I convinced them it was your front tooth, and they put it back."

"Really funny," grumbled Tinsley.

"Anyways, that's about all we know, I guess. Neighbor heard the shot and called it in…didn't see nothing, though."

"Naturally."

"Actually, they just thought someone was shooting at stray dogs, and thought they ought to report it."

"That happens a lot."

"Yeah, but when I noticed the address, I tried to call you…"

"I was busy."

"Yes, you were. I'll tell you the truth, hero, when I came up to the car, there was so much blood—well, I thought we'd lost you. Wayne…do you have any idea who did this?"

"No."

"You sure?"

"I think so. My mind is a bit out of kilter right now."

"So you're back to normal then?" He started to laugh.

"All except my eyes," Wayne said softly. "I have to admit, I'm afraid of being blind." Silence followed again, thick and heavy. Finally he added, "My tongue feels awful. It's hard to talk…"

"Well, they say you nearly bit it off when you got shot in the head," Bill said, then he added, "you big sissy."

Chapter 34

Jeff's hair looked more like a rough-stacked shock of corn than tresses. Having just bathed, he towel-dried it and left the bathroom without combing. His thoughts were miles from his appearance, and he had every hour of every day for the coming week planned.

Faye chuckled when he entered the living room. "I see you're starting a new hair style."

He felt his head, then grinned. "Guess I am." He used his hands, trying to press the hair against his scalp. It resisted. "I need you to cut this when you get time," he said. "When it's burred, it's a lot less trouble."

"Sure." She looked back down at the pieces of cloth as she sewed them together—the beginnings of the top of her next quilt. She didn't know when she'd find time for a quilting bee now, but at least she would have the tedious work done. "Jeff," she said without looking up, "Will you do me a favor?"

"Sure. What?"

"I need you to go by the hospital. I want you to visit Deputy Tinsley."

"What about?"

"I would like you to see how he is…see if he needs anything."

"Okay, but why us? Shouldn't his family…"

"Ordinarily. But while Wayne was overseas during the war his parents were killed in a car wreck. I'm sure you've heard that."

"Yes, ma'am."

"Well, he has no brothers or sisters, either. If there are any other family members, they would be distant."

"You've known him a long time, huh, mama?"

"Oh, yes. Since we were little kids. He doesn't have anyone to really do for him, now. I think helping him is the Christian thing to do. Don't you?"

"Yes, ma'am. But, wouldn't **you** rather go? You know him a lot better than me."

Faye glanced up from her work. She read no insinuation, no unanswered question on his face. "I would go myself, son, but I don't think it would be appropriate...for several reasons."

"Okay. I won't be long."

"Comb your hair first. Can't have you scaring the nurses at the hospital."

After repairing his hair, Jeff stopped again on his way out. "Why did he stay around here, do you think? No family or anything..."

"Any number of reasons. His wife is buried here...that's a comfort to some people. And, too, this is home to him. Did you know he used to own his own farm?"

"No. I guess I never thought about it."

"It wasn't very big. Maybe a hundred acres. But with the depression...then his wife's long illness and hospital bills...it was just too much." Faye noticed Jeff had settled onto the edge of the sofa, listening closely. "Why do you ask?"

"Just curious. I don't know him very well, but I've noticed some things about him."

"Really? Like what?"

"Well, when he talks to me, he talks **to** me...not down **at** me. Do you know what I mean?"

"I think so."

"Another thing is harder to explain..."

Faye stopped her sewing and placed the material pieces in her lap.

Jeff was in a rare talkative mood, and she knew she should give him her full attention. Faye had recently promised herself she wouldn't miss the slightest hidden meaning…the tiniest message from her boys, now. She had to be disciplined, tireless, and watchful for signs of anything out of the ordinary. She shouldn't have let Allen stay gone so long…

"What Jeff? What's hard to explain?"

"When he talks to people, whoever they are, it's like he's at home with them…"

"I see."

"No, that's not it. It's like, well, one day he was visiting with Mrs. Wiley at school…"

"The English teacher?"

"Yeah. They sounded like two college professors talking…books, and poetry…stuff I never even heard of, and I'm a senior."

""He likes to read, I guess."

"Yes, ma'am. But I've also heard him talking to hired hands and people who don't have no education, and he just talks to them like we're talking."

"Okay?"

"I mean it's like one of them lizards that changes colors to what they get on."

"A chameleon?"

"Yeah. But not in a bad way. It's not like he's putting on."

"You do the same thing, in a way."

"Really?" Jeff looked skeptical.

"Sure. You talk different to Randy than to me. And you're different with rough men than with ladies. You know when to speak and—more important—when to shut up."

"I didn't realize I was even doing that."

"Wayne probably doesn't either. It's something you have in common. You care about others…more than about yourself. You care if others are comfortable around you. It's a special gift. As you get older, your gift will grow with you, like Wayne's did."

"I wouldn't mind that…being more like him."

"Or maybe," she said, "he'll get lucky and become more like you."

The mellow rumble of the flat-head Ford had a pleasing sound with it's glass-packed mufflers bubbling deep tones from dual pipes into the late evening air. Jeff liked the car, but he knew he was wasting valuable time because of it. He was having to pile irrigation tubes onto the "20" Farmall tractor and haul them to the various places where they were to be set. The tractor was slow, costing him valuable time. They needed a pickup.

He hadn't mentioned it to his mother yet. They couldn't incur more debt. He would talk to her about it when he had a solution.

When he pulled into the hospital parking lot, daylight was folding itself away, and lights were coming on in various rooms of the building. The hospital was built of yellow, chalky-looking brick and stood two-stories high, making it the largest and tallest building in the County, except for the Court House.

At the front desk, a middle-aged woman with spectacles hung from a chain around her neck met him with a smile. She was average in almost every imaginable way, and Jeff couldn't remember if he had ever met her before. At the desk he changed his mind. The very ordinary woman bore an extraordinary knot on her left ear lobe, large enough to give the appearance she had two lobes on the one ear, one hanging onto the other. Jeff was certain he had not met the woman before.

"Howdy," she said.

"Hi. How're you?"

"Good, thanks. Help you?"

"Yes, please. Deputy Wayne Tinsley's room number?"

"He's in two-eleven. Go up the stairs and turn right. He's in the second room on the left."

"Thanks." Jeff jogged up the steps two at a time, locating the room immediately. The door stood ajar, and he saw Tinsley lying in the bed. At least, he assumed it was Tinsley. Big, white gauze pads were attached to the left side of his face and head, as well as smaller and widely assorted other bandages on his neck and bare shoulder.

"Who's there?" came the familiar voice from the bed.

"It's me, Jeff," he answered. Wayne was looking right at him. Why would he ask who he was?

"Jeff Cowan?"

"Yes, sir."

"Good. Come on in. You here to see someone in the hospital?"

Jeff hesitated. Wayne was looking at him…in his direction…but it was like he was looking through him. "Uh, yes, sir. I came to see you."

"Well, that's real nice. A good surprise."

Jeff knew Wayne had been shot. But he was not prepared for what he saw…so many bandages, uncovered cuts…and almost everyplace on the left side of Wayne's face not covered with bandages was bruised deep blue.

"Are you doing okay?" he asked, lamely.

"Yeah, I'm fine…except for when the pain medicine wears off. I get a little cranky then. Come on in. You're not in yet, are you?"

"No, sir," he began, stepping inside the room.

"Have a seat. I believe there's one over here by the bed. Thanks for coming."

"Sure." Jeff realized he had no idea what to say. He sat in the straight-backed chair, and cleared his throat.

"How do I look, Jeff?"

"Fine. Well, not real good. You don't know?"

"I know how I feel, but I don't know how I look."

Jeff didn't know if he should ask. "Why, Mr. Tinsley?"

"They haven't brought me a mirror yet. A friend of mine was in for most of the day, but he's the biggest liar in the world. I thought maybe you could give me an honest opinion."

"Mirror? So you can see okay?"

"Well, not at this moment. They just did this procedure where they put a dye of some kind in my eyes. Doc said if there were any tiny scratches or glass slivers in them, the dye would help him spot them."

"How did it turn out?"

"Good. I got a clean bill of health…literally. The problem, though, is that the dye they use blurs your vision something awful. I can see forms now, but that's about all. You could have been President Eisenhower for all I knew when you walked in."

"How long will that last?"

"Just a few hours. That's what they told me, anyway."

"Good. I'll bet you'll be glad."

"Sure will. Say, you didn't finish answering my question. How do I look? How 'not really good' am I?"

"Your head is…well, the left side of your head is covered in bandages, so I really can't tell about underneath them. There are several minor scratches, and you're pretty bruised up." "Sounds like I've been shot, huh?"

"It doesn't look so much like you got shot, as it looks like you were in an explosion."

"So you think my bid for the homecoming queen might be on hold?"

Jeff laughed. "I'm not sure you had the votes **before** you got shot."

That time they both laughed.

"I really am glad you came by, Jeff."

"I'm glad to do it, but I can't take credit for being thoughtful. Mama asked me to come by and check on you."

Tinsley lay still, eyes closed.

Jeff continued, "She knew you don't have any family close around here."

"No, I don't. But I do have friends. Several folks have come by for a few minutes just to check in…others have called the desk leaving messages. Good friends are almost as good as family. Almost."

"Do they know who shot you?"

"No. No idea, really."

"Did it hurt? Getting shot, I mean."

"Didn't feel a thing."

"Wow."

"It's not because I'm tough, Jeff. It just happened so fast, I didn't even know what had happened. Slept right through the whole thing. Truth is, it has been pretty painful after the fact…here in the hospital."

"I'll bet."

"But don't tell anybody. I've already been called a sissy once today."

"Really?"

Wayne laughed lightly, but it hurt his face. "It was a friend of mine."

"Can I ask you something else?" asked Jeff. Although Wayne could'nt see the young man's face, the change in his voice was apparent.

"What is it, Jeff?"

"When you saw my dad..." he paused. "It was just you in the room with him. You and him...till the others arrived..."

"What do you need to know, son?"

"Someday...not now...but some time, will you tell me about it. About what you saw?"

"Jeff, I don't think it would be good..."

"No. I didn't mean that, what you're thinking. I don't ever want to know the details. Imagining...dreaming is awful enough." Jeff became angry with himself. He knew his eyes were watering, and he wiped at them with his shirt sleeve. Thankfully, the deputy couldn't see him, he thought.

"Then what?"

"About the room. The bed. The chairs in the room. I just want to know what it was like...for him...during those last hours. Does that sound stupid...or weird?"

"No, it doesn't. Sometimes not knowing is worse than knowing. Yes, I'll talk to you when you're ready. I think it's a little early right now though. Don't you?"

"Yes, sir, I do. I just wanted to know if you could do that sometime?"

"Sure. There is one thing I can tell you right now, though. On the table by the bed, his wallet was laid out. He had a picture pulled out of it and laid on the table where he could look at it. It was a picture of you and Randy and your mother in the back yard of your place. There was also a pad of paper and a pencil. He was thinking of your family...he wanted to write...in those last moments. He loved you all very much. He was just mixed up."

Jeff's eyes no longer watered. They silently poured out onto his cheeks and onto his shirt. He didn't wipe them away. The silence in the room was intense, but not uncomfortable. Wayne felt no guilt in the lie concerning the picture or the paper pad. It wasn't in his nature to lie easily, but he heard a need in Jeff's voice.

For the second time that day Wayne felt a masculine hand on his forearm. Jeff held to Wayne for several moments as he gathered himself, his hand searching out the human contact he needed so desperately. It was so hard being the man of the house. It was difficult keeping up the appearance of strength he didn't feel.

Strangely, Jeff didn't feel uncomfortable touching the other man in a way that would ordinarily have felt far too intimate. And for several moments they remained, silent and alone together.

Wayne didn't tell him to move his hand.

Chapter 35

Disoriented and frightened, Johnny could not free himself from those same emotions at his every awakening. The rattle of a door, a boot heel striking concrete, unfamiliar voices…all were sounds that brought him wide awake, in a state of near-panic.

He tried to fight the feelings…the emotions. Maybe a light in the cell would help, he reasoned. His eyes had accustomed themselves to the absence of light days ago, but the floor and the unfamiliar corners were always in total darkness. The only light was that which managed to squeeze itself through a one foot square hole in the door.

He determined he would be brave. He would not allow them to see his fear. But, after a few days, he realized no one cared. No one came, except for when Benningfield or Deputy Tinsley talked to him. Otherwise, every day was the same. Bravery, cowardice, kindness, and evil were all the same in the darkness.

He frequently walked tight little circles in the small cell to physically tire himself. He hoped it would help him sleep on the concrete floor. They provided him with an old army blanket, but it afforded little comfort.

Jailers called his cell the hole. The hole was usually reserved for fighting or otherwise difficult prisoners, or for one who just needed to be "taught a lesson."

The hole was on the end of the jail where Negro prisoners were kept, and when white prisoners acted up, they were put there, too. That was part of their punishment, actually…being in the colored section of the facility.

Johnny was an accused murderer, and they hadn't housed one of those in years.

Besides, he had killed a white man, and tried to kill one of their own deputies. He could rot in there for all they cared.

He was fed when, and if, the old Negro trustee remembered him—and if he felt like it. Johnny Wilson didn't care. He scarcely ate the food anyway. The pinto beans weren't particularly bad, but his stomach was tied in so many knots he could hardly keep food down.

He tried to imagine what might be going on outside the cubicle. As badly as he despised the confinement, there was a warped sense of security in its never-changing solitude. It was hard for Johnny to believe, only months ago he was a high school student with a loving mother, a little sister, a really caring step-father, and a home.

His step-father, Isaac, was either in the jail near him or already in prison. They had not been allowed to see each other, and Johnny's calls in the darkness had all gone unheeded. Whatever else he lacked in information, Johnny was sure he wouldn't see Isaac for a long, long time…if ever again. And with Isaac gone, everything was gone.

Johnny allowed himself the smallest glimmer of hope Deputy Tinsley might find out who killed that old…what word was bad enough to describe Mr. Bradley? Johnny's mother would have said Satan was walking around in that man's fancy clothes. But he hadn't heard another word from the deputy, and his hopes turned to despair.

His mama had told Johnny about his real daddy, but it wasn't necessary. Johnny remembered him as cruel…a bad person, filled with whiskey and evil. Johnny secretly looked for signs of his daddy in himself, afraid he would become like him.

He would always hate the day his mama died, but he took some comfort knowing she hadn't seen her son locked up for murder. He tried to not feel sorry for himself, but as the days stretched toward his inevitable execution, depression covered him like a heavy blanket.

Every thought…every idea, had to penetrate a dark shroud of hopelessness, just to rise to a level of consciousness.

"Okay, but I don't get it," came the jailer's voice from down the hall. Johnny heard the metal lock clunk open and the squeak of iron hinges as an out-of-sight gateway was opened. Almost immediately, it swung closed with a clang. The lock was re-bolted.

"You're on your own in there, boy. I ain't got the time to be playing nursemaid."

"Yes, sir," came a voice through the darkness. The soft clacking of boot heels on concrete grew nearer, stopping short of Johnny's cell.

"Johnny. Johnny Wilson?" came a whispered call.

"Here I is!" bellowed a huge man with silver hair. "What you doin' in here, white boy…you lost?"

Other inmates joined in, taunting…but from shadows where they could not be recognized. Finally, a dark brown arm appeared through the bars of a nearby cell. A forefinger on the end of it pointed at Johnny Wilson's hole.

"Thanks," the subdued voice whispered quietly. There was no response.

Johnny stood, face against the barred hole in his door. He could not see on either side of it, and the face appeared so suddenly he jerked back, startled. They had been within inches of each other.

The sudden closeness surprised Jeff as well, and both he and Johnny eased back closer to the opening. There was some small familiarity in the white face, but Johnny didn't recognize his visitor.

"Johnny?" Jeff said again.

"Yeah. Who's there?"

"It's Jeff Cowen."

"Jeff Cowen?"

"Yeah, from across the highway from your house. We ride the same school bus. You hid in my barn." Johnny inched closer, curious but wary. Jeff spoke again. "I can barely even see you in there."

"Is that gonna' be a joke?"

"A joke? I don't understand…"

"You know, one of those smile-so-I-can-see-you jokes. That's what I was wondering."

"No, I just can't see you very well. Don't they have a light in there?"

"No, sir. No light. It's like this all the time."

"Have you been in there ever since they picked you up?"

"Yes, sir. Except for one day at court, and one day with Mr. Tinsley. Since the day you turned me in."

"Don't do that."

"Don't do what?"

"Don't call me sir. I'm your age. About. And turning you in was the right thing to do."

"What're you doin' here? You don't belong in here."

""I needed to see you. I need to talk to you about something."

"You need to talk to **me**?" Johnny was incredulous. Was it a trick, his being here? A sheriff's trick to make him say things...to get him to confess?

"Yeah. But I don't know exactly how to start..."

"What day is this, Mr. Cowen?"

"It's a...it's Tuesday night."

"Tuesday **night**? I just been wondering."

"Johnny, please!"

"Mr. Jeff, me and you don't have nothing' to talk about. Why are you here?"

"Listen, if you're gonna' call me **Mr.** Jeff, I'm gonna' call you **Mr.** Johnny. How'd you like that?" Jeff's voice showed building aggravation.

"I guess I don't rightly know how I'd feel about that. Ain't nobody ever called me that."

"Then stop it. Okay?" Johnny didn't answer. "Listen to what I tell you. Then decide if we have anything to talk about."

"Okay." Silence followed. Jeff was emotionally charging his batteries for what he needed to talk about. He would have to speak quietly enough so the other prisoners didn't hear.

"I'm still listenin,' Mr., uh...Jeff. Sorry."

Jeff sighed, then sucked in a deep breath. It was harder than he had imagined. "What would you say if I told you we was kin?" There, he said it.

Johnny's mouth opened. He would have laughed out loud, but for something in Jeff's expression. He slowly closed his mouth, looking for…for something…to explain the presence of the crazy white boy. He stared boldly into the eyes of the other. Framed in the harsh, square, barred window, Johnny could find no lie, no joke in the face of Jeff Cowen.

"What are you talking about? Why are you here? What do you want?"

"Listen, this is **hard** for me, saying this stuff. Being here. I've wrestled with this for days."

"Say what you gotta' say, then."

Jeff grabbed the two vertical bars of the small window and lowered his gaze. "My dad…Allen Cowen…he was…" he shook his head, "…you ain't gonna' believe this…he was a half-brother to your mother."

He was right. Johnny **didn't** believe it. He stood, the shock of just **hearing** such a thing held him speechless. He would not consider such a…Jeff **was** crazy!

"I've **seen** your daddy, and he's a white man. Why are you doing this? You don't bring my mama into this…" He forced himself to lower his voice. "You don't know **nothing** about my mama."

"More than you might imagine, but you're right…I really didn't know her. I'm sorry about what happened."

Johnny stared, openly unhinged. "Thanks," he muttered. Why were they doing this, he wondered again.

"Johnny, I know how you feel. I really do. I only found out about this a few nights ago myself."

The prisoner stared, but didn't respond.

"And I promise you, I resisted a lot more than you're doing right now. I raised cane and yelled and argued and kicked furniture and nearly went nuts. Everything I ever thought was real, all of a sudden, wasn't."

"I don't understand any of this," Johnny said, finally. "This is all crazy."

"It's even crazier than you think. I ain't never in my life even **heard** of anything like I'm gonna' tell you."

"Then you tell me. Start wherever you need to start and go to right now, in this jail."

"Okay."

"I'm a going to try and listen, quiet-like, till you finish."

"Okay."

"Okay. **Then** we'll call the crazy house people to come give you a ride."

"You **said** you'd be quiet. So, be quiet! You can do—or believe—whatever you want when I'm through. But first, just stay shut up so I can get this out."

"I'm shut. Go ahead."

For twenty minutes Jeff talked, explaining the ledger and its contents, the unplanned birth of Allen and his illegal adoption by the Cowens...of the unbelievable coincidence of Johnny's mother and Allen crossing paths. He even told of Allen's suicide, with great difficulty. Jeff worked hard, telling the story as accurately and as objectively as he could. He spoke in a low monotone voice, as though reciting something from memory, which helped him keep his own emotions in check.

When he completed his story, Jeff raised his head. Johnny's hands also gripped the vertical bars in the window, just below Jeff's. His head was lowered, eyes closed. The silence lasted almost a full minute. Finally Jeff spoke again.

"Johnny?"

"Hmmm?"

"Johnny, you okay?" he whispered hoarsely.

"Yeah. It's just that...I don't know...it's more than I can take in all at once."

"I know."

"Soon as I think I've got it all wrapped up in my mind, another thought comes flying in...it just goes on and on."

"I feel the same way. I still haven't settled on how I'm supposed to feel."

"You want to know something?"

"What?"

"I should be dancing a jig. This is like a Negro comedy. One where these white people find out they ain't so white after all. And it's the worse thing in the world. That **should** be funny."

"Should be?"

"Yeah, but it ain't. I feel bad, and I don't know exactly why. I'm sorry how your father...about him."

"Thanks. That's a pretty awful thing for us to have in common."

"Yeah."

"Johnny, my daddy was a good man," Jeff said. "He was good to my mama, and to me and my brother. He fed hungry people at the back door whenever they showed up..."

"That's good."

"I don't know **why** he did what he did. He always said he wasn't prejudiced. He used the word nigger—no offense—sometimes, and so have I. I never **meant** nothing by it. He didn't either. All the grownups I ever knew used that word to describe...well, colored people. But daddy never said a hateful word, a mean thing, about anyone, no matter who or what they were."

"What're you trying to say?"

"If daddy wasn't prejudiced, why did he hate himself so bad—when he found out about...you know, what he was...why did he hate that so bad that he would...take his own life?"

"Maybe it wasn't hate. Maybe it was scared."

Jeff looked through the bars at the face he could scarcely see, not answering.

"Jeff, do you ever talk to Deputy Tinsley?"

"Sometimes."

"Do you know if he's still working on this murder?"

"Shoot, I shoulda' already told you. I heard he don't think you're guilty and he has a possible suspect in his mind."

"Really?"

"No kidding. And just last week, somebody shot him…"

"The suspect?"

"No, Tinsley."

"Somebody shot the deputy? Is he okay?"

"Yeah. He's gonna' be fine."

"I sure hope so."

"I didn't know you even knew him, except he arrested you."

"I don't, really. But he's the only person out of all these cops who seems to care if I'm guilty or not—and him with less reason to care than any of them."

"Why?"

"I resisted his arrest. Judge says he should'a shot me. Hey, before you go?"

"Yeah?"

"What kin arc **we?**"

"We're cousins…half-cousins, actually."

Johnny shook his head. "I'm just gonna' sit here in my corner now and remind myself this is just a big old dream…that's all."

Chapter 36

Wayne signed a release before the hospital staff agreed to let him leave. His departure was much too soon, and they would not be responsible if he bled to death on the way home, but he was going stir-crazy lying in bed with so much to do...so little time.

"You're just asking for trouble, Wayne," nurse Richards barked, hands resting knuckles-down on broad hips. "Let someone else take care of this business. You're not in any shape to go traipsing off after the likes of those that killed Mr. Bradley and almost did the same for you."

"I'm fine Beatrice. You're very kind, but I've got things to do."

Wayne had had far too much time to think about recent events, and too little time to do anything about them. He had to do **something.** He had promised the colored lady...what was her name? Mrs. Blankenship? He had promised her he'd talk to the school teacher about her daughter's attack.

He knew that particular crime wasn't in the local spotlight—or even of much importance to most people, but he **did** give his word. He flipped his hat up automatically, only to have it slide off the remaining bandages. He smirked, shaking his head slightly. Maybe these hospital people knew a little more about his condition than he had credited them. He didn't feel very focused.

Moments later he tossed the hat absently into the seat of his squad car. He stared, surprised at the condition of the interior. He hadn't seen it since the shooting, and Bill had a new window and windshield installed while Wayne was in the hospital, but it hadn't been cleaned.

Dark blood stained the tan vinyl seat. Broken glass lay in the crack between the seat and the backrest, and more filled the floorboard. Blood splatters covered the passenger side of the car…on the dash, the door, the glass. His blood.

He felt an uneasiness in his stomach. The sight of the car was a stark reminder to him of how close he had come to dying, how nearly another human came to ending his life.

Wayne recognized the feeling in his stomach as deep, burning anger. He had seen many men lose control of their actions because they could not deal with those feelings he now felt. He would have to be careful.

Tinsley brushed away several pieces of glass from his seat and eased gently inside the car. It was just after 10:00 am, according to his *Timex,* and the wind was already picking up. He paused to wind the watch, not remembering the last time he had handled that particular chore. It was still running, so it could not have been too long ago. Time had been an oblique object for him the past couple of days.

The rear-view mirror pointed almost straight up, and he adjusted it. He had already put the transmission shifter in gear when he paused. He put the car back in Park, and readjusted the mirror, pointing it directly at himself.

He studied the image several moments, taking account of the stitches on the side of his face, and where hair had been shaved off the left side of his head. His eyes were circled with black and green bruises. Most of the left side of his face was freckled with small black scabs.

"Okay," he spoke to himself quietly. "Ohh…kay." He replaced the mirror, backing out of the hospital parking space without looking again. "First, I'll talk to the teacher…who probably knows nothing anyway…then I'm going to take care of this…this…" The roar of the engine drowned out his words, as wind whistled through the open window.

The colored school house was less than a mile from the hospital, located behind the whites' school, near the bus barn. Wayne had not achieved nearly the speed he desired before having to brake to go around the school building. Old re-capped tires squalled against the bricks as he swerved quickly around the corner. He didn't know the colored school teacher's name, but that really didn't matter. He wouldn't be hard to spot.

Wayne pulled the squad car within thirty feet of the front door of the Army barracks- turned-school. Dust boiled around the car as it slid to a stop, curled up, then drifted away on southwest winds.

Class was in session. Standing in the brightness of the sunlight, Wayne couldn't see inside the school, although the door stood ajar. He stepped to the porch, then just inside the door, the drone of a single male voice the only sound other than his lightly shifting feet. The voice stopped.

Darkness began to fade into a dim gray as Tinsley's eyes adjusted to the change. Gradually, forms took shape…tiny little people to his right—the front of the room—and ever-increasingly larger students as he looked from right to left. No one spoke. Every student had turned in their desks, staring at him. In the front of the room, Denson Shields also stared, his jaw sagging like a worn out hinge.

Wayne had not considered it, but as he looked at those looking at him, he realized it was probably the first time any of them had ever seen a white person in their school. And this particular white person—covered in bandages and stitches and bruises and a uniform—had to be quite a sight.

Wayne was stricken with the starkness of the room. He wasn't sure what he expected…perhaps a blackboard and multiplication charts on the walls. Instead, there was only a calendar with a photograph of a white woman in a bathing suit.

He addressed the teacher, who had managed to close his mouth.

"Sorry for the interruption."

"May I help you, deputy?"

There was no friendliness in the man's voice, nor in his expression. It was a strange reaction for a Negro, Wayne thought…especially when talking to a lawman. A familiar down-trodden, shuffling, beaten demeanor was far more common.

The Negro teacher displayed none of those traits, and Wayne was surprisingly a little irritated at **his** own demeanor, too. The man had an expression of, what? Pride? Not exactly, Wayne reasoned, although that was obviously present. There was something more. Something deeper. Something disconcerting.

"I need just a few moments of your time. I'm sorry…about the class, I mean. It's official business."

The teacher glanced up at a large white clock on the wall at the back of the room. "This class will be over in twenty minutes." The slightly overweight Mr. Shields spoke as to one of his students. Wayne recognized at once that the soft, almost feminine look of the man belied a strength of purpose beneath. Tinsley also knew from the man's voice he was not from the Cash, Texas, area. And it was obvious the teacher intended to make a point with the deputy.

"No, sir," Wayne responded. "The class is over now. Early recess."

Hatred blazed from the man's eyes, obvious, piercing. The classroom was his domain. No one gave orders in his classroom but him. He stood, his dark suit and white, starched shirt adding to his appearance of a controlled, professional intellectual.

"Or we can just talk at the sheriff's office," Wayne added. The teacher had picked the wrong day to go head to head with him. He was not in the mood.

"Children," Mr. Shields seethed through clenched teeth, "go to recess. Return to your seats in ten minutes." They began to rise slowly, as though an explosion were imminent and they had no idea where to go. "Mr. Washington…"

"Yeah, sir?" answered a fourteen-year-old boy in a full grown body. Wayne noticed his threadbare overalls and bare feet.

"You will be responsible for the younger children being back inside on time."

"Yeah, sir," the boy responded. He stood long beside his desk looking at the clock as he counted quietly with his fingers. When satisfied with his count, he quietly slipped past Tinsley, excusing himself when he came between the deputy and the teacher.

Tinsley walked immediately to the front of the room, expecting a barrage of verbal abuse. When he was within three feet of Denson Shields, the teacher stuck out an open hand.

Wayne grasped it, cautiously, not willing to fall victim to a sucker punch. He needn't have worried. "I have to be teaching them every moment, deputy. I trust you understand. Even your interruption gives me opportunity to teach them something."

Tinsley's brow lowered unconsciously. What are you teaching them, he wondered. Bad manners?

"You don't understand, do you deputy..." he looked at the name tag on Wayne's uniform shirt. "Deputy Tinsley? You don't understand what I just taught them, do you?"

"Can't say I got the drift, no."

"I suppose there's no reason you should," he answered. "You see, these children have no pride...no honor about themselves. They've never seen a Negro who does. They needed to see that the sky indeed did not fall down when I talked to you as an equal."

"I see." Wayne wondered if he had read the man so completely wrong. Was he—Wayne—merely shocked that a Negro man spoke to him as an equal? No, he knew that look...that look of hatred. The look didn't discern color of skin. Hate looks the same in any color.

"You needed to see me, deputy?"

"Sorry. I was injured...accident, recently. I'm still a little slow on the uptake. Yes, I just need a couple of minutes. It's about one of your students."

"The oldest student in this school is fourteen. How much trouble could one of my students be in?"

"Oh, it's not trouble. One of them...the Blankenship girl..."

"Little Shirley? What happened?"

"Somebody hurt her." Although no one else was nearby, Wayne lowered his voice. "Sexually, I mean." The words seemed cold in the antiseptic atmosphere of the dark classroom.

"Where...when?" Mr. Shields stammered.

"Recently, apparently. The girl is young, of course, and she doesn't know the exact day.

As for where, I believe the rape occurred just over there," he pointed through the wall. "…at the bus barn."

"Poor child. No wonder…"

"What?"

"She has always been so good in her attendance at school. So attentive…always one of my best little helpers…"

"That changed, I understand…attendance, I mean?"

"Yes. She has missed several days recently, including today. I should have known something was wrong. Thank you for letting me know, deputy. I'll try to be more sensitive to her needs…now that I know."

"There is something else," Wayne began.

"More?" Shields asked.

"Yes. It seems Shirley has a friend. An older friend who also knows about the attack…and who may be…" Wayne stopped, not knowing how much was appropriate to tell the girl's teacher.

"May be what?"

"She may have been victimized by that person, also."

"Raped?"

"Molested. Maybe. I'm not sure of the details, exactly."

"But, why would you think such a…?"

"She sorta' implied it…to her mama. I don't really know if she knows what to think…or how to feel. She has some kind of loyalty to this person. These lizards that take advantage of little girls can be pretty slick."

"Is it possible it's just her imagination? Or a cry for attention? Because of the rape incident, I mean?"

"I don't know what to think, Mr., uh…"

"Shields."

"Mr. Shields. I don't know many details since I haven't even spoken to the little girl. Her mama told me second hand."

"You haven't spoken to Shirley?"

"No. So do you have any ideas? Men she might have regular contact with? How often would she have opportunity to even be around other adult men…?

Shields glanced upward and to the left, slightly. He seemed deep in thought. Finally, he said, "I just can't say. I guess it could be any of the older boys. I don't know the Washington boy very well…Willy. He came here in January, maybe February of this year. Seems like a decent enough sort, though."

"She didn't say it was a boy." Tinsley's spine froze, cold as a *Popsicle*. I'm the dumbest man alive, he thought. "I didn't think you could give me a name, really," Tinsley offered. "But Mrs. Blankenship asked me to check with you." He turned and started for the door. "Thanks for your time."

There was no response. Half way to the opening, Wayne stopped and turned his head back toward the teacher. He thought Shields was glaring at him, but the man flashed a quick smile. "Mr. Shields. Why are you here?"

The smile disappeared as readily as it came. "I have no choice."

Chapter 37

Blown sand beat against Jeff's body, and he pushed back at it, head bowed. Night was near, only a soft orange glow in the West evidencing the earlier day. Frequently, with the setting of the sun came the setting of the wind as well. That was not the case today, and Jeff had done all he could to break up the ground around the young cotton.

His eyes were blood red, irritated by the sandpaper air around him, his nose clotted with dirt. A brown line circled his lips where moisture and dust conjoined. He ached from riding the bouncing, rough old *Farmall* tractor; his back remained bent from the awkward position required to keep a close eye on the rotary hoe plows. The steel seat on the tractor had vibrated him numb hours before.

If they made a crop this fall, it would be because he had done the right things and had worked hard. It would be **his** crop. Faye helped as much as possible, but with the acquisition of a second job at the grocery store, her time was spent…as well as her strength. After finishing up at the school cafeteria, she would go straight there and stock and sack and carry out groceries until they closed at 9:00.

He only saw his friends at school, and on weekends at the Bradley place where they still broke horses. It wasn't the same now, though. Sam and Ray were slacking off, irritated by Jeff constantly driving them to do more, hurry faster, go longer. It was no longer fun, and their excuses for not showing up came more and more frequently.

He was concerned Ivy Bradley would get tired of the slow progress and just sell all the stock as-is, leaving him short one pay check, small as it was. He didn't hear the squeak of the back screen spring when he pulled it open, and he pushed the door open as automatically as he breathed while sleeping. He sought out the rocker in the living room and slumped into it with a sigh.

His feet were still numb from the constant vibration of the tractor. He pulled his left leg over his right, then tugged at the worn-down cowboy boot. When that boot hit the floor, he sat back against the rocker, eyes closing briefly. The peaceful respite ended quickly when the sudden image appeared in Jeff's mind again. His dad, sitting alone in a motel room with a gun to his head...the explosion! Jeff sat up immediately, jerked the second boot off, and slammed it to the floor.

He was seeing that same image more and more. Why now? He glanced at the clock on the living room wall. It was 8:35 pm. He needed to get the pinto beans back on the stove to warm up. They were left over from the night before, and needed a little extra water, he remembered...he wanted them ready when Faye got home.

He pushed himself up from the chair with a quiet groan, plodding into the kitchen. He would just...then he saw them. Dirty dishes, still in the sink from breakfast. He stormed back through the living room, down the short hall, and into his and Randy's room. The door slammed hard against the footboard of Randy's twin bed.

"What!? You scared..." Randy began.

"What are you doing?" It was obvious Randy was lying on the bed looking up at the ceiling.

"Nothin'."

"Why aren't the dishes done?"

"I'm tired."

Jeff's face, already red, emblazoned even more. "Tired? You're tired? From what? Did you have to walk all the way across the house to get a drink of water or something?"

"Whatdayamean?"

"You're not…" Jeff was furious. Words failed him. He grabbed his brother by the shirt collar. "Outside! Come on." He jerked Randy off the bed and dragged him, stumbling and resisting, through the house and out the back door, the screen slamming behind them.

"What are you gonna' do?" screamed Randy. He had never seen Jeff like this in his life.

"I'm gonna' beat you to death and bury you behind the grape vines!" Jeff yelled down at him.

Randy's eyes were so wide Jeff could see the rising moon reflecting in them. He spoke so quietly his bigger brother could hardly hear. "Please don't kill me."

Jeff knew it was the same look Randy had used on their mother so many times…the look that melted her heart. "Why not, you little bug? Tell me one good reason I shouldn't kill you. You're worthless. You don't carry your weight around here. You're just another mouth to feed, and someone else to wash clothes for. You don't help. You're lazy! And I'm sick of you.

No, I'm sure of it. I'm going to kill you. But first, I'm gonna beat you so bad you'll want to be dead."

"Wait, Jeff! Wait. I'll be better. I'll work hard."

"Bull! You don't even do the two or three piddly little chores I gave you. None of them…"

"You're not my daddy. I don't have to do what you say."

"Yes, you do! You have to do what I say, because I'm bigger than you, and—for now—it's my job. It's your job to do what I say. Me and mama."

"No. I want my daddy." Tears welled up in Randy's eyes as he spoke. "I want daddy. Not you."

"Well you got me. And daddy's dead. He ain't coming back, so get used to it. He's dead and buried, and probably in Hell right now!"

"Don't say that! You aren't supposed to say that! Daddy's in heaven with the angels…mama said so."

"She told you that 'cause you're a baby and can't handle the truth."

"I ain't neither no baby! You're a liar."

"Well, I ain't no liar about you being a little bug who don't carry his weight around here…and I'm tired of it."

"Kill me then. I don't care." Randy spoke almost conversationally, and the tone stopped Jeff where he stood.

"Yes, you do, Randy. Don't say that."

"You can't tell me what to say, neither. You can't tell me what to do or what to say. I hate you!" With those words he pushed Jeff in the chest as hard as he could, knocking the older brother back two steps.

"Stop it!" Jeff barked. But the onslaught of his brother had only begun. Randy stopped pushing, and started hitting Jeff with his closed fists. Jeff warded off most the blows, but took a few strikes in the face and upper body.

"Stop! Randy, I said stop it! I mean it!" Finally, Jeff struck back, striking Randy in the chest, knocking him flat of his back. Randy, surprisingly, jumped right back up and charged his brother again.

His whirlwind roundhouse blows weren't physically hurting Jeff, but their intensity increased with every moment. "I hate you! I hate you!" Jeff grabbed him in a giant bear hug and held him, arms pinned to his sides for a long moment. "I hate you! I hate you! I want my daddy!" He ranted for several moments before Jeff spoke. His voice was as controlled as he could make it.

"I love you, Randy."

The tension in the younger brother eased somewhat, and Jeff slid down to the ground, onto his knees. Randy's head was higher than his, and he leaned it against Jeff's neck, suddenly quiet. Jeff still held him in a bear hug. The younger brother finally spoke.

"What?"

Through words that had become broken in Jeff's voice, he managed to repeat, "I said I love you."

Jeff heard the sudden sob from his brother, then more…gushing out as though they had been kept in a pressure cooker. He sobbed aloud for several minutes, not speaking. Jeff felt warm tears running down his own dusty cheeks. They hugged closely together for several minutes, neither of them speaking. Jeff had never heard Randy cry so…not even at the funeral.

It was Randy who broke the silence. "I don't hate you, brother."

"I know Randy. I know you don't. Things have been real hard...for all of us."

"Why? Do you think maybe we did too many bad things and God is mad at us? That happens sometimes." He sniffed.

No. I don't think that."

"Are you sure?"

"Randy, I'm not even sure which boot goes on which foot half the time these days. I'm just trying to get by. Just trying to get through each day as it comes."

"Do you miss daddy, too?" Randy's lips, still for a moment, began to quiver again.

"Yeah. More than anything."

"Why did he do that? I think it may be my fault."

"No, it wasn't your fault. Don't ever think that. It was his fault."

"Are you mad at him? You sound mad."

"Yeah, I'm mad at him. I'm mad at him for leaving us. I'm mad at him for hurting mama and you. I'm real mad at him."

"But, you said you love him."

"I do. You can love somebody and be mad at them at the same time."

"Like with me...when you was gonna kill me?"

"I wasn't really gonna' kill you...but yeah, like that. I was mad at you, but I still loved you. Shoot, if I didn't love you, I wouldn't care what kind of person you are. It wouldn't bother me seeing you act lazy and no good."

"I'll do better, Jeff."

"I will too. I'll try to not be so bossy. Make you more of a partner around here, instead of a hired hand. You think you could handle that responsibility?"

"I'll try."

"That's all I ask." Jeff realized they were still hugged closely together, which had felt right and good earlier, but was beginning to make him a little uncomfortable. He gently separated himself from his brother. He held out a hand to Randy, which he took with his much smaller hand. "Partners then?"

"Partners. Yes, sir."

"Okay, let's get supper ready. I'll help you with the dishes…this time."

"Thanks."

"One other thing, Randy."

"What?"

"We might not want to mention that killing and burying you in the back yard stuff to mama. She's got a lot on her mind already."

They started back to the house, when Jeff saw her, standing behind the screen door, watching them. How long had she been there?

"Beans are about warm. You boys get your hands washed for supper."

Randy walked by her quickly, ducking his head so she would not see his red, puffy eyes. Jeff walked slower, aware finally he was barefoot and grass burrs were all over his feet. He stepped to the screen door as Faye pushed it open. He could not read her expression. She turned as he entered the house and placed her arm around him, her hand resting lightly on his neck and shoulder. Patting him lightly twice, she removed her arm and returned to her chores.

Chapter 38

Faye stopped at the bank on her way from school to the grocery store. She put it off as long as she could, but they needed food in the house, as well as other supplies. The belt on the water-well pulley was almost worn out and needed to be replaced. There were other things, and she and Jeff had prepared a list of essentials, pricing everything they needed.

The First National Bank of Cash was small, but austere by the standards of other buildings in town. Marble was evident throughout, and the interior shined like no other place she had ever been.

"Faye!"

"Hello, Mr. Reasnor. How are you?" She smiled at the bank president.

"I'm great. It's good to see you. How're the boys getting on?"

"They're fine, thank you. And your family?"

Oscar Reasnor took her hand, shook it, and held it as they covered the standard greetings. He was still trying to prove to the entire town he was capable of running the bank every bit as well as his grandfather and father before him. Better, even. But with all the new government rules regulating banking practices, it was hard to personalize service as they once did.

"Oscar, may I speak to you a moment?"

"Of course, Faye. Come over to my desk." He led her to a chair and held it while she sat. She thanked him and took a piece of paper from her pocket book. Oscar sat, waiting quietly. Faye sighed deeply. This was a new experience for her. She held her shoulders back, chin up.

"I need one hundred and sixteen dollars and forty-two cents." There, she had said it. She waited to see what happened next.

"Okay."

"I have a list here…of what the money's for."

"I don't need to see it, Faye. It's your money. Do you have your checkbook with you? You can just write out a check for that amount, and I'll get you the cash."

Faye flushed bright red. "I'm sorry, Oscar. I didn't make myself clear. I need a **loan**. I need to borrow that much money."

He waved her apology off with a smooth, white hand. "No, no, Faye. It's me that should apologize. I just assumed…you know."

"If we had that kind of money in our checking account, I wouldn't be sitting here. I don't like to be beholden…even to a bank."

"You wouldn't be beholden, Faye. When we make you a loan, we charge interest. It's a business transaction. We make you a loan, and you pay us for it. No need to feel bad about it. Loans are good for both of us."

"Thank you, Oscar. I do understand about interest. I just can't help but feel the way I feel."

"Anyway, Faye…sure, I'll loan you the money, if you like. I just don't understand why you don't…" he paused. "Can you wait right here for just a second?"

"Of course." Faye sat, her back straight as a board, hands folded around the well worn pocket book in her lap. She could feel the stares of others around the bank lobby…they were present everywhere she went. The widow of Allen Cowen, who killed himself. Tush, tush…what a shame. Wonder how she's doing?

She could see Oscar going through a file he had pulled out of a metal cabinet. He wrote something down on a piece of paper and started back toward her. When he arrived at his desk he placed the piece of paper on the desk in front of her.

"Have you written any checks today?"

"No, I haven't." She leaned forward slightly and looked at the numbers written on it: 254.12.

"I don't understand," she told him.

Oscar looked around, assuring their privacy. "That's your bank account balance."

It was Faye's turn to stare, but her gaze was drilled into the eyes of Oscar. "You've made a mistake," she said, flatly. "I know exactly how much is in my account. That is two-hundred and fifty dollars more than I have."

He smiled. "So you **don' t** know about it?"

"About what? What are you saying, Oscar?"

"The reason your books are off is that there was a two-hundred fifty dollar deposit made recently that you obviously don't know about."

Faye frowned. "No, there's some mistake. People can't just come and put money into another person's bank account...can they?"

"They can't take money **out** of your account...can't even find out how much you have in it...but they can put all they want **in** it. And that's what happened."

"But who...?" She looked around the room, involuntarily.

"Can't say."

"You mean you don't know?"

"No. I mean I can't say. The person couldn't have put the money in without your account number. So...he...the person, asked me to deposit it."

"Then you know. Tell me who..."

"I promised, Faye. I gave my word I wouldn't tell. Frankly, I agree with the person's preference to keep it secret...for a number of reasons."

"But, Oscar...I can't take this money. It's just not..."

"Then it'll just sit there in your account, wasting away...not drawing interest, nothing. Use the money, Faye. Swallow your pride for once. Take it for the boys. Consider it a gift to them."

She lowered her head, eyes closed. When she raised her head, dignity had returned in full. "Will you thank, whoever it was, for this?" She pointed at the paper on the desk.

"Of course. Now, if you still want that loan…?"

"No. No, thank you. I believe I'll hold off on that for now."

"Good. And, Faye?"

"Yes?"

"Me and the wife wanted to tell you how sorry we are for your loss. I'm sorry I couldn't be at the service. You know, with the bank to run and all…"

"Thank you Oscar. And thank Mrs. Reasnor for me, too." She rose to leave, then asked the banker, "Why would someone do this?"

"I guess you've got a secret admirer."

She shook her head. "Unbelievable," she whispered to no one. "Plumb unbelievable."

Oscar Reasnor watched her walk across the lobby, push open the glass door, and press into the afternoon wind. Her steps seemed lighter than when she entered. He looked up and saw his senior teller, William Sorrowich, standing in front of his desk. William smiled broadly. He had watched Oscar observe Faye as she left.

"Handsome woman," William offered.

"Yes. I was madly in love with her once…in the second grade, I believe it was."

"Was she as attractive as a child?"

"I thought so. There's no denying her looks, but until you know Faye, you don't really realize just how attractive she is. With her, the beauty goes all the way through."

"Sounds like you may still be smitten."

"Don't be ridiculous. I'm married."

"Can I ask you something, Mr. Reasnor…Oscar?"

"What?"

"Did you make that deposit…were you the one who provided the money, I mean?"

"I wish I could say it was me that did it. But no, it wasn't."

"Then, who?"

"I gave my word. That's the end of it."

As Faye stepped into the stiff downtown breeze, she heard the squeal of tires on brick. She looked quickly in the direction of the sound just in time to see Wayne Tinsley's patrol car careen sharply around the corner a block away, headed out Farm to Market Highway 102. Even at a distance she heard the roar of the big *Ford* engine as it produced higher and higher rpms, accelerating away from mid-town.

She raised a hand slowly, shading her eyes from the afternoon sun. The car was already well out of sight, but she lingered. What must be going on? What would cause him to be in such a hurry? A silent prayer came to her slightly parted lips, words unspoken. Thoughts turned into a tiny movement of the mouth…all in silence…all in a moment. Watch over him.

Wayne made the sharp curve just outside of town at over one hundred miles per hour. Kids in town had named it "Dead Man's Curve" although—to Wayne's knowledge—no one had ever been killed there.

He sped past the Holland farm house and directly into the Blankenship's front yard. Dust boiled inside the open car window and was still settling across the interior as he knocked on the front door.

"Mrs. Blankenship!"

"Just a minute…hold your horses!" she called back in response to his loud battering on the door. He heard her walk heavily across the living room, and the door swung open wide. She looked quickly behind her and partially closed the door. "What are you doing here?" she whispered.

"I need to talk to Shirley. You and I together…we need to talk to her."

"I told you," she said. "She can't talk about it to anyone else…not yet. You'll scare her to death."

"It's important. I don't need to ask her about any of the details of what happened to her…I'll keep it light. But I need to see her **now**."

"Mama?" The small voice came from a room just off the living area.

"It's okay, baby. Come on in. We have company." She glared a warning at Tinsley and grudgingly stepped aside as she swung the door open for his entry.

He stepped inside just as Shirley walked into the living room. She stopped instantly, her eyes immediately wide, searching her mother for an answer.

Before Ruth Blankenship could speak, Wayne stepped closer to the little girl. He held out his hand, bending low to minimize his height over her. "My name's Wayne," he said softly.

She allowed him to shake her limp hand, but kept her eyes on her mother. Ruth nodded at her daughter. "It's okay, baby."

"You must be Shirley," he continued.

"Yes," he thought he heard her say. It was a tiny voice hidden behind mostly closed lips.

"Mind if I sit for a second?" he asked, pulling out a kitchen chair and easing himself into it. She didn't answer. "Are you feeling okay this afternoon, Shirley?"

"Yes, sir."

"The reason I asked is I know you were sick this morning and couldn't go to school. You're feeling better now, though?"

"Yes."

"Shirley…" He pulled out another chair. "I'm sorry. Where are my manners. Won't you sit down, please?"

She looked again at her mother who nodded. Shirley took the offered seat, looking down at the floor.

"Shirley, don't be upset by me being here. You're not in any trouble. Okay?"

She nodded, but did not respond.

"I need a little help with a couple of things. Easy things. Will you help me?" She sat, unmoving, silent. He continued. "Shirley…can you tell me every man you know? I mean, every grown man you know."

She looked at Wayne as though he had lost his mind. His appearance didn't help either. What **happened** to him? The silence lasted a full minute. When Wayne finally decided the awkward silence wasn't going to create a response from the girl, she proved him wrong.

"Daddy. Daddy is all. And teacher…Mr. Shields."

"You know, that's what I figured. I just needed a smart young girl like you to prove me right. So, the only men you know…men you know well enough to talk to…is your daddy and Mr. Shields?"

"Yes, sir."

"Okay, thank you for talking with me."

"That's all?" interrupted Mrs. Blankenship. "You came out here just for that?"

"It's a lot, Mrs. Blankenship." He glanced at Shirley. "Bye, Shirley. I'll see you again sometime."

"Okay." She looked at her mother who nodded toward the children's bedroom.

"Go on to your room and play. I'll be in in just a minute."

Wayne and Ruth watched the little girl quietly as she disappeared into the solitude of her bedroom.

"Nice girl," he said.

"Yes, she is. So, you think Mr. Shields…?"

"I know…it seems too awful to think about…a teacher and all. That sort of thing just doesn't happen. But one of the first things the sheriff told me about investigating crimes is that two things need to be present for a person to commit an offense: motive and opportunity."

"The motive is obvious, I guess?"

"Yes, ma'am. And today, while I was talking to Mr. Shields, I realized…Shirley lives in the country…goes to school and back with other kids…she is never around adult men…except at home and at school."

"Why do you think it's Mr. Shields, and not my husband?"

"I don't really know, Mrs. Blankenship. That's how I feel. Maybe it's nothing more than the fact I don't like Shields. But there is one other thing. I think you have an understanding…insight into what has happened that I will never have."

"What do you mean?"

"I think if your husband was molesting your daughter, you would know it. And I would be working a murder out here, instead of a rape."

"You're not as dumb as I thought," she said, without smiling.

"It took me much too long to figure this out…if I'm right," he answered. "I'm about exactly as dumb as I thought."

"I'm sorry, deputy. I'm really on edge…and I'm trying to keep my emotions from running over. I was taking out on you what isn't yours to be taken. I could kill a teacher as easy as my husband."

"I can't even imagine how you feel, ma'am."

"So, what're you goin' to do now?"

"I'm going to arrest that…Mr. Shields." He started for the door and paused, his hand on the knob.

"Are you a praying woman, Mrs. Blankenship?"

"Yes, I am."

"This isn't a very Christian thing to say, but maybe you might want to pray a little prayer concerning Mr. Shields."

"What in the world kind of prayer would I say for him?"

"Pray he resists arrest."

Chapter 39

Ivy lounged in her webbed chaise, absorbing rays through the sunlit window. Her body was tanner than anytime in her life. The petal-pushers she had worn only twice made nice shorts once she hacked the legs off. She had never owned a swim suit, but a towel served her purpose, covering as little or as much of her body as she desired. For a closer tan, she simply rolled the towel up, exposing more skin to be painted by the sun.

She never felt more free. She had finally reached Earl Smith by phone at the jail, telling the jailer she was his aunt. They worked things out, and he swore silence about their earlier agreement. He would be taken care of, she assured him. She sighed heavily, noting with some pride the degree of rise and fall of the towel.

"Okay, Mr. Deputy Sheriff Wayne Tinsley," she whispered to herself. "Next time you don't get off so easy. Next time you will **have** to notice me." She had chiseled herself, sculpted her every part, bronzed every inch he might conceivably see. She was tired of being lonely…and she wasn't a fool. She knew how men watched her when they thought she didn't notice. She had learned many things she would have preferred not knowing from her husband. Her **ex**-husband—she corrected—may he rot in some special place with all those other sick, deceitful, smelly, foul men of his ilk.

Tinsley was different. He had never looked at her **that** way. Why? Maybe because he had only seen her in those unsightly moments after Bill's death. At the hospital…no makeup…at home shortly after…in that old robe. She had never really had an opportunity to bowl him over. She did not like the fact he seemed so much in control of himself…indifferent, even…to her.

That would change, she knew. She had a couple of new dresses, ordered recently from the *Sears-Roebuck* catalogue. The black one would show off her hair and eyes better, but the red one was cut lower, enough to be provocative. She would wear the red one. Next time he came, it would be at her bidding. Stockings, high heels, makeup… everything would be perfect. **She** would be perfect.

Not only would Wayne Tinsley be unable to concentrate on that bothersome murder of her husband, he wouldn't be able to speak without stuttering. She laughed quietly at her thoughts. Like all cops, Wayne was poor. But that wouldn't really matter…not in a few weeks, anyway. She would have enough money soon to…

To what? She smiled silently. To do anything I want, she thought. She reached over to a small wrought-iron table and lifted a sweaty glass. The ice was mostly melted, and moisture ran down the sides of the smooth tumbler in tempting tiny rivers. She touched the glass to perfect lips, then slid her tongue up the side, slowly…deliberately. At its rim, her mouth caressed the glass, tilting it ever so slightly until the smell of sweet Gin touched her nostrils. She pulled in the smell, tilting the glass more, until the liquid kissed her lips, cold and numbing.

It filled her mouth, trickled down her throat, cool…mesmerizing. In the past few days, the pleasure of it had intensified for her. Bill had never let her drink, although he guzzled like a fat bear. She sipped. She savored. She loved…really loved the way it helped her feel. She couldn't be seen going in a liquor store—even if the closest one was more than fifty miles away—but their old hired hand didn't seem to mind making the trip for her.

He brought her a bottle every day or so. She paid him what he said it cost. It seemed awfully expensive to her…but well worth it. He would smile this snaggle-toothed smile, say

"Ten dollars, please," then tip his hat when she paid. She shook her head.

"Let's not think of that old Negro right now," she said aloud to her glass. "Let's keep our mind on the prize. Wonder how much a badge costs?"

Realizing her legs were crossed, she separated them, not wanting to miss a single ray of sun on skin. The loud banging at the front door startled her, and half a glass of gin splashed onto the towel, quickly soaking through to her warm skin. She didn't notice. Rising quickly, she stumbled to her bedroom, calling down the hall, "Just a sec!"

The pounding continued, a frenzied no-time-to-wait-a-sec knock.

"Just a minute, I said!" she called again, reaching for a filmy gown she had purchased the day before in Hoover. "This better not be that deputy," she mumbled. "I'm not ready to receive him, just yet."

"Open the door!" came the masculine voice. "I know you're in there!" She didn't recognize the voice.

"Hold your horses!" She jerked the door open, catching the big man's fist in mid-air, about to slam against her door again. He was muscular, dirty, and young. Sweat stained the underarms of his white tee-shirt, blended with grease across the front of it. He smelled of oil and old dust. Anger lined his face, burned through his eyes.

"Burl Patterson...what in the world...?"

"I just talked to Earl in the jail. Very interesting."

"What are you talking about?"

"You and Earl. He told me about your agreement with him. I was in on the deal from the beginning. Ain't nobody telling me how I'm going to be taken care of. Ain't nobody telling me squat!"

"When did you get out of jail? I assumed you were still locked up, too."

"I'll bet you did. I just bet you did. My folks bonded me out. Earl's folks can't afford to get him out, and probably don't really care whether he gets out or not. Maybe I don't either."

"Oh, don't be like that, Mr. Patterson...uh Burl?"

"I know a set-up when I see one. Earl been coming over here quite a bit without me, huh?"

254

"Not really. He's only…"

"Shut up! I want to know the deal. The whole deal. And I want to know how **I'm** gonna' be taken care of."

"Okay, Burl," she stifled a grin, in spite of his anger. Ivy could not help but remember thinking when she first met them together how much they sounded like someone who should be on the *Captain Kangaroo* Show…hey, kid's…it's Earl and Burl!

He crossed his arms in a defiant posture. "I'm waiting."

Then she did smile, her brightest, eye-sparkling smile. She looked straight into—through him, for a long moment. "Please don't be angry with me, Burl." She reached out a small hand and placed it on his muscular forearm. "Come, sit with me. I'll tell you everything." The touch was like electricity going through Burl, and he unfolded his arms.

"Uh, okay."

She had him. It was that easy, always had been, for her. It was that same look, that smile…that touch, that had so completely captured Bill Bradley so many years ago. Even as a child, she had the power over men. It didn't take long for her dead husband to hate that in her.

And, over time, it no longer worked with him at all.

As much as he had worshipped her in the beginning, he hated her that much in the end. She had never really analyzed the power…the gift, her mother called it. It was just a natural thing, handed down from her similarly beautiful mother…at least she had been beautiful once, when she was young. Sclerosis of the liver had killed her at age 44.

Burl sat heavily on the couch, as directed, then leaned forward and removed the *Mechanics Illustrated* magazine which had been rolled up in his hip pocket. He laid it, crumpled, on the coffee table. Ivy sat on the same couch, twisted sideways to face him, one leg crossed under the other. Her hands were folded in her lap, making a small, shallow bowl of skin. Every movement, every posturing of her body…the constant eye-contact…all created a perfect portrait of innocence…of a defenseless, beautiful woman in need…

"May I get you a beverage, Burl?"

"Uh, no, ma'am," he mumbled.

"You're a get-right-to-it sort of man, huh?"

He straightened up a little on the couch. She called him a man. At nineteen, no real woman had ever called him a man before.

"Yeah, I guess I am, now you mention it."

"Okay then," she repositioned herself a few inches closer, leaning in toward the foul-smell. "Let me tell you how I'm going to take care of you."

Burl didn't understand the sudden heat he felt in his face, or the strange feelings of his body. He knew them well...those sudden feelings...but he didn't know why they were so strong now. Mrs. Bradley was older...not really **that** old, though. And she was dressed. Completely dressed!

"Are you okay, Burl? You seem so...I don't know...distracted?" She smiled that smile again, one he took for...for, what? She really liked him, he decided.

Ivy checked his expression...his reaction to her performance. These young ones are so easy, she thought. This one, however, was more of a challenge for her than most. He smelled like her father. He acted like him, too. And the magic look she could present anytime was much more difficult to affect with Burl. What she really wanted to do was go into the bathroom and throw up.

"Burl, I'm so sorry we haven't had a chance to talk earlier. I got through to Earl by telling them at the jail I was his aunt. I knew that wouldn't work twice."

"That makes sense, I guess."

"And, to tell the truth..." she reached out and touched him again, this time on his hand, which rested uncomfortably on his upper thigh. He jerked involuntarily at the touch, but kept his hand in place. "...and please don't tell Earl this...?"

He shook his head no, without speaking.

"I trusted you. I wasn't sure about Earl. I like Earl—don't get me wrong—but I can read people really well. I read strength in you that is very rare in a man. I didn't feel that with Earl. I needed to reassure him...so he wouldn't, you know, start telling things he didn't need to be talking about."

"Okay. Yeah, I can see how that could be."

"Here's what we're going to do, Burl. It's very simple, really. There were only the three of us present that day…when we talked. Only three of us know about the conversation we had. Right?"

"Yeah."

"The cops weren't there. No one else was there but us. All we have to do is keep quiet. Deputy Tinsley knows a little, but I can convince him he misunderstood what I said the last time we talked. Don't get tricked into thinking they know anything, because they don't. If they knew of our…our agreement, it could go really bad for all of us."

"Just because we **talked** about killing your husband?"

"It's a little more than that, I'm afraid."

"Whatdayamean?"

"We didn't **just** talk about it. I made an offer…you don't know this, but Earl came back later, and agreed to do it."

"He came back after we left?"

"Yes, Burl. I don't think he trusted you to keep quiet. I told him I trusted you, but…"

"Why, that…"

"Don't concern yourself with him, now. I need you to concentrate. I wanted to keep you out of this, Burl, but when y'all got picked up by the police with the stolen things in your car…"

"He said you **gave** him that stuff!"

"I didn't. But when you ended in jail, you can see how disturbed Earl was. You knew about my offer, and you knew Bill had been murdered. And, now you have a felony charge hanging over your head. Earl was afraid you would tell on him as a—what do they call it when you tell something to get out of trouble?"

"I call it a rat fink. I wouldn't fink on Earl. I wouldn't tell on you, either."

"Oh, I know you wouldn't. That's why I had to talk to Earl…let him know everything was okay. Keep his mouth shut for a while. I'm going to give him $5,000.00 when this is all settled and I get my insurance money."

"How about me?"

"Well, of course you didn't really **do** anything. What do you think would be fair...to you and to me?"

"I was in on it from the first. And the way I see it, if I talk, you and Earl would both go to prison. I'd say I'm doing a lot...and I could get in trouble, too...just by knowing and not saying."

Ivy was growing tired of the greasy kid and of her game of manipulating him. He was far too much like her father, anyway. "Burl, I'm going to tell you a secret."

"What?"

"It's a secret no one around here knows."

"Not even Earl?"

"Not even Earl. I have a brother. We're very close. He lives in the city."

"So? Why the secrecy?"

"My brother and I are very close. He has spent most of his adult life in prison. He's been out less than a year."

"Okay, but what's that got to do...?"

"He was in prison for murder."

Burl stared at her, unaware of what any of this had to do with their conversation. "I don't get it."

"He is very protective of me. And, Burl, you just threatened me."

"I didn't! I was just saying..."

"You were just saying," she spat out, "that you were going to turn me in unless I pay you off. You are trying to blackmail me." The sparkle he loved so much in her dark eyes had become fire. He didn't like the fire at all.

"I just meant..."

"I know what you meant. Now listen to me." She leaned even closer, her breath of gin and *Listerine* penetrating his oil-lined nostrils. "Here's what I'm going to do for you. When I get my insurance settlement, I will pay you one thousand dollars. Not a cent more. You will use that money to travel somewhere a long way from here. Find a job. Start a life."

"And if I don't go?"

"I'll have a visit with my brother. If you don't go, I'll talk to him. If you talk to the cops, I'll tell him."

"You think I'm afraid of your brother?"

"If you have a single brain cell in that greasy head of yours, yes. You should be very afraid." She softened her voice for a moment, false sincerity dripping from bright red lips. "I like you so much, Burl. The thought of you lying face up in a pool of blood with…oh, say an ice pick sticking in your eyeball…that would just upset me something awful."

Burl stared at her, but only for an instant. He could not match the intensity of her glare. "One thousand?"

"That's what I said."

"Okay. How…?"

"I'll give it to Earl to pass on to you."

"Okay."

"See yourself out," she nodded toward the door.

He was already rising from the couch. It had been so comfortable only moments before. "Yes, ma'am." As he pulled the door open, he heard her voice again, calling his name.

"Yes, ma'am?"

"If I ever see your face again…ever, anywhere…"

"You won't."

She nodded, dismissing him with a flick of the wrist. The door closed quietly behind him. In a moment she heard the loud rumble of his car as he sped away. Why didn't I hear him pull up, she wondered.

Ivy lifted the glass, running her finger around the cool drizzle of its exterior, then transferred it to her neck and collar bone, loosening the lavender gown.

"Now, where was I?"

Chapter 40

"Yeah, Bill, I'm sure. What? No, I don't have a warrant." Wayne threw his hat onto the kitchen table, exasperated. "He **did** it, Bill. I **know** he did. Besides, I've wasted almost two days waiting on the Judge to get back to town. What's all this warrant business, anyway? We've never needed a warrant before."

"I know," came the gravelly voice from the other end of the line. Wayne thought he could hear a smile in Bill's remarks. "But, pard, do you know what today is?"

"It's uh…" Wayne looked at the calendar hanging on the wall next to the refrigerator. "Sure…uh, Friday? Friday. Why?"

"Friday. It's quittin' time on Friday. This can wait."

"Since when did you get to be a clock watcher?"

"Since it got to be Friday. Listen, Wayne. No kidding, if you had a lead on whoever shot you…or on the Bradley murder…that's one thing."

"But molesting a colored girl is another?"

"Not just that she's colored. It's an old case. Been goin' on for awhile, by what you told me. And that old nigger teacher…"

"What makes you think he's old?"

"Humph! Don't know. Ain't he?"

"Probably in his forties."

"Anyway, that's beside the point. He's been teaching there in Cash for how many years? Ten?"

"I think so. Ten or twelve. Maybe more."

"Then he ain't goin' nowhere. He'll be there Monday morning."

"Listen to me, Bill. Shirley's dad took her to school this morning...he didn't know what was going on."

"Why not?"

"His wife was afraid of what he might do. Get himself thrown in jail. Not that I'd blame him."

"You shoulda' told him, pard."

"I **know** that now. But he **never** takes her to school. Never."

"Can't say that anymore, I guess."

"I'm not arresting that teacher in front of the whole colored school Monday morning. Besides, Bill, I need to do this. I need to get it behind me...so I can get back to concentrating on Bradley's murder. This is like an itching place I need to scratch so I can get on to other things."

"I believe you, pard. And I don't believe you, too."

"What do you mean?"

"I believe you when you say you need to do this. I don't believe it's no more than an itch you got. You want this guy in jail."

"You didn't see Shirley Blankenship."

"Shirley?"

"The little girl. You didn't see her...her eyes. You didn't talk to her mama. You didn't see **her** eyes."

"Monday, Wayne. We can talk to the sheriff and be on firmer ground when we pick up the old—or not so old—lecher."

"Bill..."

"Bye, Wayne. See you Monday."

Tinsley slammed the receiver down, harder than intended. His temperament was more edgy of late. He pulled the chair out away from the worn pine kitchen table, looked at the wooden seat, then pushed it back. He brushed slender, strong fingers through his salty-black hair, wincing when he jerked against an unhealed cut in the scalp.

"Wait 'til Monday..." he mumbled, walking to the kitchen sink, looking out the window above it, then shuffled back to the refrigerator. He spun around, grabbed his hat, forcing it down almost to his ears, ignoring the pain. "Wait 'til Monday, huh. By Monday, that sorry buzzard will be sitting on jail concrete with a knot on his head."

He slammed the screen door open, storming outside without shutting or locking the loose-fitting front door. The *Ford* started with some hesitation, as tentative about going anywhere as Bill Lightsey had been. Wayne jammed the shift lever into the slot marked "D," had a second thought about running through the elm tree in front of him, and changed to "R," before spinning the tires on the hard gravel-packed dirt driveway.

He was almost a block away when he stomped the brake pedal. He shoved the transmission into "Park" and sat in the middle of the street. "Okay. No more pain killers." He shook his head. He had no idea where Denson Shields lived. He had felt like an idiot a lot lately, he realized. He shook his head again, removed the hat and placed it gently in the seat beside him. Who could he ask?

Okay, more to the point, he thought, who could he ask that wouldn't tell everybody in the county what a fool he was? Jeff. Jeff Cowan knew everybody in town. He's mowed half the lawns in Cash, Wayne thought, before he had to take up farming full-time.

He put the car in gear again, accelerating gingerly up to the stop sign at Main Street. I'll be lucky if Jeff's even home, he thought. He's been putting in a lot of hours.

Wayne glanced down at the western-cut white shirt he wore. He had ironed it, as usual. And—as usual—it still looked too wrinkled. Linda, the first week they were married, told him he would never iron another shirt as long as she lived. The taste of salt appeared unexpectedly in his mouth. He fought back emotions to keep the tears away.

Strange, he thought, the seemingly innocuous things in life that hit a man right in the solar plexus…unexpected things. Things that had no particular affect—at least, not consciously—at the time. Then…

It was like the morning he was getting ready for work and dropped a sock beside the bed. He had knelt down to retrieve it when her house shoe, lying upside down under the edge of the bed, caught his attention.

In an instant he broke into a torrent of sobs, broken like a big baby. How many times had he vacantly been aware of the presence of the shoe? How many sleepless nights had he spent with it lying beneath him?

He hadn't even been thinking of her that day. He had thought he was over the worse part of mourning. Then he saw that house-shoe. It held no particular significance to Wayne, at least not on a conscious level. Why had he been so torn apart then? Why, today, had a poorly ironed uniform shirt and an off-hand statement by his dead wife…dead wife…that still sounded so cold.

He hated the sound of the words in his mind. He swallowed back a lump which had lodged in his throat, and sniffed lightly. "Must be the drugs," he said aloud. "Got my mind all messed up." He had the turn-signal switched for a left turn, slowing significantly from the short ride from town. Just prior to turning in at the Cowen's driveway, he saw movement a half-mile from the house.

Mostly he saw dust, blowing around an almost invisible *Farmall* tractor. He turned off the signal and drove a short way down the two-lane highway before turning across the barrow ditch and up near the edge of the field. The cotton was already eight inches high, its leaves waxy-green.

Jeff was doing a good job, a man's job, Wayne thought. He took pride in the boy that even he didn't understand. Wayne had watched him grow up. He had attended most of Jeff's basketball and football games, and even went to a couple of rodeos in which Jeff had participated. The boy always played—and worked—over his head.

Wayne had never let on, of course, his admiration for the kid. People would think…well, they would take it wrong, he was sure.

He waved at Jeff as the tractor drew nearer. Jeff returned with an off-hand salute. As the rusty tractor terminated the row, Jeff stopped, lifted the two-row plows from the earth, and shut off the thunderously loud motor.

He leapt down from the right rear tire with a thump. Dust spouted up from around his boots as he landed. He looked back at the setting sun to check the approximate time remaining before dark.

"Sorry to interrupt," Wayne called out.

"No problem. 'bout quittin' time anyway. Everything okay?"

"Sure. Fine. I just needed some directions."

"Really?"

"Yeah. I need to talk to the teacher from the colored school. Mr. Shields. You wouldn't happen to know where he lives, would you?"

"I think so. You just need directions, or do you want me to show you?"

"Directions only. It's official business."

"Okay. Mr. Shields, did you say? I don't guess I ever heard his name."

"Yeah. He doesn't get out much...other than school, I guess."

"Well, I've seen him in and out of a place over in colored town. I guess that's where he stays."

"Okay."

"Let's see," Jeff turned toward town, getting his bearings. He raised his right arm, pointing north. "Go straight into town on Main...go on down Main about, I don't know, nine or ten blocks..."

"Um, hum..."

"Say, do you know where the old Bentley house is...there on the corner?"

"Sure."

"Turn back to the left there," he made a crooked angle with his finger, demonstrating. "Go down that dirt street three...no, four blocks...it's a dead-end anyway, where the concrete building is...the old ice house?"

"I know where it is," Wayne nodded, looking toward Cash.

"Make a right there, go one block, then a left, back through that grove of elm trees by the road..."

"Okay."

"Just on the other side of the trees, on the right side of the street, is his place. It's green...that shingle-type siding...several are missing off the front. Everything okay, Deputy Tinsley?"

"Yeah. I'm going to take him in for questioning on a case I'm working."

"Not the murder case?"

"No. That one's still simmering."

"Well, good luck." He looked back at the setting sun, orange shining through the dust on the horizon. "I guess I'd better get busy. I can still make a few rows before dark."

Wayne held out a hand, which Jeff took it without hesitation. "Thanks, Jeff. See you later."

"Yes, sir." He was back to the tractor in a moment. The crank in front hung loosely until Jeff pressed it forward against the shaft. Two hard turns had the engine roaring back to life. Before re-mounting the shuttering pile of iron, Jeff looked back over his shoulder. Wayne's patrol car was already pulling back onto the pavement, the beam of its headlights faint in the twilight.

Jeff frowned, then shuttered, a chill running through him in spite of the intense lingering heat. His eyes followed the fading red tail-lights of the car as long as he could see them. He had a terrible feeling he would never see Deputy Tinsley again.

Chapter 41

Seeing more than one tree alongside the highway every few miles was a rare occasion in the Texas South Plains. Seeing a **grove** of trees was something to celebrate. For as long as Wayne Tinsley could remember, kids had ventured to the grove to play.

Even though the grove acted as an unintentional gateway separating colored town from the rest of Cash, it was used by kids from both sides, who occasionally met there and—if very young—played together. They usually kept that fact from their parents, fearing long sermons about why they shouldn't intermingle with "those kind."

Even as Wayne considered the history and relevance of the grove, he became suddenly entombed in its darkness. His headlights, not really needed before, were necessary to pass through the narrow, winding jungle of trees, bushes, and vines. The place had always invoked mysterious visions for him. Although the gateway extended no more than one hundred and fifty yards across, it ambled almost a half-mile down what must have once been a creek bed.

Wayne's car pulled free of the trees, and-once again—enough residual light from the sun made his headlights only marginally necessary. He saw the green house immediately. Several strips of the tar-shingle surface were missing, just as Jeff had said. There was no car present, which didn't surprise the deputy.

Wayne pulled to the side of the dirt road, still fifty feet from the front of the house. He didn't really expect trouble, but there was no sense announcing himself until he was ready. He turned off the lights and reached for the door handle.

He hesitated. Regulations required he check out on the radio before getting out to make an arrest. He looked at the Motorola, hanging from the bottom of the metal dash. The green light was off. He reached over quickly and flipped the toggle switch to the "on" position. As soon as the radio warmed up, he heard the dispatcher's voice.

"…unknown to this operator, Sheriff. He's not responding."

"Have you tried his house, again?" The sheriff's deep voice didn't sound happy.

"Yes, sir, Sheriff. Still no answer. I'll try again, if you…"

"No. Don't bother. I'll go over there myself." He definitely did not sound happy.

Tinsley keyed his radio. "This is Unit 1637. Have you been trying to locate **me**, Sheriff?"

"Only for nearly an hour," he grumbled.

"Wayne," broke in the dispatcher, apparently assured the sheriff was finished. "We got a call from over there…a Mrs. Blankenship. Her little girl is missing."

"Missing? How long?"

"Over two hours, now. The other kids didn't see her after school… thought she must'a got sick and went home early."

"Ten-four. Can you call her back, and…" Wayne remembered the Blankenships had no telephone. Mrs. Blankenship would be frantic, he thought. "Disregard. I'll check it out. If she calls back, tell her I'm working on it, and find out where she is."

"Ten-four, Wayne. I think she was calling from the Holland farm."

"Okay. I'll be away from the car a few minutes."

"Ten-four."

Wayne exited the car, closing the door quietly behind him. If he was right about Shirley Blankenship's older "friend," he might be in the exact right spot, he thought.

He eased up against the front of the house and heard what sounded like two men's voices. When he heard laughter from a crowd, he realized he was hearing the radio playing an Amos and Andy bit. When he reached the first window, the room was completely dark. He could barely see inside, but it appeared to be a bedroom.

The second window was bright, beaming mottled rays onto the ground outside. It was beside the front door. Wayne was sure it would be the living room. He slid alongside the house and peeked through the lower corner glass pane. A dog barked a hundred yards away, then a cat shrieked. It was totally silent then, even the sound of the radio no more.

There was no visible movement inside. Nothing. The furnishings were old, clean and tasteful, the floor covered in old, cracked linoleum. He began to relax.

"Deputy!"

Wayne jumped, startled at the close proximity of the voice. He looked around, expecting the man to be directly behind him. He wasn't.

"Yeah?"

"Are you going to stand out there in the dark all night, or come on in?" Mr. Shield's voice was undeniable, dripping with bitter sarcasm. "Or don't you dirty yourself by coming into the abodes of people of color?"

Wayne took a bolder look into the window, but still saw no one. There was a dark room off the living room...maybe the kitchen? He may have seen movement there. He couldn't be sure.

"I'm coming in, Mr. Shields. That okay?"

"Please. I've been expecting you." His voice sounded almost friendly. "That is, **we've** been expecting you."

A chill struck Wayne. So he was right. The **we** would include little Shirley, he was certain. Although already bidden entrance, he tapped lightly on the door again. He reached for the door knob and twisted it slowly. He stopped, moving his body to the side of the door. He turned the knob again and swung the door open. Standing to the side, he called out conversationally.

"Mr. Shields, I just came to take Shirley home. Her mother asked me to stop by and get her. I'll bet she tans her hide good when she gets home."

"Tans her hide. What an interesting expression. Do you really believe Shirley's **hide** would tan?"

"It's just an expression. I don't know. Yeah, I guess. Maybe. I don't know."

"Of course her skin tans. We get darker in the summer, too, you know. Same as you whites."

"Okay. I wasn't really talking about tanning, anyway. I just meant…"

"I **know** what you meant!" he screamed. "I am not one of the ignorant field hands you make fun of and push around with your little badge and your little gun, and your little intelligence!"

"I can see that, Mr. Shields. It's very obvious you are a smart man…"

"Don't be condescending, deputy. Why can't you just be forthright. I have something you want. Can you take her from me? I don't think so. Can you talk me into giving her to you?

Of course, you can try. I hope you do try, actually. It would amuse me to see you fumbling around trying to trick me in to believing you actually care about Shirley."

"I didn't come here to trick you."

"Mrs. Blankenship didn't send you here to pick up her daughter, did she?"

"No."

"So you did come here to trick me."

"I came here to throw your arrogant, child-molesting, uppity, **tan-able** hide in jail…oh, and to put a knot on your ugly head, if you'll give me a chance."

"My, so you **do** have a temper, after all. I thought you were coming in?"

Wayne stepped into the door opening. He could see Shields, sitting at the kitchen table. On the table, a shot gun lay in front of him, although he was not touching it. His hand rested casually a few inches from the trigger. Wayne stepped closer to the opening, exposing the other side of the table and the rest of the kitchen to his field of view.

The barrel of the gun was a foot from Shirley's face, pointed directly at her. Wayne froze. He calmed himself outwardly, then redirected his attention to the teacher. "You don't need to do this."

"Oh, well done, Deputy Tinsley. Except for the faintest flash in your eyes, it was as though you hadn't even seen Shirley...or the shotgun. Very well done."

Shotgun, thought Wayne. Shotgun. "I'm glad to see you're so easily amused, Shields."

"Shields, is it? What happened to **Mr.** Shields. Have I gone down so much in your estimation?"

"No. That would not be possible."

"I think you may be playing this all wrong, deputy. You see," he moved his hand deftly to the trigger of the shotgun, "it would be the simplest thing in the world for me to pull this around and shoot you. You might be able to touch your holstered firearm before dying, but I doubt it."

"And you're telling me this because you like me so much?"

"I'm telling you this because you had better show me some respect in my own home. And make no mistake, it's not that I don't **like** you. I **hate** you. You, and all your kind."

"What kind is that?" Wayne kept his eyes on those of Shields, hoping for some opening...some way to get close enough to the gun to perhaps...

"Never mind. And...stop!" Wayne had edged a step closer. He halted at the command. "That's close enough. We can converse from where we are."

"Mr. Shields, regardless of what you think of me, I really believe you care about Shirley. Let her go home. I'll stay here with you. Let's not make her part of this."

"**We're** not making her part of this. **I** am. And I don't believe for an instant you think I care about Shirley. You believe it's just some sick..." he turned to Shirley. "Cover your ears, darling." She covered her ears with both hands. She glanced quickly at Tinsley, her eyes round and white with fear.

"You believe," he continued, to Tinsley, "it's just some sick sex thing." He motioned for Shirley to lower her hands. She obeyed without hesitation.

"You're right," Wayne said. "That is exactly what I think."

Shields shook his head, a look of sorrow crossing his brow. "It has always been so. Those of you who think you are so understanding...know nothing at all of true love." His forefinger scratched absently at the wood stock of the shotgun near the trigger-guard. Wayne glanced quickly at Shirley, trying to reassure her, then back at Shields.

The teacher was still wearing a black suit, brightly shined black dress shoes, a starched white shirt, and a thin tie knotted tightly around his neck.

"Tell me, Mr. Shields..." The other's brow furrowed, as though lost in the conversation momentarily. Wayne continued, "Tell me about that love. What you were talking about...the kind most of us don't understand."

"You don't care."

"I want to understand, Mr. Shields. I really want to know."

"I can see you do, sir." Shields looked away from the deputy, and at Shirley. Wayne wanted desperately to inch forward, but he was still well within the peripheral vision of the teacher. Shields' voice took on an aura of dreaminess, and he droned, "Look at her. She is perfect...unspoiled." His face instantly took an expression of fierceness. "At least she **used** to be."

Wayne did indeed look at Shirley. She lowered her head, eyes cast downward. He spoke to Shields while still looking at the girl. "**Used** to be?"

"Yes. Little girls, you see..." his voice began to mellow again, "they have a special character about them. Their innocence...their purity. It is to be loved, cherished...captured in the moment."

"I see."

"No, you don't! You don't see at all! You haven't thought it out enough...you haven't felt the feeling...you haven't experienced true purity."

He gazed at Shirley again. "Raise your head, darling. I can't see your beautiful, brown eyes." She obeyed reluctantly, fearfully. Leave her alone, you maggot, thought Wayne. Can't you see she's...

"It is something you will probably never understand, deputy," Shields continued. "There are many of us who do. Did you know that?" Tinsley didn't answer right away, and the man continued. "I have many, many letters from men who know—as I do—the special love a man can have for a little girl."

"Letters? Where..."

"There is a publication...underground, of course...which helps those of us who are enlightened, make contact. There are many of us, you know."

"Really?"

"Yes, really. You see, little girls like Shirley have only this small period of time in their lives...between their infancy and maturity, to experience this love. Most never have the chance. It is not just a case of my desiring Shirley's body...it's much more."

"I didn't realize." Wayne responded. His mind was whirling, trying to determine a means of escape for the little girl. He was too far inside to get back out the door, without some sort of diversion. And he was fresh out of diversions. Even if he could get himself out, Shirley would still be in jeopardy. Could he do her more good from outside? He surely wasn't helping her from where he stood.

"Of course you didn't realize," continued Shields. "You think only with your physical mind. You have no emotional depth. Most men don't."

He paused a long time, as though trying to decide something important. Then he continued. "Little girls need this. They need someone who can show them how they are supposed to be touched. With kindness. Tenderness. They need a gentle hand to learn the ways of men, so they can know the difference. They like it, once the fear is gone, once the shackles their backward parents placed upon them have been released.

"I am doing them a great service. A favor. I am teaching them love. I am showing them the greatest emotional and physical love they will ever experience. It is my duty to help them, even though society doesn't understand. It creates great difficulties for me, occasionally. But it is for them. Everything I do is for them."

"Earlier, you said Shirley **used** to be pure. Is that because you have already…?"

"Don't be a fool. It was that white man…that night in the bus barn. He raped her. He murdered her purity. Nothing can ever be the same with her again. Not between us. Not for her."

"She's the same person," argued Wayne.

"No, she not! You'll never understand!"

"You know, Mr. Shields, you're right. I'll probably never understand the way you think…or how you've convinced yourself you feel. But I do understand. I really do."

Shields only glared at him. Wayne continued.

"What I understand is that my original thought was accurate. I understand that you are a vile, evil, sick, child-molesting lizard. You don't deserve to be alive, and—hopefully—I can help you with that."

"Pretty brave words for a man who is seconds away from being blown apart by a shotgun…"

"And that's another thing! I'm also not too happy about you shooting me last week! Not only are you a belly-crawling reptile, preying on children in your care, but you're also a coward…shooting me from ambush!"

Wayne stopped his tirade, suddenly out of words. He wanted to rile the man enough to perhaps make a surprise move. But Shields was not going to be distracted. He was too crazy to be distracted.

Wayne had never been afraid of death, but he did not want to be killed by this man. And, more than that, he did not want to witness Shields blowing this little girls head into fragments right in front of him. That's what Shields was going to do. Kill the girl, so Wayne would have to watch. Then he would kill Wayne because his hate required it. Shields would then kill himself.

It would be in that order.

Chapter 42

Suddenly the room went black, and Tinsley bolted for the front door, diving after two long strides, as the shotgun boomed behind him. His left hand hit the rise at the door sill, and he crawled, scrambled, and rolled the remaining few feet, twisting to the side of the door, gasping.

As he leaned against the house front, he realized he had heard a loud "klunk" on the rooftop just as the lights went out. He also realized he was not shot. A rush of acid hit his stomach as he realized if **he** was not shot, then...

"Shirley!" he called into the darkness. Silence. "Oh, my..." he moaned. "Shirley? Shirley, honey. Are you okay?"

There was no response from the child, but Wayne heard Shields whisper, "Be silent! Don't make a noise. Do you understand me?" Relief flowed over Wayne like warm wine. She was still alive, although Shields didn't want him to know that. Maybe. Or was he whispering loudly enough to make Tinsley **think** she was alive so he wouldn't rush him?

Shields might be crazy, but he wasn't stupid. With Tinsley now outside, it would be simple for him to call in all the help he needed, then just burn the house down around the teacher...if the girl were already dead. Wayne had to focus, he decided consciously. If Shirley was dead, he could do nothing for her now. If she was still alive, she needed him to be smart and get her to safety.

"Hey, teacher!"

Silence.

"Shields?"

Nothing.

What happened to the lights, Wayne wondered. And what was that noise on the roof?

"Wayne…" came a whisper. He peered in the direction of the voice, but could only make out a shadow at the corner of the house.

"Wayne…" came the voice again, this time more frantic.

"Doggonit!" Without further hesitation, Wayne bolted from his position, directly across the still open door, and to the house corner. No shots came from inside. Wayne was banking on Shields not expecting him to be stupid enough to run right in front of the door. As he rounded the corner he ran head-on into the body belonging to the whispering voice.

"Jeff!"

"You okay, Wayne?"

"Yeah…but I don't know about the little girl. He may have shot her."

"No, I don't think so." Jeff said, still whispering, "But we need to check on…"

"Jeff…how do you know?" Wayne interrupted. "What makes you think he didn't shoot the girl?"

"I was watching through the kitchen window. Wayne, we need to check on…"

"The kitchen window? But, how…"

"Deputy Lightsey told me to throw that big chunk of concrete on the ceiling when he signaled. It was so big, I had to get close. So when I threw it up there, I looked in the window. I couldn't see inside, but the shot seemed to go straight up…into the ceiling…guess he thought somebody was up there."

Wayne stared at the young man in the darkness for a moment, gathering his thoughts and breath. "Bill? Bill's here?"

"That's what I've been trying to tell you. We need to check on Bill."

"Why?"

"Just as soon as the electricity went off, I think I heard him scream. I don't see him over around the pole now. He may be down in the grass."

"He **cut** the electric wires?" Wayne asked.

"Yeah. Used bolt cutters. He said on these old houses the fuses are on the inside...so he'd have to cut the lines."

"Good grief!" Wayne exclaimed. "Look, I hate to ask you this, but can you keep an eye on the front door...from the corner here? I don't want that guy out of the house. I can see the back door from over there." He nodded toward the electric pole.

"Sure."

"Don't do anything, Jeff. If he comes out, just get my attention. Don't even let him know you're here. I'll check on Bill, then be right back."

"Yes, sir."

Wayne stopped an instant, placing a hand on Jeff's shoulder. "I'm serious. Don't do anything. I have no intention of taking more horrible news to your mama."

"Go check on Bill."

Wayne nodded and was gone, slicing through the darkness toward the electric pole. It was now totally dark, and he had more trouble finding deputy Bill Lightsey than he had expected. When he did locate him, it was because he tripped over the man's legs.

"Bill! Bill, you okay?" he whispered frantically. He felt along Bill's prone body, arriving finally at his head. Wayne felt for the carotid artery in his neck. "Bill? Come on, man...talk to me." Wayne's own pulse was pounding so hard he couldn't determine if what he was feeling was his own or Bill's. He felt back down to Bill's feet and checked the bottoms of his boots.

He jerked back immediately. As he feared, the boot soles were hot as fresh ashes. Wayne banged his knee against something hard and metallic. The bolt cutters, he reasoned. He reached out for them, but suddenly pulled back. If they were still close to the hot end of the wire...

He felt again for a pulse. He thought there was a faint one, but he could not be certain. "Have to get you to the hospital, pard…" Wayne's teeth clenched tightly. His brain tried to present facts with which to reason, but Tinsley was unwilling to listen. You have to choose, it said. The little girl or your best friend…who lives…who dies? Maybe you can save Bill, and the girl will be alright. If you save the girl, however, Bill will die for sure. He needs help now. Wayne shook his head. He would not accept what his mind told him were his only options.

"Bill!" He shook the limp body of the overweight deputy, then slapped his face. Frustration was damming like a powerful river in Wayne. He would **not** decide between Bill and Shirley. "Hang on, Bill," he whispered to the lifeless deputy. "I'll be back."

He scurried quietly back to the corner of the house where he left Jeff earlier, finding him at his post, still…quiet. When Wayne slipped up behind him, Jeff did not look around, but asked, "How's Bill?"

"Bad, I'm afraid," he answered. "I'm not certain he's still alive. I need to get him to the hospital."

"Okay. How?"

"I'm gonna' drag him to the car."

Jeff did turn around then, staring through the darkness at the insane deputy. "He must weight nearly three hundred pounds."

"Two-seventy-five, I think."

"How can you…?"

"I was hoping you might help me with him. If we can get him into the car, you could drive him to the hospital."

"What about you?"

"I'll wait here, until the cavalry arrives. When we get Bill to the car, I'll call the S.O. and get help on the way."

Without speaking further, the two men—crouching low—slipped back through the darkness to Bill's prone body. Tinsley reached out a hand, stopping Jeff. "There are still hot wires around here somewhere," he whispered. "Follow directly behind me…in my steps. When we get to him, we'll pull him back in this same direction."

Jeff didn't answer, but Wayne thought he could see his head nod. "Once we're a few feet away, we won't have to be so careful about the wires." Wayne grimaced to himself. Then we can start worrying about that maniac in the house."

He knew moving Bill would be difficult. Dragging dead weight across unknown territory in total darkness would never be a picnic. Dragging a **lot** of dead weight across unknown territory in total darkness, and doing so silently, and safely…not getting electrocuted or shot…Wayne shook away the thoughts.

One of the most difficult things, they discovered, was maintaining silence when every movement of their heavy load demanded a grunt, a gasp…an expulsion of breath.

"Stop," Wayne said quietly, faintly…breathless. Jeff was grateful for the rest, but realized Wayne hadn't just stopped for a breather. He was feeling around on the ground for something. Jeff waited. After a few silent moments, Wayne raised himself off the ground, still crouching. With a large movement of his arm, he threw something— invisible in the darkness—toward the house.

Jeff heard gravel striking the roof with a spattering, muffled sound. "What…?"

Wayne drew near his ear. "I want to keep him on the defensive… make him wonder what we're doing. He thinks we're plotting on him now, maybe making a move."

The idea sounded good to Jeff. If the colored school teacher thought they were about to come in on him, he wouldn't be sticking his head out, or trying to figure ways of attacking them.

At least, he hoped that's the way it worked. They were already pulling on Bill's arms again, moving him one, sometimes two feet at a time, in jerking movements. Both men were sweating…soaked.

Finally they arrived at the car, panting quietly. Wayne opened the rear door on the passenger side, knowing it would not illuminate the interior light. He would have to crawl partially over the front seat to get to the radio.

"Keep an eye on the house, Jeff. I'm going to call in. Then we can load Bill."

"Okay."

Wayne fumbled a moment in the darkness, leaning over the seat, finally locating the microphone.

"Unit 1637, ten-thirty-nine!" Giving the signal for an officer emergency, Wayne knew he would have the attention of not only the dispatcher, but of every other officer in the area who could hear him.

"All officers stand-by," the dispatcher responded professionally. "Go ahead, Wayne."

"I've got a man with a gun...holding a child...held up in a house near the tree grove in Cash. Also, Deputy Lightsey has been electrocuted. He'll be in route to the hospital momentarily. Unknown, possibly D.O.A."

There was complete silence on the radio. Tinsley knew cars from every department around were racing through the night at unsafe speeds to come to his aid. It wouldn't be long, now...perhaps ten minutes or so...

"Unit 1637...Deputy Tinsley? Repeat your traffic...Wayne, can you hear me? Please respond. Unit...you're cutting out. Say again your emergency and location..."

"What!" When he heard the squelch of the radio—meaning the dispatcher had ended her transmission—he gave his situation again. He talked slowly...louder than he wanted. As he ended his second transmission, he paused, waiting.

The silence was intense in the car. Wayne could hear nothing but his own breathing, finally slowing down. Finally, there was a crackle on the radio speaker. "...gative, sir. Unable to copy any of it. Anyone out there on this channel hear what the deputy said?" Tinsley recognized the deputy's voice. It was Ralph, the young deputy from the Bradley murder scene.

"Unit 1639, I'll be en route to the Cash area...see if I can locate him."

"Ten-four," Wayne heard the dispatcher say.

"Okay, Jeff. Let's get him in here." Between the two of them, they managed to get Bill into the back seat of the car. It was like trying to stuff a two-hundred-seventy-five pound bag of water into a wall locker. Every time they got a part of him inside, another part would slip out.

Sweat poured into Wayne's eyes, blinding and burning, before they finally finished the task.

They closed the door, both pushing as hard as they could, to get the deputy sealed in the sedan. They sat a moment, both winded, sitting on the dirt with their backs still pressed against the car door.

"Jeff," managed Wayne between gasps for breath. "When you're able, slide through the window there and get him to the hospital. Here's the keys."

"What're you gonna' do, Wayne?"

"Wait for the posse, I guess. I can't leave that little girl here alone."

"I heard what they said on the radio. Nobody knows where you are."

"When you get to the hospital, get some help to get Bill out of the car...go around by the emergency room." He stopped a moment, getting his breath. "When they've got Bill inside, use a telephone and call the sheriff's office. Tell them where I am."

"Yes, sir."

"And Jeff?"

"Sir?"

"Stay at the hospital...with Bill. You've done way more than your part already."

"But..."

"No. I can't have you in more jeopardy than you've already been."

"But what if you need...?"

"No. You stay away."

Jeff sighed. "Guess I better get Mr. Lightsey to the hospital. You be careful."

"Don't start the car 'til I'm back up to the house."

Jeff waved acknowledgment. Wayne started crawling back to the corner of the house where he had met Jeff earlier. For the first time that night, he felt for his revolver. He knew it was in the holster, it's heft significant. But touching it made its presence more real...it made the probability of his having to use it shortly more real in his mind.

He could not hesitate, Wayne knew, if given an opportunity to take down the school teacher. He would have to be brutal. Hopefully, he thought, the man would be content to sit in the darkness wondering what was going on. Tinsley moved closer to the door. When Jeff started his car and began backing away into the trees, Wayne heard movement inside.

"I told you, darling." It was Shield's voice, almost conversational. "They don't really care about you. Oh, he'll be back…when he has twenty other cops with him. Not because of you, though. He'll be coming back for me, because I showed him for what he really is. A coward. A coward and a racist. White people hate it when you show them for what they are."

Please answer him, Shirley, Wayne thought. He was almost certain Shields would not be talking to her if she were dead…again, unless he had seen Wayne and knew he was still outside the house. Please Shirley, just a word.

She didn't speak, but Wayne heard her whimper, stifling a sob. She was alive!

No help would be coming for a while, he knew. Maybe Shields would just stay put…leave the girl alone. He wondered if the man was still close to the shotgun. How could he know?

"It's time, Shirley," Wayne heard from inside. "I'm so sorry. But as I told the man, you are soiled goods. It just hasn't been the same between us since you let that man do what he did."

"But, I…" There it was. Her tiny voice!

"No, dear. Don't fight it. You'll be better off in the long run. I know. I know, he forced you. But there must have been something you could have done. Besides, if you hadn't looked at him that way…like you looked at me when it was new between us…he wouldn't have thought it was okay to do what he did."

Tinsley wanted to vomit. And he wanted, more than anything, to smash that…then he heard her scream!

Chapter 43

The scream was filled with terror. Hair on the back of Tinsley's neck tingled at the sound of it.

"Teacher! Hey, teacher! You better think about it!"

"Ah, Mr. Tinsley…so you're still with us. Much better."

"Better for you, yeah. You need some advice."

"Advice? From you? What could you possibly advise me about?"

"Didn't you just dangle a participle, Shields?"

"Don't be…don't play games with me. You and I both know you have nothing about which to advise me."

Wayne's mind was spinning. He had to keep Shields talking…occupied. There had to be a trigger…a way to get Shirley out of there. "On the contrary, Mr. Teacher. I think you could use some sound legal advice about now."

"No, I don't. The last thing I need is legal advice."

"Why not?" asked Wayne, already knowing the answer.

"I have no intention of taking on your white judicial system. My career is over. My life is over. I only have to make it official."

"Then let the kid go. She's got nothing to do with any of this. Make your last act one of kindness to a girl you love."

"I warned you about treating me as though I am stupid! I still have use for this one. I didn't think so a moment ago, but when you interrupted our conversation with your presence here..."

"What are your intentions?"

"Finally. A straight question. I intend to walk out of here. I intend to do so safely...with Shirley. We will walk into that grove of trees that I know better than you know your living room. After a time, I will leave her for you to find...unharmed, if you do as I say. And I will disappear. That, deputy, is what I intend."

"I can't let you just walk away from here."

"You are not **letting** me do anything. I am in control here. It might surprise you to know you are the one who brought this plan to mind."

"How did I do that?"

"I had actually intended to dispose of this little thing in front of you earlier...then kill you. Does that surprise you?"

"Not in the least. That's what I expected. I also thought—at the time—you might then commit suicide. But, I was wrong about that, wasn't I?"

"Completely. I still have things to do. I still have little girls to educate." He laughed a mirthless laugh.

"Shields, no matter what you do here tonight, you know they will never stop looking for you...**I** will never stop looking."

"Suppose I let you live, deputy. What difference could it possibly make to you what happens to a little Negro girl?"

"Plenty. But that's not all." Wayne decided to try his trump card. "There would always be that other thing to be worked out."

"What thing?" Shields actually sounded interested.

"That **murder** thing."

"I haven't killed anyone **yet**, deputy...but you **are** getting on my nerves."

"I'm talking about Bill Bradley. You murdered him."

There was silence from inside the house. Not even the occasional whimpering of Shirley was present. Finally, the steady, controlled voice of Denson Shields emerged.

"So you intend to stick that one on me, huh?"

"No sticking to it. He raped your...your little friend. You saw him do it. He destroyed your love affair. He killed Shirley's innocence. He was a maggot. I probably would have killed him, too. That's probably what a jury will think as well. But we need to let them hear your side. Otherwise, they're just going to indict you as some unknown colored murderer who they could care less about."

"Yes, I can see how much you care about what happens to me."

"No. You and I both know I really don't care much what happens to you, but what I told you is the truth, and you know it. A man who rapes a little girl like…nobody is going to care who killed him…or how."

"But they will be okay with a man loving…what would be your word? Molesting? They would be okay with a Negro teacher **molesting** that same little girl."

"Maybe they won't have to know. Make a deal with the District Attorney. Plead guilty to the murder for a no-bill on the…that other thing."

"Interesting, Mr. Tinsley. Interesting that you would think me so naïve. We will be leaving now. And, unless you want this child's brains splattered all over the wall in here, you'll move into the doorway, where I can get a good look at you."

Wayne's heart pounded. They're coming out now!

"Just a second!" he called back. "I hurt my knee when I dove out of the house earlier."

"Time's up. In the doorway…now! You have to the count of three!"

Wayne straightened, leaning against the house next to the door opening. Quickly, he pulled the .38 from his holster and placed the barrel in the small of his back under the holster belt.

"One! Two!…"

Wayne double-checked, making sure the barrel sight wasn't snagged in his belt. It was all he could do. Then he stepped sideways, his entire body outlined in the door. The night—so dark before—seemed positively illuminated with moonlight.

Wayne braced himself for the shot he was sure would come. He had already given thought to the hope Shields still had bird-shot in the shotgun. Not that it couldn't still kill him, but his chances were a little better with the smaller caliber pellets. At this distance, it probably wouldn't matter anyway, he thought.

"That, sir, is a beautiful sight. You, lit up by the moon like a Christmas tree, right in front of my door. And, you'll be pleased to know, I have good news for you."

"Oh, yeah?" Tinsley was tensed to leap aside. Then Shields appeared before him, out of the darkness of the kitchen. The shotgun was indeed in the hands—the **hand**—of the man. He held Shirley with the other, pressed tightly against him. Her dress and socks were so white they seemed to glow in the darkness.

"Yeah. The good news is that you may get to live. I know if I kill you they'll never stop looking for me. And there's no telling how many Negroes will get walked all over in the process of the search."

"How about Bradley? Don't you think you should get that handled?"

"It **is** handled. I didn't kill him."

"But..."

"Deputy! Concentrate. Concentrate on what's important here."

"I need to know. You're either going to kill me and run 'till they find you, or you are going to let me live, and run 'till they find you. What difference does it make if you give me thirty seconds and tell me the details. I'm sure Bradley taunted you..."

"Don't bait me!" He shuffled the gun, bringing the barrel up to waist high, pointed directly at Wayne. "But, you know, you're right about something. They would look for me a long time over Bradley's murder...not like if I killed a cop...but it **would** be an inconvenience."

"So, what happened?"

"I already told you. I didn't kill him. I don't know why that's so hard for you to believe. I've been forthcoming with you about everything else."

"Granted." Keep him talking, Wayne thought. Maybe, just maybe, someone heard his call for assistance on the radio.

"I was there that night." Shields stepped another foot closer to the door and Tinsley. He looked around, checking for other cops. "I went to his barn that night with murder in my heart."

Wayne said nothing.

"When I strolled into his big, fancy barn like I was somebody, I thought he was going to have a fit. He cursed me, I accused him...told him what I saw. I even told him I had already been to the house and told his wife..."

"Did you?"

"No. He hated the way I talked to him. He hated I didn't bow and scrape and act afraid." In the faint darkness Wayne thought he saw Shields smile a crooked smile. "He really hated me. I'm glad. That made us equal in that one regard."

"What did he do?"

"He completely lost control. He had been beaten terribly already...blood was all over him...his nose was smashed. I told him maybe next time he should rape a smaller girl."

"You didn't beat him then?"

"Of course not."

"Go on."

"He was beside himself. Bradley, I mean. He started screaming at me...calling me uppity...calling me an uppity nigger. That's when I took the ice pick out of my coat pocket..."

"Then it **was**...?"

"Shush, deputy. You're not really a very patient man, are you?"

"I guess I'm not." He nodded for Shields to continue, and took a quick glance at Shirley. Her eyes were huge, afraid. They pled with him. He knew she didn't understand the longer he could drag this out, the better their chances...

"In fact," the school teacher continued, "he got so mad at me, he kicked out, trying to catch me in the groin."

"Did he?"

"No. His fury was his own undoing. Those little size-six, pointy-toed cowboy boots with the slick leather soles went right out from under him. He went up like a shot, and his head hit the floor like a ripe cantaloupe!" Shields laughed aloud. "You should have seen the look on his face right before his head exploded on that slick concrete."

"I'll bet," answered Tinsley. "But the ice pick?"

"I did indeed intend to kill him. But when I leaned over his body, blood was flowing like a river out of his cracked skull. His eyes were glazed over. He was dead as a man can get."

"But why…?"

"The ice pick? That's ease, deputy. That…that animal **looked** at my little Shirley. He **looked** at her innocence…then he destroyed it. He was stone, cold dead when I did it. I very slowly stuck the point of that ice pick against his eyeball and oh-so-gradually applied pressure to the handle."

Wayne stood speechless. He believed Shields. It was too bizarre to not believe. "I understand," he muttered finally.

"No, you don't understand. Not really. But…as you put it…now you know. I do have regrets, however. I wish I could have seen him take that beating. I wish I **had** killed him…the accident was too easy, too quick. And," he smiled down at Shirley who was still watching Wayne, "I wish I had had **two** ice picks."

Wayne nodded, then motioned toward Shirley. "Let her go, Mr. Shields. She's been through enough."

"Almost enough. It will soon be enough. But for now, start walking backward…easy…don't fall." Tinsley started backing away from the door. "And don't think, deputy, that I failed to note your firearm is missing."

Wayne glanced down at his empty holster. "All that rustling around in the dark. I guess it fell out. Didn't think you'd mind."

"No, Mr. Tinsley. You hoped I wouldn't notice. But I did. Once again, you owe me your life. I could have killed you at any time."

"I know that. I appreciate you not shooting me…again."

"I never did apologize about that, did I? When Mrs. Blankenship called me from her employer's house to let me know you were coming to see me…well, you can imagine what I thought."

"You thought I already knew about you, about what you had done."

"That's all yesterday's news. I am a man of my word. You know my intentions. So step away. Shirley and I are going for a walk "in the woods" as they say. If I hear so much as the crack of a twig behind me, I'll take her head off."

"So you said."

"I keep my word, deputy. Stay away until my escape is assured, and I'll let her live. Otherwise…"

"And you should know, too, Shields," Wayne stopped moving back. "I also keep my word."

"Your point?

"If you hurt that little girl…in **any** way, I'll hunt you down like the rabid dog you are. And I'll find you. And when I find you, I'll kill you."

Shields almost snarled. "Strong words for an unarmed man standing alone in the darkness." He raised the shotgun, pointing it directly at Tinsley's head. "Now, get back!"

Chapter 44

Wayne Tinsley could do nothing but stand and watch. He pivoted on the balls of his feet to stay aligned with Shields and Shirley. His hands rested in apparent nonchalance on his hips, his right hand four inches from the butt of the *Smith and Wesson* Revolver at his back.

One slip, Shields…that's all I need, he thought. One little distraction, one turn of the ankle on a rock…something…anything, and this will all be over. For one of us, his subconscious tried to insert. For one of us. The edge of the trees was less than a hundred feet from the front yard, and Shields—now that he was moving—covered the distance quickly, pulling and dragging Shirley Blankenship alongside him.

Wayne edged toward them without giving the appearance he was following. but the teacher dragged his pupil further and further from him, increasing the distance between them. Tinsley wanted to scream. He was helpless. He had not the slightest doubt Shields would kill the girl if Wayne rushed in after him.

If only he could be sure the man would free Shirley as promised, Wayne could live with losing him, he thought—temporarily at least. The problem was he was not at all sure the evil teacher could help himself…if he could keep himself from murdering her, could he also keep himself from murdering her spirit just a little more…just once more "for old time's sake?"

He edged closer, hearing an occasional twig break in the distant interior of the grove. He knew they were far enough away…and moving…he could get closer. Perhaps if he could just stay close enough to hear movement…

It was like walking through tar. Invisible twigs slapped his face, cutting flesh. Thorns from an unknown tree-clinging vine grabbed constantly at his clothes…his face…his arms. It was impossible to move without stepping on brittle fallen limbs and old, dried leaves. He was amazed Shields could move—and with the girl—so quietly.

He replaced the revolver in the holster, snapping it securely, fearing it would slip out or be snagged in the underbrush. An owl screeched suddenly, offended by the interruption. A large dog barked nearby. Wayne swept away sweat which trickled incessantly into his eyes.

Every two or three yards he pulled up, listening intently. He could still hear distant footfalls in the foliage. He stopped again, expecting to hear the same silent sounds of movement, but did not. There was nothing but silence. Even the dog had ceased his tirade. Wayne stood very still, trying to control his breathing…trying to control the sound of his own pounding heart in his ears. Every breath, every movement he made, seemed magnified in his pounding head.

Then, voices! Shields was screaming angrily at the girl. Was he trying to…what? What was he…? She screamed. Wayne started to run in the direction of the din, but steeled himself to maintain control. He had to be quiet. He had to be fast…really, really fast…but under control.

Then the sound of a shotgun blast smashed against his eardrums, stopping short her second scream. It had only been the beginning of a scream…an outburst of fear, followed by the hollow, and horribly loud boom of the gun. Wayne stopped in his tracks, his eyes searched for a miracle in the darkness, knowing none was there.

"No!"

He dropped to his knees without knowing he did it. They had

suddenly weakened, and his brain could no longer give him a suitable reason to stand. No words came from his lips.

There were no words. He had failed. In spite of all his game-playing and talking and trying to out-smart Shields, he had failed.

He had allowed a madman to walk away with and murder an innocent little girl.

He looked up toward the sky, searching…hoping to see the moon, the stars…something. The quietness was overbearing now, following the loud report of the shotgun. All was quiet. No moonlight was visible through the trees. No little girl saved by Deputy Tinsley.

There was only darkness.

Chapter 45

The bright lights of the emergency room hurt Jeff's eyes. Two nurses and a janitor came out to help him get Bill inside. Even with the gurney, he was difficult to load. Before removing him from the car, one of the nurses checked Bill for a pulse, then nodded to the other nurse. Jeff didn't know if it meant, "Yes, he's alive," or "Yes, he's dead."

But from the way they rushed about, getting him loaded and into the hospital, Jeff knew she must have felt a pulse. As soon as they were inside, he was gently pushed aside and pointed toward the waiting room.

"But, I…" he began, but found himself talking to the front of a swinging door. He looked around the small lobby, barely more than a foyer, for a telephone, but saw none. The sign above the emergency room area where everyone ran in with Bill said "Positively No Admittance."

He pushed it open, sticking his head inside. No one saw him.

"I need a phone!" he yelled at the entire room. There was a momentary cessation of movement. They stared at him, frozen in an instant of silence.

"Front desk," one of the nurses finally answered. Then, as though on cue, everyone resumed their tasks as if there had been no interruption.

He ran outside, cut across the grass, and circled the building. He hit the glass-framed wooden doors at full force, slamming them wide open with a bang. He was still running when he slid to a stop at the desk.

"Phone!" he gasped, pointing to the black instrument behind the high counter. "Need...phone...emergency!"

"Jeff...?" Mrs. Houston grabbed the telephone and set it on the countertop. The cord stretched tight, but held fast. Jeff grabbed the receiver and paused, his forefinger about to dial.

"Phone book? You have a phone book?"

"Who...?"

"Sheriff...Hoover!"

Mrs. Houston jerked open a drawer behind the desk, pulled out a tiny book and started thumbing through it. "Jeff!" He looked up from the phone book she was going through. "Call the operator."

He dialed the "O," waiting impatiently for the rotary dial to retract itself. The operator took four rings before responding.

"Operator...this is an emergency. I need the sheriff's office in Hoover," Jeff blurted.

"One moment, please." Her voice could not have seemed more unconcerned. Sounds like a machine, Jeff thought numbly.

Finally, a woman answered. "Sheriff's Office."

"This is Jeff Cowen," he said quickly. "I'm calling for Deputy Tinsley. He needs help."

"Oh, thank goodness. I've been frantic...trying to reach him on the radio...where is he?"

Jeff gave her directions to Denson Shields house.

"Just a moment...don't hang up," she told Jeff. He could hear her repeating directions, by radio, to officers. Help was on the way.

"Okay...uh, I'm sorry. Can you tell me your name again?"

"Jeff. Jeff Cowen. Will they be there soon?"

"Yes, they will. As a matter of fact, I wouldn't recommend you get back on the street right now. They have a tendency to drive really fast when an officer needs help."

"Okay, thanks."

The telephone went dead in his hand. He turned to go, then spun back around. "Oh, Mrs. Houston."

"Yes, Jeff?"

"Thank you. I'm sorry...almost forgot."

"It's okay. I heard what you said. I would be distracted, too."

"Yeah, but my mama still likes to hear the words."

"She's right. And speaking of her," she picked up the telephone receiver from the cradle, holding it toward him. "You think?"

He took the phone from her, gratefully acknowledging her thoughtfulness. She held her finger, poised over the dial. "Two-six-one-one," he said, and she made the call.

Before the first ring had completed itself, Faye answered.

"Hello."

"Hi, mama."

"All you all right?"

"Yes, ma'am. Just checking in."

"Two police cars just came by here with their lights on. They must have been going a hundred miles an hour. I was scared to death."

"They're going to help Wayne Tinsley..."

"Is he hurt?"

"No. At least, when I left him he was okay."

"Left him? Jeff, what's going on? I saw you get into his car earlier..."

"No, that was Deputy Lightsey."

"Lightsey? Why would you be with him?"

"He saw me outside and stopped to see if I knew the directions to a house in town. He figured Wayne was there, but didn't know how to find it. I just went along to show him."

Faye sighed a deep breath. She hadn't even realized she had been holding it in. "Okay, son...I'm going to try really hard to keep quiet while you tell me everything. Go ahead."

Jeff went through the whole story again, but with more detail. Faye, in spite of her frequent inclinations to do otherwise, did not interrupt. When he finished, Jeff waited. Finally, Faye responded with a single word.

"Men."

"Ma'am?"

"Jeff, go back to the emergency room. Check on Bill. I'll meet you there."

"At the emergency room?"

"Yes."

"Okay."

"I'll be right along."

Chapter 46

Tinsley had no idea how long he knelt there on the ground. He was aware of movement in the trees, but at exactly what point in time that awareness slipped from the subconscious to present-time reality he did not know. He only knew he heard movement and that the sound had been present for…how long?

With great effort, he lifted himself upright…at least partially upright. He struck his head against a tree limb and almost fell back to the ground. He felt the bump, which appeared immediately, and vacantly wondered where or when he lost his hat. He eased up again, moving forward quietly.

He could do nothing for Shirl…he couldn't help the little girl, now. But he could avenge her. The thought of taking Shields to jail had not crossed Wayne's mind since hearing that last shot. He didn't consciously dismiss the idea of an arrest and trial. They were just things…concepts…that had no connection to what was happening.

He crept slowly, methodically…focusing every fiber of his physical, emotional, and spiritual self into staying in some form of contact with Shields, using the man's own evil aura like a bloodhound uses a scent.

Wayne allowed the presence of only one fear to remain with him. He would not—could not—allow Shields to kill him before he completed his mission.

"Please keep her hidden from me till I'm finished with him," he prayed silently. He knew the sight of…of the girl would be a great distraction for him. It would give an even greater edge to her murderer. Strange, he thought. Praying to God that he give me the tools necessary to help me kill a man.

Not a man. A monster. Focus. Concentrate. Wayne knew a few things from military combat about himself. He knew he could actually see better now…that—because of adrenalin—his eyes had literally changed their shape…more elongated than before…improving his eyesight to the front. His mind helping his body protect itself.

He also knew, however, that the same thing that improved his eyesight, decreased his peripheral vision…he had to be more careful to avoid attacks from his flanks…

His hearing was keener, as his body seemed to slide between trees and through brush like a light breeze. The thorns no longer grabbed at him…the night was no longer the enemy. Wayne fought with his own emotions, reminding himself that many of the feelings he was experiencing was a euphoria—a false good-sense feeling about his surroundings. He also reminded himself that Denson Shields was probably experiencing the same adrenalin-based things in his own body. His hope was that Shields had never been in combat. That he did not understand the many transitions his body and mind were making…without his consent or knowledge…to protect themselves from danger perceived through impulses of the brain.

Although a combatant needs to know those things, Tinsley remembered, one can also become so tied up in thinking about them, even the self-protection system of a man's body can become the enemy. Don't over-think it. Just know it, then put it away. Shut the door. React to danger spontaneously. Be ready for everything. Expect nothing. Anticipate only that you will be surprised. And that you will win.

He could hear the sounds…silent movements in the trees. His mind could almost see the man's every step, every falter. He had told the truth about his knowledge of the grove. He seldom slipped. Then, as suddenly as the earlier shot, was silence. Wayne continued, easing himself in the direction of the last movement.

The cessation of movement by Shields was not a surprise. Wayne knew the man would have to set an ambush for him. After killing the girl, Shields would know Tinsley was coming…that he would not stop. And the man knew his way around…he knew where the best ambush place would be. He had, no doubt, been walking straight to it all along.

Tinsley started to imagine where the best place for an ambush would be. What should he look for? Some unusual object…something that didn't belong here…to draw his eyes…to stop his movement, while Shields took his shot from elsewhere?

Don't over think it, he reminded himself. Listen. Smell. Feel. Thunder rumbled in the distance, a low, rolling sound that lasted a long four seconds. His mother had said that sound was just God's potato wagons rumbling along in Heaven.

Concentrate! He stopped a second, took two deep breaths, then continued as quietly as possible in the direction where he last heard Shields walking. An occasional mosquito drew near, the sound of their beating wings loud in Wayne's ears. But they didn't land. There was something about the smell of the man…an emanation from his very pores…

Another rumble of thunder joined Wayne in the darkness, followed by a drop of rain on his forehead, feeling like a hard-striking rock. He was near, he knew…very near the evil. He closed the door. No thoughts. Nothing. A presence, perhaps…nothing more. He took a step. Stopped. Took two more steps. Stopped. He was very, very near.

And like a small island in the ocean, the opening appeared. It was no larger than an indoor bathroom, and treeless. A spot of moonlight touched the grass. Odd, thought Wayne. Moonlight and rain drops. Don't usually go together. It was the first time he had really been able to see since entering the trees.

See. With his eyes! The least likely place for an attack. He took two steps into the light, heard the footfall he expected, and dived nose-first into the ground. The scream was even closer than he anticipated, the two footsteps…running…and the sharp, sudden pain in his side as the butcher-knife split skin to the bone across three ribs.

The instant Wayne hit the ground, he rolled in the direction from which Shields had come. He rolled twice and came up immediately, lunging back at the man who was still trying to get himself off the ground.

The flash of the large blade told Tinsley which hand to go after, and he smashed into the man grabbing his right wrist. Shields stumbled backward two steps from the force of Wayne's rush, then fell hard to the ground. He pounded Wayne with remarkably strong blows to the head and body with his left fist. His own body wrapped around Wayne's back, his legs encircling the deputy as he beat him. Wayne pressed with every fiber of his body into the wrist, trying to dislodge the large knife.

Holding with all his strength to the wrist with his right hand, he released his left and smashed Shields nose with his elbow with intense force. The onslaught of blows stopped for a moment, and Wayne slammed his elbow into the man again, striking the side of his neck with little effect. The third blow of his elbow caught Shields at the side of the head.

Tinsley could feel the strength of Shields' grip on the knife lessen slightly, and he took advantage of the instant to re-grab the arm with both his hands, roll quickly out of the legs hold, and twist fiercely on the arm and wrist. Shields screamed an instant before Wayne heard the forearm snap like a broken tree limb. The knife fell to the ground.

Wayne smashed him in the face with a closed fist, knocking the teacher backwards. He jumped on him immediately, slamming fists into the man's face, neck, and upper body. Surprisingly, even as he took the onslaught, Shields reached quickly with his remaining good hand and grabbed Tinsley by the throat. Gaining leverage, he began slowly pushing the deputy off him.

Both men grunted and growled like beasts, as they struggled fiercely, not just to win, but to live. Veins exploded beneath the skin of both men as they lay in a mortal deadlock, each straining against the other…each needing for the moment to live more than to hate. Tinsley was bleeding profusely and weakening, he knew.

Shields knew it, too. His chest was covered with Tinsley's blood. If he could just hold on…

Wayne knew Shields should not be able to remove him with one hand. He was amazed at the strength of the man. He also knew he was weakening quickly, close to unconsciousness. If he passed out, he would never wake up. He grabbed Shields' left hand as it circled his throat. Grasping his little finger, Tinsley isolated it from the others and began pulling back.

It snapped, and immediately Shields' hand jerked free of Wayne's neck. But just as quickly, he knocked Wayne off, jumping quickly to his feet, and ran for the fallen butcher knife. Tinsley dove at his feet, and they both tumbled in a mass of sweaty, gasping bodies. Wayne saw the light flash an instant before he felt the sharp pain in his side beneath the ribs.

He flailed wildly at Shields, trying to locate the one good arm. He found an arm in the darkness and grabbed hold, managing to catch only the cloth of the coat sleeve. He felt the blade edge slit across his upper thigh, but it wasn't deep. He had the correct arm. He grunted loudly as he re-grasped the arm, gaining better control. When he reached for the knife-wielding hand he caught the blade, and—although it sliced deeply into his palm—he held on, twisting and angling it in every possible way to break it free from the man who was killing him.

With a final, desperate twist of the blade and a fierce bellow from what should have been already depleted lungs, he jerked the knife free, still holding it by the blade. He found himself face to face with Shields, and for the first time looked deeply into him. Into his soul. Shields had won. It showed in his eyes. He had killed Tinsley. He was just waiting for the deputy to lie down.

Wayne exploded suddenly into Shields groin with his knee. Then again and again. Shields screamed like a scalded goat, and…finally… slumped over trying to protect himself from another crushingly painful assault. Wayne grabbed Shields' hair, as he bowed before him in pain, flipped the butcher knife over, and deliberately sliced deeply into

Shields' throat, from one carotid artery to the other. Blood immediately pulsed thick, five-foot long streams from his neck.

Wayne slowly released the death-grip he had held on the man's hair. Shields looked up at him, surprised. He sat down, hard, on the ground in front of Wayne. Even in the darkness, Wayne could see the enormous amount of blood coming from the man. A sudden wave of nausea struck him and, Wayne too—his knees buckling—crumpled to a seated position, facing his attacker. He eased himself over, groaning in pain, to a nearby tree. Leaning against it, he sighed heavily.

He noted, without particular interest, his revolver still snapped in its holster. It didn't concern him. He knew there hadn't been time. Had he hesitated one second...even the amount of time it would have taken to try to draw his gun...Shields would have beaten him.

He watched Shields as he slowly slumped over to one side and lay in a partially bent position, his life flowing into the grass. There was no longer the look of arrogance on his face. No longer did hatred burn from every glance of his eyes. He was a child molester...and a murderer. Wayne felt no pity for him. No remorse. He was tired.

He looked down at his chest and stomach...covered in his own blood. It looked just like Shields', black and thick in the night, flowing out of him onto the grass in the tiny moonlit spot where nobody won. Not far from them, a little girl...he couldn't think more about her now. At least, when they found him here, they would also find the body of Denson Shields.

So tired. He rested his head back against the tree. It had begun to rain very gently. He wondered absently why Shields hadn't used the shotgun. Then he heard police sirens in the distance...coming to help. Coming too late.

He closed his eyes, as consciousness slipped away.

Chapter 47

Ivy watched the car for more than a mile as it approached her house. In a rare outing to her front yard, she discovered her long absence from it had left the place looking ragged and unattended. Weeds had taken over the lawn. The once beautiful flower garden could brag of nothing but dead stalks, leaning limply over dried earth.

She would have to hire someone to take care of the things, she thought, just as soon as that money...

It was a police car! A sheriff's car, actually, and it was pulling into her driveway. She looked down at herself, self-conscious in that she had applied no make-up. Her shirt, a yellow chiffon, should have been washed a couple of days ago. Her cut-off shorts showed her legs well, but, they too were wrinkled and soiled. She was barefoot.

As the car pulled to a stop in her drive, she realized immediately she did not know the driver. He was very young, obviously. And somewhat attractive. When he exited the patrol car, he removed the western style hat, revealing a shock of sandy-brown hair.

"Mrs. Bradley?"

"Yes, deputy. That's me." She smiled her biggest smile. Then, quickly she blew into her cupped hand and sniffed.

"My name is Deputy Palmer."

"Pleased to meet you, deputy. Won't you come in out of the sun?"

"Thank you ma'am, but no. I don't have a lot of time. Maybe we could just sit here on the porch a moment. I have something for you."

"Doesn't look something like a check, does it?" she asked, a coy smile on her lips.

Ralph looked at her, unknowingly. He held out a sealed envelope with her name on it. "It's from Deputy Tinsley, written a few day ago."

"Oh, I heard on the radio. I'm so sorry, Ralph."

He nodded. "Please, sit down. I'll join you."

She motioned to the letter, "When did you say...? Why?"

"Don't know ma'am. He left directions...I was instructed to bring this to you...in the event he couldn't. Actually, Deputy Lightsey was supposed to bring it, but he's still a little under the weather. Anyway, Deputy Tinsley wanted you to have this."

"That dear man, thinking of me, even when..." she tore open the envelope. She held it so Ralph could not see, although he had already turned away. It read:

Dear Mrs. Bradley,

The following is my official conclusion concerning the murder investigation of your husband, Bill Bradley. These conclusions are the same ones I will report to the insurance company. The letter will not be mailed to the insurance company, however, until certain provisions are met by you.

Item 1. Bill Bradley was not murdered. His death, though initially bizarre on the face of it, was an accident...the result of a violent fall. The autopsy report (attached in the letter to the insurance company) will support my findings.

(Ivy, the insurance company will receive only item 1 if you comply with my instructions. If you do not, the second report (already prepared) will be submitted by a deputy friend of mine. It adds, as follows:

Item 2. Mrs. Ivy Bradley, wife of the deceased, did, in combination with Earl Smith and Burl Patterson—both of Cash, Tx, conspire to cause the death of Mr. Bradley.

Item 3. Mrs. Ivy Bradley, after the fact, conspired to and did in fact withhold evidence in this case, promising funds from the payoff of your insurance company to Patterson and Smith in exchange for their silence concerning essential information.

Item 4. Mrs. Ivy Bradley is being charged with felony criminal offenses regarding this matter, thereby rendering her— according to my understanding of your company regulations— no longer a viable recipient of her ex-husband's insurance funds.

Etc., etc.

(I added the Etc. because I'm sure you have no interest in the legal mumbo-jumbo.)

Here's my deal, Ivy. You are about to receive a legal form which will transfer the insurance money into your account at the bank. You will also be given another form, which you will sign, immediately transferring 40% of the gross amount from the insurance company to another account.

That's it. You will still have more wealth than you will be able to deal with wisely. And you will be helping someone in need. I am giving you this opportunity for a couple of reasons. I like you, and I feel sorry for you for what you went through with Bill. You committed several felonies (as mentioned above), but I am willing to let them slide if you sign the forms mentioned.

Whether or not you agree to my terms, I would recommend you destroy this letter immediately, for both our sakes. Now, if you agree to my terms, tell the deputy with you "Yes." He has the forms with him. If you do not, and want to go to trial, just tell him "no." He will then show you his handcuffs.

He has his orders. It's up to you. I'm banking on you to play it smart.

     Sincerely,

       Wayne.

Ivy folded the paper quietly and stuck it in her front pants pocket. She sighed deeply, trying to not shutter or faint. The silence was long, deputy Ralph Palmer in no apparent hurry to leave now. She wanted to scream at the top of her lungs. She wanted to fight. She wanted **all** the money. But most of all, she wanted to go inside and take a nap.

In spite of all her dreams of wealth...and she could **still** be wealthy...she felt a sense of immense relief it was over. She had thought all along Earl Smith had killed her husband. The coward had been there that night...at the barn. She saw his car. But not only had the little weasel backed out, he let her believe he had done it so she would still pay him.

No wonder he acted so strangely. He had no idea who killed her husband...except that, apparently, no one did.

"Are you all right, Mrs. Bradley?"

She turned toward Ralph, boring into him with her beautiful eyes. "Yes."

"Yes, you're all right? Or, **yes?**"

"Yes, Ralph. I'm all right. **And,** 'yes'." She smiled at him.

He removed two documents from his shirt pocket, unfolded them and handed each to her, indicating where to sign. She signed both without reading, as casually as signing a post card.

"Okay, ma'am. That about does it for me." He turned to leave.

"Deputy..."

"Yes, ma'am?"

"Do you know what this is about?"

"Ma'am, all I know is I was to bring you Wayne's letter and to give you these documents when you finished reading."

"And the handcuffs?"

"I don't understand, ma'am. I was just told to give you the forms to sign. Nothing about handcuffs."

She really smiled then. "Deputy, please, will you do me the greatest favor?"

"Sure, if I can."

"Come inside with me. This has been a very stressful day for me...you can't imagine. I lost my husband recently. I guess you already know that?"

"Yes. I was here that day."

"Anyway, if you'll just stay with me a few minutes...I'll get you some iced tea. I simply **must** get a shower, if you don't mind...oh, I'm sorry. I didn't embarrass you, did I."

"No. It's okay, ma'am."

"Good. You come on in. It won't take me but a minute. I don't have nearly the skin to wash as a big man like you. Then we can talk a minute...I just need a professional to help me through this. Please?"

He was already allowing her to lead him through the open front door. "I can't stay a really long time, though."

"Of course, Deputy. I understand." She shook her head, involuntarily.

"What is it, ma'am? Something I said?"

"Oh, no. I'm sorry. I was just thinking about Deputy Tinsley. He really was quite a man, wasn't he?"

"Still is, far as I know."

Her head jerked up in time to see Ralph's smile, and the twinkle in his young, blue eyes.

Chapter 48

There were only four of them at the beginning. Randy, Jeff, and two of Jeff's friends—Sam and Ray—from school. It takes more players than that to have a really good scrub baseball game, but they were bored.

It was a rare summer day, the wind not blowing. Sand was not something they were eating, but something they walked on. The sun was bright, the temperature in the high eighties. It was a day made in heaven. It was perfect...except four people can't play scrub baseball.

The batter was always chasing after a ball he missed, or that was pitched so badly he didn't even swing. The other three spent most of their time standing around waiting for nothing to happen. They had had about enough when the beat up old Plymouth pulled off the shoulder of the road in front of house.

"Johnny! Hey, Johnny!" Jeff called out when the boy stepped over the folded front seat. "Come on!"

Johnny waved at him, a broad smile flashing across his face. "Be right there."

"Hurry up. We're dying out here." The presence of just one more player was creating a little excitement for the day, already.

"What're y'all playing?" Johnny Wilson called back.

"We're **trying** to play scrub," answered Ray.

"There's probably ten kids over there," he pointed to the houses across the highway, "that can play ball better than Jeff."

Everybody laughed, including Jeff. When the laughter stopped Randy shrugged. "I'll see."

"What?" asked Jeff.

But Randy was already off, sprinting to the highway's edge. "Hey!" he screamed at the top of his lungs.

An eight year old boy walking into his house across the road stopped abruptly. When he turned back, he saw Randy staring directly at him. The boy pointed his finger toward his own chest, a "who me" gesture.

"Yeah!" responded Randy. "Any a' yall know how to play scub?"

The boy nodded.

"Come on. We need more players!" He spun around and returned to the field without awaiting a reply.

Johnny Wilson walked to the front porch of the house and stood in front of the large swing which hung from it. "Mr. Tinsley, sir?"

Wayne slowly opened his eyes and looked at Johnny. "Was I sleeping again?" he asked.

"I don't know for sure. Sure looked like maybe you was."

"I've been doing a lot of that lately. Those pills they gave me for pain makes sleeping really an easy thing to do." Wayne smiled at the boy. "You want to sit down?"

"No, sir," he looked back at the other boys. "I'm gonna' play some ball, I guess. I just never had a chance to tell you 'thank you'."

"Just doing my job, Johnny. I'm glad you're out, though. Wish I could a' been there to turn the key myself…but like I said, with all this sleeping and stuff…"

"No, sir. Lots of people could have done their jobs. Lots of people didn't. I think you did a lot more than your job. I won't forget."

"Nor will I, Johnny. Do you know what you're gonna' do now? Where will you go?"

"Folks across the street are gonna' let me work with them through this fall…harvest time. After that…" he shrugged his shoulders.

"Good luck. I hope things work out."

"They will, Mr. Tinsley. It's been a real hard year, but things are going to get better."

"I believe you're right."

Johnny turned and started to trot to the other players, then suddenly stopped. Without turning he spoke, "Mr. Tinsley, I never knew no white man I admired before…" then he was gone.

As he ran to meet the other boys, Wayne looked at their faces, all young, tanned, healthy…and all with smiles on their faces as Johnny Wilson approached them. Even Sam and Ray beamed with the prospect of another player joining the game. As he turned his eyes from them, movement was visible at the highway.

"Faye! Faye, can you come here?"

In an instant the screen door creaked open. "What is it, Wayne? Is something wrong?"

"Look." He pointed with some difficulty toward the highway.

"My Dear Lord!" She put a hand over her eyes, shading them, as she peered toward the apparition. Five kids from across the highway were crossing over toward them. Three had mitts. One flipped a baseball into the air and caught it as they walked. Two were girls. Their ages ranged from eight to what Faye guessed at about sixteen.

She started out to them when Wayne stopped her. "Just a second, Faye." She paused, but continued to stare. Wayne sat up straighter in the swing. The five kids joined the five already standing around, and a few words were spoken between the groups. The adults on the porch couldn't hear what was said, but as though on cue, the group broke up and children ran in all directions, filling the holes in the field.

"Guess they had to decide on the rules," Faye said. "Why didn't you want me to go out there?"

"I just figured we grown ups have things pretty messed up already. They can't possibly do much worse." He nodded toward the playing field. "They seem to have struggled through that terribly political moment pretty good on their own, huh?"

She laughed. "Yes, they did. But I wasn't going to butt into their business." Wayne looked up at her. She was pulling off the full-length apron she had worn while finishing the dishes. "I'm going to show them how to hit a baseball!" She strode off to join the others.

He smiled after her, admiring her spirit. He couldn't hear what she or the boys were saying, but suddenly all around her burst into laughter. Such a beautiful sound, he thought. They all resumed their positions except Jeff, who stayed on the pitcher's mound to strike out his mother.

He taunted her, laughing all the while, warning her to not get caught up in her skirts when she swung and missed his "dark pitch."

"Bring it on!" she called back.

He brought it. It wasn't nearly Jeff's best pitch, and it wasn't very "dark." He was taking it easy on his old mama.

She smashed the first pitch, carrying the ball high into—and out of left field. It landed on the center stripe of the highway, and bounded across the road. She held the bat up in her best 'sissy' impression, and let it fall. Then, in a falsetto voice, "Was that okay, Jeffie?" It took a moment for the kids to close their mouths, but when they finally did, they couldn't keep them closed, blasting Jeff with a flurry of "pitcher's got a rag-arm" and worse.

Johnny Wilson was jumping straight up and down, laughing. He couldn't have caught a grounder at that moment if it had been a basketball.

Faye pranced back to the porch. She sat primly beside Wayne, watching the others play. Finally, she turned to him. "What?"

"What? What do you mean 'what'? You just got yourself a spot on the New York Yankees. How did you…?"

"Shhh. Don't tell, and I'll let you in on a secret." He closed his mouth, smiling. She continued, "I can't do that. I've never hit a ball like that in my life, and there's not a chance in the world I ever will again."

"That's why you got out of there so fast. So they wouldn't ask for a repeat?"

"Yep. I'll never pick up a bat again as long as I live. I've had my moment in the sun, and the boys can just believe their mother is the home run queen of the world."

They sat for a long while, watching the baseball players, not speaking. Silence, to Wayne and Faye, was not uncomfortable. Neither was conversation. They listened to the voices, the sounds. Occasionally a car or pickup drove by, and more often than not, passengers craned their necks…looking at either the strange mixture of ball players, or the banged up deputy and the suicide widow.

"Guess we're quiet a sight, huh?" said Tinsley.

"Yes, we are." She nodded in the direction of the ball game. "Why can't it be like that? Look at them. Listen. All they see are other ball players…a first baseman…a catcher. I see no hate out there."

"I'll give you my twenty-five cent theory, if you like."

"Please. But you'll have to take an I.O.U. on the quarter."

"You got it. They **love** baseball. Right? Or, at least they love to **play** baseball."

"Okay."

"It is my very intellectual opinion, Faye, that the only thing that can replace hate is love."

"Now that's really deep," she smiled. "I expected a little more for my twenty-five-cents."

"Well, you're operating on credit, so the money doesn't go so far."

"Okay, Wayne. I know there's more on your mind than that. Give."

He lowered his head, thought a moment, and continued. "That night…in the grove with Denson Shields…"

"Yes?"

"When things were, you know, really bad…he wasn't trying to kill me because he hated me…and he **did** hate me."

"Well, he certainly didn't **love** you." she offered.

"No. But he loved life. Even in his sorry, miserable mind, when it came right down to it, he was fighting me with all he had so he could live…not so I would die."

"Wasn't that the same thing. You die, he lives?"

"Sure. But that's not what I mean. He did hate me. But that was replaced by a stronger emotion…the emotion of love he still held for life."

She twisted her lips slightly and raised one eyebrow. "Love is stronger than hate? Is that what you want me to believe?"

"It **has** to be."

"I hope you're right, Wayne." She looked back at her boys. "They need you to be right. They all do. Maybe this looks like they care about each other…this game. But if it's only the love of playing a game, that'll have to do, I guess, until the right thing comes along."

"It's better than nothing, Faye. Maybe a start."

They sat for awhile again, not speaking…lost in their thoughts. Faye finally asked, "Wayne, may I ask you something about that night? I know it's been difficult for you…"

"What is it, Faye?"

"It's about you. How you felt. When you still thought Mr. Shields had killed the little girl, did you intend to kill him regardless of whether he resisted or not?"

He hesitated. "I had good reason to believe he killed her."

"Of course you did. I understand that. But…"

"I don't know, Faye. I wish I could tell you for sure. I wish I knew. To the best of my knowledge, I think I intended to kill him, no matter what."

She touched his hand as it lay beside him on the swing. "I'm sorry, Wayne. I shouldn't have brought it up. I just…"

"No. No, it's okay. I need your questions. I need to think about that night…about who I am."

"That's not why I asked, Wayne. I already know who you are. I'm just not sure who **you** think you are."

"When you get that figured out, let me know, will you?"

"I'll tell you a couple of things you may not know about yourself…"

He looked cautiously at her, and found her expression serious. "Okay."

"First, if the events of that night had not unfolded as they did…if Mr. Shields hadn't stopped to relieve himself, little Shirley could never have grabbed the shotgun and ran off. If she hadn't tripped, screamed, and the gun discharged…well, your frame of mind would have been different. He probably would have killed you."

He nodded assent. "I believe you're right."

"I also know that you think you're pretty smart, acting like you know nothing about that 'anonymous' gift made to me and the boys at the bank."

He shrugged. "Where would I get that kind of money? Have you still not told the boys?"

"I haven't. I'm a little old fashioned, I guess. They'll know, soon enough. But, in the meantime, I still believe they can build character earning what they spend."

He laughed lightly. "Jeff may shoot you when he finds out y'all have all that money. He's about to kill himself trying to keep this farm going."

"He'll be okay." She returned her hand over his. "Have you noticed how much he's matured?"

"Yes, I have." Wayne used every ounce of control he possessed trying to maintain the conversation. Faye's touch still rattled him. He knew his face was red. He was on fire.

"And the last thing I can tell you, Mr. Wayne Tinsley, is that you have been in love with me for a long time."

He could only stare.

"Wayne, close your mouth."

Her quiet laugh had to come straight from the angels, he thought. "But, why would you say that?" he finally stammered.

"It's one of those big secrets of a small town, Wayne. Everybody in Hensley County knows you love me but you."

"I could just never...it was never the right..."

"It's okay, Wayne. I know the timing has never been there for us. We could never speak of it, or even allow ourselves to think it. But it's been hiding in the background a long, long time."

"And now...?"

"The timing is still not right," she said, the light fading somewhat from her face. It's too soon...for both of us."

"I know. You're right, of course. Anyway," he added, trying to insert some levy into the conversation, "I only love you for your money."

She laughed a deep, happy laugh. Her eyes sparkled, and Wayne knew she was right. He had always loved her, but didn't realize how transparent he had been.

"I need one more favor from you Wayne," she said, her face suddenly serious again.

"Of course."

"It may be too soon for us. It may take a long time. But I need you to promise me one thing."

"Anything."

She smiled again, her face bright as the sun, "Never give up."